Storms and
SECRETS

A SMALL-TOWN ROMANCE

CLAIRE
KINGSLEY

Always Have LLC

Published by Always Have, LLC

Edited by Eliza Ames and Michelle Fewer

Cover Design: Lori Jackson

ISBN: 978-1-959809-14-2

www.clairekingsleybooks.com

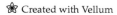 Created with Vellum

To my cat, Westley, who was very jealous after I dedicated my last book to a dog.

Actually, I don't think he has any feelings in his cold, feline heart.

But I love you anyway, Westley. Even though I did not put a cat in this book.

(It's because you peed on my favorite boots. That's what you get.)

About this book

He's always loved her. Now he'll fight to save her.

Zachary Haven has been living a lie.

He's stuck in a rut, pretending to hate the woman he's always loved. He didn't mean for things to turn out that way. But sometimes life gets out of control, especially when you're young and stupid.

Not that he ever had a chance with her. She's gorgeous and smart, talented and kind. And Zachary? He can't seem to keep himself out of trouble.

Marigold Martin just met the man of her dreams.

Blowing into her life like a storm, he sweeps her off her feet. She can't help but wonder if he's the one. He's a dream in a bespoke suit—and he says he wants her heart.

But nothing is as it seems.

A brush with death wakes Zachary up to the reality of his life. And his feelings for Marigold. He's determined to make her his—convince her they were always meant to be.

But secrets run deep, and Zachary fears the man who's after Marigold could be more than a romantic rival.

He could be the devil himself.

And Zachary might be too late to save her.

Author's note: A troublemaker turned small-town hero risks everything for the love of his life. A soft-hearted heroine who finds her strength. An accidental body piercing, brotherly shenanigans, the Squirrel Protection Squad, and lots of big feels. This small-town romantic suspense will leave you breathless, with the romantic happily ever you've been waiting for.

NOT a love triangle

Content warning: this book contains references to sex trafficking

CHAPTER 1

Zachary

ANOTHER SHOT of tequila was probably a mistake.

I tossed it back anyway. Rocco gave me the look. The one that said don't even think about ordering another, because I ain't serving you.

That was fine. My head was pleasantly fuzzy, my limbs loose, and I still had a beer to finish. I wasn't drunk. Close, but I knew how to walk that line.

Granted, I probably couldn't walk an actual straight line at that point, so I either needed a ride or I was walking home. Again.

That wasn't ideal, considering it was raining enough to drown every squirrel in Tilikum. In early October, the weather in the mountains was basically drunk. It could go from sunny and warm to stormy and miserable in an afternoon.

Still, my place wasn't far.

I shifted on my stool, turning so I could survey the action. Saturday night at the Timberbeast Tavern could either be fun or boring, it was anyone's guess. My brother Garrett was there, hanging out with a couple of other off-duty deputies. Boring. Garrett was the boy scout of the family. He was basically a robot. It drove me nuts. And those guys wouldn't know fun if it hit them in the face. They'd probably arrest it.

The two girls at the table beneath the old Tilikum Trading Co. sign, though? They looked like fun.

Tourist season had wound down, but they looked like out-of-towners. I wondered what they were doing there. The Timberbeast wasn't nice enough to cater to most visitors. It was one step above a dive bar, really—rusty timber tools and old signs on the walls, and a bartender who looked like he'd come straight out of the woods.

They were dressed nice. One blonde, one brunette. Both hot. Looked to me like they needed a little Z Haven in their lives.

I hopped off my stool and paused while the room spun a little. Shit. That was fine, I had this. I grabbed my beer and sauntered to their table.

"Hey." I grinned and took them both in, judging their first reactions to me. The brunette smiled but the blonde looked bored—even skeptical.

I liked her disinterest. Challenge accepted.

Not that my goal was to take her home with me. I had a reputation in this town, and it was partially well-earned. I was a world class flirt. If hitting on girls were a sport, I'd have every gold medal. But, unlike what people assumed, I wasn't quick to jump in bed with every girl I met.

It was all part of my charm.

"Zachary Haven." I held out my hand to the brunette. She shook my hand and batted her eyelashes a little. Cute, but she was making it way too easy. The blonde, though? She looked me up and down a couple of times before shaking my hand. It gave me a little punch of adrenaline, swirling with the alcohol in my system.

"I'm Julia," the too-eager brunette said. "This is my friend Lynnette."

"Mind if I join you?"

Lynnette's eyes flicked from me to Julia and back again. "Sure."

Score one for Z. I pulled an empty chair from a nearby table and straddled it backwards. They both had drinks, so I didn't bother offering to buy one yet.

I started chatting them up. Basic stuff, just asking easy questions to get them talking about themselves. They were friends, had met in college, and were in town enjoying a weekend getaway. Julia was single and although Lynnette admitted she'd recently been on a few dates with a guy back home, that didn't bother me. This wasn't going anywhere. I just liked knowing it could.

A few jokes had them laughing, loosening up. Lynnette wasn't looking so skeptical anymore, her eyes lingering on mine.

Score another one for Z.

The door opened and my sister, Annika, walked in, followed by one of her longtime friends, Isabelle.

Audrey came in right behind them. She'd moved to town a while back and was engaged to my brother, Josiah. When the door shut behind her, I let out a sigh of relief. Maybe it was just the three of them.

I thought I was safe until the door opened again. And she walked in.

Marigold Martin.

There went my night.

I tried to turn my attention back to Lynnette, but all I could do was compare her with Marigold. Damn it, that always happened. Marigold was the standard. Whether I wanted to or not, I compared every woman to her.

And they all fell short.

Lynnette and Julia were hot. But Marigold? She was gorgeous. Her long brown hair fell around her shoulders and her flawless skin seemed to glow in the dim light of the bar. She wore a long-sleeved shirt—hard to tell what color from where I was sitting—with jeans and heels. Casual for her, but she looked great.

She always looked great.

"Who's she?" Lynnette asked.

I tore my eyes away. "Who?"

"The girl you're staring at."

"I'm not staring."

"You were. Let me guess. Ex-girlfriend?"

I scoffed, hoping I could blow this off. "No. I don't even know her."

Lynnette raised her eyebrows, clearly seeing through my bullshit. "Now that's a lie if I've ever heard one."

"Fine, she's friends with my sister."

Julia leaned closer, her eyes brightening, as if somehow that information made the situation more interesting. "Really? Like childhood friends?"

"Yeah."

"How long have you had a crush on her?"

I chuckled. "I don't have a crush on my sister's best friend."

Lynnette's expression had changed, too. Her posture was open and her gaze flicked between me and Marigold. "Why? Did your sister insist you not date her friends or something?"

My brow furrowed. "No. If my sister had told me not to date her, I would have just because she told me not to."

Lynnette laughed. She had a cute smile, but it lacked Marigold's radiance.

I was doing it again.

"I'm so invested in this," Julia said.

"I know, right?" Lynnette glanced at Marigold again. "Does she know you like her?"

"No. What? I don't." This was going downhill fast.

"I bet she doesn't know," Julia said to Lynnette as if I wasn't there. "Do you think she's married to someone else?"

Lynnette shifted in her seat. "I don't see a ring."

"She's not," I grumbled.

"Oh good, then you still have a chance," Lynnette said.

I shook my head, then took a drink of my beer. Not that I'd ever admit I wanted one, but I didn't have a chance with Marigold. I'd blown it with her a long time ago. Now I moved between aggressively ignoring her and pretending I didn't like her. It was stupid, really. And not a great way to live. Especially in a small town where we couldn't avoid each other.

Marigold went to the bar to order and I looked away so they wouldn't catch me staring at her again.

Pink. Her shirt was pink.

"We should probably get going," Lynnette said. "But it was surprisingly fun to meet you."

"I hope you get together with her someday," Julia said. "You two would make a really cute couple."

I flashed her a crooked grin. "We would, but it helps when one half is me."

Julia laughed, then stood and started toward the door.

"If you do get together, I hope she's tough." Lynnette joined her friend, calling back over her shoulder. "You need someone to keep you in line."

She wasn't wrong.

But I was never getting together with Marigold.

I watched them go, not sure if I was disappointed or indifferent. I finished my beer, idly wondering if Rocco would serve me another one. Probably not.

Maybe I'd just go home and drink myself into oblivion. While I wasn't scheduled to work in the morning, I couldn't be sure my current client wouldn't call me in on a weekend. It had happened before. And as much as I did not want to admit I was getting older, I wasn't as resilient as I used to be. At twenty-one, I'd been able to party all night and sober up enough to be sharp at work by eight. Now that I was in my mid-thirties, recovering from a night of drinking took longer.

And being sharp wasn't optional when you were an electrician. A mistake could literally kill me.

Although that was part of why I liked my job.

A male voice, rising in anger, caught my attention and I glanced over my shoulder. Cory Wilcox was at a table with some girl I didn't know. Neither of them looked happy. His face contorted as he spoke and she leaned away, as if trying to put more space between them.

Cory was a jerk. I knew him from way back. We hadn't exactly been friends in high school, but we'd run with the same crowd. Nowadays, he was a loud-mouthed dick with the beginnings of a beer gut. The girl he was with had blond hair with dark roots and she was dressed in black.

He leaned closer and lowered his voice, saying something I couldn't quite hear. Her eyebrows drew together as she replied.

I turned around. Not my problem, not my business.

Except Cory would not shut up. His voice rose again. "That's bullshit, Katrina, and you know it."

"Why do you always have to be like this?"

"Because you pull this shit constantly. I work my ass off and what do you do all day? Sit around doing nothing. You're useless and you think you can complain about me?"

My back tensed.

"You shouldn't talk to me like that."

"I'll talk to you however the fuck I want."

I glanced in Garrett's direction. He and his buddies were on the other side of the bar. They'd probably intervene if it came down to it, but they were too far away to hear what was happening.

Katrina started to say something else, but Cory laid into her, calling her a long string of expletives. I didn't know her, and hell, maybe she really did sit around all day doing nothing while he worked, but that didn't mean he had a right to treat her like that.

I wasn't necessarily known for being a nice guy, but I had a very short fuse when it came to pieces of shit like Cory. You didn't talk to a woman like that. Ever. I glanced at them.

Her chair scraped across the floor as she got up to leave.

"You dumb bitch, get your ass back here."

Cory grabbed her arm.

Okay, I was done.

I stood and, thankfully, the room didn't spin. I was steady as I walked over to Cory. He was right in Katrina's face, but not yelling loudly enough to attract the attention of the cops in the room.

That was fine. I'd handle it.

And I was going to enjoy it too.

I poked Cory on the back of the shoulder a few times with my index finger. Hard.

Without letting go of Katrina's arm, he whirled around, face contorted with anger. "What the fuck?"

"Let her go."

"Back off, Haven."

"I would love to." That was a lie. I didn't want to back off, I wanted to punch him in the face. "But you're pissing me off."

"Mind your own fucking business."

He tried to turn away—as if he could get out of it that easily—so I grabbed him by the shoulder and spun him toward me.

"I don't like the way you're talking to her and I really don't like the way you grabbed her when she tried to leave." I leaned closer, trying not to wobble, but the room was starting to spin again. "So prick being a stop. No. Stop being a prick."

"Fuck you, Haven."

Without warning, I balled my fist and popped him in the mouth. Katrina screamed and he staggered backward into an empty chair.

I could have left it at that. Should have left it at that. But of course I didn't.

Heedless of the commotion, and the three off-duty cops in the room, I went after him. Blood trailed down his chin but I hadn't hit him hard enough to knock him down. He swung and his fist glanced off my jaw. I didn't even flinch. I grabbed him by the shirt and punched him in the face.

That one did it. He dropped to the sticky floor. I licked my bottom lip and tasted the metallic tang of blood.

Katrina fell to her knees next to him. "Oh my god. Baby, are you okay?"

Was *he* okay? A minute earlier he'd been calling her every derogatory name in the book. Now she was worried about him?

Someone grabbed me by the upper arm and shoved me toward the door. "Let's go."

It was Garrett.

Cory was on the floor groaning. I hadn't even knocked him out.

"What the hell?" I tried to wrench my arm away but Garrett tightened his grip. "Dude, what are you doing?"

"Getting you out of here."

"They can't kick me out." I twisted around and raised my voice. "You deserved it Cory, you douche."

"Shut up, Z," Garrett growled.

"What are you going to do? Arrest me?"

He opened the door and shoved me outside. "Do you want me to? Because it seems like you do."

"How am I the bad guy?" I gestured toward the bar. "He was being a total prick."

"Being a prick isn't a defense for assault."

"You expect me to sit by and let a guy talk to a woman like that?"

"Standing up for a woman is fine, but you can't go around punching people in the face."

I grinned. "Yeah I can. I just did."

Apparently that was the wrong thing to say. His expression hardened and he grabbed my arm again. "Let's go."

"Wait, are you actually going to arrest me? It was just a little bar fight. I didn't even knock him out."

He hauled me toward his car. "I probably should arrest you. You're lucky I was there, otherwise you'd be spending the night in a cell. I'm taking you home."

For some reason, I got in his car without protesting. Maybe punching Cory had taken the fight out of me. For now. And if I argued, Garrett might change his mind and haul me in.

Wouldn't have been the first time.

We pulled out of the parking lot and I flexed my hand. My knuckles were starting to hurt and I still tasted blood in my mouth.

I was glad of one thing, though. I hadn't seen the look on Marigold's face when Garrett hauled me out of the bar.

CHAPTER 2

Marigold

THE DOOR SHUT behind Zachary and Garrett, but the tense energy in the bar remained. I glanced around, wondering what had just happened. It looked like Zachary Haven had punched Cory Wilcox out of nowhere.

Why would he do that?

Then again, it was Zachary. He didn't need an excuse to start trouble.

He *was* trouble.

Rocco helped Cory get to his feet while his latest girlfriend, Katrina, pawed at him, sobbing. Kade, one of the off-duty deputies who'd been sitting with Garrett, went over to talk to them.

"Oh, Z." Annika shook her head. "What are we going to do with you, big brother?"

"I wonder what happened," Audrey said.

"Who knows," Annika said. "Cory probably said something stupid and Zachary has no impulse control."

That seemed likely. Cory Wilcox was a jerk. I didn't know Katrina, but I wanted to pull her aside, give her a big hug, and gently suggest she consider breaking up with him. Then make her an appointment to fix her roots.

Leave it to me, the salon owner, to notice someone's dye job in the aftermath of a bar fight.

But honestly, those roots. She deserved better.

She deserved better than Cory Wilcox, too.

I was a little surprised Annika hadn't followed her brothers outside. When we were younger, she'd been the family peacemaker and often stepped in to keep her brothers out of trouble. Maybe becoming a wife and mother had changed things. She had her own kids to worry about now. Her brothers needed to take care of themselves.

The mood in the bar shifted and the hum of conversation resumed as people went back to their drinks. The Timberbeast was no stranger to the occasional bar fight. I figured it was a small-town thing. Sometimes the guys around here insisted on settling things with fists.

So unrefined.

No wonder I was still single.

"Well, that was fun," Isabelle said. "Nothing like a Saturday night out on the town."

Audrey sat up straighter, trying to see. "Do you think he's okay?"

I glanced at Cory. He looked more mad than hurt. "He seems fine."

"Probably hurt his pride more than his face," Isabelle said.

I took a sip of my wine and my gaze flicked to the door. Was he gone? He wouldn't come back after that, would he? Not tonight, at least. Garrett would take him home.

That was good.

Wasn't it?

I put down my glass and let out a sigh. Zachary Haven. He was the one man I couldn't seem to get out of my head. I'd been best friends with his sister Annika since we were little, and that's all I'd ever be to him—his little sister's friend. Nothing more. He'd made that clear a long time ago.

So why did my heart still flutter when he was around?

Why did my cheeks flush and my brain stop working? Was it his careless brown hair? His mysterious blue eyes? His sharp cheekbones, stubbly square jaw, and the little dimple in his chin? I was graceful enough around men in general, but around Zachary Haven? I was a mess.

Which was utterly ridiculous. Especially because there were two major problems with him. One, he was not my type. My dream man was refined and gentlemanly. The type who opened doors and pulled out chairs as a matter of habit. Zachary was a sarcastic and snarky man-child who still started bar fights.

And two—which, to be fair, was the bigger problem—he hated me.

I didn't know what I'd ever done to make him dislike me, but I'd stopped trying to solve that mystery a long time ago.

So why couldn't I get beyond my misplaced crush? I'd had a nice childhood, my parents were good people. Nothing should have made me crave the attention of a man who hated me. How toxic was that? And yet, there I was, stuck in a loop of blushing and butterflies whenever he was around.

But I never talked about it, not even to my friends, because it made me feel so pathetic.

Which was why I was glad he'd left.

Not glad that he'd left after an altercation involving fists. But at least I could relax.

"I'm loving the rose gold and wine vibe," Audrey said. "Especially for winter."

"It's going to be so elegant," Annika said.

While I'd been momentarily lost in thought, the conversation at our table had turned to the big topic of the season—at least for the four of us. Audrey's wedding.

Audrey had moved to town earlier that summer, and we'd become instant friends. It was fun to have a friend who was in a similar stage of life. I adored Annika and Isabelle, but they were both married with little ones. They had different responsibilities and concerns. Initially, Audrey and I had bonded over being single in our thirties, although for her, it hadn't lasted long. She'd recently gotten engaged to Annika's brother, Josiah.

They made the cutest couple and it was so good to see Josiah, who was not exactly a people person, soften up a little bit. They'd recently moved into a house Josiah had remodeled. And because I was a little bit wedding obsessed, I'd been helping Audrey put together the details of their big day.

I nudged my attention back to my friends. "I love the colors too. They're perfect for you."

"We picked the invitations," Audrey said. "Well, I did. Josiah didn't have a strong opinion about it, so that was fine. The envelopes are sparkly rose gold on the inside and there's a gorgeous wine-colored ribbon around the invitation itself."

"I remember seeing those," I said. "They were one of my favorites."

We talked dresses and the relative merits of a DJ versus a band. They'd already decided on a venue—Salishan Cellars Winery down in Echo Creek, a town not too far from Tilikum. It was the best place for weddings anywhere in the central Cascades. I'd been there for wine tastings many times and always found myself daydreaming about having my own wedding there.

Of course, a groom would help. And in that, I was very much lacking.

It was funny, in a way. I loved all things love—romance novels, love stories, bridal showers, weddings. My life aesthetic could be summed up as romantic. Everything from my clothes to the decor in my house and salon exuded romance. And yet, I'd been remarkably unsuccessful at finding my own happily ever after.

Not that I hadn't tried. I'd dated off and on. A few of those relationships seemed as if they had potential to be the one. But none of them ever worked out. There was always something in the way; something not right. I didn't want to settle just to get married. But I did wonder if my dreams of marriage and babies and family and a future with a partner were just that—dreams.

My phone buzzed with a text, which was odd. I was with the people I texted most frequently. I talked to my parents regularly, but they were phone call people. I peeked at my phone, concerned when I saw it was the landlord for my salon.

"Is everything okay?" Isabelle asked.

My friends knew me so well. "Yes, fine. It's my salon landlord."

"Why is your landlord texting you on a Saturday night?" Annika asked.

"The light fixture in the restroom went out." I tucked my phone back in my purse. "He's just telling me he'll have someone out to fix it in the morning."

"That's good," she said.

"It's very good. He was supposed to have someone out days ago. I had to put in flameless candles and ask my clients to use a flashlight if they needed more light. The last thing the salon needs right now is another barrier to returning clients."

"You're a hair genius," Audrey said. "I'm sure your clients don't mind a dim restroom. It's totally worth it to have you as a stylist."

"You're so sweet. I appreciate it. But business has been tough, especially this last year. With inflation, people are cutting back, and their beauty routines are often one of the first things to go."

"That's definitely familiar," Audrey said. "When I was unemployed, I totally neglected my hair."

"Sometimes we have to make hard choices," I said. "It's understandable. And difficult for everyone, including me. Just don't mention anything in front of my parents. If my dad gets an inkling that my business has issues, he'll overreact."

"Your dad is so sweet," Annika said. "But yeah, the next time you had dinner with your parents, you'd probably find out he bought the building so you wouldn't have to pay rent anymore."

I shook my head. "I don't know if he'd go that far, but he'd definitely do something."

"This is probably a dumb question," Audrey said, "but could your parents actually do that? Could they afford it?"

"Not that I'm aware of," I said. "They do fine, but I don't think they have buy-a-building money sitting around."

"You never know," Isabelle said. "Your mom's paintings might have caught the eye of a rich, eccentric art collector who bought her latest masterpiece for millions."

I laughed. My mom was a painter, and she did sell her work, but mostly at a local art gallery in town. "That would be amazing. But if that ever happened, I'd much rather handle my business challenges on my own and let my parents bask in their newfound millions."

The conversation shifted from my salon to Annika's latest craft project. She was busy making Christmas ornaments to sell at Tilikum's Christmas Village during the holidays. How she had time to create such beautiful designs when she was a busy, working mom of four, I had no idea. But maybe she simply made time because crafting brought her joy.

That was a good lesson. I needed to remember her example. It also helped that her husband, Levi Bailey, was such a hands-on and involved husband and father. She'd married a really great guy and they'd built a beautiful life together.

So had Isabelle and her husband, Elias. Her family owned and operated Christmas Village, which was the highlight of the holiday season for the entire town. They were busy running her family farm and raising two kids while Elias managed a successful business of his own.

It reminded me how lucky we were to still live close

enough to get together once in a while. These girls' nights weren't frequent, but they were always so bucket-filling.

"I just need to pause to say how much I love you three," I said, my throat tightening with a rush of emotion. "I know you're all so busy with your careers and weddings and husbands and kids. I'm so grateful you made time for this tonight."

Annika leaned over and hugged me. "We love you so much."

"You're going to make me cry." Audrey wiped a few tears from beneath her eyes.

Isabelle raised her glass. "To our friendship."

We all lifted ours and clinked. "To our friendship."

Our moment of big feelings passed and we laughed at our happy tears.

"Hi, ladies."

I smiled at the voice behind me. Luke Haven. He approached our table and put his hand on the back of his sister's chair.

"Hey there." Annika twisted in her seat to look up at him. "What are you up to?"

He rested his other hand on my chair and winked at me. "Just hanging with some friends."

Luke was a good guy. A little lost, maybe, but he'd always been sweet to me. Once in a while I wondered why I wasn't attracted to him. On paper, Luke and I could have been a good match. Was it my unrealistic expectations keeping me from seeing what was right in front of me?

No, it wasn't. Luke and I had no spark. A few years ago, we'd even had a very blunt conversation about whether we should be a couple. He was single. I was single. We'd known each other forever. Maybe it made sense.

But he'd reluctantly admitted that he wished he was attracted to me, but he just… wasn't.

Which had been a relief because I felt exactly the same way. And neither of us wanted to settle.

He acted flirtatious toward me, but he acted that way toward every girl. That was just his personality. And I had a feeling he paid me a little extra attention because he felt bad about the way Zachary treated me. It was like he was trying to make up for his brother.

Sigh.

"No hot date tonight?" Annika asked.

"Afraid not," he said.

"Careful," Isabelle said. "Josiah found someone. Maybe you'll be next."

He chuckled. "Not likely. Anyway, I'll stop interrupting. Just figured I'd say hi. Have a good night, ladies."

"Night, Luke," we all said in a chorus.

"Why is he still single?" Isabelle asked, tilting her head as she watched him walk away. "He's a nice guy. Good looking. Owns a successful business. It seems weird that no one's snatched him up yet."

"My theory is his radar's broken," Annika said. "He's always attracted to the wrong women."

"Or maybe he goes for the wrong ones on purpose," Isabelle said.

"Some guys do that, if they're trying to avoid commitment," Audrey said.

I wondered. Garrett was the only Haven brother to have been married, but his marriage had ended several years ago—which was a good thing. His wife had been... interesting. And by interesting, I mean awful.

Was it just a Haven thing to wait to settle down? They came from a blended family. Three of the boys were Paul Haven's sons, and three were from Marlene Haven's first marriage. Annika was the one child they had together. The boys had all been quite young when Paul and Marlene had gotten together, but maybe those early experiences of divorce and brokenness had left their mark on the Haven brothers.

It was hard to say. But I hoped Luke would find his person someday. He deserved it.

As for me, I had to admit, I was stuck in a rut. I loved my career, but my business was struggling. And my personal life wasn't exactly exciting. My friends were all living their dream lives, complete with weddings and husbands and babies. They were building families. I loved that for them. I adored their kids and loved being the favorite auntie.

I just couldn't help but wonder if my turn would ever come.

Just a Ride

BRIELLE

THE WALK WOULDN'T HAVE BEEN SO bad if Brielle's hoodie hadn't been soaked. But it had started raining right after she'd left the apartment, and getting a ride was proving to be harder than she'd thought.

It was midday, but the sky was dark, the sun hidden behind black storm clouds. Those hadn't been there when she'd left. It had been gray, but no sign of a storm brewing.

Great. She better get a ride because the rain was about to go from annoying to torrential.

She adjusted the straps of her backpack and kept walking. The highway didn't have much of a shoulder along this stretch. The last guy who'd passed had been hugging the turn and almost hit her. She'd flipped him off but she doubted he'd even looked. Probably hadn't even seen her.

Headlights flashed in front of her, but the car was going in the wrong direction—toward Tilikum. She needed to get away from town, regardless of the weather. Even if that meant walking all the way to Pinecrest.

Could she make it on foot before dark? Probably not. She just hoped someone would stop and give her a ride sooner rather than later. Especially because of the rain.

Once she got to Pinecrest, she could take a bus to Vegas. There was a bus station in Tilikum, but she wanted to disappear, and the stupid nosy townspeople would make that impossible.

It was their fault she was out in the rain.

That, and her stupid ex-boyfriend. She'd thought moving in with him would solve her problems. Living with her parents was a total nightmare. She was nineteen, they couldn't tell her what to do anymore. He had his own apartment, and everything had been great.

Until she'd caught him with her supposed best friend.

Where did that leave her? She couldn't stay with him. Couldn't go back to her parents' house. And she didn't have any friends she could trust.

It was time to bail. Get out of Tilikum. Away from her parents who treated her like garbage. And away from the jerks who'd betrayed her.

When she made it to Vegas, she'd disappear. Find a new job, start a new life. She was never going back.

A gust of wind made her blond hair swirl around her face. She put her hood up and hunkered down in her hoodie, wishing she had a decent coat. It was only October, why was it so freaking cold?

A car approached behind her. She turned and stuck out her thumb, hoping they'd take pity on her and stop.

They didn't even slow down.

"Asshole," she called out.

Not that it helped. It wasn't like they heard her.

She crossed her arms, put her head down, and kept going. Rain fell steadily, soaking her hoodie and making her shiver. It was so cold, her teeth chattered and she wondered if her lips were turning blue.

When she heard the sound of another car, she turned, hoping to flag them down, but they were already slowing.

Hope soared as the vehicle pulled over. It was a nice car—

a sedan, black or maybe dark gray. But her hopes were dashed when the car got closer. A guy was driving and it looked like he was alone.

She'd hitchhiked before and she didn't get in cars with men unless they had women or kids with them.

He rolled down the window. "Hey, are you okay?"

She took a better look inside, hoping there was someone else in the car she hadn't seen. But the rest of the vehicle was empty.

"I'm fine."

"Do you need a ride or anything?"

The way he said that caught her attention. There was a hesitance in his voice, like he wasn't sure how this worked. Like he'd never stopped for a hitchhiker before.

She stepped closer. "I don't get in with men."

"Yeah, I don't blame you." His brow furrowed with concern. "There are a lot of bad people out there."

Wow, he was gorgeous. Older than her, but no gray in his dark hair. He had warm brown eyes and neatly trimmed stubble. He wore a button-down shirt with the top unbuttoned and the sleeves cuffed. She could imagine him loosening a tie after work, sliding it through the collar to take it off, and unbuttoning the first couple of buttons.

Water dripped down her cheeks and her feet were well on their way to going numb. The way his forehead creased with concern, and with no lust or malice, made her want to trust him.

Or maybe it was the storm and the potential warmth of his car.

"I'll be okay." She tried to keep her teeth from chattering. "I just need to get to the bus station in Pinecrest."

He looked forward, then back at her. "That's a long walk."

"Yeah."

Another gust of wind hit her and rain pelted her face.

"Okay." He hesitated. "If you're sure. I won't force you into anything, but if you want a ride…"

She didn't get in cars with men. But she was wet and freezing and he looked nice. He had kind eyes. One corner of his mouth turned up and he nodded toward the passenger seat as if to say, come on in. It'll be fine.

Trust me.

She glanced around the storm drenched highway. At the rain pelting down and the trees bending in the wind.

And she ran around to the other side of his car and climbed in.

CHAPTER 3
Zachary

MY PHONE WOKE ME UP. Groaning, I rolled over and forced my eyes open. Who the hell was calling me this early on a Sunday? And why weren't they texting like a normal person?

"Hello?"

"Zachary, it's Joe Rodriguez."

I did jobs for him sometimes. Maybe he had something quick and easy for me. I scrubbed a hand over my face, trying to wake up. "Hey, Joe. What's up?"

"Sorry to bother you this early on a weekend, but I'm in a jam. I have a bathroom light fixture that needs to be replaced in my building on Main Street. Any chance you could get over there today?"

Bathroom light fixture? Definitely easy. "Sure, no problem."

He let out a relieved breath. "Thanks so much. I promised I'd have someone out there this morning, so this is a big help."

We said goodbye and I dropped the phone on my bed. I rubbed my face again and pinched the bridge of my nose. I was hungover as hell. Which was stupid. I hadn't had that much to drink last night.

I worked my jaw a few times, expecting it to be sore, but Cory hadn't hit me all that hard. Barely felt anything. My fist was sore, but I figured it was worth it.

Wait. What had Joe said? Which building?

He owned several, all of them downtown. But the one on Main Street?

That was Timeless Beauty. Marigold's salon.

Shit.

For a second, I thought about calling Joe back and telling him I couldn't make it after all. Her salon was open on Sundays. She'd be there. Spending time in close quarters with Marigold was worse than a hangover.

But if I didn't do it, I wouldn't just be leaving Joe in a bad spot, I'd be screwing over Mari.

I promised myself I'd never do that again, so I threw off the covers, got my ass up, and headed for the shower.

———

A little bell tinkled when I opened the door to Timeless Beauty. The place was so Marigold, it was ridiculous. Everything from the fancy framed mirrors to the velvet chaise to the vintage art on the walls were perfect representations of her.

"I'll be right there." Her musical voice came from the back and my chest tightened.

She came around the partition behind the front desk wearing a navy-blue dress that brought out the blue in her eyes. She stopped and I didn't miss the look of surprise on her face.

"Oh. Hi." She absently clasped her hands, as if she were suddenly unsure what to do with them. "You must be here to replace the restroom light."

"Yeah."

Yeah? That was all I could say? *Smooth, Z. Real smooth.*

A hint of pink crept across her cheeks, giving me an instant hard on. Which made me feel like a total creep.

"I already tried changing the bulbs in the existing one and that didn't help, so Joe bought a new fixture. Hopefully that works. It's the only restroom I have and it's pitch black in there without a light."

"I'll take care of it."

"Thanks." She gestured toward the back of the salon. "It's back there."

I walked past her, through the empty salon, and tried to ignore how good she smelled.

She was right, the restroom was dark as hell. Not even a tiny window to let in some light. I propped open the door and looked up at the light fixture while I flipped the switch a couple of times. Not that I expected it to turn on, but you just never knew.

"Do you know where the electrical panel is?" I called out, then winced. Hangovers were a bitch.

"I think it's in the back."

Her voice was soft. And too close. I assumed she hadn't followed me, but she was in the doorway of the restroom.

"Sorry. Didn't see you there."

She glanced away with an awkward smile.

I was such an idiot.

I followed her through a doorway into a work area. A wide bank of cabinets with shelves above it lined one wall and there was a small desk in one corner with an open laptop and a mug with a little blot of lipstick on it.

My eyes lingered on the red print of her lips.

I needed to stop that. *Focus, Z.*

The electrical panel was on the back wall. I opened it and even though the labels were faded with age, they were legible.

"If you need anything else, let me know," she said, and I didn't miss the hesitance in her voice, like she wasn't quite sure how to talk to me. "I have a client coming any minute, so I'm hoping the rest of the electricity can stay on."

"I can turn off the power to the restroom. If anything is on the same circuit, it might not work, but I'll get you up and running as soon as I can."

"Okay. Um… thanks."

The bell on the front door tinkled and without another word, she disappeared out into the salon.

I shook my head. It was my fault things were awkward between us. I was the one who'd screwed up in the first place —because of course I was, screw-up was my middle name. It wasn't like we'd dated. She wasn't an ex-girlfriend. I'd just done something stupid. Something I could have put behind us years ago.

But then I'd made it worse by avoiding her. She'd walk into a room, I'd walk out. It hadn't taken long for it to feel like I had to stay away from her, otherwise… I don't know, the sun would go supernova or something.

So there we were, years later, and I never knew what to say when I was around her. She probably thought I hated her, which just made me avoid her more.

Vicious cycle.

Regardless of how I felt about being in close quarters with Marigold, I had a job to do. I flipped the breaker to turn off power to the restroom, then went back out to my truck and grabbed my ladder and tools.

Marigold had her client, Sandra, in a chair. She ran her fingers through her short silver hair as she talked to her in the mirror.

I took my ladder to the restroom, trying not to be too intrusive. After setting up the ladder and strapping on my tool belt, I climbed up to start taking the old fixture down.

Drywall dust fell as I finished unscrewing the old fixture

and pulled it down from the ceiling. It was heavier than it looked, so I rested one end on my shoulder while I tested the wires to make sure they weren't hot, and got to work on the wiring.

Marigold's voice got a little louder. It sounded like she'd moved Sandra to the washing sink on the other side of the wall. I tried to focus on what I was doing, not on the sound of her voice.

It wasn't easy.

Out of nowhere, my vision went black. It was like driving too fast in a blizzard late at night—dark, but bright white flashes were everywhere, moving so rapidly they ran together. A mechanical crackling sound filled my ears, drowning out everything. It took me a few seconds to recognize what was happening.

Oh, fuck. Am I being electrocuted?

I couldn't let go of the wires. Somehow my brain was working well enough to recognize electrical current was flowing through my body, probably burning me from the inside—although I didn't feel any pain—but I couldn't move.

This might kill me. And I never told Marigold how I feel about her.

As quickly as it started, the noise stopped. The silence hit me like a blow. I couldn't breathe. My vision was dark, nothing but vague shadows.

Wait. I wasn't on the ladder anymore. I was on the floor.

Then the pain hit.

My arms and chest were on fire but I still couldn't move. I sucked in a breath, finally drawing air into my lungs, and my heart pounded in my chest. Pain radiated across my back. I must have fallen off the ladder and hit the ground. Hard.

"Zachary?"

I blinked a few times, trying to clear my vision.

"Zachary, can you hear me?"

The fog started to clear and through the haze of pain, a

face took shape. She had to be an angel. No human could be so beautiful. Clear blue eyes filled with concern. A soft mouth with full pink lips. Dark hair spilling around fair skin.

"Are you an angel?"

"What?" Her voice was so concerned. Almost panicked. "No. Sandra called 911. They're on their way. Don't move."

I reached for her face and touched her cheek. I had to know if she was real. "You're so beautiful."

"Don't, Zachary, you're hurt. You fell off the ladder."

The room around her wouldn't come into focus. Everything was hazy and indistinct. It was as if nothing existed except this beautiful woman looking down on me.

"Wires shouldn't have been hot," I mumbled.

"What? The wires? Oh my god, did you get shocked?"

The edges of my vision darkened, like black clouds closing in on her. I reached up again, trying to cling to her. She took my hand and I couldn't understand why it hurt so much.

"I think I'm going to pass out." I hardly recognized my own voice. I almost sounded drunk.

"Stay with me, Zachary." She touched my cheek. "Stay with me."

————

I jerked awake to the sound of beeping. Everything was out of focus, my eyes watery. Where was I?

Vague memories of an ambulance ride came back to me. They'd taken me to the hospital. I'd been at Marigold's salon and fell off the ladder. Why did I fall?

Right, the fixture. I'd been reaching up to finish disconnecting the old light and put my hand on the box. But nothing should have been hot. I'd turned the circuit off at the breaker. I'd tested the wires.

"Something must have been wired wrong," I mumbled.

"It's okay," a soft voice spoke. "I'm so glad you're waking up. They told me you would, but I was starting to worry."

That voice. *Stay with me, Zachary.* "Marigold?"

She moved closer and her face came into focus. "Are you in any pain?"

I was in a ton of pain, but somehow it didn't matter. "What are you doing here?"

"They brought you here in the ambulance and I followed. Do you know where you are?"

"ER?"

"Yeah. Do you remember what happened? They said you might not."

It was hard to keep my eyes open, so I let them drift closed. "I tested the wires. Don't know why it was hot."

"So you know you were shocked?"

I nodded. That was a mistake. Hurt like hell. I groaned.

"You are in pain, aren't you? The nurse gave you something but she said you might need more when you wake up. You have burns and you fell pretty hard."

Opening my eyes, I tried to focus on her face. Burns. That was what I felt. My hands felt like they were on fire. So did my shoulder and chest. Current must have gone through one arm and out the other.

I was lucky it hadn't stopped my heart.

"Let me call the nurse."

"No." I needed to talk to her first, before the pain meds knocked me out. I might never have an opportunity like this again. "Marigold, wait."

"She'll be here in a second. Just hang in there."

I had to tell her. I could have died and she never would have known. "No, Mari—"

"Oh good, he's awake." A nurse dressed in blue scrubs came around the curtain. She had gray in her hair and a motherly smile.

My vision was clearing but my head wasn't. Everything was still too fuzzy.

"How are you feeling?" she asked.

"Hurts," I said. "But—"

"Don't worry, honey, I can take care of that." She started doing something with the IV. "They're going to admit you, so we'll move you to another room once it's ready for you. My guess is, you'll go home tomorrow. You have some burns and you'll be sore from the fall, but you got very lucky. Your injuries could have been much worse."

To my increasingly hazy brain, that sounded like a good thing. I could feel the drugs start to course through me. It felt great, erasing the pain like it had never been there.

But I still needed to talk to Marigold. I needed to tell her. "I love you."

The nurse laughed. "That's what they all say. This will help you rest and we should be able to wean you off by morning. For now, just get some sleep."

"No." My voice sounded far away, like someone else was speaking, and I realized I'd closed my eyes. I forced them open, trying to find Marigold. "Love you. Always you."

"You are a cutie," the nurse said. "This is going to make him really drowsy, so don't worry if he just sleeps. He'll be fine."

There were more voices. Talking. I couldn't make it out. Too tired. I wanted to stay awake, but my body wouldn't cooperate.

I sank into the depths of pain-free bliss, hoping Marigold would be there when I woke up.

CHAPTER 4

Zachary

WHEN I WOKE up the next morning, Marigold was long gone. I had a vague memory of her touching my face and telling me to get better, but that could have been a dream. It was hard to tell. Soreness set in as the pain medication wore off, but I wanted a clear head, so I refused more.

The fall had messed me up more than the shock. I had minor burns, but I'd gotten lucky. Those could have been a lot worse. Fortunately, I hadn't broken any bones, but I was bruised and beat up. I felt like I'd been run over by a truck. Repeatedly.

My head was also a mess, but it wasn't from the shock or the fall. It was Marigold.

I could still hear her voice, like a seductive whisper. *Stay with me, Zachary.*

For a moment, when electricity had been coursing through me, I'd thought I was going to die. And who had I thought about? My parents, my brothers, my sister, my nieces and nephews, my friends?

Nope. Marigold Martin.

What the hell was I supposed to do with that?

I couldn't go back to pretending she didn't exist. She very

much did exist. And of all the regrets I had in this life, the way I'd treated her was the one that hurt the most when I'd thought it might be the end.

That was huge.

I had to face reality. I had a thing for Marigold and it was never, ever going away.

It wasn't because she felt unattainable, although she did. And it wasn't because her friendship with my sister made her off limits. Hell, if Annika had ever said I couldn't go for Marigold, I'd have married her by now just because she told me not to.

No, I was crazy about Marigold because of who she was. Because she was smart, and sweet, and drop-dead gorgeous. Because she was the type of woman who'd follow an ambulance to the hospital and sit with a guy who'd spent more than fifteen years ignoring her. That was just who she was.

Granted, I wasn't good enough for her. She absolutely deserved better than me. But that excuse wasn't going to fly anymore.

The question was, what was I going to do about it?

I didn't have an answer and before I could think about it much, the doctor came in to let me know I was being discharged. She told me to rest and take some time off work. I could tell by her tone she wasn't sure whether or not I'd listen.

Neither was I.

My truck was still at Marigold's salon, so while I got dressed, I debated who I should call for a ride. It was midday on a Monday. My friends were all at work. So was my brother Theo. He was a teacher and football coach at the high school. I had no idea if Garrett was on duty today and I didn't want to find out. I'd walk home first.

I didn't want to call Annika either. She was busy juggling work and four kids. Josiah was a good bet. He and I generally got along. And since he worked for himself, it wouldn't be a huge hassle for him to come give me a ride.

Mentally running through my list of siblings made me think of my brother Reese. Which was weird because the jerk had left Tilikum years ago and hadn't been back. Although I could have sworn I saw him once, about seven years ago, give or take. I'd seen a guy in town getting into a black SUV and for a second, it had looked like Reese.

Probably hadn't been him, but I thought about that once in a while. It made me want to punch him in the face. I didn't give a shit if I ever saw Reese again, but Mom did. If he'd been anywhere near Tilikum without going to see her, he deserved to be knocked on his ass.

I got out my phone and was about to call Josiah when my mom, Marlene, came around the curtain. Her hair was up and she adjusted her blue-rimmed glasses.

"There you are." She wrapped me in a gentle hug, then pulled back and touched my face. "Are you okay? Why are you up?"

"I'm going home."

Dad came in behind her, dressed in his typical flannel and jeans. Paul Haven was a lumberjack looking dude with big arms and a thick beard peppered with gray. He looked me up and down but his expression didn't betray anything. For all I knew, he was disappointed the shock hadn't killed me.

He crossed his arms. "Did they really release you, or are you just walking out?"

"I wouldn't just walk out of a hospital."

Dad's brow furrowed. Mom raised her eyebrows.

"Okay, fine. But it was only once, and I was like twenty. Do you need to see my discharge paperwork?" I picked up the packet the nurse had given me and held it up.

"Of course not," Mom said. "But I think you were older than that when you wrecked the dirt bike."

I'd been thinking about a different incident—a four-wheeler accident—but I decided not to point out that I'd been stupid enough to leave a hospital against doctor's orders not once, but twice.

But hey, who was counting?

"How did you guys know I was here, anyway?"

"They called to let us know," Mom said. "I came to the ER last night, but you were asleep."

That was a little bit creepy. I had no memory of my mom being there. I must have been out cold.

I wondered if Marigold had still been there.

"Well, let's get you home," Dad grumbled.

"We're not taking him home," Mom said.

"Then what are we doing here?"

Mom put a hand on his arm. "We're taking him to our house. He can go home when I'm sure he's okay."

"The doctor said I'm okay," I said.

Dad shot me a look. "Don't argue with your mom."

Why did these two still have the ability to make me feel like I was a ten-year-old kid? I put up my hands. "Not arguing."

Mom stepped closer and touched my cheek again. "You gave us a scare, Zachary. That could have killed you."

I grinned. "Can't get rid of me that easily."

Dad grunted. Mom just shook her head.

I put my work boots back on, trying not to groan. I didn't want my mom to worry more than she already did. And I didn't want to admit I was in pain in front of my dad.

We left and headed for the exit. I smiled at the nurses as we walked out, winking at a few of them.

Habit.

The bumpy drive up to my parents' place wasn't pleasant. Too many bruises. They lived in a hand-built log home at the end of a long gravel driveway on a hill with views of Tilikum through the pine trees. It had been a cool place to grow up, especially for a restless kid like me.

My truck was parked outside the house. How had it gotten there?

"Did you guys get my truck?" I asked.

"Josiah and Audrey brought it up," Mom said.

Huh. That was cool of them.

We went inside and I headed straight for the kitchen. I hadn't eaten much in the past twenty-four hours and I was on the verge of getting hangry.

"Go sit down," Mom said, shooing me out. "I'll get you some lunch."

I wasn't going to argue with that. I kissed the top of her head. "Thanks, Mom."

Dad seemed annoyed, although sometimes that was just his face. I went into the living room and gingerly lowered myself onto the couch. My phone buzzed with a text, so I got it out to check. It was a reply from the general contractor on the job I'd been working on. Finally. I'd texted him hours ago to let him know what had happened and that I wouldn't be there today. True to form, his only reply was, OK.

Whatever. I didn't expect him to give a shit about my brush with death.

Dad followed me in but he didn't sit down, just leaned against the kitchen doorway. "So what happened yesterday?"

"Other than I got shocked all to hell?"

"I mean why did it happen?"

Defiant anger rose from the pit of my stomach. Of course he assumed it was my fault.

For once, it actually wasn't. "Joe called me this morning. Turns out some genius ran two sets of wires through a shared pipe in the wall and managed to short the switch leg to the box. Marigold must have turned on the other light while I was touching it. Not her fault. She couldn't have known."

"Your mom was right, that could have killed you."

I flashed him a cocky half-grin. "Could have, but didn't."

My flippant tone clearly pissed him off. His thick

eyebrows drew together in a glare. I braced myself for him to blow up at me, but this time, he didn't. Just grunted and left out the back door.

I didn't know which was worse. When he yelled at me like I was still a teenager, or when he didn't, like I wasn't worth the trouble.

Lately it was hard not to feel like he'd given up on me.

I might have blamed my friction with Dad on the fact that, technically, he was my stepdad. When my parents had married, they'd each been a single parent to three boys. And despite the fact that my biological father popped up now and then, Paul was my dad. As far as I was concerned, he always had been. I was a Haven, end of story.

But that didn't mean we got along. And I doubted my genes were the problem.

I was the problem.

Story of my life.

Mom brought a plate with a huge sandwich and handed it to me. "He's not mad."

"Could have fooled me."

"You scared him."

"Interesting response to fear." I took a big bite.

She sat down next to me. "He doesn't know how to deal with big feelings. You two have that in common."

I met her eyes, my forehead tightening with confusion. "I'm not the one who walked out."

"True, but you both hide in your own way. He's gruff. You use humor." She raised her eyebrows. "And sarcasm."

"I do not." That was a lie. I totally did.

She just shook her head. "So I heard you're in love."

I almost dropped my sandwich in my lap. "What?"

She smiled. "You told the nurse in the ER you loved her."

I groaned. I'd been trying to tell Marigold, but clearly my timing had been awful. Now it was a joke, like one of those viral videos of someone proposing to their nurse when they came out of anesthesia.

"How'd you hear about that already? Were you there?"

"No, it was before I got there, but I talked to Aunt Louise." She shrugged, as if that explained it.

Who knew how Aunt Louise had heard. Tilikum gossip line strikes again.

I grinned. "From what I remember, the nurse was pretty hot for her age. And the drugs she was giving me were awesome."

"What's not to love? By the way, I saw Gavin Bailey at the store this morning. He asked if you were all right."

"Gavin? How'd he know?"

"He was one of the responders."

How did I not remember that? Gavin Bailey had been one of my sworn enemies from the time we were born. The Haven and Bailey families had been feuding for generations, until my sister had gone and married Levi Bailey. I was still getting used to not hating them. Old habits die hard.

"I must have been really out of it. Did I try to punch him or anything?"

"I don't think so. I'm not sure if you were conscious when they got there."

"That's probably good. You shouldn't punch the guy trying to save your life. Even if he's a Bailey."

She patted my leg. "Can I get you anything else?"

A date with Marigold? "No. When are you going to let me go home?"

"Maybe tomorrow."

I laughed and shook my head. "Mom, you don't have to do that."

"Give me this. I don't get to take care of you boys very often anymore. It reminds me of when you were little."

"If you want to be reminded of when we were little, just

go in the spare bedroom. Why do you still have those old bunk beds?"

"We have grandkids." She paused and cracked a smile. "And hopefully we'll have more someday."

I almost blurted out that I was pretty sure Marigold and I would give her a tiny army of grandchildren. But I was getting ahead of myself. I needed to convince Marigold to give me a chance first. We'd get to all the babies later.

Mom patted my leg again, then got up and disappeared out the back door. I inhaled the rest of my sandwich, then laid down on the couch. Considering what my body had been through, a nap was probably a good idea.

But I couldn't sleep.

I stared at the ceiling, thinking about Marigold.

What was she doing today? Was she at work?

Was she worried about me?

I wondered if I should call her. Thank her for getting me to the hospital and let her know I was okay.

But I wanted to do that in person.

What was it going to take to undo years of being shitty to her? It wasn't ideal, but I wasn't afraid of the odds. My rebellious streak ran deep and this felt like an unspoken challenge. Get Marigold Martin to fall in love with me?

I was Zachary Haven. I never struck out with women. How hard could it be?

CHAPTER 5
Marigold

IT WAS weird being at the salon again.

Rain pattered against the windows and the world outside was shrouded in gray mist. I took a sip of my tea, enjoying the warmth of the mug in my hands. It wasn't cold in the salon, but watching the storm outside sent a shiver down my back.

Or maybe it was the memory of Zachary's accident.

I felt horrible about it. The electrician Joe had sent to fix everything had explained that when I'd turned on the light above the washing station, it had somehow shocked Zachary. He'd said it shouldn't have happened—there was something wrong with the wiring—and it certainly wasn't my fault. But I still felt awful.

He could have been killed. For as long as I lived, I'd never forget the sight of him lying on the floor. He hadn't moved and I'd been terrified he was dead.

Most of the incident was a blur in my memory. Yelling for Sandra to call 911. Rushing to see if he was breathing. The relief I felt when he took a gasping breath and I knew he was alive.

I blinked to clear my head. Reliving that awful experience

wasn't doing any good. Zachary was okay. I'd heard from Annika that he'd been released from the hospital that morning. No major head or spine injuries and his burns weren't as bad as they could have been. His parents had taken him to their place to help him recover.

They were such a sweet family.

"Hey, Mari, Amy just called," Stacey said from her spot at the front desk. "Her daughter is sick, so she has to go pick her up at school. I rescheduled her for next week."

I glanced at the time. That meant I didn't have any more appointments today. I let out a sigh. Things had really slowed down in the last month.

"Okay, thanks. You might as well go home early. I doubt we'll get any walk-ins, but if we do, I can take care of it."

She smiled, her eyes bright, the caramel highlights we'd recently added to her long, dark hair to give it more dimension enhancing her perfect complexion. "That actually works out great. Jason is already home for the day."

Stacey had worked for me for the last few years and I adored her. Her husband, Jason, owned his own plumbing business. But he wasn't the pants-hanging-down-too-low type of plumber. He was a former football player turned weightlifter, a Greek god of a plumber.

Stacey was a very lucky woman.

She tidied up the front desk a little before grabbing her things and leaving out the front door.

I took my empty tea mug to the back to rinse it out, wondering if I should just close early. With the weather the way it was, it was doubtful anyone would come in. But I did have some bookkeeping to get done—business owner problems—so I decided to stick it out until closing time.

The wind howled outside as I worked. Bookkeeping wasn't a fun task, especially when finances were so tight. How had everything gotten to be so expensive? It seemed like everything from color to toner to laundry detergent had doubled in price in the last few years.

Things had been better when I'd had another stylist working for me, but she'd married the man of her dreams and moved to Colorado. I really needed to find someone to fill her chair or I wasn't going to be able to keep paying Stacey's salary.

The bell on the front door tinkled, drawing my attention away from the depressing numbers. Maybe it was a walk-in. That would be a positive way to end the day.

"I'll be right there," I called out.

I stood and fluffed my long hair, then walked out to greet my potential customer.

A man stood just inside. His back was to me and he ran a hand over his hair, wiping some of the rain off. When he turned to face me, I blinked in surprise.

Tall. Thick, dark hair. Mesmerizing brown eyes. His bone structure was exquisite, his stubble neatly trimmed. He looked like he'd stepped right out of an ad for designer men's cologne.

"Hi." His voice was deep and smooth, flowing over me like rich maple syrup. "Are you open?"

It took me a second to answer and I felt my cheeks flush. "Yes. Yes, I'm open."

He gave me a subtle grin, puckering dimples in both cheeks.

Both. Cheeks.

"Do you do men here?"

"Um, what?"

His smile grew. "Men's haircuts? Both barbershops are closed, so I thought I'd try here."

"Oh, yes. Of course I do. Yes. Come in." I was so flustered, I needed to pull myself together. But oh my goodness, he was so handsome. "Can I take your coat?"

"Thanks."

He slid his coat from his shoulders, revealing a button-down shirt and a pair of dark slacks. I took his coat, trying not to be further distracted by his obviously toned body.

Honestly, where had this man come from?

I hung up his coat and directed him to my chair. The first thing I usually did was run my fingers through a client's hair while I asked them what they wanted. But I was so nervous, I wasn't sure I could bring myself to touch him.

"So, what can I do for you?"

His eyes met mine in the mirror. "I just need a trim. Keep it short on the sides and back, but a little bit of length on top is fine."

I nodded and finally compelled myself to touch his hair. It was healthy—thick and soft. I ran my fingers through the top and grabbed a comb.

"Preston," he said.

"What?"

"My name." There were those dark eyes in the mirror again. "Preston Bradford. And you are…?

"Marigold Martin."

"Beautiful name." One corner of his mouth lifted. "It's nice to meet you, Marigold Martin."

"Thanks. You too."

I swallowed hard. It would be all too easy to get lost in those mysterious eyes. I tore my gaze from the mirror and grabbed a cape. I was a professional. I just needed to do my job.

I put the cape around his shoulders and fastened it at the nape of his neck. "If you'll follow me, I'll wash your hair and then I can get started."

From the corner of my eye, I saw him smile again.

Swoon.

I led him to the washing station and he leaned back in the chair. Turning on the water, I waited a few seconds for it to warm up, then tested it on him. "How's that temperature?"

"Perfect."

I wet his hair and washed it, pretending he was just another client and my stomach wasn't filled with butterflies. It worked well enough until I started massaging his scalp, like I always did, and he groaned.

He chuckled softly. "Sorry. That feels good."

I pressed my lips together and kept massaging, willing myself not to say something embarrassing. His eyes were closed, so mine roamed over his handsome features. He groaned again, the noise low in his throat. Normally I would have stopped massaging by that point, but I kept going a little longer.

But honestly, could you blame me?

Finally, I had to stop or I was going to make things awkward. I had him sit up and pressed a towel to his hair to get the excess water off.

"That almost put me to sleep," he said. "You have talented hands."

I laughed and my cheeks blazed with heat. This man was going to kill me right here in my own salon.

Oddly, that made me think of the way Zachary had looked lying on the floor.

Strange thought to have at that moment.

"We can go back over to my station."

Preston followed me and sat in the chair. And I got to work.

"So, you must be new in town," I said, attempting a normal conversation while I started cutting. "Or visiting?"

"I don't live here full time, but I'm building a place about an hour northwest of here. Kind of a mountain getaway. It's fairly isolated, so Tilikum is a convenient place for me to stay when I'm in the area."

That was interesting. The Tilikum gossip line had been buzzing about someone building a mansion on the river. A lot of local tradesmen had been hired to work on it, including Stacey's husband. This had to be the owner.

"Where do you live the rest of the time?"

"Seattle."

That was common. There were quite a few out-of-towners, mainly from the Seattle area, who owned vacation homes in the area. Most of them rented them out when they weren't using them.

"What about you?" he asked. "Are you from Tilikum?"

"Born and raised. I went to beauty school in Wenatchee, but otherwise, I've always lived here."

"It's a nice town. I like it."

"Me too. Small-town living isn't for everyone, but it suits me."

His eyes caught mine in the mirror again and he smiled.

Focus, Marigold. Don't screw up his hair.

"What do you do for a living?" I asked, letting my 'make conversation with the client' habit take over.

"I'm a lawyer."

"What kind of law do you practice?"

"Corporate law. It probably doesn't sound riveting, but I like it."

"As long as you enjoy what you do, that's what matters."

"I prefer working behind the scenes. Mostly I try to poke holes in contracts. Find the loopholes and make sure my clients don't get screwed over by them."

"Sounds complicated."

He shrugged. "It is at first, but I guess I have a talent for it."

I put my scissors down and ran my fingers through his hair, testing the length, then continued cutting. I wanted to ask him if he was married, but I couldn't think of a way to casually slip it into the conversation. I never asked my male clients if they were married or dating someone. It just wasn't something I needed to know.

But I really, really wanted to know.

"How long do you think you'll be in town?" I asked.

"Not sure. The house I'm building is taking longer than I expected. My assistant has been handling most of it, but I decided to make a trip over here and see if I can get things back on schedule."

"I've heard the house you're building is beautiful."

"Where'd you hear that?"

I shrugged. "It's a small town. People talk. An out-of-towner building a big house is front page news here."

I caught his smile from the corner of my eye.

"It's going to be nice."

Does your wife think so? Is your girlfriend helping you pick colors?

Nope, I couldn't do it. I just kept cutting his hair.

I finished his trim, resisting the urge to lean closer and breathe in his scent as I cleaned up the back of his neck with the clippers. The shampoo I'd used smelled incredible on him.

After putting a little pomade in his hair, I took off the cape and brushed him off. I handed him a mirror and spun the chair around so he could see the back.

"What do you think?"

He touched the front and moved his head around. "It looks great. Thank you."

"You're welcome. I'll get your coat and meet you up front."

My stomach felt jumpy as I retrieved his coat from the hook and brought it to the front desk. I was glad I'd sent Stacey home early. There was no way she'd have missed the flush in my cheeks or the way I fumbled trying to ring him up. He stood on the other side of the desk, watching me with a slight smile on his face.

I gave him the total and he tapped his credit card to pay.

"You're all set," I said. "Do you want a receipt?"

"No, I'm good." He paused, his eyes lingering on mine for a long moment. "I'd like to take you out sometime."

I blinked in surprise, my mind racing. My lips parted but I couldn't seem to get any words out.

He raised his eyebrows. "Yes?"

I closed my mouth and took a deep breath. "Sorry. Yes, I'd love to."

He gave me that subtle smile again as he got out his phone. "Can I get your number?"

I gave it to him. Was this really happening?

"I'm busy tonight. But tomorrow?" he asked.

"Tomorrow would be great."

"I'll call you." He smiled again. "Bye, Marigold."

"Bye, Preston."

He slipped on his coat and left, disappearing into the storm.

I watched him go, dumbstruck. Had the dashing gentleman of my dreams just walked into my salon and asked me out?

It seemed like maybe he had.

The Cabin

BRIELLE

THE CABIN WAS NICE. Luxurious, even. Leather couches, a big fireplace, a loft bedroom with the most comfortable bed Brielle had ever slept on.

By the time they'd gotten to the bus stop in Pinecrest, the last bus had already left. She was stuck without a place to stay in the middle of a storm.

But the guy who'd picked her up—he'd told her his name was John—had come back. He'd actually circled the block a few times while she tried to buy a ticket. When he saw her standing, despondent, on the side of the road, he'd offered her a place to crash.

The storm had been getting worse and she'd been desperate. She'd figured it was either go home, die of exposure somewhere, or take her chances with John and possibly become a murder victim.

Home was a hard no. Whether she froze in the storm or was murdered, she was dead either way, so why not try for a warm place to sleep?

He'd told her the cabin was a bit of a drive, but at that point, she'd been committed. And so far, nothing bad had happened. No threats, no tying her up, nothing. He hadn't even hit on her. Just explained that he owned a cabin no one was using and she was welcome to stay there until she figured things out.

When he'd left her there, alone, she'd wondered if he was either going to come back and kill her in the morning, or if he somehow knew who she was and her parents were going to show up.

Once again, he surprised her. No parents. And he obviously hadn't murdered her. He just brought her some groceries, showed her how to use the old DVD player, and talked her into staying longer, just to be safe.

After all, there was another storm outside. Vegas could wait.

Brielle wasn't stupid. She knew people weren't nice for no reason. John had a motive. She just hadn't figured out what it was yet.

For now, she was warm and dry. She'd left her phone at the apartment, and felt sort of naked without it, but someone could have used it to track her. And if John really wanted to hurt her, he would have. He'd had plenty of opportunity. It wasn't that she trusted him—she didn't really trust anyone— but she'd take advantage of his hospitality for as long as possible, then have him take her back to Pinecrest to catch a bus to Vegas.

She held a bag of chips in one hand and absently ate while she watched the rain come down through the back window. All she could see were pine trees and clouds. In the summer, it was probably pretty.

A little fantasy came to mind—a simple daydream. John keeping her there, not because he was a rapist or a murderer, but because he liked her. She could be his princess in a tower, hiding away in the woods while he kept her safe. He'd let her live there and take care of her, keeping her tucked away like a treasure.

She knew it was a stupid daydream. But it was nice to imagine anyway.

A knock on the door roused her from her thoughts and she turned to find John coming in.

"Hey." He shut the door behind him and smiled at her. "I figured I'd check on you. See if you need anything."

She gave him a quick once over as he took his coat off and hung it on a hook by the door. He was wearing a sweater and slacks and although he could have been concealing a weapon, she didn't notice anything obvious. And he hadn't brought a duffel bag full of plastic sheeting and a butcher knife or anything.

"I'm fine. I don't think there's anything I need."

He took a step and instinctively, she stepped back. He paused but didn't give any other indication that he'd noticed. "Good. Just making sure. Are you bored? I know there's not a lot to do."

"No, I slept in and then I started watching your collection of The Office."

"Good show."

"Yeah, it's funny." She put her bag of chips down and sucked the salt off her fingers. "Why are you being so nice to me?"

"You're not used to that, are you?"

She crossed her arms and shook her head.

"I get it. You weren't out on that highway in a storm for fun. You said you were going to Vegas, right?"

She nodded.

"Why?"

"I'm moving there."

"With just a backpack?"

"It was easier that way. Once I get to Vegas, I'll find a job and a place to live. But you still haven't answered my question."

He glanced away. "I had an older sister. She took off one

day and never came home. When I saw you, it reminded me of her."

So that was why he was being so nice to her. Brielle's heart swelled with sympathy. "I'm sorry. That must have been awful."

"It was. I was just a kid, but I'll always wonder if I could have done something."

"I'm sure it's not your fault she left."

"No." He paused. "I don't make a habit of picking up hitchhikers and bringing them out here, in case you're wondering. You're my first."

That made her laugh a little. "Thanks for giving me a place to crash. But I should probably get back to Pinecrest so I can get a bus ticket and get out of your way."

He looked away again and nodded slowly, as if he were trying to figure out what to say. "What if you just... stay a little while?"

"Stay here?"

"Yeah. I'm not going to try to talk you out of going to Vegas if that's what you really want. But it's dangerous out there. The weather is terrible."

She took another step back. A part of her—a big part—wanted to stay. She felt safe.

But she couldn't stay in some random guy's cabin forever. Her little daydream of being his hidden treasure was stupid.

Wasn't it?

"How long?"

He shrugged. "I don't know. I'm making this up as I go along. I'm just worried if I drop you off at the bus station, something horrible will happen to you. Something I could have prevented if you stayed here."

He was thinking about his sister again. Brielle could tell. Maybe he saw her as his second chance. A way to make up for the sister he'd lost.

Would it be so bad to hide out there for a little longer? No one would find her—if anyone was even bothering to look, which was debatable.

"I know you don't have any reason to trust me," John said, meeting her eyes. "But I can tell you've been through some hard stuff. I just want to help."

Tears welled up. The way John looked at her, it felt like he saw her. Truly saw her for who she was. Not someone to yell at and belittle. Just Brielle.

Maybe he really wasn't a rapist or a murderer. He'd certainly had plenty of opportunities to hurt her. If that was what he was planning, wouldn't he have done it already? Why keep offering to help?

Had she simply run into the right guy at the right time?

It was about time she got a break.

She swiped the tears from her cheeks as he cautiously approached her, and let him put his arms around her. She sank into his embrace, resting her head on his chest. He smelled good, like cologne and clean laundry.

"I'm sorry for whatever you've been through," he said.

She let him hold her for a long moment. It wasn't exactly a fatherly embrace, but he didn't do anything inappropriate, either. She relaxed, feeling safer than she'd ever felt in her entire life.

"Okay. I'll stay for a while."

He squeezed her, then let go and stepped back. "Good. I'll help you figure out a plan. But this is good."

Brielle agreed. It was good. Even better than going straight to Vegas. She could take her time. Hide out where no one would find her. Where she was safe.

And later, when he left her alone again, she was so grateful to be there, she didn't notice he'd locked her in from the outside.

CHAPTER 6

Marigold

I PASSED a truck on the way to my parents' house, and for a second, I thought it was Zachary. My heart fluttered, which was so silly. It wasn't even him, just an older man driving a similar truck. And who cared if we drove past each other? It was a small town, I saw him out and about from time to time.

Maybe I was just worried about him after the incident at the salon. It wasn't my misplaced crush, just friendly concern.

That didn't really account for the heart flutters, but I pushed it out of my mind.

I had a break between clients, so I'd decided to stop by and visit my mom. She'd had a minor medical procedure on her left wrist a few days earlier and I knew from experience I needed to check on her in person to make sure she was recovering as well as she claimed on the phone.

My parents, Craig and Alyssa Martin, lived on a quiet street in the house I'd grown up in. When they'd bought it, it had been a modest three-bedroom, one bath starter home. My dad had later added a second story, expanded the garage, and built an art studio for my mom. In the chilly fall weather, the light in the windows made it look warm and inviting.

I knocked and let myself in. "Hi, Mom. It's me."

"Hi, flower," she called. "Back here."

I moved through the familiar space, past old family pictures and my mom's paintings, making my way toward her voice at the back of the house. My dad was forever working on the house, but the furnishings hadn't changed much in the last twenty years. They had the same comfortable furniture in earth tones, the same moss green dishes in the kitchen, and the same white tea kettle perpetually on the stove, ready for visitors.

A beaded curtain hung in the doorway of my mom's studio, and the hardwood floor was covered with years worth of paint splatters. Several easels held in-progress paintings and huge windows let in light from the backyard. Dressed in denim overalls and a white tank top, her dark hair pulled up in a haphazard bun, Mom stood in the middle of it all, her head tilted, one hand on her hip.

"Mom?"

She held up a finger and tilted her head in the other direction.

I waited while she contemplated the half-finished painting in front of her. She grabbed a wide paint brush and a tube of paint, then squeezed a glob of light blue on the canvas. With exaggerated strokes, she smeared the paint all over the picture she'd been working on.

"Is everything okay?" I asked.

"No." She kept brushing the paint back and forth across the canvas. "This one's junk."

"I'm sure it wasn't junk. Did you have to ruin it?"

"Yes." She put the brush down and turned. "Sometimes there's no other way but to start over." Her face broke into a wide smile and she opened her arms. "Come here, flower."

I hugged her, breathing in her familiar perfume while she held me.

"What are you doing here?" She pulled away, her brow furrowing with mild confusion.

"I told you yesterday I'd stop by." I gestured to the brace on her left wrist. "I want to make sure you're okay."

She picked up an almost-empty mug and peered into it, as if she expected it to be full. "You told me? Sorry, I must have forgotten."

My mom was something of a hot mess. Dad called her a flighty artist, and although he meant it with affection, it was also true. It seemed like her memory wasn't the best and she was constantly losing things, but I tended to think her memory was fine. She just didn't pay attention. Her mind was forever in another world.

And it wasn't as if she were old. Not even close. She'd been a young mom when I was born, and was only in her fifties now. And she looked it. Her dark hair only had a few sparkles of gray and the smile lines around her eyes gave her a cheerful appearance rather than aging her.

"So how is your wrist?" I asked.

"It's fine. A little sore, but that's to be expected." She took a sip and made a face. "Ugh. Cold. I should make more. Do you want some tea?"

"Sure."

I followed her through the beaded curtain and into the kitchen. She tossed the last of her cold tea into the sink and filled the tea kettle.

"Where's Dad?" I asked. "Is he working today?"

"Who knows." She made a flippant gesture with her hand. "You know him. Can't sit still."

That was true. He owned a construction company and had built many of the newer houses in Tilikum. When he wasn't working, his idea of relaxation was building or fixing something around the house.

I helped her make tea for the two of us and we took our mugs to the table.

"What else is new?" Mom asked and blew on her tea.

For a second, I contemplated telling her about Preston

Bradford and the date he was taking me on that evening. But it was just a first date, and, dreamy though he was, I didn't want to give my mom any ideas before I'd had a chance to get to know him. "Not much. I've been busy with work and helping with Audrey's wedding plans. That's been fun."

"How's Zachary?"

"Apparently fine." I shrugged and took a careful sip of my tea. "Annika said his injuries weren't as serious as they could have been."

"That's good. Oh! Did you hear about the squirrel war?"

"Squirrel war?"

"You know how we tend to think the squirrels around here are all in cahoots."

"Okay…"

"Apparently there's trouble in paradise. A few squirrels had a stash of nuts out behind Tilikum Hardware. The employees would watch them on their breaks. And then, just the other day, there was a raid."

"A squirrel raid?"

Mom nodded. "Another group of squirrels rushed in, dug up the nuts, and took off with them."

"How do they know it wasn't the same squirrels? Maybe they were just moving their stash."

"I don't think so. The original squirrels were there, squeaking and squawking from the trees while the intruders descended. The Squirrel Protection Squad is up in arms over it. They don't know whose side to take."

"Does the SPS really need to get involved?"

She wrapped her hand around her mug. "That's what I said."

I laughed. I honestly wasn't sure if she was talking about a real thing that had happened or if she'd heard bits and pieces of a squirrel story and made up the rest.

Then again, this was Tilikum. A squirrel war wouldn't be out of the ordinary.

The door to the garage opened and my dad came in. He was tall and fit from years in construction with tanned skin and bright blue eyes.

"Look at this, my two best girls." He gave my mom a quick kiss. "Hi, lovebird. I missed you."

My parents were ridiculously cute. They'd known each other since preschool, started dating in high school, and the rest was history. To an outsider, they might have seemed like a poor match—too different. But my dad's steadiness and sense of duty was the perfect balance to my mom's flightiness.

"I missed you too," she said. "What have you been up to all morning?"

"I was over at Marigold's."

I blinked in surprise. "Why were you at my house?"

He pulled out a chair and sat. "I replaced your range."

"Why did you replace the range? It worked fine."

"It was gas," he said, as if that explained it.

"I know it was gas. I like having a gas stove."

He shook his head. "A new study came out saying you shouldn't have gas ranges. Causes asthma or allergies or something."

"I don't have asthma or allergies."

"Yet."

I stared at my dad for a moment. My parents had a key to my house—I'd given it to them for emergencies—and this wasn't the first time he'd taken it upon himself to complete a home repair that may or may not have been necessary. Without telling me first.

"Dad, you didn't have to replace my range. If I decided I needed an electric one, I would have done it myself."

"Flower," he said and booped me on the nose, "I don't want my little girl to have to worry about these things."

I sighed. I appreciated my dad and his willingness to help. I really did. But he had a way of making me feel like I couldn't take care of myself. Like he couldn't accept I was a grown woman. Or that he didn't trust me to handle my own life.

But I didn't have time to convince him of that. I had to get back to the salon.

"Sorry, but I have to get back to work." I took my mug to the sink and rinsed it. "Mom, thanks for the tea and I'm glad your wrist is okay."

"Oh yes." She looked at the brace on her wrist as if she'd forgotten it was there. "Thank you, flower."

"Bye, Dad. Love you."

"Love you too," he said absently, already fussing over Mom's wrist.

I drove back to the salon, parking in the lot next to the building. The sky was gray with clouds threatening rain and the breeze was cold.

"Hey, Marigold!"

That voice. It reached inside me and made my heart flutter. My stomach tingled at the sight of Zachary Haven, dressed in a black coat and jeans, his hair a little messy from the wind, jogging down the sidewalk toward me.

Breathe, Marigold. Breathe.

Why did he have to be so cute? His blue eyes were like the sky on a sunny day and his lips always seemed to be on the brink of a mischievous smirk.

As usual, my tongue decided to stop working and all I could do was blink at him.

He stopped. And then he did the strangest thing. He looked at me.

Zachary Haven never looked at me.

In the rare instances he was forced to actually interact with me, he wouldn't meet my eyes. He'd look away, say what needed to be said as quickly as possible, and brush by me.

This time, he didn't. He stood still on the sidewalk and

looked me in the eyes, subjecting me to the full force of those gorgeous blues.

The intensity of his gaze made my heart race. What did he want? Why wasn't he saying anything?

Several awkward seconds later, he finally said, "Hi."

"Hi."

He opened his mouth as if to speak, then closed it again before muttering, "Sorry, um…"

"Are you okay?"

"Yeah." He shifted on his feet and looked around, blinking like he was confused.

What was going on?

Oh no. Did he have a head injury from the fall?

I stepped closer. "Are you sure? Should you be up and around already? Maybe you should go home and lie down."

"No, I don't need to lie down." He met my eyes again. "I just wanted to say thank you."

That was nice of him. "You don't need to thank me. All I did was call an ambulance. And I didn't even do that. Sandra did."

His brow furrowed. "Weren't you at the hospital? Or did I dream that?"

"You didn't dream that. I was there."

"Are you sure?"

"Yes. Maybe you should go home and lie down."

"No." Glancing away, he rubbed the back of his neck. "What's wrong with me? I don't know why this is so hard."

"Why what's so hard?"

"This." He gestured between the two of us.

A gust of wind blew my hair around my face again.

"See," he said, as if the wind explained everything. "It's all wrong."

"Do your parents know you're up? Did the doctor say it was okay?"

"Yeah, that's not the problem."

This was so strange. Why was he acting like this? "What problem?"

He threw up his hands. "I don't know."

"Marigold, we have to talk," a woman said behind me. It was Gina Hembree, my next client. I hadn't even noticed her approach. "My ends are fried and I really think we need to go darker this time."

I tore my eyes off Zachary. "Okay, Gina. Go ahead inside and Stacey will get you checked in. I'll be there in a minute."

She checked her watch. "I hate to rush you, but I have another appointment after this."

"No problem." I smiled at her and turned back to Zachary while she went into the salon. "Sorry, but I have to go."

The pained look in his eyes didn't make any sense. What was going on with him?

His gaze moved from me to the salon door then back to me. "Okay. Work. I get it. I'll talk to you later."

"Zachary, I'm serious, are you okay? You're worrying me."

"Yeah." He started backing away, his brow still furrowed as if he were confused. "Fine."

He was not fine, but there wasn't anything I could do about it. The first drops of rain pattered on the sidewalk around me and the cold wind cut through my jacket. He turned and walked the way he'd come, not looking back at me again as I watched him go.

"Mari?" Stacey stood with the salon door partially open. "Are you okay?"

I startled. "Yes. Fine. Sorry. I'm coming."

She held the door for me while I hurried inside out of the wind.

"Gina, I'll be right with you."

I went to the back office, took off my coat, and hung it on the back of the chair.

"Who were you talking to out there?" Stacey asked. "Was that Zachary Haven?"

"Yes."

"Is he okay?"

"Honestly, I don't know." I grabbed a brush and ran it through my hair, trying to tame it after all that wind without totally destroying the loose waves I'd done this morning. "He was acting strange, but he's also Zachary Haven, so who knows."

"Don't worry about your hair. You look gorgeous as always."

I smiled. "Thanks, Stace. Can you distract Gina for a second? I need to make a quick call."

"Of course."

I pulled out my phone while Stacey went to chat up my client. I needed to call Annika.

"Hey, Mari," she answered.

"Have you talked to your brother today?"

"Which one?"

"Sorry, Zachary."

"No, I thought he was still at my parents' place."

"Maybe he was, but I just saw him and he was acting strange."

"Strange, how?"

"Not himself. It's hard to explain. He came up to me outside the salon and at first he just said thank you, I guess for helping him when he fell. Then it seemed like he wanted to say something else, but he was acting confused."

"Uh-oh. My mom said he didn't hit his head, but maybe he did and the doctors missed something."

"Head injury was my first thought. But I don't know, that wasn't even the weirdest part."

"What was the weirdest part?"

"He looked at me."

"What do you mean? Why was that weird?"

"He never looks at me. He made eye contact."

"Okay, that is weird."

"Right? I don't know what's wrong with him, but maybe you should track him down. Or tell your mom or something."

"I will. Thanks for the heads up."

"No problem. Listen, I have a client waiting, so I have to go, but I'll talk to you later."

We said goodbye but before I could put down my phone, it buzzed with a text.

It's Preston. Looking forward to seeing you tonight.

I took a deep breath. Preston Bradford was taking me out tonight.

Putting Zachary firmly out of my mind, I went out to deal with Gina's hair with a little extra spring in my step.

CHAPTER 7
Zachary

DAMN IT.

Damn it, damn it, damn it.

I hurried my ass back to my truck to get out of the rain. What the hell was wrong with me? I'd never been so awkward around a woman in my life. But the sight of her had been dazzling; she was the sun shining through the storm clouds. For a second, it had been like the moment I'd come to on the floor of her salon.

Stay with me, Zachary.

And then I couldn't get my brain and mouth to work together. I'd managed to thank her, barely, but when I'd tried to say more, it was like I'd blown a fuse. Broke the circuit. And that was that. No words.

She probably thought I had a head injury. Great.

I got in and smacked the steering wheel. That had not gone the way I'd thought it would. I talked to women all the time. Hell, I'd made a sport out of hitting on girls, and I was the grand champion. I always knew what to say. A little smirk, a wink, crack a joke. I was great with women.

Not with Marigold, apparently.

Maybe the shock had fried my brain a little.

Or maybe it was just her.

I blew out a breath. Should I have followed her into the salon? But then I just would have made a fool of myself in front of a bigger audience. And she wasn't the type of girl to think a guy being a bumbling idiot was cute. Marigold liked guys who were charming and suave.

The exact opposite of my performance.

Damn it.

Not one to back down from a challenge, I decided I just needed to regroup. Try again. I'd figure out what to say to her —maybe even practice. That way if my brain decided to stop functioning again, I'd be prepared.

I glanced at the time. I'd decided to partially listen to doctor's orders and put in a half day. The job site was about an hour away, but I had time to grab a quick bite to eat. The Steaming Mug was just up the street, so I ventured back into the rain and jogged up the sidewalk.

The smell of coffee greeted me as soon as I walked in. There wasn't anyone in line and only a few of the tables were full. I eyed the pastry case, hoping they still had a breakfast sandwich even though it was basically lunchtime.

The barista took my order and although my luck with Marigold had been shitty, my luck with food was better. They had my favorite sandwich—croissant with egg, bacon, and cheese—and I ordered a large coffee.

"Hi there, honey."

A group of older ladies crowded around a set of three tables they'd pushed together. A big grin stole over my face. Among them was one of my favorite people in Tilikum. Aunt Louise. She was hard to miss. The only clothing she seemed to own were velour tracksuits in a rainbow of colors—today's was bright yellow.

My aunt Louise Haven had been married to my dad's brother for about a hundred years and was one of my favorite people for two primary reasons. One, she gave absolutely no fucks and said whatever she wanted, usually with hilarious results. And two, she regularly baked me cookies. What was not to love?

"Hi there, beautiful." I sauntered over to her table, took her hand, and kissed her knuckles.

A few of the other ladies laughed softly and exchanged glances.

"Zachary, you are too charming for your own good."

"I'd say it does me a lot of good. Morning, ladies."

More giggles.

Aunt Louise rolled her eyes and batted a hand at her friends. "Don't encourage him. He's incorrigible enough as it is."

"What are you up to on this…" I glanced out the window at the rain, "not so fine day?"

"Just updating the Tilikum bachelor hierarchy."

"What's the bachelor hierarchy?"

"It's a ranking of eligible Tilikum men. There are far too many bachelors in this town. Especially Haven bachelors, although the hierarchy isn't limited to our family."

"Okay, but what do you do with it?"

"It's a tool that helps us focus our matchmaking efforts. And we might have a little wager now and again."

I shook my head. Apparently Aunt Louise was notorious for trying to set my brothers up with women. Weirdly, she never tried to set me up with anyone. I still wasn't sure whether to be relieved or insulted. My brothers all claimed I was lucky. Her attempts at matchmaking usually ended badly.

But why didn't she even try with me?

I pulled up a chair and straddled it backwards. "How do I rate?"

She exchanged a knowing look with the woman sitting across from her. "That's confidential information."

"Come on, you can tell me. I'm at the top, right?" I flashed her a grin. "It's fine, you can admit it."

"You could be, but you have a certain reputation around town."

I scoffed. "Rumors."

"Are they? Didn't you break Cory Wilcox's nose?"

"I don't think I broke his nose. I don't even think I hit his nose."

She raised her eyebrows.

"Hey, I was being chivalrous. He was being a jerk to his girlfriend. Someone needed to stand up for her."

"Hmm." She opened her little spiral notebook and jotted something down. "Interesting."

"Do I get points for that?"

She shut the notebook. "Confidential information."

"At least tell me I'm ahead of Garrett."

"Garrett has a stable, respectable job and is a good father to Owen."

"I have a stable, respectable job. And the fact that I don't have any kids should be points in my favor."

"Honey, you know I love you." She patted my hand. "I'm just not sure if you're the settling down type."

I placed a hand over my heart. "Aunt Louise, I'm hurt. I'm completely the settling down type." Or I would be, once I convinced Marigold to go out with me.

She tilted her head and narrowed her eyes. "Maybe I've been wrong and all you need is the right woman."

"That's exactly it. I need the right woman."

Her eyes lit up. "I know! Doris Tilburn's niece. She doesn't live here in town, but that's perfect. She wouldn't have any preconceived notions about you. I'll find out from Doris if she'll be visiting soon."

"Whoa." I held up my hands. "Slow down, Aunt Louise. I don't need you to set me up with anyone's niece."

She leaned across the table toward her friends. "Don't you

think? I've only met her once or twice, but I bet she could handle him. She seemed like she had spunk."

A few of the other women agreed, nodding and murmuring their assent while Aunt Louise flipped open her notebook and started writing again.

Uh-oh. What had I started?

I put a hand on Aunt Louise's shoulder and leaned closer. "Don't worry. I already know the right woman. Just wish me luck because she's going to take some convincing."

She whipped her head around. "Really? Do tell."

I grinned as I stood and pushed my chair back to its place. "That's confidential information."

"Zachary Haven, you're terrible."

"Yeah, but you love me. I need to get to my stable and respectable job." I pointed to her notebook. "Just make sure I'm ahead of Garrett."

She smiled. "Have a good day, honey."

"Bye, Aunt Louise. Bye, ladies."

My order was waiting for me, so I picked it up and headed out to my truck.

Bachelor hierarchy? I had to be ahead of Garrett.

I ate my sandwich and sipped my coffee as I drove out to the job site. It was a long way to go every day, but it paid well, so I didn't mind. Whoever the owner was—I'd never met him, I'd been hired by the general contractor—he was obviously loaded. The house he was building wasn't really a house. Not in the normal sense of the word, anyway. It was a mansion. Over fifteen thousand square feet with a massive kitchen, multiple living areas, and at least a dozen bedrooms, each with a private bathroom. It was set back from the highway, down a long, winding driveway, making it almost hidden.

I had no idea what it was for. Not quite a hotel, not quite a typical vacation home. Maybe the owner planned to rent it out for corporate retreats or weddings or family reunions or something. Although, it was too far outside Tilikum—or any town—to allow convenient access to the restaurants and amenities I would imagine those situations required.

But I didn't care that much. If this guy wanted to build a fifteen thousand square foot vacation home for himself, that was his business.

Besides, I had more important things to worry about. Like making Marigold fall for me.

CHAPTER 8

Marigold

THE LITTLE BLACK dress was a good choice. Classic, chic, timeless. I turned to check a different angle in my full-length mirror. It was a simple sheath dress with short sleeves and a low neckline. Flattering, and made me feel pretty.

Perfect.

I took a picture in the mirror and sent it to Audrey. She replied in seconds.

Audrey: *GORGEOUS! I love that dress on you.*

Me: *Thank you! Which shoes?*

I tried on a few different pairs and sent her a photo of each.

Audrey: *Those are all cute but don't you have red ones?*

She was right, I needed to try the red ones. I got the red heels out of my closet and as soon as I stepped into them, I knew they were exactly what I needed for my date tonight.

Red lipstick to match? Definitely.

I added the lipstick before sending another picture.

Audrey: *I hope you're ready for him to fall madly in love with you because that's amazing.*

Me: *You're too sweet.*

The thought of Preston Bradford falling in love with me

made me a little giddy. Was it possible? I was just a small-town girl. What could a guy like him possibly see in me?

I looked myself up and down in the mirror. Well, I felt great in my outfit, so that was a start. Whether or not something was going to happen between me and Preston remained to be seen.

But the red lipstick and sexy heels couldn't hurt.

Audrey and I texted back and forth a few more times and she wished me a great night. I didn't want to get my hopes up too high, but I had a feeling it wasn't just going to be great—it was going to be magical.

I wasn't one to believe in things like fate, but there had to be something to how Preston and I had met. It had been such a long time since I'd met anyone new. It was like the storm had blown him into my life.

There was a knock on my door, so with one last look in the mirror, I tucked my lipstick and phone into my clutch and went to greet my date.

He stood on my doorstep in a full suit, tailored to perfection. Not a hair was out of place and his stubble was neat, but he didn't look like he'd fussed over his appearance either. He was drop dead gorgeous and he made it look absolutely effortless.

His eyes swept over me, taking me in before looking straight into my eyes. "Wow. You look incredible."

My cheeks warmed. "Thank you. So do you."

"Ready?"

"Yes."

I grabbed my wool trench coat and before I could put it on, Preston was there to hold it for me while I slid my arms in. His closeness was intoxicating, especially when I caught a whiff of his scent. I didn't know what cologne he was wearing, but it was warm and masculine, making my insides swirl.

Taking a second to blink away the effects of his manliness,

I made sure I had everything before shutting and locking the door behind me.

With a light touch on my back, Preston led me to the passenger side of his black Audi. He opened the door for me, offered his hand to help me in, and closed it when I was seated.

How did he know how much I loved all those gentlemanly gestures? We'd only just met, he couldn't have known ahead of time.

Which meant it must have been normal for him.

Swoon!

He got in and flashed me a dimpled smile. "I was thinking, there aren't a lot of good restaurant options here in town. Are you up for something a little more adventurous?"

"Sure, adventurous sounds fun."

His eyes swept up and down again, making me feel as if he liked what he saw. "Good."

My stomach tingled with anticipation as we drove through town. What did something a little more adventurous mean? Where were we going?

We made light small talk and I noticed he was good at keeping the conversation going. He turned down a road I didn't take very often. There wasn't much out that way except a small, rural airport. There was a restaurant at the airport, but it didn't seem like the sort of place Preston Bradford would take a date.

Then again, maybe he would. The food was good and it was fun to watch the planes take off. I'd had lunch there with Annika and Isabelle and their kids a few times. The kids certainly loved it. Maybe I'd been expecting too much—something too fancy—and I needed to bring my imagination back down to earth.

When he turned into the parking lot of the small airport, I was a mix of confused and curious. He didn't offer an explanation, just came around to my side of the car, opened the door, and offered his hand to help me out—all with a little knowing smile.

"What do you have up your sleeve, Mr. Bradford?"

His smile grew, puckering his dimples. "You'll see."

He offered his arm and we headed toward the main building.

The airport was so small, it didn't have an actual terminal. There were no commercial flights coming in or out, just private planes. He led me inside and walked right past the bar and grill with a view of the runway. At a door on the far side, he pulled a card out of his inside jacket pocket and swiped it to gain access.

I had so many questions, but I pressed my lips together. He obviously had a plan and I wanted to see how it would play out. Were we going flying? Was he a pilot? I was pinging with excitement and a little bit of fear. I'd never been in a small plane before.

The air was cold but still as we walked outside. Several small planes were parked nearby, but we didn't head toward any of them. Instead, he led me to the right, away from the runway and toward a large hangar.

A helicopter was parked in the middle of a large concrete square. Without meaning to, I squeezed his arm. Were we going up in *that*?

We stopped and he glanced at me. "Have you ever been in a helicopter?"

"Never."

"I'm your first." His mouth hooked in another smile. "Good."

My breath caught in my throat. I didn't know if the flutters in my stomach were because I was about to climb into a helicopter for the first time, or because of Preston.

Probably both.

A man dressed in a black suit approached. "Mr. Bradford. We're ready to go."

"Excellent."

The pilot opened one of the doors and Preston once again offered me a hand to help me in. The interior was lavish with four leather seats facing each other in pairs. Preston got in behind me and gestured for me to choose a seat. He took the one next to me and reached for my hand.

"Where are we going?" I asked.

"Seattle."

I crossed my legs at the ankles and waited while the pilot got in the cockpit and put on his headset. Preston held my hand with a familiarity I enjoyed, rubbing his thumb along mine.

"How long is the flight?" I asked.

"About an hour. Are you nervous?"

"A little."

"Don't worry." He squeezed my hand. "I've got you."

His voice and his touch were both reassuring and exhilarating.

The pilot started the engine and I was surprised at how quiet it was in the cabin. The luxury didn't just extend to the seats, it was in the entire experience. The surroundings, the comfort. I tried not to fixate on what this kind of extravagance said about Preston's bank account, but it was impossible not to notice. He was clearly a man of means.

We rose into the air and I leaned toward the window to watch the ground fall away beneath us. The view was breathtaking.

"Beautiful," he said, but he wasn't looking out the window.

He was looking at me.

"It's incredible," I said, gesturing toward the view. "Is this how you go back and forth to Seattle?"

"It saves time. And it's not a bad way to impress a girl."

I raised my eyebrows. "So you dazzle all your dates with helicopter rides?"

He met my eyes. "Just you."

I wasn't sure if I believed that, but the heat in his gaze sent tingles down my spine nonetheless.

We flew over mountains with rocky outcroppings and pine forests that seemed to stretch on forever. It wasn't long before the land below us turned into fields and farmland. A river cut through the landscape, and eventually streets and neighborhoods replaced the forests and fields.

"Tell me about you," Preston said, drawing my attention away from the view.

"What do you want to know?"

"Everything."

I laughed softly. "I don't know if there's that much to tell. I grew up in Tilikum. My dad owns a construction company and my mom is an artist. I'm an only child. After high school, I went to beauty school and eventually opened my own salon. What about you?"

"It's all pretty generic. I grew up in the Chicago area. Divorced parents, both remarried. My father is a physician, which is probably why I went to law school."

"He wanted you to follow in his footsteps?"

He shrugged. "I wouldn't have made a good doctor anyway. So, small-town girl turned salon owner. What else?"

I hesitated, searching for something halfway interesting to say. "I love to read. I guess I've always been a bookworm. And I spend a lot of time with my friends and their families."

"They have kids?"

"Two of them do. Another is getting married soon. I also love weddings, but I don't want to scare you off on the first date."

He met my eyes again. "You're not going to scare me."

"Weddings are just so lovely. I love it all. The flowers and the dresses and what it all symbolizes. I'm kind of in love with love, and weddings are like the biggest celebration of love we have. Sometimes I think I missed my calling as a wedding planner. But I've basically planned all my friends' weddings, so I get to indulge my passion."

"Are you passionate about your salon?"

"Oh, yes. This probably sounds silly, but doing hair is like creating art that my clients get to wear every day. I especially love it when I can make someone feel great about how they look. You see it in the way they carry themselves when they walk out the door."

"That doesn't sound silly. That's beautiful."

Did he mean that or was this just his first date persona? I didn't know him well enough to be sure, but he seemed genuine. At least he actually seemed interested in getting to know me. The last first date I'd been on, the guy had talked about himself the entire time.

He hadn't gotten a second date.

As our conversation continued, Preston asked more questions and his interest in my answers never waned. He really did seem to want to know everything about me.

More than anything else about our date so far—the suit and tie, the helicopter, the small romantic gestures—his attention was intoxicating.

The sun was setting as the city came into view and the result was stunning. City lights twinkled to life below us, set against a color-stained sky.

"We're almost there," Preston said. "Enjoying yourself so far?"

"So much. The sunset is incredible."

"I hoped you'd like it. We're lucky the weather over here cooperated. It could easily have been socked in with clouds."

"I guess it was meant to be."

He stroked my hand with his thumb again. "I like to think so."

Looking out over the skyscrapers and traffic, a little thrill ran through me as I saw we were going to land on the top of a building. I leaned closer to the window so I could watch our descent. The pilot clearly knew what he was doing. The entire ride had been surprisingly smooth and the landing was no exception.

The perimeter of the circular landing site was surrounded by lights, making it easy to see. We touched down with a little bump, and a moment later, the muffled whir of the engine quieted.

Preston got out and offered me his hand. The outside air was cold and the wind whipped my hair around my face. With his hand on the small of my back, he guided me to a circular staircase that led below the landing site, where another man in a black suit waited for us.

Without a word, he turned, and we followed him into an elevator. The doors opened onto a parking garage where a black Escalade waited.

"I've got it," Preston said to the driver and opened the door for me before going around to the other side and getting in.

The driver took us out of the parking garage and into the city. I'd forgotten how tiny I felt among the skyscrapers. From ground level, they towered above us, rising into the sky like modern castles of light and glass.

I was probably gaping at the view like a country bumpkin. I made sure my mouth was closed and tried to pretend I wasn't awed by the experience.

But I was awed. How could I not be? Not by the city, I'd been there before. But a helicopter ride that ended at sunset? And now a driver to take us to dinner?

Who was this man and how was it possible he'd wandered into my salon?

We arrived at the restaurant and things only got better. The ambiance was elegant without being garish. Soft music played in the background and the low light made everything feel luxurious and intimate. We ordered drinks, appetizers, dinner. Preston encouraged me to try the scallops, and it was one of the best things I'd ever eaten in my life.

It was, hands down, the best first date I'd ever been on. And it wasn't even over.

Preston was charming and attentive, the setting was romantic, and I couldn't help but feel swept away by the entire experience.

After lingering over drinks and dessert, the same driver picked us up outside the restaurant and took us back to the building where the helicopter had landed. We took the elevator to the top and Preston once again guided me gently to the aircraft. His chivalric gestures never ceased—the soft touches, the hand to help me in.

I loved it all.

The ride home was quieter. I was full and relaxed from the wine. Preston didn't seem to need to fill the silence. He just held my hand. Once in a while, our gazes would meet and he'd give me a subtle, contented smile.

It was late and the little airport was deserted when we landed in Tilikum. We went to his car and he drove me straight home.

He parked in my driveway and opened the door for me, then led me to my front door. His eyes sparked with heat, but I could already sense he wasn't going to ask to come in. He was too much of a gentleman for that.

"Did you have a good time?" he asked.

"Yes, more than a good time. It was incredible."

His mouth twitched, puckering his dimples. "Good. Can I see you again tomorrow?"

"Definitely."

"I have a lot going on, so we'll have to stick closer to home. But I need to see you again."

"I'd love to."

He leaned in and I tilted my chin up to meet his kiss. His

lips pressed against mine, soft but firm, emphatic but not force-ful. I could feel the tension in his body, as if he were holding himself back. The display of self-control only made him sexier.

"Goodnight, Marigold," he said softly.

"Goodnight."

He took a step backward and I felt a little tug of relief. Despite the heady evening, I wasn't ready for him to come inside. Maybe I was old fashioned when it came to sex, but I needed a level of trust even a romantic whirlwind of a date couldn't supply.

I was glad he seemed to understand that.

When I went inside, I shut the door behind me and my knees nearly buckled. Had that been real? If I'd dreamed up the perfect date, I wouldn't have come close to the reality of my evening with Preston Bradford. I spun around and leaned against the door, sighing. It had been real. He was real. And he wanted to see me again tomorrow.

I hoped no one would pinch me, because if this were a dream, I didn't want to wake up.

CHAPTER 9
Zachary

"MARIGOLD, this is going to come as a surprise to you, considering what an ass I've been all these years. But you're the most beautiful, amazing woman I've ever known and I think I've been subconsciously in love with you for a really long time."

A horn honked behind me. Shit. I pulled through the intersection to get out of the way and checked my reflection in the rearview.

"Nice one, Z. Real smooth."

Was I really practicing my potential make-Marigold-fall-for-me speech in the rearview mirror while I drove up to my parents' place?

Yep, that's exactly what I was doing.

Maybe *subconsciously in love with you* wasn't the right way to phrase it. That made it sound like I'd been unaware of my feelings for her.

I hadn't been unaware of my feelings. Just aggressively suppressing them.

"When I thought I was dying, the first thing I thought of was you." I paused, thinking about how that sounded when I said it out loud. Not bad. "My one regret was not telling you how I really feel."

Somebody laid into their horn and I whipped my head around, looking for what was going on.

Oh, shit. I'd just run a stop sign. They were honking at me.

Oops.

I probably needed to pay better attention to the road, not my make-Marigold-fall-for-me speech.

But the only regret thing was good. That had to work on her.

Best of all, it wasn't a cheap line. It was true.

I kept going, still pondering how to open the conversation —but with a bit more focus on the here and now—until I turned up my parents' long gravel driveway. With no more stop signs to worry about, I tilted my rearview again and spoke into it.

"Marigold, I've been a total jerk to you for a long time, so I know I don't deserve anything from you. But when electricity was coursing through me and I thought I might be about to die, the one regret I had was not telling you how I really feel."

I nodded. That was a pretty good start.

Speaking of people I'd been a jerk to for a long time, Levi's SUV was parked outside my parents' house. When my sister had married him—a freaking Bailey—it had felt like whiplash. One minute we were happily hating on and pranking each other, the next we were supposed to be family. How was a guy supposed to deal with that?

Looking back, I felt kind of stupid for holding onto my grudge for as long as I had. Levi was actually a great guy. He'd stepped up as a dad to my nephew Thomas, and treated Annika like gold. What more could a brother ask for?

When that realization had hit me, I'd decided to stop being an actual asshole and just pitch him shit like a normal brother-in-law. We'd gotten along fine ever since.

I parked next to him and got out. The squeal of tiny

human laughter came from the side of the house. I grinned. I'd always had a soft spot for kids, and having nieces and nephews was the best. Levi and Annika had four—Thomas, who was nine, five-year-old twins Juliet and Emma, and the tiny terror himself, two-year-old Will.

Every family has a kid who's largely responsible for their parents' gray hair. I was probably that kid in my family. Will was definitely that kid in his. Kinda made me feel like we had a special bond.

Levi stood near the playhouse and swing set he and my dad had built for the grandkids. It was a pretty cool setup. I'd spent countless hours pushing the girls on the swings. And the playhouse was a favorite with all of the kids. It was on a platform high enough for the kids to go under. A ladder led up to the second level on one side and a homemade rock-climbing wall was on the other. A green slide was the favorite way down.

Thomas was at the top of the playhouse with Emma, while Will was perched halfway up the rock wall. He looked too small to be able to climb it, but he didn't seem to let the fact that he was only two stop him from doing anything.

Juliet was happily swinging until her eyes landed on me. "Uncle Z!" she shouted and dragged her feet in the wood chips to slow down.

I crouched and held my arms out while she jumped off the swing. She ran to me while the others scrambled off the play structure. Juliet jumped into my arms, followed closely by Emma.

"There's my princesses."

"Hey, Uncle Z," Thomas said. He was a little more subdued than his sisters.

I grinned at him. "Hey, chief."

"Daddy, Will down," Will said from the bottom of the rock wall with a proud smile. For some reason, he'd recently started referring to himself in the third person. "Will get down."

"You sure did, buddy," Levi said. "Good job."

I let go of the girls as Will dashed over to me. He collided with my chest and I pretended he almost knocked me over. "Oof. Will, you're too strong."

"Will big boy."

"You are a big boy." I scooped him up and stood. "You know how to climb that rock wall like a champ."

The girls started giggling and a second later, they each latched onto one of my legs.

"Oh no, the princesses are shapeshifters! They've turned into the dreaded Bailey leg monsters!"

They squealed with laughter as I dragged them across the ground. Levi still had his arms crossed, but he smiled at his kids' antics. Thomas stood in an identical posture, arms crossed like he was getting too old for this stuff, but still smiling.

"Annika must be inside?" I asked.

"Yeah," Levi said. "I figured I'd let the kids burn off some energy while she visits."

"What energy?" I asked, looking at Will. "You guys don't have too much energy, do you?"

"No!" the girls said in unison.

Will tapped his chest. "Will big boy."

"Yes you are, my dude." I looked down at the girls, still wrapped around my legs. "Okay, leg monsters, I need you to go back to being princesses so I can go inside and see Grandma and Grandpa."

"Come on, girls," Thomas said, grabbing Juliet around the waist to pull her off my leg. "Listen to Uncle Z."

Juliet let go, allowing her big brother to drag her away. Emma kept clinging to me until Thomas grabbed her too. I put Will down and he went straight for the rock wall.

Those kids were so great.

Levi tipped his chin to me and then scrambled to grab Will before he climbed on top of the beam holding the swings. I had no idea how he'd gotten up there so fast. The kid was a tiny monkey.

I said goodbye to the kids, promising I'd come play later, then wandered inside and shut the door behind me. I could hear voices coming from the kitchen. One was Annika. I didn't hear what she said, but I recognized her voice. Then Mom's. Someone else replied and I got this weird jumpy feeling in the pit of my stomach.

Marigold.

A slow grin spread across my face. Marigold was here?

I hadn't seen her car, but she'd probably come with Annika. She was certainly no stranger to this house. Usually, seeing her at the kitchen table with my mom and sister was such a normal sight, I barely thought about it. I still ignored her, like I did any time we ran into each other.

But that was about to change. It was like fate had delivered her right into my hands.

Granted, I needed to find a way to get her alone so I could talk to her. I didn't want to deliver my speech in front of Annika and my mom. But that didn't have to be hard. Annika would totally have my back. All I had to do was pull her aside and tell her I was secretly in love with her best friend and I needed the chance to come clean. She'd find a way to get Mom out of there and I'd have Marigold all to myself.

Foolproof.

"A helicopter?" Annika asked. "You're kidding me."

"No, he took me out to that little airport outside town and there was a helicopter waiting," Marigold said.

Wait, he? Some guy took Marigold in a helicopter? What the hell was she talking about?

"Where did you go?" Mom asked.

"Seattle. He flew me all the way to Seattle just to take me

to dinner. He said it was because there aren't a lot of good restaurants in town."

"He had to be showing off, at least a little bit," Mom said.

"I'm sure he was, but it wasn't in a bad way. He didn't seem conceited about it. It was more like he was excited he could give me that experience."

"Oh my gosh, it sounds amazing," Annika said.

Marigold sighed. "It was. It was the absolute best date I've ever had."

I balled my hands into fists. Someone had taken Marigold on a date? And not just a date, the best date she'd ever had?

Well, it was time to plan a murder.

"I can't even describe it," Marigold continued. "He was such a gentleman, from the first moment he arrived."

Crossing my arms, I rolled my eyes.

"He did all the things I love. Opened doors, offered me his arm. He was well dressed and smelled so good I wanted to rub myself all over him just to keep his scent on me."

I didn't even know who the guy was, but that image made me gag a little.

Annika sighed. "I love it when they smell good. Sometimes when Levi gets off duty and I haven't seen him for a while, I have to just hold him and smell his neck. It's like a drug."

"I love that," Marigold said.

"Anyway, go on."

"It wasn't just his manners or the helicopter or the private car in Seattle. Or the fancy restaurant, even though the food was delicious. He really seemed to want to get to know me. He asked questions and kept the conversation going so easily. I felt like he was genuinely interested in hearing what I had to say."

"That kind of attention is hard to beat," Annika said.

"It really is. And I don't remember a man ever being that way with me before. Usually they just ask a few questions and then either start talking about themselves or their favorite sports team or something. But Preston listened. He looked me in the eyes and listened to everything I had to say, as if I were the most interesting person in the world."

Preston? Who the fuck was Preston? I searched my memory but I didn't know anyone with that name. Where had she met this guy? I inched closer so I could see into the kitchen where she sat at the table with my mom and sister.

"I can't believe he just walked into your salon," Annika said.

That answered the where she'd met him question. Thank you, sis.

"I know. I keep wondering if he's real and if it all actually happened. But the flowers he sent to the salon this morning were real."

"Aw, he sent flowers?"

"Right after I opened. Here, I took a picture."

I scoffed. Flowers? Who cares?

"Whoa," Annika said. "That's not a bouquet of flowers, that's a masterpiece."

"Those are incredible," Mom agreed.

"Aren't they amazing? Stacey couldn't stop gushing about them all day."

Okay, maybe flowers were worth caring about. But still. I could send her flowers at work. That didn't make this Preston guy special.

"There's just something about him," Marigold said. "He has this quality I can't quite put my finger on. He's confident without being arrogant and funny without being obnoxious. And the way he looked at me. It felt so good to have a man look at me like that."

The soft wistfulness in her voice felt like a knife to the chest. She sounded so dreamy. And it wasn't me who'd made her feel that way.

"I'm so excited for you," Annika said. "He sounds like he's perfect."

"He's either the perfect man for me or he's too good to be true. There can't be any in between."

Perfect for her? No way. That was me.

The sound of a throat-clear behind me almost made me jump. I slowly turned to look over my shoulder.

"Hi, Dad."

His brow was furrowed, his thick eyebrows knitting together. "You okay?"

"Yeah, fine."

His eyes flicked to the women at the kitchen table, then back to me. "You sure?"

The conversation in the kitchen had stopped. Everyone was looking at me.

Mortifying. This was fucking mortifying.

I swallowed hard and shrugged, both to appear casual and to try to release the knotting tension in my shoulders. "Yeah, I'm good."

The solution was simple. Do what I'd always done when it came to Marigold. Ignore her. Pretend she wasn't there. Look away. She wasn't important, she wasn't beautiful, she wasn't mine.

I couldn't do it. That old pattern of behavior should have fit like an old pair of jeans, but apparently I'd outgrown them. Couldn't get them on if I'd tried.

My eyes locked on hers for a long moment. Her lips parted and a hint of color flushed her cheeks.

I could see Annika watching me. She knew. My sister knew and she was staring at me, horrified, like I'd just murdered someone in front of her.

This was a disaster.

"I just remembered I gotta go." I spun around and walked out the door.

I was halfway home before my brain started working

again. I didn't remember getting in my truck or backing up or going down the driveway. It was like coming to after being shocked, except I was driving through town, eyes fixed on the pavement instead of looking up into Marigold's beautiful face.

"Pull yourself together, man!"

I let out a long breath. I didn't know what had just happened to me, but something about hearing Marigold describe the best date of her life—one that had not been with me—and my dad catching me staring at her, and my sister's horrified expression, had completely short-circuited my brain.

I had an ache in my chest. Why did that hurt so much?

So she'd been on a date with a guy who clearly had bank. I wasn't rich, but I had something he didn't. Something better than a big-ass bank account.

I was Zachary Haven. And I was the one who was in love with her.

This wasn't a problem. It was a challenge. A dare. A battle.

All's fair in love and war, and I was going to win.

No matter what.

Such a Cool Guy

BRIELLE

WITH A YAWN, Brielle stretched like a cat, then glanced at the time. A little after six. She hadn't meant to take such a long nap, but it probably didn't matter. After all, she didn't have anywhere else to be.

John had brought her more clothes, along with some makeup and other girly stuff. She had some cash, but he'd insisted she keep it. He said he didn't mind paying if it would help her out.

He was such a cool guy.

More and more, she was starting to feel like she really was his princess in a tower. Except she wasn't a real princess and the tower was a cabin. But it was like something out of a fairy tale.

Vegas was still the goal, obviously. But the more Brielle thought about it, the more staying through the winter seemed like a good idea. She wanted to see what it looked like when the cabin was covered in snow.

And if one of the times John came out to check on her, he got snowed in and couldn't leave, would that be so terrible?

She heard him knock and sprang out of bed so she could

smooth down her hair and fix her clothes. She didn't want him to think she was lazy and just sleeping all the time.

"Brielle?" he called from downstairs.

"Yeah, coming."

She glanced down from the loft. He set something on the floor and peeled off his coat. He always dressed nice. Name brands, not the stupid generic knock-off crap her mom always made her buy. And he smelled good too. Clean and masculine, like his cologne was expensive.

He picked up his stuff—looked like more groceries—and took it all to the kitchen. Brielle went down to help.

"How was your day?" she asked.

"Busy. Kind of frustrating." He pulled a six-pack of beer out of a bag. Fancy beer, in bottles. Not the cheap stuff her dad and ex-boyfriend drank. He took one, opened it, and held it out to her.

She accepted it, wondering if this meant he thought she was over twenty-one, or just didn't care. He'd never asked her age and she certainly wasn't about to tell him now. Not if he was going to let her drink.

"Thanks," she said.

He opened one for himself and took a long pull, then gave her a subtle smile. "No problem."

"It's probably not a big deal, but the front door seems like it's stuck or something. I couldn't get it open."

"Did you want to leave?"

"No, I was just going to go outside and the door wouldn't budge."

"It sticks." He took a drink. "I'll see if I can fix it. But I wouldn't go out there alone. There's a lot of wildlife. It isn't safe."

Brielle hadn't thought about that. There were probably bears. And moose. Moose could be even more dangerous than bears. She didn't want to come face to face with a wild animal.

She followed him to the couch with her beer and sat next to him. Tipping the bottle to her lips, she took a swallow. It was smooth with just a bit of a bite to it. She'd never had a beer that actually tasted good before. It was amazing.

From the corner of her eye, she could see John watching her. His expression was hard to read. She licked her lips and took another sip, enjoying the way he observed her mouth as she drank.

"You seem tired," she said.

He nodded. "Yeah. I've just had a lot going on."

"Sorry if I'm making things hard on you."

"No, it's not you. You're a bright spot. It's mostly work stuff."

"Where do you work?"

"I just have a boring office job." He took another drink. "Can I ask you a question?"

"Sure." She followed his lead and drank more.

"Do you think anyone's looking for you?"

She shrugged. "I'm sure my parents wonder where I went, but they won't look too hard."

"What about friends?"

"They'll just assume I took off. I doubt they'll worry about me. They knew I was planning on leaving at some point."

"No boyfriend, then?"

"No." She took another drink, hoping to bring on the buzz faster. "No boyfriend."

John shifted so he was facing her and draped his arm along the back of the couch. "That surprises me."

"That I don't have a boyfriend?"

"Yeah."

She tried to hide her smile as she went fishing for a compliment. "Why does that surprise you?"

"Come on. You know you're beautiful."

Hearing him call her beautiful was more potent than the beer. "I am not."

"Of course you are. Have you had a boyfriend? A serious one?"

"Yeah, a couple. The last guy cheated on me, so I dumped him."

"Asshole."

"He totally was."

He hesitated, his eyes moving up and down. "Can I ask you another question?"

She took another drink and nodded.

"Have you ever been with a guy?"

Her lips curled in a smile. "John, are you asking me if I'm a virgin?"

He nodded.

She met his eyes and shook her head slowly.

"Good to know."

She wasn't sure what that meant. Had he been hoping she was a virgin? Or had he been hoping she wasn't?

"Does it change how you think of me?"

"No. I was just curious."

"Are you a virgin?" she teased.

He smiled. "No, definitely not."

She liked this. The buzz and flirty banter. The attention. She wanted more of it; craved it. "What about you? Do you have a girlfriend? I see you don't have a ring."

He held up his left hand. "Nope."

"And I'm really the only girl you've kept out here."

"The one and only."

"Why are you keeping me out here, John?" she asked, leaning closer.

He didn't move. Just held her gaze in his. He didn't seem uncomfortable but he didn't invite her closer, either. Her last boyfriend would have had her shirt off by now if she'd given him the same look. But John wasn't a boy. He was a man. A man with self-control.

God, it was sexy.

He took her empty beer bottle out of her hand. Had she finished it already?

"Want another one?"

"Sure."

He went to the kitchen and brought back another beer, then handed it to her and sat down again.

"Thanks." She took a drink. Her buzz was coming on fast, but she wanted it. The thought of getting drunk with John was fun. So was the thought of getting drunk and not having to worry about getting caught.

He didn't say anything for a long moment. Just watched her with interest in his eyes. Was he into her? Did he want to make out?

What would it be like to make out with a man, not a boy? She'd never kissed a guy who had stubble on his jaw before.

"What are you thinking about?" she asked.

He pulled his phone out of his pocket. "Can I take your picture?"

That almost killed her buzz. Take her picture, why? To show to the cops? Because someone was looking for her?

"Why?"

"You're pretty."

"You want a picture of me because I'm pretty?"

"Yeah. And then I can look at it when I'm away."

"Not so you can identify me to the cops or something."

"Brielle, I'm letting you stay in my cabin. If someone's looking for you and they find out, I'm the one who'll be in trouble."

He had a point. It didn't make sense that he'd turn her in now. Not after everything he'd done for her. Even with a beer buzz, she knew that was true.

"Okay, you can take my picture."

He held up his phone and she smiled for him.

"Here." He took her beer and set it on the coffee table, then brushed her hair back from her face before taking a few more.

"Is that good?" she asked.

"Can you stand up for another one?"

"Okay." She stood and only wobbled a little.

He got up and held out a hand to steady her, then stepped back and lifted his phone. "Unbutton your shirt a little."

She did what he asked, unfastening the top two buttons and spreading the collar to show off more skin.

"Good." He took a few more. "Turn and put your hand on your hip."

She kept following his instructions, playing it up with a lip pout and moving her hand down to touch her backside.

"Oh yeah," he said, his voice going low and growly. "That's good. Unzip your jeans and pull them down."

She giggled, her head swimming, and did what he said.

"Take them off."

That made her pause. He wanted her to take off her pants so he could take pictures?

But what was so bad about that? They were for him. Why not give him what he wanted?

She made a show of undressing, taking them off slowly, posing for the camera as she did. Pouty lips. Sultry eyes. When he asked her to take off her shirt, she almost hesitated, but told herself to just do it. Have fun. It was John. It was fine. He'd done so much for her, she could do something for him in return. Make him happy.

And he certainly looked happy.

"Good girl. That's my kitten."

His praise was like a drug.

Her bra came off and she forcefully silenced her questions before they could come anywhere near her lips. She did what he asked. Posed how he wanted. Touched herself the way he told her to.

"You're really fucking sexy, Brielle. I love this."

When he finished, she assumed he'd want sex. After all, he'd gotten her mostly naked. Taken provocative pictures.

She could do it. She wanted to. It wasn't that she was drunk, although she was. John was hot. It didn't matter that he was older than she was. They were both adults. And why not thank him for everything he'd done for her?

But he didn't touch her. Didn't try to kiss her or lie her on the couch or take her upstairs to the bed.

Tears stung her eyes as he swiped through the photos. She started picking up her clothes, but he came closer and put a hand on her wrist.

"What's wrong?"

"I thought you wanted me."

He touched her cheek. "Kitten, you're everything I hoped you'd be. Such a good girl. I know you're going to please me."

Her heart fluttered. Please him? That sounded so sexual. So grown up and erotic. She wanted that. "Why can't I please you now?"

His mouth turned up in a grin. "You did. You pleased me very much. Do you want to please me again, next time I visit?"

She nodded. "Yes. How?"

He didn't answer. Just smiled, puckering the dimples in his cheeks, while she put her clothes back on. He hadn't said or done anything funny, but her buzz made her want to giggle.

She felt good. Drunk felt good. It was fun to take her clothes off for him—exciting and dangerous. He was such a man, not a boy like her ex who'd cheated.

John wouldn't do something like that. She knew he wouldn't.

So why not have fun with the man who'd rescued her. He was hot and he'd called her sexy. And he certainly wasn't forcing her to do anything against her will.

She sat down with her beer and took a long drink. He said she could please him. She liked that and decided not to worry about what he'd want her to do and why.

CHAPTER 10
Marigold

I WAVED goodbye to my client as she left the salon. Her new chin-length bob suited her so well. I was excited she'd finally taken the plunge and trusted me enough to give her a new look.

"She sure was happy," Stacey said. "I love that cut on her."

"I'm glad she's happy with it." I lowered myself into the other chair behind the front desk and took a drink of my water. "Who's coming next?"

"Betty Newman, but not for an hour."

While too many breaks between clients wasn't a good thing, a little break was always nice. I sat back and inhaled deeply. The scent of flowers filled the air, but not because I'd brought in fresh blooms to greet my clients. Preston had sent flowers again. Even though the first one still looked beautiful, another arrangement had arrived at the salon not long after I did.

I'd gone out with him again the night before, this time without the glamor of a helicopter and fancy restaurant. He'd taken me to a late dinner at a cute place in town, a little Italian bistro with my favorite eggplant parmesan.

Even with the contrast in the setting, it had been a lovely date. I was relieved at the simplicity and normalcy of it. I didn't want to be swept away by expensive displays of extravagance, fun as they were. It was good to get to know Preston better in a more casual setting. Although looking back, it felt like I'd done more of the talking than he had.

Still, his gentlemanly manners had been on full display and I'd had a nice time.

I picked up my copy of the local newspaper, the Tilikum Tribune, and started thumbing through it. I hadn't paid much attention to our local paper until I'd become friends with Audrey. She worked there and was on her way to taking over for the current editor when he retired in a few years. Out of support for my friend, I'd started buying it, and found I really enjoyed perusing the stories. Now I had two subscriptions, one for my personal use and one to keep out for salon clients.

A headline on the front page caught my eye. There was a missing person. Brielle Thayer. The photo showed a young woman, probably in her late teens or early twenties, with blond hair and bold lipstick. She looked familiar, but I didn't recognize her name. I'd probably seen her around town, but I didn't know her personally.

"Did you see this?" I asked, angling the page so Stacey could see it.

"Missing girl? I did hear about that. Apparently she ran away from home a few times when she was younger, so I'm not sure why they're acting like she was kidnapped or something. She's probably just at a friend's house or with a boyfriend."

"Do you know her?"

"No, but my friend works with her mom. Lots of family drama, I think."

Poor thing. The article said she was nineteen and a friend had reported her missing. Hopefully she'd be found soon.

Even if there was conflict with her family, her parents had to be so worried.

The front door opened, tinkling the bell above the door, and I looked up hoping to see a walk-in. But it was a delivery guy with yet another bouquet of flowers.

"More?" Stacey asked. "Wow, he's really trying to make an impression."

The delivery guy glanced at the two large arrangements already on the front counter. "Um, where do you want this?"

I stood. "I'll just take them. Thanks so much."

He handed me the flowers. "No problem. Have a good one."

Interestingly, the new bouquet was completely different from the first two. Those both had red and white roses mixed with other white flowers and greenery, creating a coordinating, if not identical, set.

This one had deep red roses, but also bright yellow sunflowers and an assortment of purples, oranges, and greens. It was a lovely mix of romantic and cozy, and sunflowers were my favorite. I'd never seen anything like it.

"What does the card say?" Stacey asked.

I put it down on the front desk and pulled out the card. I had to read it twice before the words made sense.

"What's wrong?" she asked.

"This isn't from Preston."

"What? Who else is sending you flowers?"

"Zachary Haven."

"Why is Zachary Haven sending you flowers?"

"I don't know."

"What does it say?" She plucked the card from my hands. "For Marigold. Love, Zachary. That's it?" She turned it over. "Nothing else?"

"I'm as confused as you are. Unless they're to thank me for going to the hospital with him when he got hurt."

"You'd think he'd make that clear. But maybe he does that

guy thing where he assumes you know what he's thinking. My husband does that all the time. I have to remind him I'm not a mind reader."

She held the card out and I took it. *For Marigold. Love, Zachary.* What would have made him suddenly decide to send me flowers at work?

The other day, when I'd run into him outside the salon, I'd thought maybe things had changed between us. I didn't know why or what that meant, but he'd been so different. Then I'd been at the Havens' yesterday afternoon and it had been back to the same old Zachary. One look at me and he was out the door.

And now he was sending me flowers?

I was so confused.

The door opened again and this time it was a walk-in. But not just any walk-in. Louise Haven.

Louise was Annika and Zachary's aunt. She was dressed in her signature velour tracksuit—today's was royal blue. Her silver hair was in a loose bun and she wore peach lipstick and a little more blush than she really needed. She was a sweet lady who spent her time flitting around town, either doing good deeds like taking casseroles to friends in need, or looking for opportunities to play matchmaker for her nephews.

"Hello, sweetheart," she said. "I know I don't have an appointment, so if you're busy I'll just make one. But my hair is driving me batty."

"Your timing is perfect. I can take you right now."

"Wonderful." She sniffed. "What lovely flowers. Do you have a suitor, Miss Marigold?"

I smiled. "I guess I do."

"She might have two," Stacey said.

Louise's eyes brightened. "Two? How exciting."

"That's not true, I don't have two suitors. Someone else sent flowers, but they're just a thank you."

"Keep telling yourself that," Stacey mumbled.

Ignoring Stacey, I gestured to my station. "I'll take you back."

"You're such a dear," Louise said.

Once she was settled in my chair with a cape around her shoulders, she took her long silver hair out of its bun.

"So what are we thinking?" I asked, running my fingers through her tresses. "Just a trim?"

"A bit more than a trim, my ends are horrific."

I held up a strand of hair to show where I'd cut it. "About like this? If I take off a few inches, I think you'll be happy with how it looks and feels."

"I trust you, honey."

"Great."

I took her to the washing station to wash and condition, then got to work. It was a simple cut, and I knew Louise well enough to know how long she'd want it. She usually wore it up, so it needed enough length to make a pretty bun.

"Tell me about this suitor," she said.

I pressed my lips together in a smile. "His name is Preston Bradford. He's from out of town, but he's building a vacation home nearby. We had our second date last night and it was fairly normal. We had a nice dinner together."

"But what about the first date?"

"A dream. He took me to Seattle in a private helicopter."

"Did he, now? That's not something you hear every day."

"It was a total surprise. And we had such a great time."

"Who's the poor chump trying to compete with that?"

"Oh, no. No one's trying to compete with Preston. The flowers were for something else."

"Who are they from?"

"Zachary Haven," Stacey called from the front.

I shot her a look. She just smiled back.

"My Zachary?" Louise asked. "Not a chump at all. And isn't that an interesting bit of information."

"He had a minor accident here at the salon recently. The flowers are just a thank you for helping him."

"Oh, I see," Louise said, but I could tell she didn't believe me. "You know, you could do a lot worse than Zachary. I'm sure your rich out-of-towner is exciting, but nothing beats a good hometown boy."

With a wry grin, I pulled down the sides of her hair to check the length. "And you wouldn't have any bias when it comes to that, would you?"

"I'm just saying, a Haven man is an excellent choice. They're solid. Well built, if you know what I mean." She winked at me in the mirror.

With a soft laugh, I rolled my eyes.

"I mean in the manhood area, dear. In case that wasn't clear."

Stacey laughed out loud.

I felt my cheeks flush slightly. "Louise!"

"What? These are the sorts of things a woman ought to know. Obviously I don't have firsthand knowledge of anything an auntie shouldn't see. But I have been married to my George for most of my life and let me tell you, I'll never regret that choice."

I checked the length of her hair again. Zachary wasn't a Haven by birth, but I decided not to point that out. She'd probably just say it didn't matter. "That's good. But I'm looking for a lot more than a man who's um, well built."

"I'm just saying, it's a perk." She met my eyes in the mirror. "Keep in mind, honey. Once Zachary sets his mind to something, it's hard to dissuade him."

"Zachary Haven doesn't have romantic feelings for me," I said, my voice firm with conviction. "Marlene probably sent the flowers on his behalf anyway. They're just a thank you."

"All right, dear."

I fluffed out her hair a little. "How's this length?"

"Just right."

"Okay, I'll get you dry and then finish up."

Fortunately, Louise didn't go back to the subject of Zachary, or the merits of her husband's manhood. I blew out her hair and added a little curl. She left happy and I went on with my day.

I put Zachary, and his flowers, out of my mind. My next client needed my full attention. She'd been coming to me for color correction after a botched bleach job at a different salon. Her hair was so damaged, we were restoring her color gradually so we didn't do more harm than good.

She also left happy, which was always the goal. By the time Stacey and I cleaned up after she left, it was time to go home for the night.

I drove home, looking forward to taking my shoes off and enjoying a cup of decaf tea. The weather had finally broken and the sky was clear, the fall air crisp and refreshing.

When I pulled up to my house, someone was parked in my driveway.

Not just any someone. Zachary Haven.

What was he doing there?

He leaned casually against the driver's side door, his black coat open to reveal a blue flannel and jeans. His shirt looked soft.

Why was I thinking about what his shirt might feel like?

The half smile on his face grew as I approached. But I was not going to let that sexy smirk do anything to me. Not anymore.

I parked next to him and before I could open the door, he was there to open it for me.

"Milady." He offered his hand.

I hesitated before taking it and letting him help me out of the car. "Thanks?"

"You're welcome." He gave my hand a tiny squeeze before dropping it. "Did you get the flowers?"

"Yes, but I'm not quite sure why you sent them."

"Because you like flowers," he said, as if that explained everything. "Listen, I know this is all coming out of left field, but I need to talk to you about something important."

"Okay."

He glanced around. "Here? That's fine, we can do this here." He paused to take a deep breath. "Marigold, I think I'm in love with you."

My eyes widened and I took an involuntary step backward. What had he just said?

"No, you're not."

"Hang on, I didn't mean to lead with that. I don't know what it is lately, but I can't seem to think straight when I'm around you."

"Zachary, you're not in love with me."

"No, that's the thing. I am. When I was shocked in your salon, there was a moment when I thought I was going to die. And the first thing I thought about was you. My only regret was not telling you how I feel."

I took another step backward, a sick feeling spreading through my stomach. "This isn't funny."

"I'm not trying to be funny."

"Is this some kind of prank? You're bored with messing with the Baileys so now you decide to mess with me?" I glanced around. "Is someone filming this to see my reaction?"

"No, of course not. Mari, I'm not messing with you. This is real."

"We've known each other almost our entire lives, and for most of it, you've ignored me. You haven't just ignored me, you've made it very clear that you hate me."

"I *never* hated you."

"Now I know you're lying."

"I'm not lying. I didn't hate you, I just thought I had to avoid you. And once I started avoiding you, it was like I couldn't stop."

"You expect me to believe that? You've been treating me like I have a communicable disease since high school."

"You're right. I know." He put his hands up. "I've been a jerk and it was stupid and I'm sorry."

Did I believe him? Maybe he really was sorry. But that didn't explain why he was sending me flowers and claiming he was in love with me. That, I couldn't believe.

"Okay, well, thank you for apologizing and I forgive you. I don't need to hold a grudge over it. But you're not in love with me."

"That's where you're wrong. I really am." He raised his eyebrows. "Didn't you hear the part about my one regret when I thought I was dying? Because I thought that was pretty good. And it's true."

"That's not love, that's a traumatic experience."

"A traumatic experience that made me realize how I feel."

I stared at him for a moment. Zachary Haven was standing outside my house, claiming to be in love with me. Once, this might have felt like a dream come true. And I knew with a sinking feeling in the pit of my stomach, I would have fallen for it. I would have believed him because it was everything I'd secretly wanted to hear.

But I wasn't falling for it now. A guy didn't go from constantly ignoring someone for so many years to being in love with her just because he got shocked and fell off a ladder. That was ridiculous. I wasn't going to let myself be so naïve.

I wasn't going to let him hurt me again.

"Zachary, you can't just come over here and claim you're in love with me like this. I just started dating someone." As soon as the words left my lips, I grasped what was really happening. He knew I was dating Preston. He wasn't in love with me, he just didn't want someone else to have me. "You're unbelievable, you know that?"

"What?"

"I don't know why you would choose now to pull this

stunt and not when I was dating someone else in the past. Maybe you realize Preston could be the one and that's why you're doing this."

"I don't even know who Preston is."

"It doesn't matter. You were ready to keep on ignoring me forever until you found out about my helicopter date."

"No." He put up his hands again. "That's not what happened."

"Seriously? For the first time in years, a nice guy is interested in me, and that's when you decide to send me flowers? When I might have found the one? Why are you trying to screw this up for me?"

"Because you should be with me instead of him. Speaking of, will you go out with me tonight?"

My mouth dropped open. "This is low. You can't mess with a woman's emotions like this. You're not in love with me and I'm dating Preston."

He shrugged one shoulder. "You've been on one date with the guy. That doesn't mean you're dating."

"Two dates."

"Two? Damn it." He blew out a breath. "Look, this isn't going the way I thought it would, but all I'm trying to say is that almost dying made me see I've been an idiot and you're amazing and if you give me a chance, I can prove I'm really in love with you."

"No."

"Wait, what?"

"No, I'm not giving you a chance. You've been a jerk to me my entire adult life and now that I'm dating someone great, you swoop in and try to mess it up for who knows what reason. It's not nice and it's not funny and it's not happening."

I stormed past him toward my front door, a heady swirl of emotions battering me from the inside. I was angry and confused, and as much as I didn't want to admit it, a little bit charmed.

Which only made me more angry and confused. There was no way he was serious. Not only was his timing atrocious, he couldn't mean it. He couldn't have feelings for me. It was just my stupid, misplaced crush trying to get my attention. I wasn't going to give it, or him, a chance to hurt me.

Not again.

"Marigold."

I stopped with my hand on the door.

"He's not the one."

I whipped my head around. "How would you know?"

The corners of his lips turned up in a smile. "Because he's not me."

"You arrogant jerk."

"And because he doesn't know you. I do. But don't worry. I'll fix this."

Gritting my teeth, I let out a frustrated groan. Zachary Haven was officially the biggest jerk on the planet. Why was he doing this to me? Why now? Why was he trying to mess things up when a world of possibility had just opened up to me?

Before Preston, I would have fallen for it. And what would I have gotten out of it? Nothing but heartbreak. I wasn't going to let that happen.

Without another word, I unlocked my door, and went inside.

CHAPTER 11
Zachary

MY ATTEMPT TO win over Marigold had fallen apart pretty dramatically. I hadn't meant to lead with *I think I'm in love with you*. I'd opened my mouth and it had just come out. Apparently practicing in the rearview mirror had been pointless. And it hadn't been the right way to open the conversation. It had left her confused and upset.

Hell, she was more than upset, she was furious.

A lesser man might have been discouraged. Not me. If anything, I was more sure. More confident. Because as soon as I'd told Marigold the truth about how I felt, everything had clicked into place.

I just had to convince her I wasn't lying, messing with her head, or only out to sabotage this Preston asshole.

Okay, I was out to sabotage him.

But I didn't want Marigold just because someone else did. I wanted her because she was always meant to be mine. I'd just been too much of an idiot to see it. This Preston dude was just a minor detail. A pebble in my path. I'd kick him out of the way and move on. Like I'd told Marigold, I was going to fix this.

Instead of continuing to be an idiot—which I had to

admit, tended to be my default—and beating my head against the wall, I decided to call in reinforcements. I was man enough to know when I needed an assist, and this was too important. I didn't want to keep screwing up.

Which was why I was sitting in a booth in the Copper Kettle diner, waiting for my sister and my soon-to-be sister-in-law to arrive.

Audrey showed up first, my brother Josiah plastered to her side. He tipped his chin to me, then pulled Audrey in for a kiss. Apparently he wasn't staying. I never would have figured Josiah would become the mushy for a girl type, but my grumpy-ass brother turned into a teddy bear with her. It was weird.

She said goodbye to Josiah, then waved at me and came over to my booth.

"Hi, Zachary." She was her usual cheerful self. Her long dark hair was pulled back, and she was wearing a gray sweater, jeans, and her signature easygoing smile.

"Hey, almost sister."

That made her smile bigger. "I love that. You know, I always wanted brothers."

"You're about to get a bunch of them."

She slid into the booth across from me and scrunched her shoulders. "It's so exciting."

Audrey was about to say something else, but Annika swept up to the table in a navy blue sweatshirt and jeans, with three macaroni necklaces around her neck.

"Those are so cute." Audrey pointed at Annika's mom bling.

Annika lifted her hand to her neck and rolled her eyes before taking them off. "I forgot I had these on. I was crafting with the girls, then Will wanted to make one too." She sat next to Audrey, then pointed a finger at me. "You have a lot of explaining to do."

"What happened?" Audrey asked.

"You must not have talked to Mari yet," Annika said.

"Not for a few days, I guess."

Annika leveled me with her best sister glare. "Why did you tell Marigold you're in love with her in the middle of her driveway? What kind of crappy game are you playing?"

Audrey gasped. "It's you?"

I put up my hands. "I'm not playing a game. Wait, what do you mean, it's you?"

"I've just had this theory that Marigold is either in love with you or Luke. Except… uh-oh. What if she's in love with Luke? If you're in love with her, and she's in love with your brother, this just got very complicated."

I blinked at her a few times. Marigold was not in love with Luke. No way.

Was she?

No.

"No, no, no." I chuckled and shook my head. "Marigold isn't in love with Luke."

"How do you know?" Audrey asked.

Annika raised her eyebrows. "That's a good question. How do you know?"

"Because…" I wrinkled my nose, like the very idea smelled bad. "Why would she be in love with Luke?"

"Why wouldn't she?" Annika asked. "He's a good guy."

"Yeah, but he's not me."

"Are you actually that conceited?" Annika asked.

"I'm not conceited. Okay, I am, but I just mean I'm better for Marigold."

"Since when?" Annika asked. "I thought you didn't like her. You always act like you hate her."

Damn it, that whole ignored her for a million years thing again. "I know, that was just me being stupid. I never hated her. I tried to explain that to her, but I don't think I got the message across very well. Especially considering she stormed inside and slammed the door."

"Can we back up?" Audrey asked. "Why did you act like you hated her?"

"It's a long story."

They watched me silently, eyebrows raised, as if waiting for me to continue.

Damn it. Again.

"I did something stupid and I hurt her. And then I made it worse by avoiding her because I felt like shit about it, which made her think I hated her, which made me avoid her more."

"But now you're claiming you're in love with her?" Annika asked.

"I'm not claiming anything, I'm telling you I am. I told her too, but she didn't believe me. That's why I need the two of you."

"You think I'm going to help you convince my best friend you're in love with her?" Annika asked.

"Why do you make that sound like the worst thing you've ever heard in your life?"

"Because you can't be serious."

"Why not?" Audrey asked, turning to Annika. "He could be in love with her."

I grinned at Audrey. "I knew I liked you."

Annika sputtered for a second before answering. "She's my best friend."

"Thanks, captain obvious, we're aware of that," I said. "That's why you're here."

"No, I mean I can't take your side."

"I'm your brother."

"And Marigold is… Marigold. She's too sweet."

"Too sweet for me? I'm trying not to be insulted here, but it sounds like you're saying you don't think I'm good enough for your best friend."

"No, Z, I don't mean it that way." She blew out a frustrated breath. "You're my brother, and I love you, but let's be honest. Your track record with women isn't the greatest."

"This is different. And my track record isn't as bad as you think it is."

"When was the last time you had a serious girlfriend?"

I opened my mouth to answer, but I couldn't quite remember. It had been a while. And what did *serious girlfriend* mean, anyway?

"See, you can't even tell me," she said. "You flit in and out of women's lives like they're entertainment."

"No, I don't." I rolled my eyes. "Okay, I do that sometimes. I like to have fun. And women are the best kind of fun."

She raised her eyebrows and damn, she looked like our mom when she did that.

"Not just to sleep with," I said. "I don't sleep with every woman I meet. I don't even sleep with every woman I could." My voice quieted and I glanced away. "One-night stands aren't all they're cracked up to be. I figured that out a long time ago."

"Wow," Audrey said, and I couldn't tell if she was impressed or confused. "I think he means that."

A deep truth hit me and I blurted it out without thinking. "The problem is, girls I've dated weren't Marigold. She's always been the standard, even when I wouldn't admit it. I wasn't trying to use them to get over her or something shitty like that. I just thought, or I knew, I didn't deserve Marigold, so I was out of luck. But how could I fall for another woman when Marigold was out there, just existing in the world. How could anyone ever compare to her? It would have been nice if it hadn't taken almost dying to figure that out, but what can I say, I'm hard-headed."

Annika stared at me, her mouth slightly open. Audrey was giving me that big-eyed gaze that made it look like she might tear up at any moment.

"What?" I asked.

"I've known you my entire life and I had no idea this side of you existed," Annika said.

I leaned back a little. "Is that good or bad?"

"Good," she said. "I would have loved to have seen it sooner."

"Maybe he's been hiding it beneath his veneer of sarcasm and smart-assery," Audrey offered.

"That must be it," Annika agreed. "I wonder if he did it on purpose or if it was an unconscious coping mechanism."

"I'm right here."

"Where do you think the urge came from?" Audrey asked, ignoring me. "It seems like you all had a pretty good childhood."

"We did, but it wasn't without ups and downs. Especially for my brothers. I'm the lucky one with parents who are still married. They all had to deal with loss when their other parent left."

"That's true," Audrey said. "That definitely left scars on Josiah."

"I'm sure it did. I always wondered if his mom leaving was why he was so grumpy and aloof." She grabbed Audrey's hands. "I love seeing him with you so much. He's so much more, I don't know, himself. Like the guy underneath all that defensiveness finally broke free, and it's amazing."

"Aw, thank you." Audrey sniffed. "I love him so much."

"And we love you so much."

They threw their arms around each other in a hug and I waited for them to finish their sisterly love-fest.

"Sorry." Annika wiped a few tears off her cheeks. "Where were we?"

"I think your brother was being surprisingly convincing that he really does care about Marigold."

"Right." Annika turned her sister-glare back on—full

power. "Whether or not I help you, if you hurt her, I'll make you regret it for the rest of your life."

"Sorry, Z, but I'm with Annika," Audrey said. "Marigold is one of the sweetest people I've ever known. I don't want her to get hurt either."

"Neither do I. I'm not going to hurt her. I'm not going to screw this up."

I hated the way Annika was looking at me, with something like pity in her eyes. She wasn't going to say it out loud, but I knew what was going through her head. She wanted to believe me, but she wasn't sure she could.

Because I always screwed it up. That's who I was in our family. The screw-up. We all knew it, even if no one said it in front of me.

Well, not this time.

"I just need a chance to show her that I really am in love with her." I paused, looking them each in the eyes for a second. "And I need to get rid of the helicopter guy."

"Oh boy." Audrey looked away. "That's definitely a complication."

"Why? It can't be that hard. She's only gone out with him a couple of times."

"Yeah, but he seems pretty amazing," Audrey said. "And kind of perfect for her."

"I don't want to jump to conclusions too quickly, because we haven't actually met him yet," Annika hesitated, "but Audrey is right. So far, he seems like her dream man."

I rolled my eyes. "So he has money, so what?"

"I don't think it's the money," Annika said.

"It's the whole package," Audrey agreed.

I shuddered. "Please don't talk about his package."

Audrey laughed. "No, I mean he's the whole deal. From what Mari said, he's refined and acts like a gentleman."

"And he seems like he's really into her," Annika added. "She couldn't stop talking about how attentive he was."

"Plus, he's not pressuring her into anything," Audrey said. "He swept her off her feet in a huge way on their first date and none of it meant he expected her to do anything she didn't want to do."

A sick feeling spread in the pit of my stomach, making me want to gag. "She didn't want to, right? I mean, she didn't…"

"I don't think so," Audrey said. "That's what I mean, he took her on this lavish, expensive date and it wasn't to manipulate her into bed."

I leaned back in my seat and crossed my arms. I hadn't thought the helicopter guy would be much of a problem. They'd been out on a couple of dates, so what? That didn't mean he was actually a threat. They weren't exclusive. And I was confident if she really gave me a chance, she'd kick that guy to the curb and choose me.

But what if I was wrong? What if she was already on her way to choosing him?

That wasn't good. I couldn't let that happen.

Which meant I had a twofold mission. One, get rid of Preston so he couldn't get in the way. Two, convince Marigold I was in love with her and give her the chance to fall in love with me.

"That look on your face is worrying me," Annika said.

"What look?"

"That one." She pointed at me. "The one that says you're up to something."

"I am up to something. I thought I was being pretty transparent. I'm trying to figure out how to get rid of the helicopter guy and make Marigold fall in love with me."

"Oh, Z." She closed her eyes for a second. "I have such mixed feelings about this. Not about you having feelings for Marigold, that's kind of amazing. But I don't know how I can be involved without putting myself in an impossible situation. I can't help you sabotage my best friend's relationship with a guy she really likes."

"Why not?"

"Because it's not right. Yes, you're my brother, and if you really love her and you wind up together, that would be incredible. But I feel like you're about to ask me to feed you information about their dates or something, and I'm not comfortable with that."

I glared at the table. Damn it. She was right, I was thinking she could feed me information about their dates.

"Girl code," I muttered. "I get it. You have best friend loyalty you can't break." I glanced at Audrey. "What about you? You haven't known her as long."

Audrey shifted in her seat. "I can't help you sabotage her relationship either."

I groaned. "Stop calling it a relationship. Two dates isn't a relationship."

"I know that isn't what you want to hear, Z, but—"

"I'm not giving up." I looked them each in the eyes. "If she really doesn't want me, not because of some other guy, but because of me, fine. I can't force her to fall for me. But I gotta try."

Audrey sighed. "You have to admit, this is really romantic."

"I did not see this coming," Annika said. "Look, I'll do what I can without compromising my loyalty to you as my brother and to her as my best friend."

"Same," Audrey said. "Except for me, it's almost-brother."

It wasn't exactly the inside job I'd been hoping for, but at least they believed me. I'd have to make it work.

"Thanks, ladies."

"Just promise me something," Annika said.

"I already told you, I'm not going to hurt her."

"No, that's not what I was going to say."

"Then, what?"

"Don't do anything crazy."

I grinned at her. "What would make you think I'd do something crazy?"

"You have the look again."

"The one that says I'm up to something?"

She nodded. "That's the one."

A slow smile spread across my face. She was absolutely right. I was up to something. I was going to ruin things for the helicopter guy and make Marigold mine.

My sister didn't think I could do it?

Hold my beer, Annika.

CHAPTER 12

Marigold

SINKING INTO THE COUCH CUSHIONS, I let out a long sigh and put my feet up. It had been a long day. A good day. One client after another at the salon was a welcome change. But my feet were paying the price.

I'd already changed out of my clothes into a tank top, pajama pants, and cardigan. Fuzzy slippers, a good book, and a cup of decaf Earl Grey tea completed my evening relaxation ensemble.

Sometimes a night with no plans was just what a girl needed.

Preston was out of town. He was hoping to be back tomorrow and we'd see each other then. I was looking forward to it, idly pondering what I'd wear on our next date. Maybe the red dress I'd bought last year and still hadn't worn. It had been a splurge, and the fact that it was hanging in my closet with the tags still on was a little bit depressing.

But no more need to be sad about an unworn dress. Not when I had another date to look forward to.

My phone rang and Preston's name on the screen gave me a little tingle of anticipation.

"Hi."

"Hi, beautiful. How are you?"

"I'm fine. Work was busy, but that's a good thing."

"Excellent. Are you still there or home already?"

"I'm home."

"Good. Listen, I just got back into town. I'm still at the airport, and I have a few things to take care of, so how about I pick you up for dinner in an hour."

I paused, feeling the slightest bit flustered, and looked down at my pajamas and slippers. "Tonight?"

"If you need more time, I can try to move the reservation, but they might not have a table."

He'd already made a reservation? I moved my feet from the coffee table to the floor and set down my tea. "No, an hour is fine. I just wasn't expecting to see you tonight."

"My plans changed." His voice got quiet, like he was talking to someone else. "Sorry, beautiful, I have to go. I'll see you in an hour."

He ended the call and I set my phone on the couch. So much for pajamas and tea. But it would be worth it to get dressed up for a date with Preston, even if he hadn't given me much notice. Maybe he was just so anxious to see me, he couldn't wait until tomorrow.

I could imagine him calling restaurants from the cabin of the helicopter, trying to find one that would take a last-minute reservation. Setting things up so everything would be just right when he arrived.

And I couldn't deny how nice it felt to be wanted.

So I nudged aside the ping of disappointment at losing my relaxing night in, and gathered some excitement for dressing up.

I went to my room and took my hair down, fluffing it in the hope I wouldn't have to start over. It still had some curl; I could work with it.

My phone buzzed with a text, but the number wasn't in my contacts. That was odd.

Hey, it's Zachary. Full disclosure, I tortured Annika into giving me your number.

I wanted to be annoyed. And I was.

But I also wasn't.

Zachary Haven was so confusing. He always had been.

Me: *Why do you need my number?*

Zachary: *So I can talk to you*

Me: *What makes you think I want to talk to you?*

Zachary: *You answered*

I groaned in frustration. I had answered. Immediately. I should have ignored his text for two days first. But I'd never been good at those kinds of games.

Zachary: *Can I just call you? I hate texting.*

I hesitated. I needed to get ready. Even if I'd wanted to talk to Zachary, I didn't have time. And I didn't want to. Not at all. I could just toss my phone on the bed and go do my makeup. That would be the smart thing to do.

My phone buzzed, this time with a call. Zachary. I pressed my lips together and squeezed the phone, wracked with indecision.

You shouldn't answer. Don't answer. This is a bad idea.

I answered. "Hello?"

"Hey," Zachary said with his typical casual confidence. "How was your day?"

"It was fine."

"Glad to hear it. What are you up to?"

I went to my closet, pulled out the red dress, and scrutinized it. "I'm getting ready for a date, actually."

"Are we going out tonight? You should give a guy more notice. What should I wear?"

Pressing my lips together, I tried not to laugh. I decided against the red dress and put it back.

"This is so much pressure," he said.

"My date isn't with you."

"It should be."

"No, it should be with the guy I'm actually dating. Not my best friend's brother who's ignored me since high school."

"Ouch. But are you really dating, though? This is what, date number three?"

"None of your business." I kept looking through my closet. Maybe the navy wrap dress.

"As the guy you should be dating, it is my business."

"Stop."

"Unlikely."

"Zachary, you can't expect me to believe this isn't some kind of game to you. I don't want to be your plaything." I tossed the navy dress on the bed. It would have to do.

"Trust me, this is not a game."

"Why should I trust you?"

"You know what, you're right. I don't expect you to trust me. I have to earn your trust. And I will."

"Well, not tonight because I have a date."

"Where's he taking you?"

"I don't know and even if I did, I wouldn't tell you."

"You can tell me. It's not like I'd do anything."

"Yeah, right."

"I wouldn't," he said, but I could hear the laughter he was trying to hold back. "Okay, maybe I would."

"At least now you're being honest."

"Marigold, I'll always be honest with you."

I sighed. Why did I want to believe that? What good would it do to give even an ounce of trust to Zachary Haven? I did that once, and it had blown up in my face. But this sudden attention from him had my head spinning.

"I have to go. I need to finish getting ready."

"Okay, sure. Have a good time tonight."

A surge of frustration swept through me. "Have a good time? This is why I can't trust you. Well, this and a million other reasons. First you tell me I should be going out with you instead of Preston, and now you're telling me to have a good time? Why do you have to be such a smartass?"

"I'm not being a smartass. Usually I am, but not now. I care about you, of course I hope you have a nice evening. Granted, I hope he screws it up and you never see him again. But I still hope dinner is good."

What was wrong with me that his logic almost made sense? "Goodnight, Zachary."

"Goodnight, Marigold."

Note to self. Don't answer when Zachary calls. Especially when you're getting ready for a date.

Glancing at the time, I groaned in frustration again. I needed to get ready. Preston would be here soon.

———

The navy dress was fine. I turned in the mirror. Yes, fine. Maybe not the nicest dress I owned, but it fit me well, and best of all, it was comfortable. If I was going to go from pajama pants to date attire, at least I could wear something that felt good.

Besides, it was just dinner. And at this hour, we'd certainly be staying in town. No extravagant helicopter rides to the city tonight.

Preston knocked. He was right on time. Because of course he was. Punctuality was an attractive trait in a man. It meant he respected my time.

I opened the door and a slow smile spread across his face.

"Wow. You look amazing."

My cheeks flushed. "Thank you."

He stepped closer, slipped a hand around my waist, and gave me a light kiss. "Ready?"

"Let me just grab my coat."

He helped me into my coat, then led me to his car. As soon as I'd taken a few steps, I knew I should have chosen different shoes. My nude heels were pretty, and complemented my dress, but my feet were already tired. I had the tiniest twinge of longing for my couch and slippers.

But this was fine. A date with Preston was worth it.

We drove into town and parked outside Alchemy Bar and Grill. I'd been there before and the food was good. In fact, the owner was one of Zachary's cousins, Eric Haven.

Why was I thinking of him as Zachary's cousin? I'd known him through Annika first, not Zachary.

I needed to get that man out of my head.

Preston held the door for me and I stepped into the lobby. Another man in a suit stood with a smile of recognition, but I'd never seen him before. A woman with long blond hair—they were extensions, but very well done—stood next to him. He held out his hand to shake Preston's.

"You made it," he said.

"This is Marigold." Preston placed his hand on the small of my back. "Marigold, this is Drew and his wife, Tess. Drew and I have been colleagues for a long time."

I tried to smooth over the surprise in my expression as I shook hands with Drew, then Tess. "Nice to meet you."

"Preston can't stop talking about you," Drew said with a know-what-I-mean smile. "It's great to see you actually exist."

I wasn't sure how to reply, but managed a polite laugh.

"Stop teasing her." Tess nudged Drew, then gestured over her shoulder. "Our table is ready. We were just waiting for you."

As Drew flagged down the host, I took a deep breath. *Our* table? Preston hadn't said anything about meeting friends. Was this a double date?

My feet moved in response to the light pressure of Preston's hand on my back. Like usual, he guided me to the table and pulled out my chair. I noticed Drew did the same for Tess.

The host gave us menus and explained the specials. Drew went straight for the wine list and ordered a bottle for the table.

The men started talking about what sounded like work. Under different circumstances, I would have happily engaged Tess in conversation. I chatted with people all the time at the salon. But that was the thing, I'd been chatting all day. I couldn't quite seem to muster the motivation to attempt small talk, which left me feeling shy and awkward.

After several long moments, Tess made eye contact and smiled. "So, Preston tells us you do hair."

Was her tone condescending or was it my imagination? Maybe I was just being sensitive. "Yes, I have a salon here in town."

"How sweet. Good for you."

"What do you do?" I asked.

"Mostly volunteer work."

"That's code for daddy pays the bills," Drew said with a wink.

Tess just smiled.

"How long have you been married?" I asked.

Drew looked at his wife. "Five years?"

"Yes, honey, five years."

He grinned at her. "It's been so perfect, I lost track of time."

She rolled her eyes.

"I keep telling Preston he needs to settle down," Drew said.

Preston glanced at me, his dimples puckering. "Let's not scare her off."

Drew and Tess both looked at me, as if they expected a reply. But I didn't know what to say. As dreamy as Preston was, and as enjoyable as our first couple of dates had been, we barely knew each other. What was I supposed to do, give his friends an indication as to whether I was wife material?

Thankfully, the server came to my rescue, bringing four wine glasses and the bottle Drew had ordered. He poured for each of us. I took a small sip, although I felt like I needed something caffeinated.

"How's the construction coming along?" Tess asked.

"Slow." I could hear the irritation in Preston's voice. "If we don't make significant progress in the next week or so, I'm firing my contractor."

"We drove out there earlier today," Drew said. "Only saw it from the outside, but it's looking good so far."

Preston put his arm around the back of my chair and turned to me. "I'll have to take you out there soon."

"I'd love to see it."

Drew lifted his glass. "To plans coming together."

Preston and Tess followed, so I lifted mine as well. I tipped my glass to meet theirs even though I wasn't quite sure what plans we were toasting. Preston's vacation house, I supposed, although it seemed like something had passed between Preston and Drew that I didn't understand.

Then again, maybe not. I was among people I didn't know well and feeling rather brain fried. I was probably reading too much into everything.

The server still hadn't taken our dinner orders. While a slow-paced dinner could be nice, I was already so tired, and trying to keep up appearances in front of Preston's friends was draining the rest of my energy. I took another sip of wine, hoping that would help.

The room went dark and, for a second, silent, as if the shock of darkness made everyone stop eating or talking to take a simultaneous breath.

"What the hell happened?" Drew asked no one in particular.

A buzz of concerned voices filled the darkness and the staff began flitting from table to table.

"I'm so sorry about this," our server said. "We seem to have lost power. I'm sure it will come on again any second."

"Why would the power have gone out?" Tess asked.

"Good question," Preston said.

The front door opened and shut again. Someone had looked outside. I heard him tell the rest of his table that the lights were on in the neighboring buildings.

Preston stiffened and moved his arm from the back of my chair. He looked around and I could feel the agitation coming off him in palpable waves. He was not happy about this.

I touched his arm. "It's okay. I bet it will come back on. We'll just wait."

He glanced at me, then looked away, shaking his head. "This is unbelievable."

"At least we have wine," Tess offered cheerfully and held up her glass.

The moments ticked by with agonizing slowness. No power. A few people got up and left. Others set up their cell phones to light their tables and continued eating, making the best of it.

"Too bad they don't have candles on the tables," Tess said. "That would have been pretty."

Preston stood and held out his hand for me. "We're leaving."

"Are you sure?" I asked as I got up from my chair. "I don't mind waiting."

"No. This is unacceptable."

I didn't want to admit how relieved I was. This surprise dinner date wasn't at all what I'd expected and getting out of there early sounded fabulous. "Okay, that's fine."

"You do what you gotta do," Drew said, and gestured to the bottle of wine. "We'll at least finish this."

Tess slid my glass toward her. "Can I finish this for you?"

"Yes, please do. It was nice to meet you."

"Nice to meet you too."

I glanced toward the kitchen and saw the owner, Eric Haven. He shrugged, either by way of apology or as if to say he didn't know what was going on. Maybe it was both.

Preston took my hand and led me outside to his car.

"I'm sorry about all that," he said. "I didn't want to sit there for who knows how long only to find out we can't even order dinner."

"It's really fine. Honestly, I'm pretty exhausted anyway."

He looked at me as if trying to decide what to do. "Can I still salvage this? Take you somewhere else?"

My entire body longed for home. For that mug of tea and my fuzzy slippers. Did I actually want that more than I wanted an evening with Preston?

At this point, yes. I was tired, and that attempt at dinner with people I didn't know had sucked what energy I had left right out of me.

"Actually, I wouldn't mind calling it a night and going home. I'm not upset or anything. I just had a very long day and my head is killing me."

Okay, so the headache was a bit of a white lie, but I didn't want him to get the wrong idea. And as much as I wanted to be home, I wasn't ready to invite him over. That meant I needed a diplomatic way of ending our evening.

"Fair enough," he said. "I have an early morning tomorrow anyway. I'll take you home."

I let out a relieved breath. He didn't seem insulted. That was good.

He took me home and didn't try to invite himself in. Just walked me to my door like the gentleman he was and gave me a soft kiss goodnight.

Not the best date I'd ever been on, certainly. But it hadn't been a total disaster.

I went inside and had to suppress the urge to text Zachary to tell him what had happened. Why was that my first instinct? And why, once I was back in my pajamas on the couch with a hot mug of tea, did I dreamily imagine what he'd say when he heard the story of the power going out at the restaurant, essentially ruining my date with Preston.

He'd probably say it was the universe telling me I should have been with him instead.

But I was not going to listen to the tiny voice in the back of my head, whispering that maybe he'd be right.

CHAPTER 13

Marigold

STACEY STOOD to say goodbye to my latest client. The front desk was filled with so many flowers, she couldn't see over them.

"Maybe we should move some of these," I said as the front door shut.

"They're beautiful, but hard to see over." She sneezed. "And I might be slightly allergic."

"Oh no, I'm so sorry." I grabbed the bouquet on the end and moved it to a console on the side wall.

"It's okay, it's not too bad. And they really are pretty."

They were pretty. And also... a lot. Preston had sent flowers every day the salon was open. And on my days off, he'd sent them to my house.

It was wildly romantic.

Or... it had been wildly romantic at first. Now it was getting to be a little bit overwhelming.

But maybe he was done. He'd made his statement. After all, it was well past midday, and a new bouquet hadn't arrived.

I grabbed another vase and moved it to the console table.

"I think the one on the other end can go in the garbage at this point. It's looking sad. And he hasn't sent any more, so this is probably it."

"I don't want to say I hope so, because it's very sweet and he obviously wants to make an impression." She sneezed again. "But, yeah."

"You know what, I'll just mention to him that they're beautiful but making you sneeze."

"That's okay, you don't have to do that."

"There's no reason to let the guy I'm dating inadvertently make your work day miserable."

The front door opened and Vicky Surrey, the mayor's wife, poked her head in. "Hi Marigold. Can I put one of these in your window?"

She held up a Missing Persons poster with a picture of Brielle Thayer.

"Of course," I said. "Is that poor girl still missing?"

"Afraid so," Vicky said. "It's a sticky situation, what with her parents and all."

"What about her parents?"

"Well, a friend reported her missing, but her parents tried to get them to call off the search. Said we shouldn't bother. You didn't hear it from me, but I'd say they don't particularly seem to want her back."

I felt a pang of sympathy for the young woman. "Are the police still trying to find her anyway?"

"The police are doing what they can. The SPS is stepping up to fill in the gap."

That made me smile. The Squirrel Protection Squad had been formed when someone had been stalking my friend Audrey—and had harmed a couple of squirrels in the process. They genuinely cared about Tilikum's infamous squirrel population, but they'd done their best to look out for Audrey too.

"I'm so glad the SPS is helping. Hopefully someone hears from her soon. And yes, please put the poster in the window. The more we get her face out there, the better."

"Thank you kindly, Ms. Martin." She used a roll of tape she produced from a pocket to stick the sign to the window, then said goodbye and left.

I grabbed two more bouquets and took them to the back. The front door bell tinkled as I set them on my desk. I wondered who it was. I didn't have another client until this afternoon.

After taking a second to fluff my hair and straighten my blouse, I went out to the front to see who had come in. I rounded the corner just in time to see the flower delivery guy leaving and Stacey holding yet another large bouquet.

My shoulders slumped. Again?

"Let me take those." I hurried to the front to grab the vase from Stacey before she started sneezing.

"Don't take this the wrong way, but what is he trying to accomplish with all this?"

That was a good question. Was he just a little over the top? If one bouquet was nice, daily flowers would be even better?

"I think he's just a romantic at heart." Was he, or was that my wishful thinking? "I'll move the rest and we can just leave today's on the front counter. Will that be okay?"

"Yeah, I'll keep them over in the other corner. One shouldn't bother me."

We rearranged the flowers so they weren't all in Stacey's face while she worked. Before I could pop out for lunch, I had a walk-in. Fortunately, it was just Olive Hembree in for a quick cut. I took her back to my station and got to work. I'd have her styled and on her way in less than an hour.

The door opened again, making the bell tinkle. I paused and shut my eyes while I took a deep breath. If it was more flowers, I didn't know what I was going to do. And if it was another customer, I had to decide whether I'd take them, which would mean no break at all today, or ask them to make an appointment.

"Wait, what are you doing?" Stacey asked.

Opening my eyes, I looked toward the front, then blinked in disbelief.

Zachary Haven grinned at Stacey, then lifted a set of large pruning shears and proceeded to cut the new flowers. With a few snips, they were all on the floor.

With another smile, he winked at me, then walked out the door.

Stacey turned around, her mouth gaping.

Olive giggled in the chair. "Why did he do that?"

"She has two men fighting over her," Stacey said.

"No, I don't."

"Then what was that?" She gestured toward the door.

I sputtered for a second. "I don't know. He's a Haven. It's probably supposed to be some kind of prank."

"They're pranking beauty salons now? I thought they just pranked the Baileys."

"They do." I let out a frustrated breath. "You expect me to understand Zachary Haven? No one does."

"He sure is a snack, though," Olive said.

Despite myself, that made me laugh.

But what was Zachary thinking? If he was trying to win me over, how was cutting my flowers going to help? It just made me mad.

Although, was I mad? I should have been, but it was kind of funny. The way he'd waltzed right in and snipped them off, then left without a word. And that wink? He was ridiculous, but that wink had sent tingles down my spine.

I went back to Olive's hair. What on earth was wrong with me? "Give me a few Stacey, and I'll clean it up."

"That's okay, I can do it." Shaking her head, she laughed.

"I probably shouldn't think that was funny, but it was hilarious."

I knew exactly how she felt.

The door opened again and I thought it might be Zachary. Maybe he'd decided he ought to at least clean up his prank.

But it was definitely not Zachary. It was Preston.

The subtle smile on his face melted away when he saw the remains of his latest flower arrangement all over the floor.

"What the hell happened?"

I opened my mouth to answer—there was no way I was telling him it had been Zachary—but Stacey beat me to it.

"Oh, just Zachary Haven. He strolled in and cut them." She laughed again. "Sorry, they were so pretty, but it was really funny. I don't even know why."

Preston's gaze moved to me, his eyes intense. "Who's Zachary Haven?"

The hardness in his voice sent a chill down my spine. "He's just… um… my best friend Annika's brother."

"Why did he cut up the flowers I sent you?"

Anger? Possessiveness? What was that in his voice? "I'm sure he meant it as a joke. He's like that sometimes."

With his eyes locked on mine, he took slow steps toward my station. "Is this a problem I need to handle?"

Handle? What did that mean? "Oh, no. It's just Zachary. And I have so many other beautiful bouquets. We had to start moving them because they were making Stacey sneeze."

I wanted to interpret the hardness in his eyes as thrilling. A possessive man who didn't want anyone to interfere with his woman. That was exactly what I wanted, wasn't it? Shouldn't that look have been melting me from the inside?

But it wasn't. It was scaring me a little.

"Preston, I'm sorry, but I'm with a client. It was just a harmless prank. I wouldn't give it another thought."

His expression softened and his dimples puckered with a

small smile. "Of course." His gaze flicked to Olive. "I apologize for the interruption."

"Did you need something?" I asked.

"You weren't answering your phone. I wanted to be sure everything was okay."

"I'm fine, just working."

He moved closer and held out an arm. I stepped in and he drew me against him, brushing my lips with a quick kiss. "I have to leave town for a little while. Probably just for the rest of the day, but possibly a little longer."

"Back to Seattle?"

"No. Other business. But I'll call you later."

"Okay."

He turned and left. I let out a long breath.

"Wow," Stacey said. "That was Preston?"

I stepped back behind the chair and tried to focus on Olive's hair. "I'm so sorry, I forgot you've never met him. I should have introduced you."

"Don't apologize. I don't think he had any idea I was even in the room. That was a man on a mission."

I caught Olive's expression in the mirror. She was pressing her lips together, clearly trying to stop herself from grinning from ear to ear. I'd just given her quite the show—enough for a week's worth of Tilikum gossip. She looked like she was in heaven.

And the entire town was going to hear about all of it within hours.

I finished up the last few touches on Olive's hair, Stacey checked her out, and she picked her way around the cut flowers to reach the door.

"Leave those there, Stace," I said. "Give me a minute and I'll clean them up."

"I'll help in a second. I just need to give my husband a quick call."

I went into the back office. I needed a minute. Between Zachary's antics—and the fact that I wasn't furious at him—and Preston's response, my head was reeling. I didn't even have room to worry about the gossip line. It was what it was. Once a story got going, it was like a boulder rolling downhill. There'd be no stopping it. At least until the next salacious story started going around.

The bell tinkled yet again and I closed my eyes. Who was here now? I steeled myself for it to be my dad with a construction crew, ready to remodel the salon in the middle of a workday because he read somewhere that hair dryers were an electrocution hazard.

Stacey didn't call for me, so I waited. Maybe it was just a client popping in to make an appointment.

Another few breaths and my heart rate returned to normal. More or less. It clearly wasn't my dad. I heard what might have been a man's voice, but just as quickly, it was gone. The bell tinkled again.

I went out to see who had come in and found the front lobby clean. The remnants of the cut-up bouquet were gone, the floor clear of the mess of flowers and loose petals.

"Oh Stace, you didn't have to do that."

"I didn't."

Had Preston come back to clean it up? Had his chivalric instincts told him to take care of the little mess for me? How sweet.

"Then who did?"

"Zachary."

"What?"

"He came back with a broom and a garbage bag. I have no idea where he got them. He didn't say much, just cleaned it up and left." She picked up a cup from the Steaming Mug. "And he left this. It has your name on it."

She handed me the warm cup and I took out the stopper

and sniffed, then took a careful sip. It was a London fog, my favorite drink, especially on a cold day.

I stared out the front windows, but he was nowhere to be seen. Rain pattered against the street. Another storm was rolling in.

And Zachary Haven was more confusing than ever.

Bringing a Friend

BRIELLE

JOHN SAT CLOSE ENOUGH that his leg touched Brielle's. They were watching an episode of The Office, but she found it hard to pay attention. His closeness was too distracting.

She wished he'd turn and kiss her. But so far, despite taking pictures of her with her clothes off, he'd never made a move.

Today he just drank his beer and watched TV.

Maybe he wanted her to make a move. Maybe this was his way of giving her a chance to have agency. That's what the influencers online called it. Sexual agency. She needed to take control and show him what she wanted.

He'd like that, wouldn't he? It would please him?

She really wanted to please him. He'd done so much for her.

"People are looking for you," he said out of the blue.

"Really? What people?"

"People in town. You've been reported missing."

Brielle didn't know how to feel about that. She didn't want anyone to look for her. She didn't want to be found. She could go on living in John's cabin forever, as far as she was concerned. Although she still had the vague notion that she ought to go to Vegas so she could get a job.

But did she really need to if John wanted to keep her there?

She wasn't worried anyone would find her. Not there. She didn't know exactly where they were, but it had been a long drive to get there. She was safe.

"They won't find me."

"No, they won't."

The way he said that, so definitive, sent a chill down her spine. Which was silly. She didn't want to be found. It was good that John was so certain.

"Are you worried about it?" she asked.

"No."

"If anyone does, you know I'm not going to throw you under the bus, right?" she asked. "You didn't kidnap me or anything. And I'm an adult, there's nothing they can do."

"I know."

She leaned back into the couch cushions and took a long drink of her beer, hoping to chase away the unsettled feeling. Let her buzz melt it away to nothing.

They watched the show a little longer, then John dug something out of a pocket and held it out to her in the palm of his hand. It was a small pill.

"What's that?" she asked.

"Take it."

"But what is it?"

He produced another one and popped it into his mouth. "It'll feel amazing."

She picked up the pill and looked at it. She'd smoked weed tons of times, but this was different.

"Trust me," John said. "You'll love it."

He smiled at her and she couldn't help but smile back. She put it in her mouth and washed it down with a swig of beer.

"How long does it take to work?"

"Not long."

He grabbed his empty beer bottle and stood. She expected him to offer to get her another, but instead he stopped and tilted his head, looking at her.

"Stand up for a second."

She laughed a little and glanced around, then did what he said. "Okay?"

"Change into the pink tank top."

She looked down at her clothes—a gray t-shirt and joggers. "Why?"

His brown eyes seemed to darken. "Because I told you to."

A tingle of fear made the hairs on the back of her neck stand on end. But why? John would never hurt her. He didn't even look scary, just serious.

Her head spun a little, but she wasn't too drunk. Just buzzed. And she didn't feel the pill yet. She hurried upstairs and dug through the drawers to find the pink tank top. Apparently that was what John liked on her. She'd have to remember that and try to be wearing it the next time he came to the cabin. Not that she knew when he'd stop by. Maybe she'd just wear it every day.

She thought about calling down from the loft so he'd look up, let him watch her change. A little striptease could be fun. And show him she had agency.

But when she looked over the balcony, ready to peel off her shirt, she saw John go to the front door.

Oh no. Was he leaving?

He opened the door and Brielle's heart felt like it stopped. Fear gripped her and she clutched the tank top to her stomach. Someone was there.

Who was he? Had they found her?

She needed to hide.

Trying not to make a sound, she backed up into the loft. Where could she hide? What if John couldn't get rid of him?

"Brielle?" John called from below.

She heard the front door close.

"Kitten, where'd you go?"

Letting out a long breath, she quickly changed into the tank top. He got rid of him so easily. She should have known she didn't need to worry.

But when she came out, she stopped at the top of the stairs. John wasn't alone. Another man stood next to him. Similar build, slim but fit, probably around the same age.

"It's okay, this is a friend of mine." John glanced at him. "Andrew."

Andrew looked up to the loft and gave her a slight smile. "Hi, Brielle."

Relief poured through her. "Sorry, I thought it was someone else."

"Come down," John said.

There was something slightly disconcerting about the way Andrew watched her walk down the stairs. His eyes moved up and down, taking her all in.

But guys usually found her pretty. It was why she knew she'd find a job in Vegas. There were always jobs there for pretty girls.

"Wow," Andrew said. "Nice. I can see why."

John smiled, like he was proud of her. It made her feel better.

"Go get Andrew a beer," John said, nodding toward the kitchen.

"Oh, sure." She almost asked if she could have another one, but decided to just take one herself. She didn't want to make them think she was a child.

She grabbed three beers out of the fridge and opened them, then brought them to the other room. John and Andrew were already sitting on the couch, each in one corner with space in the middle.

Then it hit her what was happening. John wanted to introduce her to his friends. Well, friend. But maybe this was his best friend. And he'd told him all about the girl he had staying in his cabin and maybe even how he felt about her. And now Andrew wanted to meet this girl who'd captured his friend's attention so thoroughly that he was hiding her there.

It was all so romantic and exciting.

John took the beer from her and nodded toward the empty spot on the couch. She happily plopped down. The Office was still playing, so she sat back and watched for a few minutes.

From the corner of her eye, she could see Andrew cast a few glances at her. She didn't mind. He was just checking out his friend's secret girlfriend.

No wonder John had asked her to change into the pink tank top. It was sexy, and he wanted her to make a good impression.

It was about then she felt the pill starting to work. Warmth spread through her and her eyes felt droopy. Her lips turned up in a smile. She didn't know why she was so happy. She just couldn't help it.

"There you go," John said, his voice soothing. "That's my kitten. How do you feel?"

"Really good."

He stood and moved so he was facing the couch with his arms crossed. She started to get up but he motioned for her to stay where she was. If he felt like she did, he wasn't letting it show. Had he really swallowed his pill? Maybe it was just that Brielle's head was so fuzzy.

"Wow," she said, leaning her head back. John was right, it felt incredible. She was happy and relaxed like she'd never been before.

She heard a sound but it didn't make sense. A zipper? Why was she hearing zippers? Must be the drugs. Her head lolled a little. It was Andrew unzipping his pants.

"Okay, sweetheart," Andrew said. "Get over here."

What was happening? She looked at John for guidance.

He nodded toward Andrew.

Her addled brain was struggling to keep up. What was he doing?

"Come on," Andrew said, a hint of irritation in his voice. "On your knees in front of me."

"No," John said.

"No? What the fuck, man?"

"She can get you off, but she's not putting your dick in her mouth."

"Seriously?"

"Yes, seriously."

"Why the fuck not?"

"It's a process. You know this."

Andrew groaned. "I came all the way out here for a fucking hand job?"

John didn't answer. Just leveled him with a hard glare.

"Fine. Still, I don't know why you're being so careful." Andrew took her by the wrist and squirted something slick and wet into her hand. "Come here, honey. I know you're a little out of it, but can you make a fist? That's a good girl."

She looked up at John. Did he really want her to do this? Right in front of him?

His eyebrows lifted as if to say, go ahead.

She blinked, trying to clear her head, but she couldn't think straight.

"Kitten," John said, his voice commanding. "Do it. Do it for me."

Do it for John?

Even looking at Andrew with his pants pulled partially down, she felt so good. Her body was warm and tingly. He guided her hand where he wanted it and she did as she was told. She couldn't think why she wouldn't. John was watching. She felt good.

She could please him like this. It was just the one time. It would be fine.

CHAPTER 14

Zachary

THE FOREMAN'S voice boomed across the job site. Someone was getting their ass chewed out. Luckily, it wasn't me. Even better, I was done for the day. He'd been on a rampage, yelling at just about everyone as if the delays were their fault. I was just glad I was getting out of there before he had a chance to lay into me about shit I couldn't control.

I was also glad I was almost finished with this job. So far I'd flown under the radar, but it was me we were talking about. With a foreman like that, it was only a matter of time before we butted heads. Once I butted heads with someone, it tended to escalate. And that was the last thing I needed.

After packing up my tools, I headed out to my truck. The yelling had stopped and I wondered if anyone had gotten fired.

The foreman stalked out of the garage, his face still red from shouting. I hesitated, in no mood to deal with his temper, but I was on the wrong side of my truck to get in. Hopefully he'd turn around.

He didn't, just stood there with his arms crossed while a car came down the long driveway. Not just any car, a black

Audi. I wondered if it was the owner. Word on the job site was that he'd been in town, but I still hadn't seen him.

The man who got out matched the car. His suit screamed money, and he glanced around with an arrogant, I'm better than everyone vibe. And there was no way to miss his look of mild irritation as he surveyed the front of the building.

Wait.

Holy shit.

Was that Preston?

I saw him with Marigold at the restaurant the other night, but not up close. I hadn't gotten a good look at him, but that had to be the same guy.

"Mr. Bradford," the foreman said.

"Are we back on schedule?" he asked.

"Not exactly. But most of the delays are supply chain issues. There's only so much I can do."

The Bradford guy narrowed his eyes, as if he didn't like that answer. "How are you going to make up the time?"

"I've got a second crew coming to work on the east wing."

"Which is going to cost me."

"I can do it fast or I can do it cheap. I can't do both. Do you want to see the progress on the main living areas?"

Bradford glanced at his phone. "No time. I have to fly back to Seattle."

"Fair enough. When should we expect you back?"

"I'll be back and forth all week. I have things to see to here."

They kept talking but I stopped listening. I felt like such an idiot. I should have known. Of course the guy with enough bank to fly Marigold to Seattle in a private helicopter was the same guy building the monstrosity of a mansion I was working on.

I eyed him and my jaw hitched. Something was off about him, and it wasn't just the fact that he was trying to take my woman. Granted, that was enough to make me hate him, but my gut told me something was wrong. I couldn't explain what. I just knew.

My body practically shook with the desire to do something obnoxious. To saunter up to the guy and tell him I was going to steal Marigold right out from under him. It would probably get me fired, but it would be worth it.

Something made me stop. I'd love to think it was reason and maturity overpowering my smartass instincts. But it wasn't. I just figured the longer Preston went without knowing who I was, and that I intended to crush him, the better. I could get away with more if I didn't get in his face.

Yet.

So I got in my truck, just another electrician heading home after a long day on the job site. I didn't call attention to myself and the prick didn't look, as if I were beneath his notice.

Worked for me. Before this was all over, he'd know it was me. He'd know it was a small-town, blue-collar guy who'd beaten him.

As soon as I was back on the highway, I called Annika.

"Hey, Z," she answered.

"What's the helicopter guy's name? The one who took Marigold out."

"Preston?"

"Yeah but what's his last name?"

"Why?"

"I just need to know."

"What are you going to do?"

"Other than steal Marigold from him?"

"Z, it's bad enough I gave you Mari's number. I can't keep helping you."

"All I'm asking for is the guy's last name. Is it Bradford?"

She hesitated. "Yes."

"I knew it. Thanks, sis."

"Please don't do anything crazy."

I grinned. "Come on, this is me we're talking about."

"Hence my concern."

"Trust me. I've got this."

"Wait. Before you do anything, run it by Garrett first."

"Why would I do that?"

"So you don't get yourself into trouble."

I rolled my eyes. "I'm not going to do anything illegal."

"Z, I already know you cut the power to Eric's restaurant."

"What? I didn't have anything to do with that."

"You don't have to pretend. I saw Eric at the Steaming Mug this morning. He told me."

"There was nothing illegal about it. I had his full cooperation."

She sighed. "He did laugh about it, but that's the problem. He shouldn't be encouraging you."

"He was just helping a guy out. He knows where his loyalty lies and it isn't with some rich out-of-towner."

"My loyalty isn't with him, either."

"That's not what I meant. Besides, I know you're secretly rooting for me to win. And if you're not, you should be. There's something off about that guy."

"Of course you think that. You also think you're in love with the woman he's dating."

I groaned in frustration. "I am in love with her, and they're not dating. They've been on like two and a half dates. But that's not it. My gut tells me there's something shady going on."

"Z, what are you talking about?"

I hated it when she talked to me like I was one of her kids. I mean, I understood why, but I still didn't like it. "I don't know, I just don't trust him."

"I guess I can't defend him when I've never met him. But I trust Marigold and she really likes him."

I gagged a little. "Yeah, I get it. I'll talk to you later."

"Bye, Z. Love you."

"Love you, too."

I ended the call. Ask Garrett first? Right. I'm sure my robot brother would be a big help. She might as well have told me to talk to Dad.

But that did get me thinking. When I'd told my cousin Eric I wanted to cut the power to his restaurant to mess with Marigold's date, he hadn't hesitated. He wasn't a fan of some rich out-of-towner swooping in on one of our local girls. He'd been happy to help.

This was my town, damn it. Who else could I get to help me out?

Luke would have my back. So would Theo. Josiah might help if I bugged him enough, but he was busy. I'd call him in as backup if necessary.

And there was one other guy who came to mind. I didn't know if he'd help me, but this stuff was right up his alley.

One way to find out.

I drove home and made some calls. Then cleaned up a bit and headed to the Timberbeast.

———

Luke and Theo were already there when I arrived. Luke's light brown hair was a little longer than usual, practically brushing the neckline of his black t-shirt. Theo's faded blue hoodie and shorts made him look like he was ready to step out onto the football field and coach. He and I had always looked a lot alike—he was bigger than me, but we had the same blue eyes and square jaw. We got the eyes from our mom. The jawline was one of the only good things our biological father had given us.

I grabbed three beers from Rocco at the bar—the least I

could do for my brothers for showing up—and brought them to the table.

"What kind of emergency is this?" Theo asked as I took my seat.

"The most important kind." My tone was grave. "A love emergency."

"I told you he was fucking with us," Luke said.

Theo took a sip of his beer. "Figures."

"So what's really going on?" Luke asked. "Or were you just bored? Thanks for the beer, by the way."

"I'm not bored. This is serious. Marigold's been going out with the guy I'm working for."

"And this is a problem, because?" Theo asked.

"Because she should be with me."

"Since when?" Luke asked with a laugh.

I rolled my eyes. Did I really have to go over this again? "I'm in love with her. I've been a dick to her for years because I'm stupid. But now I'm done being stupid and I tried to tell her how I feel but she already started seeing this rich guy, Preston Bradford."

Luke and Theo glanced at each other.

"He took her out last night and I sort of made sure the date sucked," I said. "But that's not enough. I need to figure out how to get rid of him and also how to spend time with Marigold so she realizes she should be with me. Plus, I'm pretty sure he's shady as fuck, I just don't know why."

"Shady, how?" Luke asked.

"I told you, I don't know. It's just a gut feeling."

Luke leaned back in his chair. "So you want to sabotage his relationship with Marigold and swoop in as the hero."

"Basically, yeah."

"Childish with a high chance of failure," Theo mused. "I'm in."

"Same," Luke said.

I grinned. I knew these guys would have my back. "I tried

getting Annika and Audrey to help, but they have girl code best friend stuff getting in the way."

"That's fair," Theo said.

"Yeah, it is what it is."

"How did you ruin her date last night?" Luke asked.

"I cut the power to the restaurant she was in. Impatient bastard didn't wait five minutes before leaving. It was too easy."

Theo's eyebrows drew in. "How did you know where they'd be?"

"I followed them."

Luke laughed and Theo shook his head.

"So I guess we know stalking isn't off the table," Luke said.

"I wasn't stalking her. I just followed her to a restaurant." I paused. "Okay, that was basically stalking. But that's the thing, I can't follow her around all the time. She's going to catch me at some point and it'll just make her mad. I've already done enough shit to piss her off, I need to make her like me."

"Yeah, ruining her dates is probably not going to win you any points," Theo said.

"What if you do the opposite?" Luke asked. "Take her on better dates."

"Isn't this the guy who flew her to Seattle in a private helicopter?" Theo asked.

"How do you know about that?" I asked.

"Everybody knows."

I rolled my eyes again. "Yes, that's the guy. And he sends her flowers every day. Like every fucking day. What the hell?"

"So send her better flowers," Luke said.

"That's not going to help. And before you say it, I know I can't keep up with a guy with deep pockets. What am I going to do to compete with a private helicopter?"

Theo started to smile. "What if…? No."

"What?"

"I was just thinking, what if she has a date with him but he has to cancel at the last minute. She'd be pretty disappointed."

My eyebrows lifted as I realized what he was getting at. "And I could swoop in to make her feel better."

"You won't have to stalk her, since she'll probably be home if her date cancels," Theo said. "And the other guy will be out of the way."

"I like where this is going," I said.

"But how will you know if he has to cancel a date?" Luke asked.

I grinned at him.

"Oh," Luke said. "I see what you mean."

I knew my instinct was right. Luke and Theo did have my back. And so would he. This was totally his area.

As if on cue, the door opened and Gavin Bailey walked in. Our eyes met and we tipped our chins.

Luke looked slightly concerned as Gavin came over to our table. I didn't blame him. I'd been the last holdout when it came to the feud with the Baileys, and Gavin and I had almost come to blows more times than I could count. We were both a little hot headed.

Gavin had calmed down a lot since becoming a husband and father, but I hoped he'd jump at a chance to go back to his pranking roots, only this time with a new target.

He spun a chair around and straddled it backward. "Hey, jerks."

Luke raised his eyebrows at me. "Did you call him?"

"I told him I need help getting rid of an asshole who's trying to steal my girl. He said he was interested."

"You know she's not really your girl, right?" Theo asked.

"Can we focus?" I turned to Gavin. "As much as it hurts

me to say this, and I mean causes physical pain, I need your help."

"Why me?" Gavin asked.

"Because you're the only guy I know who's as crazy as I am." I shrugged.

A slow smile spread over Gavin's face. "All right. Let's do this."

CHAPTER 15

Marigold

A HINT of nervousness spread through my stomach as I got ready. It wasn't a last-minute date this time, but I also didn't know if we'd be meeting up with Preston's friends again. His friends had seemed nice enough, and I didn't have any reason to avoid them, but I had an odd feeling I couldn't seem to shake.

I put on lipstick and pressed my lips together. I hadn't even spent an entire meal with Drew and Tess. How could I come to any conclusions? I knew very little about them, so why did the thought of spending an evening with them make me so anxious?

My phone rang. It was Preston.

"Hi," I answered.

"Hi— Hang on." His voice got slightly muffled, as if he was holding the phone away from himself. "How the hell should I know? Do something about it."

"Is everything all right?"

"No. Everything is not all right. My entire job site is infested with vermin."

"Oh no! Rats?"

"Squirrels." He spit out the word as if it tasted bad.

I held in a laugh. The Tilikum squirrels were infamous for their antics. "How did they get there?"

"No idea, but they're everywhere. Fuck, there's another one. No, four more. Seriously, where the hell are they coming from?" His voice got quiet again. "You found what? How did they get there? For fuck's sake. Marigold, I'm sorry, I have to cancel so I can deal with this. It's a nightmare."

"That's okay, do what you have to do."

"I'll call you later." He ended the call.

That had been abrupt, but apparently he had a squirrel emergency. Only in Tilikum.

I thought for a minute about what I wanted to do. I was all dressed up, ready to go out. Maybe my friends were free for a spontaneous girls' night. It wouldn't hurt to check. I sent a message to our group chat.

Me: *Hi, ladies! I'm all dressed up with nowhere to go. Anyone free tonight?*

Annika: *I wish but the girls are both sick*

Isabelle: *Something must be going around because my kids are sick too*

Me: *Oh no! I'm so sorry. Give your sweet kiddos big hugs from Auntie Mari*

I waited, hoping Audrey would be free. She didn't have kids—yet—just dogs.

Audrey: *That would be so fun but we're having dinner with my mom*

My shoulders slumped with disappointment. Even a night in with friends would have been fun. I'd have happily traded my dress and heels for an evening in yoga pants with my friends. But no such luck tonight.

Me: *That's fine, I totally understand! Have a nice evening, besties!*

I put my phone down, then grabbed a tissue to wipe off my lipstick. Instead of pouting about canceled plans and busy friends, I decided to make the best of it. I could enjoy an evening in just as well as an evening out.

Ten minutes later, I was in a t-shirt and yoga pants with fuzzy slippers on my feet, a steaming mug of tea in my hand, and a good book at the ready. A hint of discontent gnawed at me, but it wasn't because I was home. I couldn't decide if I was disappointed that Preston had canceled, or relieved.

I wanted to be disappointed we'd missed another chance to spend time together. And I was. But as soon as I'd washed off my makeup and changed out of my dress, I'd felt a surge of relief. And that left me feeling mildly uncomfortable because I wasn't sure what it meant.

My phone rang again as I was settling on the couch with my tea. This time, it was Zachary. And instead of sending it straight to voicemail, I hesitated.

Since I was already in a mood for self-reflection, I took notice of the way my heart jumped, and the little tug of longing and excitement at the thought of hearing his voice.

Not good.

But I'd harbored a crush on Zachary Haven—misplaced as it was—for so long. The currents of emotion I had for him ran deep.

"Hello?"

"Hey, I'm glad you answered. What are you up to?"

"Just sitting at home."

"Yeah, me too. Do you want some company?"

I closed my eyes. An emphatic yes tried to bubble its way up my throat, but I swallowed it before it could pass my lips. I couldn't spend an evening with Zachary. It wasn't even about Preston. He and I weren't exclusive. I wouldn't be doing anything wrong.

But Zachary Haven was dangerous.

"I don't know if that's such a good idea."

"Hmm. What if it's not a date? Not even me trying to turn it into a date. Just two friends hanging out."

"Not a date?"

"It wouldn't even resemble a date."

"And you won't try anything?"

"I told you, you can trust me."

His voice was different—not even a trace of snark. He sounded honest.

"Okay. We can hang out. But just as friends. And you have to come here because I'm already comfortable."

"Done. I'll see you in a little bit."

I ended the call and let out a long breath. Was I making a monumental mistake? I was about to find out.

———

It took a while for Zachary to arrive, but when he did, I understood why. I answered the door to find him dressed in a hoodie and joggers, holding a pizza box and a bag from the grocery store.

He grinned and the warmth that flooded my veins and the way my heart fluttered was impossible to ignore. But he'd always made me feel that way. I was probably just conditioned to get jumpy when he was around.

"I grabbed pizza in case you're hungry." He held up the bag. "And ice cream. Because ice cream."

I laughed and stepped aside so he could come in. His joggers had a hole in the knee. Definitely not date attire.

That was good.

"Thanks." I inhaled the scent of pizza. "I'm glad you did. I'm starving."

"Same. Let's eat."

He brought the food to the kitchen and I put the ice cream in the freezer. It was mint chocolate chip—the kind without the green dye. My favorite. I took two plates out of the cupboard and set them on the counter.

"Pepperoni." He opened the pizza box. "It seemed like

fancy pizza would be too much like a date thing, so I kept it simple. Plus, you like pepperoni, so there you go."

"How do you know I like pepperoni pizza?"

He met my eyes and grinned again. "We grew up together. Pepperoni, never sausage."

That was true. I'd spent countless nights at the Havens' for sleepovers with Annika, often with pizza. Still, it was touching that he'd remember, especially about the sausage. I'd eaten pizza with sausage at their house once and been sick that night.

"I still can't eat sausage on pizza," I said. "I must have been ten when that happened."

"Sounds about right."

"Do you actually remember that?"

"You puked all over Reese. How could I forget?"

I put a hand to my forehead. "I did throw up on him, didn't I? Oh my gosh, that was horrible."

"We were all kids. What are you gonna do."

I grabbed napkins and we took our pizza to the couch.

"Your house was always so fun," I said.

"Was it? I just remember it being loud."

"It was, but that was what I loved about it. You had this big, boisterous family and there was always something going on. It was so different from my house."

"What was yours like?"

"Quieter. It was fine, I just didn't have other kids around."

"My poor parents had more kids than they knew what to do with."

"You guys weren't that bad."

"We were pretty bad." Zachary glanced away. "Especially me."

"You did get in trouble a lot, didn't you?"

He chuckled. "All the time. I kinda still do."

I didn't know why that admission made me smile, but it did. He was so endearing when he wasn't showing off.

"Like when you hit Cory Wilcox in the Timberbeast?"

"He had that coming. You didn't hear what he was saying to his girlfriend."

"Is that why you hit him?"

"Yeah. What did you think, I picked a fight for no reason?"

"I just didn't know. I was too far away to see what was happening."

"He was treating her like garbage. As far as I'm concerned, he deserved it."

I didn't want to condone a fist fight, but there was something slightly—dare I say it—gentlemanly about Zachary. At least in the way he stood up for people. I'd seen him do it before. Although he tended to rush in without thinking, his heart was in the right place.

"What did Garrett do after you guys left?"

"He took me home."

"That's good. I was a little worried he'd arrest you."

"You and me both," he said with a grin, then glanced at my empty plate. "More pizza, or are you ready for ice cream?"

"I think I'm ready for ice cream."

"Let's do this."

I followed him into the kitchen and put our dishes in the sink while he started scooping ice cream. We bumped elbows and the brush of contact was electrifying. It made my breath catch in my throat, but he didn't seem to react at all. Just kept scooping ice cream into a bowl.

And that was what I wanted. I'd told him we were hanging out as friends. This wasn't supposed to be date-like at all. He was simply respecting my wishes.

Which made me want more accidental contact.

What was wrong with me?

He handed me a bowl of ice cream and I took it to the couch, firmly telling myself to keep my distance. Whatever my hormones were doing, it had nothing to do with my head —or my heart.

Zachary was dangerous. I couldn't forget that.

He casually flopped on the couch and rested his feet on the coffee table, then nodded toward my ice cream. "How is it? Still your favorite?"

"How did you know it's my favorite? Another childhood sleepover memory?"

"Nope. I ran into you once at the Zany Zebra. You were with some guy and when you told him they didn't have your favorite flavor, he tried to argue with you about it. As if mint chocolate chip shouldn't be anyone's favorite."

"I remember that. He did not get a second date."

"I figured. You're too smart for that."

I waited for him to say I was too smart to be dating Preston, too, but he didn't take the opening.

Maybe Zachary Haven had manners after all.

Instead, he changed the subject, going back to funny stories from when we were kids. He told me about the fort he and his brothers had tried to build out of sticks and his favorite pranks they'd played on the Bailey brothers.

We laughed about the time the Baileys hijacked the drive-in movie theater with their homemade version of *Dirty Dancing*. I'd been there that night, with Isabelle. We'd pretended to be outraged with everyone else, but really, we'd thought it was hilarious. It was interesting to discover Zachary and his brothers had found the humor in it, too. Zachary even admitted he and Gavin had struck up something resembling a friendship.

I told him things too. About my dad replacing my range without asking and how my mom was always forgetting things. I shared a few of my worst first date stories and told him about what it was like to watch Annika fall in love with Levi Bailey during the time of the feud. I gushed about my non-biological nieces and nephews—Annika and Isabelle's kids—and even admitted how much I hoped I'd be a mom someday.

Through it all, he kept it friendly. He listened and talked and laughed with me, but never made an excuse to move closer. Never tried to brush his hand against my thigh or move into my space.

We were so absorbed in conversation, neither of us noticed the hours passing until I covered my mouth while I yawned. He helped clean up and when he left, he simply said goodbye.

As I shut the door and listened to the sound of his truck pulling down the driveway, I couldn't help but think how easy that had been. I hadn't thought for a second about my lack of makeup or my outfit. I'd enjoyed an evening of greasy pizza and ice cream with someone I'd known forever.

I'd seen a different side of Zachary Haven. And I liked it.

I liked it a lot.

Maybe he wasn't the unattainable bad boy I shouldn't want. He was a man who'd known me for years. A man who was comfortable and easy to talk to.

And a man who seemed to care more than I thought he could.

CHAPTER 16

Zachary

GAVIN TOSSED me a jar of peanut butter.

"You sure this will work?" I asked.

"The Fiona method? Oh yeah. It's foolproof."

I twisted the lid to open it and pulled off the inner seal, then dug out a scoop of peanut butter with a spatula. I smeared some on the tree limb.

"Just make sure it's thick enough for the cookies to stick."

"Got it."

The Fiona method was named after Gavin's sister-in-law, Fiona Bailey, who was known around town as the squirrel whisperer. She'd trained the ones out at her house to go through an obstacle course, and although none of the Baileys would admit it—even years later—she had to have been involved in the nut bomb prank at the Timberbeast.

Granted, we'd deserved it. We'd hit their hangout, the Caboose, with a similar prank.

But Fiona had also figured out the best way to clean up a squirrel situation without hurting any of the squirrels. Which was why I was out in the woods with my former enemy building a giant squirrel lure.

Only in Tilikum.

We'd loosed the squirrels on Preston's job site, but I didn't want them to stay there. He'd probably start picking them off. Sure, they could be a nuisance, but I didn't want any of them to get killed for the sake of a prank. I wasn't a total asshole.

The best part of the prank, though, had to have been the goats. I wished I could have been there to see it. Somehow Gavin had brought in an entire herd of goats and set them loose among the squirrels. They'd wandered in and around the half-finished building, sniffing out the squirrel treats we'd planted and trying to head butt Preston's crew.

I didn't want to admit Gavin had one-upped us, but he'd nailed it.

I laughed at the mental image of the chaos as I kept spreading the peanut butter. Apparently the key was not just the peanut butter, or the birdseed we'd use with it, but the cookies from Nature's Basket. Fiona called them squirrel crack. Something about the combination of the cookies stuck to the trees made the little suckers go nuts.

Pun intended.

It would distract them from looking for more of the similar treats we'd hidden all over Preston's job site. They should have cleaned those out by now anyway, so a new stash would get them out of harm's way.

"You didn't tell me if it worked," Gavin said. "Did he cancel on her?"

"It worked perfectly. He canceled and guess who just happened to have nothing to do last night?"

Gavin smiled. "Nice."

"I finally got to hang out with her. She's trying to friend-zone me, but that's another issue. I can handle it. Thanks again for your help."

"Yeah, why not? It was fun. I haven't tried to pull off a prank this big in a long time. I was worried I'd be rusty."

"It's like riding a bike."

"Exactly."

"You gotta tell me. How did you get the goats in and out?"

"A magician never reveals his secrets."

"Come on, man. Whose goats were they?"

He grinned. "Harry Montgomery."

"He just let you take them?"

"It was fine. I left a note."

I chuckled. It was probably a good thing Gavin and I had grown up as sworn enemies. We'd have gotten into a hell of a lot of trouble if we'd been friends.

"Well, I owe you one."

He tossed an empty peanut butter jar on the ground. "Nah, we're good. Skylar and I ran into that Preston guy in town the other day. I did not like the way he looked at my wife."

"See? There's something off about that guy."

"Agreed."

"Gavin Bailey gets it," I muttered to myself. "I don't know why she doesn't get it."

"This might be enough." He stepped back and put his hands on his hips, surveying our handy work. "But if you want to be sure, you could do another tree up that way. Give them something else to do after they find this one."

"Might as well. But you should get home to your family."

"All right. Thanks, Haven."

"You too, Bailey. See you around."

I grabbed all the empty containers and put the trash bag in the back of my truck. I'd take it straight to the dump—had to get rid of the evidence. Like Gavin had said, what we'd done was probably enough. I didn't need to make another squirrel lure. But we'd gone overboard on the prank, I figured I might as well go overboard on the clean-up.

Especially because Marigold wouldn't want any animals getting hurt. Even squirrels.

I headed into town and parked at Nature's Basket grocery.

It was still early enough that there weren't many people around. Theo and Luke had helped buy the supplies for the prank, spreading it out so it wouldn't look suspicious. Now I just needed to grab more peanut butter and cookies without raising any eyebrows.

I grabbed a cart and added a few things so the squirrel crack supplies wouldn't be obvious. Turning down the peanut butter aisle, I paused. Craig Martin was walking up the other way.

Marigold's father.

For a second, our eyes met. Then he walked right by, as if he didn't have a clue who I was.

Typical. He ignored me as hard as I'd ignored Marigold all those years.

That was going to get awkward later, but there wasn't anything I could do about it now.

I grabbed a bunch more peanut butter and tossed it in the cart. It was a lot more than one guy could possibly need, but I could go through the self-checkout to avoid questions.

The cookies were on another aisle, so I headed that way. I rounded the corner and stopped again.

Marigold.

It was as if the roof opened, allowing a single sunbeam to shine on her, making her glow with golden light. She was busy looking for something, so I waited, watching her. She was dressed in a pale blue wool coat and brown knee-high boots. Her hair was down around her shoulders and, for a second, I got lost in a fantasy of fisting my hands in all that hair while I—

"Zachary?"

I blinked. "Hey."

The smile she gave me was friendly. Too friendly for my taste, but at least she wasn't looking at me like I'd confused the hell out of her.

"What are you up to?" she asked.

"Just grabbing a few things. I saw your dad."

"Really?" She glanced around. "I didn't know he was here. Maybe I'll see him on my way out."

"Are you working today?"

"Yeah, I'm headed there after this. I like to keep snacks on hand for me and Stacey, but I don't see the cookies she likes."

"Do you have plans tonight?"

Her gaze snapped to me. "Why?"

"I thought we could hang out again."

"As friends, like last night?"

One corner of my mouth lifted. "No. This time it would be a date."

"You said you wouldn't try to make it a date."

I stepped closer, wishing the stupid cart wasn't in my way. "No, I said I wouldn't try to make last night a date. I didn't say anything about today."

She was trying to hide a smile. I could see it, dancing at the corners of her lips. She looked down and her expression changed, her eyebrows drawing together.

"Why do you have so much peanut butter?"

Uh-oh. Damn it, I couldn't lie to her. But I couldn't tell her the truth, either. "Gavin Bailey told me to get it."

Dude, Z. That was a terrible answer.

"Why did Gavin Bailey tell you to buy that much peanut butter?"

I shrugged.

"What are you hiding?" She looked at the shelf and grabbed a box of peanut butter cookies. "Are you here to get these?"

"Maybe."

"Oh my god. It was you, wasn't it?"

I clamped my mouth shut.

"You loosed the squirrels on Preston's job site. That's what the peanut butter is for."

"If I loosed the squirrels on the job site, why would I need peanut butter now? That already happened."

She practically threw the box of cookies into my cart. "The Fiona method."

"How do you know about the Fiona method?"

"Everybody in Tilikum knows about the Fiona method."

"I didn't until yesterday. Why am I always the last one to find out everything?"

"Zachary, look at me."

I kept my eyes firmly on the ground.

"Look at me. Look me in the eyes and tell me you didn't fill Preston's construction site with squirrels."

Lifting my eyes to meet hers felt like trying to lift a car over my head. "I did, but the goats were Gavin's fault."

"Goats? There were goats, too?"

"Gavin brought the goats. I didn't even know he was going to do that."

"So last night was a setup. You made sure Preston would have to cancel and then just happened to call me. I'm such an idiot. Of course I fell for it."

"You didn't fall for anything. I just wanted a chance to spend time with you."

"This really is just a game to you, isn't it?"

"No. This is not a game. I swear."

"Next you're going to tell me you cut the power to the restaurant the other night." Her eyes widened. "You did, didn't you? You turned off the power so we'd have to leave."

"To be fair, it was only out for a few minutes. It's not my fault your date was that impatient."

"Zachary, I can't believe you. Why would you try to sabotage my dates with Preston?"

"Because you shouldn't be with him. You should be with me."

She stared at me for a long moment and I couldn't read her expression. The raw honesty of what I'd just said hurt like hell. I wanted to take it back. Not because it wasn't true; it was. And I'd even said it to her before. But somehow this was different. It was too true. I wanted to wrap it in sarcasm and make a joke and pretend like I was untouchable. But I'd blurted it out and now I couldn't take it back.

"I don't know what to say to you right now." She took a step back. "This is a lot and I need to get to work."

She turned around and I watched her disappear around the corner at the other end of the aisle.

It wasn't just a lot—as in, the situation. *I* was a lot. That was what she meant.

And maybe I was.

Maybe I was just too much.

CHAPTER 17

Marigold

EVERYTHING WAS WRONG.

In my head, at least. Or maybe it was my heart. I wasn't sure.

I was nestled on the couch at Audrey's house, her dog Max—the sweetest dog in the history of ever—cuddled up next to me. Her other dog, Maggie, slept near the fire. It was raining outside, but we were cozied up with tea and cookies, and my binder for their wedding was open on the coffee table.

It had been a few days since I'd seen Zachary at the store, but my feelings remained a constant distraction. It wasn't that I was angry at him—not exactly. I just didn't know what to think.

My date with Preston last night hadn't helped. The date itself had been fine. No squirrels, no surprise double date, no electricity issues. He'd brought flowers to apologize for being short with me on the phone when he'd had to cancel—unnecessary, but nice of him—and taken me to dinner. Good food, handsome man, pleasant conversation.

What more did I want?

"Mari?"

I blinked. "I'm sorry. Did you say something?"

"No, but you were staring out the window."

"Sorry. We should be talking about your wedding and here I am zoning out on your couch."

She smiled. She was so cute dressed in one of Josiah's too-big-for-her flannel shirts. "I'm not worried about the wedding. It's coming together. But what about you? Are you okay?"

"Honestly? I don't know."

"Do you want to talk about it?"

I pulled the knit throw blanket Marlene Haven had given Audrey into my lap. "You know I've been seeing Preston. And he's great. He's handsome and interesting. He's exactly the sort of man I've always dreamed of meeting."

"So it's going well?"

"Yes." My hesitation was obvious in how long I drew the word out. "But there have been a couple of things that have given me pause. Which is fine, we're still getting to know each other. I just wish I could keep getting to know him without Zachary getting in the way. So I could really decide whether I want to continue dating him at all."

She winced. "Has Z been causing trouble?"

"It's Zachary Haven, when is he not causing trouble?" I sighed. "Apparently he teamed up with Gavin Bailey to fill Preston's construction site with squirrels. All so Preston would have to cancel our date and Zachary could make it look like a coincidence when he called to ask if I wanted to hang out."

Her eyes widened. "That was Zachary? I heard about that, but I didn't know he was behind it."

"Oh yes, it was him. He came over, promising we'd just hang out as friends, and the whole time it was a setup."

Audrey smiled. "I'm sorry, but that's kind of cute."

"He pretended like he just happened to call me when he knew I'd be home because he'd made sure of it."

"I know, I know. But the effort is impressive. Go back to Preston, though. You said there have been a couple of things that give you pause. Do you mean you're unsure about him?"

It was hard to admit there were potential flaws in my dream man. But I wasn't stupid. For one thing, everyone has flaws. For another, I didn't want to be blind to his just because he looked great in a suit and opened doors for me.

"He's been sending me flowers every day. The first few times, it was amazing. These big, beautiful bouquets kept showing up and it felt like wow, he really wants to make an impression. But it's starting to feel like a little much."

"Every day is a lot."

"And he brought more last night when he picked me up. He said it was to apologize for being short with me on the phone when he had to cancel because of the squirrel problem."

"Was he short with you?"

"A little, but I wasn't worried about it. It almost seemed like an overkill apology."

"What else?"

"I feel like he makes assumptions. We're not in a committed relationship, but he almost acts as if we are."

"How?"

"There was one night when I didn't expect him to be in town, but he came back early. He called from the airport and didn't so much ask me to have dinner with him as tell me when he was picking me up."

"That could be a little bit of a red flag."

"And then it turned out to be a double date with another couple—friends of his. I didn't know until we got to the restaurant and they were there waiting."

"That sounds like something my mom would do. Invite me over and not tell me it's a dinner party with other people."

"So it's not just me? That would have bothered you too?"

"That definitely would have made me uncomfortable."

I pulled the throw blanket higher up my lap and reached over to pet Max between the ears. "The evening got cut short because of Zachary, so I don't know how it would have turned out. Maybe Preston would have realized he'd forgotten to tell me it was a double date. He's very busy, traveling back and forth from here to Seattle all the time."

"But you can't ignore that it happened, either."

"No. Just because I really want to meet the perfect man, and he seems like it on the outside, doesn't mean he is."

"What does he do for a living?"

"He's a lawyer."

"I guess that kind of makes sense. Lawyers can make good money."

"What do you mean?"

She brushed her hair back off her face. "It's just something Annika brought up. We were wondering where his money comes from. You haven't said straight up that he's wealthy, but he sure acts like he's rich. Most people can't afford a private helicopter. And apparently the mansion he's building is no joke."

I'd been trying not to think about Preston's money. I wanted to be infatuated with him, not his wallet. Admittedly, with my present financial circumstances, I'd have been lying if I said a man with money didn't appeal to me. Who wouldn't be at least a little bit drawn to the security of wealth? I wasn't immune to that.

But did his job explain his extravagant lifestyle?

"Maybe he's the type of lawyer who makes mansion and private helicopter money," I said.

"He might be."

"You don't sound very confident."

"Don't get me wrong. I'm not saying I think he's lying. But Annika and I are your friends. We can't help but worry about you."

"I know you do." I leaned back and Max let out a doggie grunt, so I started petting him again. "I think I could figure out how I feel about Preston if Zachary wasn't making things complicated."

"Because you like him."

I opened my mouth to deny it, but stopped. She was right. "I shouldn't like him. Audrey, I'm the stupidest of stupid girls. I've had a crush on him for so long, I don't even know when it started. And he's never, ever been interested in me. Why do I want a guy who's been ignoring me since high school?"

"What is that about, anyway? He told me he did something to hurt you, but he didn't say what."

Closing my eyes, I rubbed my forehead. It was a painful memory, but I had no reason to keep it a secret from Audrey. She'd probably hear the story eventually anyway.

"My senior year, I didn't have a date for prom. I wasn't exactly popular with the boys, but I really wanted to go. And then, out of nowhere, when I was at their house with Annika, Zachary casually asked if I needed a date. I said yes and he said he'd take me. He was older, not even in high school anymore. It was like all my dreams had come true. He was the quintessential best friend's older brother. Confident, good-looking, a little bit dangerous. I don't even blame teenage me for crushing on him like I did."

"What happened?"

"It was a joke. He didn't want to take me to prom. Someone had paid him to do it."

Her mouth dropped open. "Are you serious?"

"Yes. Garrett found out a few days before the dance and told Annika, who told me. I was absolutely crushed."

"Who paid him to take you to prom?"

"I don't know. I figure it was one of his friends or something. From then on, he treated me like I had a communicable disease."

"Maybe he felt like a huge jerk for what he did and avoided you because he didn't know what to do with his guilt."

"Ever since high school?"

She shrugged. "I didn't say it made sense according to logical human behavior. But men don't always make sense."

"That's true."

"I don't know why he would have done that, or why he avoided you the way he did afterwards, but I do think he cares about you now."

"It feels like I'm the butt of another joke."

"I don't think it's a joke to him. I don't know him like you do—I didn't grow up with the family—but I think he really means it when he says he's in love with you. Or he thinks he is, at least. I can't vouch for how real his love is, but I don't think this is the same as your high school prom. No one else is behind this. It's just him."

"But even if it is, what am I supposed to do with that? I start dating someone else and then he decides to change his mind? Why now? It's all so confusing."

"Did you ask him why now?"

"He said when he got shocked in my salon he thought he was going to die, and I was the first person he thought about."

Audrey started to sigh, like that was so romantic. And maybe it was—or should have been—but it was Zachary. He was not a romantic.

"Before you tell me how sweet and romantic that is—"

"It's extremely romantic."

"It would be if it were true."

"You think he made it up?"

"No. I don't think he lied. But I do think he was mistaken. It wasn't some mystical near-death experience that showed him his true feelings. He thought of me because I was the one who was there. I was in the room."

"You're awfully sure about that."

"Because it's Zachary. He's not serious about anything. That's why I can't understand why he affects me the way he does. He's the complete opposite of my type."

"I'm no help there. I didn't think big, surly lumberjack was my type, but apparently I had my type all wrong."

I stared at Audrey for a second. She had her type all wrong. Was I doing that? Had I been dreaming of a Mr. Darcy when he wasn't the right type of man for me at all?

Even if that were true, that wasn't the problem. "Regardless, I don't know if I can take Zachary seriously."

"Maybe it would help to think of Zachary as a secondary problem. Whether or not you keep dating Preston doesn't have to hinge on Zachary. And the way you talk about Preston, it seems like you're unsure."

"That's a very good point."

"Trust your instincts. If your relationship with Preston feels like it's heading in a good direction, that's great. But if not, don't worry about what that means for you and Zachary."

It was good advice. I needed to decide if Preston and I had potential. Was he a man I wanted to keep dating? Did I want to take things to the next level with him?

My heart whispered an answer, but I wasn't quite ready to listen. Because the implications scared me.

CHAPTER 18

Zachary

I TOOK A SLOW DRINK, swallowing the last of my tequila, and set down the glass. Rocco didn't ask before bringing me a second. I'd never been any good at hiding my moods, and tonight was no exception. I felt like dog shit and it probably showed.

I'd been in a bad mood since I'd run into Marigold at the market. I would have told her it was me who'd pranked Preston's job site. Eventually. But it would have been nice if she was a little more into me when I did. Then it would have just been a funny story I could have told her, grudgingly admitting the lengths I'd gone to for her. She would have laughed and said she should have known.

Then I'd have kissed her laughing mouth and made her forget she'd ever gone out with that douchebag.

Instead, I was wallowing in my failure at the Timberbeast.

I'd gone too far. Because of course I had. I always went too far. It didn't matter if I tried to do what was right, or just what I felt like doing in the moment, somehow, it was always wrong.

Josiah and my dad walked in. Great, that was exactly what

I needed. I took a drink of my beer, hoping they wouldn't notice me.

No such luck.

Josiah walked over and nudged me. "Hey. What happened? You look like shit."

"Thanks."

"What's going on?"

"Nothing."

Josiah glanced at Rocco, as if he'd know. He just shrugged. He wasn't the kind of bartender who listened to people's problems. And I wouldn't have told him anyway.

Dad slid onto the barstool next to me. "You sure you're okay? You don't look it."

"I've had a bad few days."

"You didn't get fired, did you?"

"I'm glad that was your first instinct. No, I didn't get fired."

"I was just asking."

"Maybe just leave him alone," Josiah said. "We all have bad days."

Dad nodded and got up from the stool. They moved to a table and sat down together. Work meeting, most likely. They were business partners, buying old houses and remodeling them together. Mom liked to tease them about having work meetings at the bar.

I glanced over my shoulder at them, jealousy eating its way through my gut like termites in old wood. Josiah had always had such an easy relationship with our dad. Was it because Josiah was his biological son, and I wasn't?

That wasn't really fair. Dad had never treated us any different than his other kids. I couldn't blame it on him.

It was me. I was a lot.

Too much. Both for him, and for Marigold.

I wanted to tell myself I was being dramatic. That the fact

that she wasn't happy with me right now didn't mean I'd totally blown it. I'd done worse. I could fix this.

But it wasn't that she was mad about the prank that felt like a knife wound. It was the way she'd looked at me. Like she was seeing me through new eyes, and what she saw was disappointing.

Dad digging into the wound by asking if I'd been fired had not helped my shitty mood.

Thanks for the vote of confidence, Dad.

I motioned for Rocco to settle up and paid my tab. I didn't want to be there anymore.

Outside, the cold air bit through my jacket. The night sky was clear, stars twinkling in the darkness. I headed for my truck, but I didn't want to go home. I'd just wind up sitting around brooding.

On a whim, I headed for the Caboose. Traditionally, the Caboose was the Bailey hangout, while the Timberbeast was ours. Those lines didn't really exist in Tilikum anymore. My brothers and I frequented Rocco's bar out of habit, not feud loyalty. Maybe I just needed a change of scenery—and another drink.

True to its name, the exterior of the Caboose looked like an old railroad car. The inside was decorated with vintage railroad signs and model trains, and a jukebox pumped out music.

Ignoring the pool tables and dart boards, I headed for the bar. A woman with a silver pixie cut caught my eye. What was Sandra doing there?

Sandra O'Neal was probably in her fifties and worked with Audrey at the newspaper. More importantly, she was dating Rocco. Why would she be hanging out at someone else's bar?

I took the stool next to her and nudged her with my elbow. "Hey. What are you doing in here?"

"Pouting. What about you?"

"Same."

"Must be something in the air."

The bartender came over and I ordered a tequila shot and a beer.

"Want another drink?" I asked Sandra.

"Sure, why not? But no tequila for me. I'll take a shot of whiskey instead."

We got our drinks and lifted the shot glasses.

"What should we drink to?" she asked.

"To drowning our sorrows."

We clinked the shot glasses and drank.

A few moments passed in silence before I decided to speak up. "Wanna talk about it?"

"To you?"

"Why not?"

"I just didn't think you'd be interested."

"Try me."

"Rocco and I had our first fight. Turns out, he's a walk away from conflict guy and I'm a stay and fight it out gal. Not the best combination. So now he's at work, probably not thinking about it at all because he's busy, while I'm here, wondering what it all means."

I took a drink of my beer. "That sucks."

"Right? If he wouldn't have walked away, we could have hashed it out. He claims he hates drama, but he sure is causing a lot of it."

"I hate that shit. Why drag something out when you can just talk?"

She looked at me as if she wasn't sure what to think. "Do you mean that or are you just telling me what I want to hear?"

"I mean it. My dad pulls that same crap and it drives me up the wall. He gets mad, walks away, and I'm like, okay Dad, go ahead and hide in your shop. That will make it all better."

"Yeah." She nodded slowly. "So what are you pouting about?"

"It's kind of a long story."

"I've got time." She motioned for the bartender. "Tell you what. I'll buy our next round and you can tell me all about it."

I couldn't argue with that.

The beer kept flowing and the words kept coming. I probably wouldn't have told her the entire story if I hadn't been drinking. But I was, so I did. From my screw-up back in the day, to how I spent the next however many years avoiding Marigold, to the moment when I thought I was going to die in her salon. Then I told her about my attempts to beat out the douchebag she was sort-of-dating so I could win her over and finally be with the woman of my dreams.

She laughed a lot more than I thought was necessary.

"I'm glad my train wreck of a life is amusing," I said.

"I need another shot just to process that story." She waved for the bartender again. "You're a mess."

She wasn't wrong.

We drank more and she laughed at me more. Not that I was insulted. I was probably too drunk for that. Besides, it felt better to laugh about my mishaps than brood about them. Sandra was right, the whole situation—from ignoring Marigold for so long to the squirrel prank—was ridiculous.

Or maybe it was the alcohol. I couldn't tell anymore.

"The question is," Sandra said out of nowhere, "what are we going to do about it?"

"About what?" I asked, my speech only slightly slurred. "Marigold?"

"About our problems." She punched me in the shoulder. "We can't let them get us down. We have to do something."

I held up my beer. "This is what I'm doing 'bout it."

"No, no." She shook her head and slid off her stool, then held the edge of the bar until she was steady on her feet. "I know what I'm going to do."

"What?"

"Something Rocco's gonna hate." She smiled. "Wanna come?"

I hesitated, blinking in confusion. She couldn't mean... My head was fuzzy, but even drunk me wouldn't do that. Not a chance. "Wait, what?"

She laughed so loud the bartender shot her a glare. "Don't worry, kid. I'm mad, and probably drunk, but I'm no cheater. Besides, you're too young for me. I'mma do something I've wanted to do for a long time. Just need a friend along to keep me brave."

Keep her brave? I had no idea what that meant, but the bartender was eying us with a look that said our welcome was wearing thin. Laughing too loud, probably.

"Can we get chips first?" Drunk me always wanted potato chips. Something about alcohol and salt.

"Sure." She patted me on the back. "Let's go."

I followed Sandra out the door and up the sidewalk into town. I wasn't sure what she had in mind, but I had a feeling it was going to make a good story.

CHAPTER 19

Zachary

MY HEAD WAS KILLING ME.

There'd been a time when I could be drunk off my ass, fall into bed for a few hours, and get up like nothing had happened.

Somewhere along the way, I'd gotten too old for that kind of bullshit.

Damn it.

Groaning, I covered my eyes to block out the little bit of daylight filtering through the blinds.

"Stop," I said to absolutely no one, as if the sun would quit shining and let me go back to sleep.

It didn't listen. And I needed to go to work eventually.

With a disgruntled exhale, I rolled over. Searing pain gripped me and I almost yelled out loud. What the hell? Something hurt. A lot.

Shit. Had I tried to ride a bike down the hill downtown again? I'd done that once and wound up in the river. And with a lot of bruises to show for it the next day. But I didn't remember falling into the river. This time of year, there was no way I'd have forgotten. The shock of cold water would have sobered me up quick.

Wincing, I sat up and wiped the crust out of my eyes. Maybe I'd tripped off the sidewalk or something. I pulled the covers back and checked the obvious places—knees, elbows. No injuries. I stretched out my arms and twisted my wrists, then rolled my shoulders. Nothing.

A hazy memory tickled the edge of my mind and I cracked a smile at the absurdity of it. It wasn't a memory, it was a dream. Had to be. There was no way I'd…

Except…

Oh shit.

Sandra's crazy stunt? She'd gotten her nipples pierced. I distinctly remembered turning around so I wouldn't see her with her shirt off, but reaching back to hold her hand while the guy did it.

And then I'd thought it would be a great idea to…

Fuck.

Slowly, I lifted my shirt. Something definitely hurt. No, I couldn't have. I wouldn't have. There was no way.

I had. I'd gotten my left nipple pierced.

With a shriek, I dropped my shirt. Who the fuck would have done that? I'd been drunk off my ass. That was some shady shit, right there.

Then again, I was pretty good at pretending to be sober. Maybe I'd been that convincing.

"Fuck," I muttered. What the hell had I done to myself? I was not a nipple piercing kind of guy. And once I realized what it was, the pain was just plain stupid. The entire left side of my chest throbbed, the ache running deep. It felt like I'd been stabbed.

Of course, I had been.

I was such an idiot. How did I get myself into these situations?

More importantly, how was I going to get rid of it?

There was only one thing to do. Take it out. I'd deal with the pain of it healing, but I was not leaving that thing in.

I took off my shirt, moving it gingerly over my head so it wouldn't brush against the piercing. How had I gotten my shirt back on afterward? Thank goodness I had. I vaguely remembered getting a ride home from one of the few Uber drivers in town. Hopefully he hadn't seen it.

Glancing down, I felt slightly nauseated.

"Come on, Z. You can do this."

I looked again but couldn't seem to make my hands go anywhere near it. I decided I needed to pee first, and I should probably wash my hands before I touched it anyway. I wasn't avoiding the problem. I was just being smart about cleanliness. The last thing I needed was a nipple infection.

Vaguely wondering if Sandra was also in pain, I went to the bathroom. I washed my hands and stood in front of the mirror. My left nipple and the surrounding skin were an angry red. The gold barbell stuck through it looked awful. Other people were into that sort of thing, and that was fine. I wasn't judging. But this was not my jam.

I touched my chest near the piercing, close to the edge of the redness. It hurt, but I didn't flinch. No problem. I could get it out. I poked around the circumference a little more, working my way closer. I had a pretty high pain tolerance. This wouldn't be an issue.

Except every time I tried to unfasten the barbell, I started to get dizzy. Sweat broke out on my forehead and the throbbing pain intensified.

"Fuck," I muttered again. I couldn't do it. I couldn't get the damn thing out.

This was stupid. I'd picked gravel out of my knees a thousand times as a kid. Why couldn't I take out a simple nipple piercing?

I splashed cold water on my face and tried again. No go. I was going to wind up passing out on my bathroom floor if I kept at it. My face was white as a sheet, my lips turning gray.

The only spot of color was my one bright red nipple, the redness looking angrier by the minute.

What the hell was I going to do?

My first thought was Marigold. But I couldn't show her this. It was humiliating. Besides, she was angry at me and I didn't want her to think I'd done this on purpose just to get sympathy or attention.

There was only one real option. Only one person I could trust with a screw-up of this magnitude.

My mom.

———

The nipple pain got worse as I drove out to my parents' place. I'd called my mom to make sure she'd be home, but I hadn't told her what was going on. Just that everything was fine but I needed her help with a problem.

No extra cars were parked outside their house, which was a good sign. Hopefully that meant none of my siblings were there. I had to keep this under wraps. They'd never let me hear the end of it if they found out.

I went inside and found my mom in the living room. Her hair was up and her glasses had slid down her nose as she worked on her latest knitting project.

She looked up and smiled, but I didn't miss the concern that touched her eyes. "Hi. Is everything okay?"

I rested my hands on my hips and took a deep breath. This was fine. I could trust her. "I accidentally got my nipple pierced last night and now I can't get it out."

She didn't laugh at me. Didn't scoff or scold. She just looked at me as if she weren't sure she'd heard me correctly. "You did what?"

"Accidentally got my nipple pierced." I lifted my shirt to show her my shame, then let it drop.

"Okay," she said slowly and set her knitting on the couch next to her. "How was that accidental?"

"There might have been alcohol involved."

Her lips pressed together and I could see her trying to stop herself from smiling. "When you said you needed help with a problem, this wasn't even close to what I was expecting."

"Yeah, well, I didn't expect to wake up with a piece of metal stuck through my nipple this morning, but here we are."

"Why do you need my help?"

"I can't get it out."

"Is it stuck?"

"No," I admitted. "I can't touch it without feeling like I'm going to pass out."

She adjusted her glasses, another amused smile on her lips. "Oh, honey. Okay, let's go take care of it."

Relief poured through me. Yes, I was a grown man, and yes, I'd gone to my mom to get an accidental nipple piercing taken out.

Don't judge. I have sensitive nipples.

I followed her into her bathroom, grateful Dad didn't seem to be around. I took off my shirt and leaned against the counter while she washed her hands.

"Thanks for not lecturing me," I said. "I feel stupid enough as it is."

"That looks like it hurts plenty." She dried her hands. "Natural consequences."

"How do I get myself into these things? I'd blame you and Dad, but you weren't terrible parents."

She laughed. "I guess I'll take that as a compliment. And as for why, you'll have to figure that out for yourself. All I know is you have a strong combination of impulsiveness and stubbornness, and that can be dangerous."

It was dangerous. I did things without thinking them through all the time.

Like pranking the helicopter guy so I could hang out with Marigold and not telling her.

"Hold still," Mom said. "How does this thing work?"

"I think you have to unscrew one of the ends."

I looked up while she unscrewed it, clenching my teeth against the pain and wondering when I'd turned into such a weakling. This wasn't that bad. Why hadn't I been able to do it myself?

"What are you doing?"

Dad's voice.

Great.

I glanced at the doorway. His big frame almost didn't fit and he was watching us with a look bordering on horror.

"I'm taking out Zachary's nipple piercing," Mom said, as if it were the most normal thing in the world.

She finished unscrewing the ball and I tried not to wince.

"I can't look." Dad averted his eyes.

"What do you mean, you can't look?" Mom asked, adjusting her glasses again. "It's just a piercing."

Dad kept his gaze away from my image in the mirror. "Why did you do that to yourself?"

"I was stupid. And maybe a little drunk."

"You'd have to be." He tried to look again but couldn't seem to make himself do it. "I don't know why that thing is making me feel like puking."

"You big baby," Mom said. "You're as bad as Zachary. He couldn't even take it out himself."

"Don't blame him." He shook his head. "That's a hell no."

Despite the way my nipple throbbed from Mom unscrewing the ball on one side, that made me laugh. Paul Haven was a big, tough guy. The fact that he couldn't look either was hilarious.

And a little bit vindicating.

"Hold still," Mom said.

"Sorry, Dad's distracting me. I can't—ow!" The dull throb became a searing streak of fire across the left side of my chest as she slid it out.

"See? Just like taking off a bandage." She held up the piercing.

I hunched over, gingerly cupping a hand over my mutilated nipple. "Ow! That was *not* like taking off a bandage!"

"Best done quick." She screwed the ball back on and held it out to me. "Make sure you keep it clean until it heals."

I took the piercing and stuffed it in my pocket. She patted my cheek while Dad shuddered and walked out.

Blowing out a long breath, I moved my hand and looked. It was still an angry red, but at least now it could just heal closed. I still didn't know what I'd been thinking. Yeah, drunk, and that mostly explained it. But why did I always jump at the first chance to cause trouble, even when it was only trouble for myself?

That wasn't the kind of man Marigold needed.

And the truth of that hurt a hell of a lot more than the piercing.

Last night I hadn't been drinking because Marigold was mad at me. I'd been drinking because I finally understood something. I wasn't good enough for her.

I'd admitted that to myself before, but I'd been thinking about all the time I'd wasted ignoring her. How I'd treated her. That was just external—the dumb decisions I'd made. But I could fix that. I could stop being stupid.

This was different. This was the realization that maybe I wasn't right for her after all.

She deserved better.

Locked?

BRIELLE

THIS WAS FINE. Everything was fine.

Brielle was safe. Her parents weren't there to belittle her and fight with her about every little thing. She wasn't going to walk in on her ex-boyfriend with her ex-best friend.

She had everything she needed. Clothes, food, shelter, entertainment.

She even had a friend. John was so good to her.

But she couldn't stop looking at the front door.

The thing she'd done with John's friend wasn't a big deal. Brielle wasn't a prude. In fact, she'd enjoyed it. He hadn't made her do anything she didn't want to do. Granted, she'd been pretty high at the time and didn't really remember the details, but John certainly hadn't done anything wrong. He'd been right there, ready to protect her the whole time.

And it wasn't like it had happened again. It wasn't a big deal at all.

She was so close to believing that. But not enough that she could ignore the front door.

John had said it tended to stick. She'd taken him at his word. Why would he lie to her? She was his kitten, kept safe in his cabin. His secret. She liked being his secret. His special one.

The front door still beckoned. Was it locked? Was he keeping her there, locked inside? Or did the doorknob simply stick?

She was sober, her mind unsettlingly clear for the first time in a while. She didn't have to stay that way. There was beer in the fridge—plenty of it. He'd left a bottle of whiskey in the cupboard, too. If she wanted to get drunk, it wouldn't take long. She could drown her doubts. Stop worrying. Enjoy her little cabin in the woods. Enjoy being safe.

But was she safe?

And what was going on back home?

She didn't want to care what her parents thought—didn't want to think about whether they were worried. When she'd left, she'd assumed it wouldn't take long for them to give up looking for her. How much did they even love her, anyway? They treated her like garbage. She was an adult. It wasn't like they could control her anymore.

But the more time that went by, the more she thought about them, and her friends back home, wondering if they missed her.

John had told her people were looking for her. Had they stopped? Would she become another Tilikum tall tale? A hundred years from now, would people tell the story of Brielle Thayer and how she went missing, never to be seen or heard from again?

Maybe she should ask John to let her call her parents. Just so they'd know she was somewhere safe.

But what if he said no? What would that mean?

And what if the door really was locked?

There was only one way to find out.

She marched over to the door and grabbed the handle. It wiggled but wouldn't turn. Her heart sank. Had John locked her in? Why would he do that?

But as she kept turning it back and forth, it seemed to give a little. She pulled up and in, trying to loosen the door from the frame.

The knob turned. She had to push hard, but it opened.

Cold air rushed into the toasty cabin, making her shiver and the hairs on her arms and neck stand on end. The forest outside was wet but the sky was clear.

She wasn't locked in. She could leave whenever she wanted. It really had just been a stuck door this whole time.

Leaving the door open, she ran up to the loft, taking the stairs two at once. She grabbed her hoodie and went back down, stepping outside and shutting the door behind her.

The outside world seemed strangely big and ominous. How long had she been inside? She'd lost track of time. She wasn't even sure what day it was.

It didn't matter. The weather was decent—dry at least—and she could simply follow the ruts that served as a road out to the highway. From there…

She didn't know what she'd do from there. She didn't actually know where she was. They'd driven a long time the night John had picked her up. Well over an hour from the bus station in Pinecrest. It wasn't as if she could walk into town, find a phone she could use, and call home to let them know she was okay.

What was she doing out there? She should just go back to the cabin.

But her feet carried her away from her little hideaway in the woods. Her shoes picked up smears of mud as she walked and a lump formed in her throat. She couldn't stop thinking about the pictures. About John's friend Andrew. About why John let her drink and gave her drugs.

Was it because he was a cool guy? Or because he wanted her out of it so she'd do things.

What else was he going to ask her to do?

She kept walking, trying to ignore the cold and the

nagging feeling that she was going to get in trouble for leaving the cabin. Where was she going to go, anyway? If she made it to the highway, what would she do? Hitchhike again? Why? Why leave the warmth and safety of John's cabin? She hadn't even grabbed her backpack.

Still, she didn't stop. She moved faster.

The road was overgrown, hardly a road at all. Was she still following it? The sound of her heartbeat seemed to echo in her ears. What would happen if she kept going? Would anyone find her? Could she ever get back to civilization?

Did she want to?

The trees grew thicker. There wasn't room for a car anymore. She must have veered off the road somewhere. Fear was making her stupid and she didn't even know why she was afraid. John was taking good care of her, she didn't need to leave.

Too late. Panic had taken over. She couldn't think straight, couldn't reason her way through what she was doing. She just kept hurrying through the woods, too overwhelmed to stop.

A voice called out and her panic intensified. They were going to catch her. She'd left the cabin and someone else was going to find her. They'd take her home to her parents and they'd never let her live this down. They'd call her an ungrateful whore. She didn't even know if they'd let her back in the house. She'd be worse off than she was before she'd left. At least out here, she had a place to stay.

She'd made a terrible mistake.

"Brielle!"

Her heart rate skyrocketed. Whoever was out there, he knew. She'd been found and now her safe place was ruined. John would be furious.

"Brielle, wait!"

Her foot caught on something, sending her flying through the air. She hit the ground with a thud. The impact almost knocked the air out of her lungs and she gasped for a breath, her face smashed against the cold, wet pine needles.

She squeezed her eyes shut. No. This couldn't be happening.

Someone crouched next to her and touched her face. "Kitten. What happened?"

Kitten? Opening her eyes, she looked up.

It was John.

His forehead was creased with worry, no anger to be seen. He took her hands and helped her up.

"What are you doing out here?"

"I don't know." She sniffed. Her knees hurt and she wondered if she'd torn her leggings. "I got scared."

John's eyes hardened, the soft brown seeming to darken. "Was someone there?"

"No." She didn't want to admit to the truth, but she knew from experience that lies were best kept vague. "I thought I heard something and went out to look. I'm sorry I didn't go back inside. I got scared and I ran."

"Don't do that again, kitten. It's not safe out here." His dark eyes glinted with a hint of anger. "I told you to stay in the cabin."

"I know. I'm sorry."

He held her in his gaze for a long moment. Panic still gripped her—made her want to run again. But there was something in his eyes that kept her still, almost as if she were being hypnotized.

He moved a step closer and gripped her chin, keeping her face tilted toward his. "I need to know you can be a good girl, kitten. I can't have you running off like this."

She swallowed hard. "I can be good."

"Are you sure?"

She nodded as best she could with her chin still in his grip.

He let go and his expression softened. "That's my girl.

Come on, let's get you back where it's safe."

Safe. Yes, that was what she needed.

John would keep her safe.

CHAPTER 20

Marigold

DISHES CLINKED in the background at the Copper Kettle and the whole place smelled like buttery toast. My parents had invited me to breakfast and my mom sat across from me dreamily gazing at the menu while my dad had his arm around the back of her chair.

"What sounds good, lovebird?" Dad asked.

"I was just thinking about that time we had blueberry pancakes at that place near Yellowstone. Do you remember that?"

"I do. That was a fun trip."

"Was that the time we saw a moose?"

"No, that was different."

She glanced at him. "Where did we see the moose?"

"Banff."

"Oh, right." Mom's eyes got a faraway look. "It was so pretty there. I'd like to paint it."

"That can probably be arranged." Dad's gaze moved to me. "What about you, flower? Blueberry pancakes?"

"No, I was thinking an omelet."

The server came back to our table with a coffee carafe in

hand. She topped off Dad's mug with a smile. "What can I get going for you folks?"

"My wife and I will have blueberry pancakes with a side of bacon," Dad said. "And my lovely daughter would like the cheese omelet."

"Actually," I said, "the pancetta omelet, please."

Dad gestured toward me. "What she said."

"Got it." The server smiled again. "Coming right up."

Mom was still staring off into the distance. Probably remembering the scenery of Banff and imagining how she'd capture it on canvas. I wondered if she really wanted blueberry pancakes. She hadn't protested, but she hadn't been paying attention either.

I tried not to bristle at the fact that Dad had ordered for me, too. He ordered for Mom all the time and she never seemed to mind. But I didn't need him doing the same for me.

"How is everything at the salon?" Dad asked. "Any luck finding another stylist?"

"To be honest, I haven't been looking. But everything is fine."

I could tell by the way his brow furrowed he didn't believe me. "The right person isn't going to just walk in one day. You need to at least advertise."

"I know, Dad. I've just had other things occupying my attention."

He pulled out his phone and started scrolling. "I saw an ad the other day. Let me find it for you."

"An ad for what?"

"A hair stylist. I think the salon was down in Wenatchee, but we could just change the wording a little."

"Dad, it's fine. I can write an ad myself."

"Of course you can," he said, his tone soothing. "I'm just trying to help."

"Thanks, but I'll take care of it."

"Elk!" Mom exclaimed out of nowhere.

Dad glanced at her and raised his eyebrows.

"We saw elk on the trip to Yellowstone. Do you remember that, flower?"

"I don't think so. Maybe I was too young."

"Of course you were. You couldn't have been more than three." She touched Dad's arm. "That's what we should do next summer. A family road trip."

"Love it," Dad said.

I opened my mouth to say I didn't know if I'd be able to take time off for a family road trip—and I was in my thirties, not a ten-year-old—but I closed it again. Mom got ideas like that all the time. She'd probably forget as soon as something else caught her fancy. I didn't need to make waves by saying no to a vacation that probably wouldn't happen.

Her eyes moved to me, coming into focus. "How have you been lately? I sense something is wrong."

"Are you okay?" Dad asked, his voice suddenly laced with concern.

They had no idea.

But I really didn't want to get into any of it with them.

"I'm fine. I've been busy, but I'm all right."

"And what about this man you've been seeing?" Mom asked.

Dad's expression hardened. "What man?"

"I've been sort of seeing someone, but it's very early. Nothing to get excited about."

"Nothing to get excited about? Flower, everyone in town is talking about how you landed the rich out-of-towner. Isn't he the one building the mansion up north?"

"I don't know if it's a mansion."

"I heard it has fifteen bedrooms." She put her hand over mine. "Honey, I would never tell you to go for a man for his money. But if a good man happens to have money? There's nothing wrong with that."

Dad still looked skeptical. Strangely, I was glad for the

concern in his expression. Mom was the furthest thing from a gold-digger, and I knew she meant what she'd said—she'd never encourage me to chase a man for his money—but I didn't like the idea that she already had heart eyes for Preston because he was wealthy.

"I'm honestly not sure where it's going," I said. "If anywhere."

"You've always been so careful with your heart," Mom said. "I admire that."

"Good thing you weren't or I'd have been screwed," Dad said with a chuckle.

She leaned against his arm. "You had my heart from the beginning."

"You two are so cute," I said. "I love it."

Mom smiled. "Just don't be too careful with your heart. You have to be vulnerable enough to give it to someone. Love is a risk."

"But one worth taking," Dad said. "If it's the right person."

That was the question, wasn't it? Who was the right person?

The waitress came with our food and set our plates in front of us. I was glad for the distraction and opportunity to change the topic. Mom seemed happy with her blueberry pancakes and Dad divided up the bacon between them. They started talking about a possible trip to Banff so she could paint, apparently having already forgotten the idea of the family road trip to Yellowstone.

The door opened and three uniformed sheriff's deputies walked in. One of them was Garrett Haven. I'd known Garrett for most of my life, and, like Luke, he felt like a brother to me.

He met my eyes and tipped his chin. Despite his friendliness—he was a great guy—there was always a remoteness in his eyes. He looked tired. I wondered if it was the pressures of his job or being a single dad. When he'd left his wife a few years ago, everyone who knew him had let out a collective sigh of relief. That marriage had been a train wreck.

But somehow, Garrett didn't seem happier. He seemed haunted.

As he went to his table, I wondered why all the Haven brothers seemed so darn brotherly to me—except Zachary. Why did he have to be the one to get under my skin?

I went back to my food while my parents chatted. The waitress came back and asked if we wanted more coffee.

"None for us," Dad said.

I still had my tea, so I shook my head.

"Your boyfriend was in here again the other day," she said, giving me a knowing look. "He's quite the looker."

"Was he?" Mom folded her hands under her chin.

"He's a handsome one," she said.

Hearing Preston being referred to as my boyfriend bothered me. I shifted uncomfortably in my seat. "He's not really my—"

"You're a lucky girl," she said with a smile, not letting me finish, then moved on to her next table.

Mom raised her eyebrows but Dad had concern in his eyes. He opened his mouth as if to say something, but a commotion near the front caught our attention.

A couple stood talking to Rob Landon, the owner, and the woman raised her voice.

"I'm her mother and I say it needs to come down."

Rob glanced around, clearly uncomfortable. "Now, Mrs. Thayer, I don't think there's any harm in leaving it here."

"She's an ungrateful snot, not some tragic missing girl," Mrs. Thayer said.

"Her parents," Mom whispered. "Brielle, the girl who went missing."

"If she wanted attention, she sure got it." Mrs. Thayer's voice rose. Her husband stood next to her with his arms crossed and an angry furrow in his brow. "This town needs to stop playing her game."

The diner had gone silent, all eyes on the Thayers. Garrett stood and walked to the front.

"Oh, look at you, big man in uniform," she said. "Stop wasting your time. She'll show up eventually, but this time I ain't taking her back."

Mr. Thayer ripped the Missing Persons poster off the window. "We're taking them down. We're her parents, we have the right."

"Go solve a crime or something," Mrs. Thayer said, glaring at Garrett.

"Why don't you folks move on." Garrett's voice was controlled. "No need to disturb everyone's breakfast."

"If you're looking for her, it should be to arrest her," Mrs. Thayer said. "Getting a whole town all worked up. Probably ran off with some guy. We all know it."

"All right, Mrs. Thayer," Garrett said, gently ushering them both toward the door.

They left but the incident left an uneasy feeling in my stomach. If Brielle had left her family, it wasn't hard to see why.

"Shameful." Mom shook her head. "She's their daughter."

Dad's face was flushed with anger. "They're taking her posters down? How could they do that?"

Mom put a hand on Dad's arm. "Maybe she left for a good reason."

"Clearly." Dad gestured the way the Thayers had gone. "If she were my daughter, I wouldn't rest until I found her."

"It's so sad," I said. "I wonder where she is."

"Hopefully somewhere safe," Mom said.

Dad twisted in his chair to face the table where Garrett had gone back to his seat. "You'll keep looking, right?"

"The investigation is still open," Garrett said.

"Let me know if there's anything we can do to help. The

SPS have numbers. We can form search parties, whatever you need."

"Appreciate that, Craig," Garrett said. "We'll let you know."

Dad turned around and went back to his food.

Something about Brielle's disappearance was disturbing. Maybe there was an explanation—she'd left with a boyfriend or gone to stay with friends in another town. But why hadn't she told anyone where she was? It was like she'd vanished without a trace.

Her posters were everywhere in Tilikum, but I wondered if her parents were really going to try to take them all down. How could they stop looking? She was their daughter.

I just hoped she was okay, wherever she was.

As we finished our breakfast, the conversation turned to easier topics. Mom couldn't seem to get Banff out of her head and Dad mused about when the first snow would come and whether he needed to re-insulate any of the pipes in the garage before it froze.

They never let me pay for anything when we were out together, and this time I didn't bother arguing. We said our goodbyes and I decided to make a quick trip to the restroom before I left.

I fluffed my hair and applied some lipstick, then headed back into the restaurant. But when I caught sight of the man in the lobby, my breath caught and my heart began to race.

Zachary.

The hostess handed him a bag. He must have come in for a to-go order. Indecision gnawed at me. I could duck into the bathroom and avoid him. He was probably about to turn around and leave anyway. Or I could keep walking and talk to him.

Did I want to talk to him?

The decision was made for me when our eyes met. But instead of puffing out his chest and flashing me his usual cocky grin, his smile looked different. Subdued. He looked almost dejected.

Someone walked past him and he winced, as if in pain. He mouthed *ouch* and gingerly picked at his shirt. Then he met my eyes again and jerked his thumb over his shoulder, indicating he had to go.

He turned around and walked out the door.

I told myself he must have to get to work. He was probably running late. That was why he didn't stay to at least say hello to me.

Then again, the last time I'd seen him, I'd walked away upset. Maybe he just didn't want to deal with me after that.

Whatever his reason, it made me inexplicably sad. I went out to my car, telling myself it was fine. What did I expect, that he'd keep chasing me when I'd told him I was dating someone else and we needed to stay just friends? That was awfully selfish of me, to assume he'd keep trying.

Was that what I was assuming? Was I hoping he'd keep at it until I made up my mind? Keep himself in the running as an option while I hemmed and hawed and complained to my friends about being confused?

I was a horrible person. Absolutely horrible.

And to make things worse, I had a date with Preston tonight.

CHAPTER 21

Zachary

I TOSSED my takeout bag on the passenger seat and started my truck. My chest hurt, but it wasn't from the piercing. Granted, that did hurt, but I wasn't worried about the physical pain. It would go away. This ache was deeper.

My earlier confidence was shot. I'd convinced myself I was the right guy for her, but why? She was smart and beautiful and put together. What the hell did I bring to the table besides impulsiveness and sarcasm?

In the diner, I'd smiled at her so she didn't think I was back to ignoring her, but then I'd left. She was probably still mad at me anyway. I hated to admit it, but the right thing to do was leave her alone.

I'd also decided I was going to quit. I couldn't keep working for the guy Marigold was dating, even if it was indirectly. The job paid well, but it didn't matter. If anything, I needed to keep myself from the temptation of screwing up the job on purpose just to fuck with him.

I ate my breakfast sandwich as I drove up the highway, not really tasting it. When I got to the job site, I parked and went looking for the foreman. I wasn't quite sure what I'd say to him. How did you tell the contractor who'd hired you that you had to quit because you hated the owner with the furious heat of a thousand suns?

Probably better to tell him I had something else come up that interfered. Keep it vague. It wasn't his business anyway.

I walked through the sprawling building toward the far side where I could hear the noise of power tools. Floors were being installed in that part of the house but I didn't see the foreman anywhere. I went up to the second floor but it was deserted. He wasn't in the multi-car garage, either.

Finally, I went out a door that led to the back. The sound of the river was a gentle hum and it pissed me off that Preston owned this land. It was too nice for him, with the beautiful view and the slope leading down to the rocky riverbank. The mountains rising in the background.

Fuck that guy.

But if Marigold stayed with him, wouldn't all this be hers?

Maybe if I were a better person, that would have made me feel better. But it didn't.

I was about to go back inside and just text the foreman since I couldn't find him, when I realized I wasn't alone.

Speak of the devil. Preston Bradford himself was out there, facing the view of the river.

My instinct for trouble went absolutely crazy. Should I confront him and punch him in the face? Rush him and tackle him into the freezing water? I'd get wet too, but it would be worth it. My hands twitched and I clenched my jaw while adrenaline pumped through my veins.

"Preston." The voice of another man stopped me from springing into action. He came through another door, closer to where Preston was standing, and I stepped back into the shadow of the building.

Preston turned toward the other guy. He looked vaguely familiar. About the same age, dressed in slacks and a button down shirt.

"Can I get the keys to the cabin?" he asked.

Preston crossed his arms. "Why?"

"I need to blow off some steam."

"No."

"What the fuck is going on with you?"

"Nothing."

"Then why are you keeping her all to yourself?"

Keeping who to himself? Was he talking about Marigold? I resisted the urge to charge in and punch them both in the face. Barely.

"I have plans for her," Preston said. "But that means I need to be in control of the situation."

"So you're just going to keep her out there?"

"Until this place is done."

"You shouldn't have picked her up, man. You should have stuck to the plan."

"I saw an opportunity and I took it. And it's going to pay off."

"How?"

"She's smart. Not educated, but she isn't stupid like most of them. I can teach her things. Eventually, she'll be doing the recruiting for us."

"Huh." The other guy rubbed his chin. "That's intriguing. But how can you trust her with that?"

"That's why I'm taking my time." Preston shrugged. "It's like the Marines. I'm breaking her down, then I'll build her back up. She's practically a blank slate. I can make her into anything I want."

"How's your girlfriend going to feel about that?" The way he said that implied he already knew the answer; his girlfriend wouldn't know.

But that also meant the other girl they were talking about wasn't Marigold.

Preston just shook his head, as if that question didn't require an answer.

"She's a risk too, you know," the other guy said.

"You don't have to worry about her. She doesn't know anything."

"I know she doesn't. That's obvious. But how long do you think you can keep it from her?"

"Long enough."

"You better be like heroin to her. Get her good and addicted or she's going to bolt on you. She doesn't strike me as the type who'll look away."

"Not like Tess," Preston said.

The other guy laughed. "Tess doesn't want to know. She sees what she wants to see. My gut tells me you won't have that luxury with Marigold."

"Marigold is not your concern."

He held up his hands. "You know I won't get involved there. I'm still skeptical about your little experiment, but I won't get involved there either. Just don't screw it up. If something happens and she turns on you, we'll all be fucked."

"She won't. I already have her eating out of the palm of my hand. Won't be long before she'll do anything I say, whether she's doped up or not."

"Okay. You've been right before. You were certainly right about this place."

"I'm always right. Trust me, I'm going to make you a shit ton of money."

Their voices faded and eventually disappeared as they wandered into the building. I thought about trying to follow—see if I could keep listening. I was many things, but subtle wasn't one of them. I'd probably get caught.

And I had no idea what I was really dealing with.

I slipped back through the job site, careful to avoid the areas where work was being done. What I'd overheard didn't make much sense. I'd hated—fucking hated—hearing them refer to Marigold as Preston's girlfriend. But who was the other girl? Was he cheating on Marigold?

I went out to my truck and called Garrett.

"What's up, Z?" he answered.

"Can you arrest someone for me?"

"No."

"What if there's a good reason?"

He hesitated. "At the risk of hating myself for asking, what's the reason?"

"There's this guy, Preston Bradford. He's building the mansion on the river north of town."

"And?"

"He's up to something shady."

"Z—"

"No, listen. I overheard him talking to his buddy about some girl and molding her to do their recruiting for them. I'm telling you, something was off about it. Can't you make up an excuse to pull him over and search his car?"

"No," he said, his voice sharp with exasperation. "I can't pull him over because you think he's up to something."

"Damn it, Garrett, I know I'm right. Can't you at least look into him? Do some research or whatever?"

"On what grounds?"

"I don't know. There's apparently a girl in a cabin and the other guy wanted to go blow off steam with her and Preston wouldn't let him."

"Nothing you're saying makes sense."

"I know. I don't know what he was talking about either, but my gut tells me there's something going on out here."

"I can't arrest someone on someone else's gut feeling, Z. Especially yours."

I groaned in frustration. "Fine, but when it turns out I'm right, I'm absolutely throwing it in your face."

I ended the call and tossed my phone on the passenger seat.

My phone buzzed with a call. It was the foreman. That was weird. Was he here? Didn't matter, it was good timing. I needed to tell him I was off the job.

"Zachary Haven," I answered.

"You're fired."

Wait, what?

"Excuse me?"

"You heard me. You're fired. Don't come to the job site again or you'll be escorted off. Final check is in the mail."

Before I could ask why, he hung up.

A jolt of anger surged through me. That asshole. He couldn't fire me. What the hell?

The hairs on my arms stood on end. It felt like I was being watched. I lifted my gaze and there he was. Preston Bradford stood not twenty feet away, arms crossed, staring at me. His eyes were narrowed in a hard glare.

It was him. He'd told the foreman to fire me.

But why the fuck did he care about some random electrician working on his stupid mansion?

And then I realized, this was about Marigold. I was the competition and somehow he knew it.

In that moment, something inside me changed. I could have decided to beat this guy because I wanted to win. Because I wanted to show him I was the better man. He could fire me, I didn't give a shit, I was going to get the girl. Marigold was going to be mine.

But that wasn't it.

I was still going to win Marigold. But not for myself. It wasn't about me anymore. In that face, I saw evil. I didn't know how I knew, but I was sure of it. There was a malevolence in his face that went far beyond jealousy over a woman. In that moment, I got a glimpse of the devil.

And I made a choice.

I'd get Marigold away from him. Even if it ruined any

chance I had left of being with her. She might hate me when this was over, but it would be worth it to protect her.

Zachary the troublemaker was back in business. And he was going to be relentless.

CHAPTER 22

Marigold

THE DARKNESS OUTSIDE seemed ominous as Preston and I drove through town. I'd thought about canceling. Give myself time to think things through. But I'd decided to keep our date. Audrey had said to trust my instincts, and she was right. I felt like I needed to see him again to cut through all the mental clutter and confused feelings.

If tonight felt right, I'd know. And if not, I could go from there.

He looked impeccable, as always. Full suit, well groomed. He glanced at me, a subtle smile playing on his lips. There was heat in that look. Desire.

It made my heartbeat quicken. Was that anticipation, or something else?

He'd gotten tickets to a musical adaptation of my favorite book of all time, *Pride and Prejudice.* The helicopter ride and luxurious dinner in Seattle had been extravagant and exciting, but this was close to perfection. He knew I loved to read and how much this story meant to me. I didn't know if this was something he'd enjoy himself, so it showed a willingness to do things I liked. That was certainly a mark in his favor.

I'd been to shows at the theater at Tilikum College before,

usually with Annika and Isabelle. It was charming and inti-mate, with rows of plush seating, a good-sized stage, and not a bad seat in the house. Preston led me in with his hand on the small of my back. Nights were getting chillier, so I'd chosen a sweater dress and tall boots. Clouds blotted out the stars but cheerful lights leading to the front of the building welcomed theatergoers in out of the cold.

The lobby was crowded with people. I waved to Mrs. Leary, who'd been my client since I'd first opened my salon. Mayor Bill was there along with his wife, as were Sheriff Jack Cordero and his wife, Naomi.

Preston slipped his hand around my waist and pulled me closer. His touch almost made me flinch. I glanced at him but he wasn't looking at me. His dispassionate gaze was on the crowd around us, but it was impossible to tell what he was thinking.

The doors to the theater opened and people lined up to take their seats. Preston didn't seem to notice the line. Or maybe he didn't care. He pressed forward, leading me toward the usher taking tickets. No one complained, but I felt my cheeks warm with mild embarrassment. We could have waited an extra minute or two. It wasn't as if we were late.

It was such an odd contrast to his usual manners. But when I thought about it, his gentlemanly gestures were always directed at me, not other people. I'd never seen him be overtly rude, but he didn't go out of his way to be gracious to others either.

Our seats were several rows back from the stage, roughly in the middle. We sat and people began filling in the spaces around us.

Preston took out his phone and his brow furrowed, as if something was bothering him.

"Is everything all right?" I asked.

He nodded. "Just work issues."

I folded my hands in my lap and let my attention wander.

Naturally the stage curtains were closed, but I could see the shadows of the crew's feet as they walked around, prepping things for the opening act. The hum of conversation grew as people took their seats and I wondered if the show was sold out.

I was about to try to make conversation with Preston while we waited for the show to begin, but someone at the entrance to our row caught my eye. I'd only seen him for a second, in my peripheral vision, but it had looked like Zachary.

No, it couldn't have been.

I turned, but all I could see was a couple with their backs to me. They seemed to be talking to someone, but it couldn't have been Zachary. Why would he be at the theater?

The man shook hands with whoever he was talking to, then he and the woman he was with headed toward the exit.

Zachary Haven stood at the entrance to our row, a triumphant smile on his face.

He was here.

My eyes widened as he sauntered toward me. If Preston was polished, Zachary was raw manliness. He'd combed his thick hair so it was off his forehead and the stubble on his square jaw was somehow both neat and rugged.

A few people stood so he could move past them. He smiled and thanked them, then turned his attention back to me. I could have sworn I saw an actual twinkle in his blue eyes.

A thrill ran through me and I had to press my lips together to keep from smiling. My stomach did a belly flop, my cheeks flushed, and my heart raced.

This was terrible. I was on a date with another man. But I couldn't help it.

Zachary Haven had always left me breathless.

"Hi," he said, lowering himself into the seat next to me. "Imagine running into you here."

My eyes widened and I could feel the tension snapping off Preston, the waves of his anger breaking over me.

"What are you doing here?" My voice came out as an embarrassing squeak. Then I noticed what he was wearing. A suit, but there was something sparkly on the lapel, catching the light. "And what are you wearing?"

He glanced down at himself. "A suit?"

"Are those sequins?"

"Oh, yeah." He smoothed down the lapels. "My mom dressed it up for that masquerade we all went to. I guess I haven't worn it since."

"But why are you here?"

His eyes flicked past me, toward Preston. I didn't even have to look to know Preston was seething. "I could make something up about what a funny coincidence it is that my seat is right next to yours, but I won't lie to you. I paid the couple sitting here double their ticket value to give up their seats so I could sit next to you."

I had no idea what to say to that.

"You need to leave," Preston said, his voice low.

"Yeah, I'm not going to do that." Zachary leaned back in his chair with an air of casual confidence. "You're welcome to try to make me, but Sheriff Jack is sitting right over there and somehow I don't think you want to give the local sheriff a reason to notice you."

I let my eyes move to Preston. His features twisted with rage. Something about his expression made my stomach turn. I wouldn't have blamed him for being annoyed with Zachary, but this was something else. The pure hatred in his eyes was disconcerting.

It felt like I was truly seeing him for the first time.

With a dismissive glare, he turned away, as if he'd decided Zachary was beneath his notice.

Zachary just kept grinning.

The overhead lights flashed, letting people know the show

was about to begin. I leaned closer to Zachary and lowered my voice to a whisper. "You shouldn't be here."

"I know. I'm doing it anyway."

"Why?"

"Because I don't trust him. I want to tell you why but I don't have proof. Yet."

"What are you talking about?"

"I'll explain later. The show's about to start."

I let out an exasperated breath. Preston turned toward me, but I kept my eyes forward.

This was so awkward.

And yet, somehow I felt calmer with Zachary sitting next to me. Which made no sense whatsoever. If he hadn't been there, Preston wouldn't have been angry. I wouldn't have had any reason to feel uncomfortable. If anything, this was all Zachary's fault. How could his mere presence make me feel better?

But it did.

The curtain opened and the director came out to introduce the production. Preston put his arm around the back of my chair and kept it there, like he was marking his territory. I couldn't ignore the way I bristled at his nearness. I tucked that away for further reflection and kept watching the show.

The tension heightened during the intermission. Preston stood but made no move to go to the lobby to use the restroom or get us drinks. He crossed his arms, alternating between casting angry glares at Zachary and pretending he didn't exist.

Zachary made small talk with me about the show, commenting on the actors and costumes, and asking me a few questions about the story. He seemed to ignore Preston, but I could tell he was aware of him.

I was just glad neither of them decided to pick a fight.

Yet.

At the flash of lights, people began returning to the theater and Preston took his seat. When he put his arm around my shoulders and drew me closer, I shifted, giving myself a little more space.

The show continued and, despite the absurdity of the situation, I was able to enjoy the production. The musical adaptation was unique and charming and I found myself sighing and swooning in all the right places. The actors were so talented and the man playing Mr. Darcy was perfect.

At the end, the cast came out to a standing ovation. Preston stood and clapped with the rest of the audience, but he looked mildly disinterested. Or maybe he was just distracted. I wondered if he'd spent most of the show seething at Zachary.

Zachary, on the other hand, clapped with enthusiasm and whistled through his fingers.

A sense of dread stole over me as the curtain closed and the lights came on. Somehow I had to navigate my way through the lobby and outside with two men who might very well try to kill each other as soon as they had the chance.

Preston's face was stony and he gripped my elbow as we made our way out of the theater. Zachary walked slightly ahead of us, his posture casual, hands in his pockets, as if he wasn't the least bit concerned about anything.

Typical Zachary Haven.

Once we made it to the parking lot, Zachary stopped and turned to face me. "Mari, can I talk to you for a second?"

Preston's grip tightened painfully around my arm. I snapped my gaze to his, making no attempt to hide the shock filling my expression.

Without a word, he loosened his hold, then turned a glare on Zachary.

I stepped away, the feel of his fingers pressed into my arm still lingering. Zachary moved back and, to my surprise, Preston didn't close the distance as I followed him. I cast a glance over my shoulder and, although he looked like he was ready to explode with rage, he didn't stop me.

"What are you doing?" I whispered. "Other than making my date absolutely furious."

"I'm sorry about that. I really am." He kept his voice low so Preston couldn't hear. "But you need to know he's dangerous."

"Just because you don't like him, that doesn't make him dangerous."

"I overheard some things he said and they weren't good. I can explain more later." His eyes flicked to Preston, then back to me. "This isn't about me, Mari, I swear. This is about you. I haven't given you any reason to trust me, but I know I'm right about this. He's dangerous. Please be careful."

I stared at him for a moment. The sincerity in his voice was disarming, validating something I already felt deep inside.

"Marigold, we need to go," Preston said.

"Be careful," Zachary said again. "And call me if you need anything."

My back and shoulders tensed when I heard Preston's footsteps behind me.

"We're done." He took my elbow in his hand again. "You need to get the fuck away from her."

I braced myself for Zachary to charge in. If this was going to turn into a fight in the parking lot, I needed to get out of the way.

But Zachary didn't lose his temper. No clenched jaw or balled fists. He regarded Preston calmly, no trace of his usual bravado.

"She's smarter than you think," he said. "And she's going to figure you out."

With one last glance at me, he turned and walked away.

Preston took a long breath and his grip on my arm tightened again.

I wrenched it away and swung around to face him. "Don't grab me like that."

For a second, his expression darkened with anger and a hint of fear swirled through me. But just as quickly, his features softened.

"I'm sorry." He gently touched my arm where he'd held it. "I didn't mean to hurt you."

I nodded in acknowledgment of his apology. "I need you to take me home now."

Did I imagine the flash of anger that once again darkened his features? It was gone so fast, I couldn't be sure.

"Of course."

The fear in the pit of my stomach wasn't soothed. If anything, it spread, making me wonder if I should get in the car with him.

I wanted Zachary to take me home.

But if I said as much to Preston, I'd only be fanning the flames. I didn't want to create a confrontation when, miraculously, one hadn't happened.

We walked to Preston's car and he opened the passenger door for me. I got in, swallowing hard. Preston wasn't actually dangerous, was he? He'd never given me a reason to think he might hurt me.

And if Zachary was so convinced he was dangerous, why had he left me alone with him?

He hadn't. He was going to follow me home.

I didn't know how I knew—I couldn't see him or his truck —but I was sure of it. Zachary was going to watch over me until Preston was gone.

Headlights gleamed in the side mirror the entire trip home from the theater, trailing far enough behind us that Preston didn't seem to notice.

I did.

We parked in my driveway and Preston walked me to my

front door. Despite everything, I was strangely calm. He looked me up and down, his eyes calculating. And suddenly it was as if I could see through his sophisticated façade. Could tell what he was really thinking. He was gauging my reaction—my body language, my expression—and deciding how to proceed.

How to get what he wanted.

Like the anger I'd seen in the parking lot at the theater, the look passed quickly. But I couldn't unsee the truth—the cold, hard calculation behind his eyes and in his actions.

He wanted to be in control, but I wasn't going to let him.

"A lot happened tonight," I said, my voice steady, "but I don't want to discuss it right now. I'm going to go inside."

"Marigold." He took my hand gently in his and lifted it to his lips. "I don't want to end the night like this."

I slipped my hand from his grip. "I do. I need you to give me space right now. I'll talk to you tomorrow."

Was he going to back down? I could see the war in his eyes, the desire to overpower me. To manipulate the situation so he could be sure he came out the hero.

I don't know why he chose to step back, but he did. A few weeks earlier, I would have been fooled—characterized this moment as another sign of his gentlemanly nature. But, that wasn't what it was, and I could see it now. It was a strategic retreat, for his benefit, not mine.

This had been our last date, but I decided not to say anything yet. The atmosphere was too charged and that tingle of fear still persisted. I wanted to be in public when I told him. My vague sense that Zachary was out there somewhere wasn't enough. I couldn't risk it.

"Thank you."

He took another step back, probably wondering if I was really going to leave him out there in the cold.

I was. I unlocked my door and went inside.

The click of the deadbolt as I locked it behind me eased a

tiny bit of my fear, as did the sound of his car leaving a few moments later.

He was gone.

I let out a long breath then checked the rest of my windows and doors to make sure they were locked. I didn't really think Preston would break into my house in the middle of the night.

But I wasn't totally convinced he wouldn't.

I'd seen something tonight, something he'd been expertly hiding from me. There was another layer to Preston Bradford, a different man under the smooth charm.

Zachary may very well have been right. Preston was dangerous.

I went to my front window and peeked out. He was indeed gone, and I didn't see another car. No sign of Zachary. Maybe he'd gone home when he saw Preston leave.

Zachary.

I probably should have been angry at him. He'd crashed my date with Preston, trying to sabotage us yet again. What kind of man would do such a thing and think it was okay?

Another realization hit me. It was like stepping out into the light after being in darkness. Everything was illuminated and clear.

Zachary Haven was absolutely ridiculous. And also the man of my dreams.

He was like the most charming, silly, over-the-top book boyfriend in any number of my favorite stories. Cocky, spontaneous, and impulsive. And he'd turned all that chaotic energy on me.

He hadn't been manipulating me. I wasn't the butt of the joke. Zachary Haven probably hadn't been serious about much in his life. Until now.

Until me.

I grabbed my phone from my purse. I didn't want to have this conversation now, either. I wanted to see him in the light of day, face to face. And I really wanted to officially end things with Preston before I saw Zachary. That felt like the right thing to do.

But I didn't want him to go to bed tonight wondering if I was mad.

Me: *He's gone and I'm okay. Thank you for tonight.*

Zachary: *Of course. You sure you're okay?*

Me: *Yes, positive. Can we talk tomorrow?*

Zachary: *Definitely. What time?*

Me: *I have something to take care of first thing, but I'll text you after. Does that work?*

Zachary: *Whatever you need*

Me: *Goodnight, Zachary*

Zachary: *Night, Mari*

I put down my phone and exhaled. I'd see him tomorrow. And I had a feeling everything was about to change.

CHAPTER 23
Marigold

NERVOUSNESS TIGHTENED my stomach as I got ready to leave. I'd asked Preston to meet me for coffee this morning so we could talk, and I would have been lying if I'd said I wasn't dreading it. I needed to end things with him, officially. And as tempting as it was to hide behind a text, I knew that wouldn't be sufficient.

Plus, a guy had broken up with me over text before. I knew it was common in this day and age, but I didn't like it. Whether or not Preston deserved more of my time and attention, I was going to do this the right way.

I also knew there was a possibility he'd choose differently than he had last night—that the malevolence I'd seen behind his eyes would come out. Which was why we were meeting downtown at the Steaming Mug. I wanted witnesses, just in case he decided to cause a scene.

I'd skipped breakfast and only had a few sips of tea, but my nervous tummy didn't seem to want anything. So I grabbed my purse, tucked my phone inside, and set it on the console table while I grabbed my coat from the hook near the door.

I heard a car pull into my driveway and before I could

look out the window to see who it was, someone knocked on my door.

My heart jumped a little as I answered.

Preston stood on my doorstep, his expression hard. There wasn't a trace of warmth in his eyes. Just cold, hard steel.

Involuntarily, I took a step back. "We're supposed to meet at the Steaming Mug."

He came in and shut the door behind him. "I want to talk now."

I took a deep breath. If this was how he wanted it, I'd just get it over with. "Fine. I'm not going to see you anymore."

One corner of his lip twitched in the hint of a smile. "Yes, you are."

"Excuse me? No, I'm not."

He didn't seem angry. The rage I'd seen in his face the night before was nowhere to be seen.

Somehow, this was worse.

He stepped past me and went into the living room, looking around at my things. "This place is nice. Quaint. Kind of like your town."

"I don't think you heard me properly."

"No, I heard you. I just disagree."

"You don't get to disagree with me on this."

He paused and met my eyes. "Of course I do."

"You can't force me to date you."

"No?" He clasped his hands behind his back and kept taking slow steps around the room. "I get what I want, Marigold. Always."

I wasn't sure how to reply to that. This wasn't going the way I'd expected. I'd assumed he'd be angry. Not so utterly dismissive, as if I had no say in the matter.

"I've been very patient with you." He reached up to straighten one of my mom's paintings on the wall. "In fact, you have no idea how patient I can be. And I don't think you appreciate what you're trying to give up."

"There's no point in having this conversation. You're not going to change my mind."

His brow furrowed slightly. "I don't think you understand. This doesn't end until I say it does."

"I don't think *you* understand. It's over. And you need to leave."

He moved closer and I took another step back.

"It doesn't have to be like this, princess. I'm the best thing that's ever happened to you. Do you really think that small-town moron can compete with anything I can give you?"

"I can't be bought."

His lip twitched in a smile again. "Don't be naïve. Everyone has a price. I can make all your problems disappear, like that." He snapped his fingers. "If you want to keep your salon, great. But you'll never have to worry about paying the bills again. And this house? This is nothing. I'll give you extravagance you've never dreamed of. You have no idea who I really am, Marigold. I rub elbows with the elite. I live in luxury you can't imagine. And I want to bring you into that world."

"That's not what I want."

"Of course it is. It's what everyone wants, whether they're brave enough to admit it or not." He stepped closer and brushed my hair back from my face. "I can give you everything you've ever wanted. You'll never have to worry about anything."

I flinched away from his touch. "No."

Anger twisted his features and an edge crept into his voice. "Is this actually about him? You can't seriously be thinking of choosing him over me."

"This doesn't have anything to do with him."

"He's nothing but a worthless, blue-collar nobody. You really want to be stuck in this random corner of nowhere with a guy like him? What kind of life is that? I want to elevate you above all this."

"I don't want you to do anything for me, and this isn't about Zachary."

His jaw hitched. "Don't say that fucker's name in front of me."

"Don't speak to me that way." My spine straightened. I wasn't giving him another inch. "I told you how I feel. I don't want to see you anymore. Now you need to respect my wishes and go."

"You still don't get it." He moved into my space, forcing me to back up. "This doesn't end until I say it does."

"Yes, it does, and if you don't leave now—"

His palm struck my face with a sharp sting. Shock reverberated through me as I clutched my cheek and staggered away.

He hit me. Preston had actually hit me.

I'd never been slapped before, by anyone. I didn't know what to do, how to react. I just stood there in shocked silence, my heart hammering in my chest, one hand covering the side of my face.

"Get out." It was so monotone, it didn't even sound like my voice.

"Marigold, no. I'm so sorry. I overreacted."

"Get. Out."

"You don't understand, I didn't mean to." His voice had lost all its edge. "I would never hurt you. I'm sorry."

I lowered my hand enough to look at him. My cheek blazed with the heat of where he'd struck me and my stomach roiled with nausea. I didn't want to cry in front of him, but tears gathered in my eyes. I couldn't stop them.

"Get out of my house. Now."

He pressed his lips together and, for a second, I thought he was going to keep arguing with me. My phone was in my purse and I'd have to get past him to reach it. Would he let me make a call? Certainly not.

If he didn't leave, I was going to have to run out the back door. I'd go to a neighbor. Call the police.

In the time it took me to formulate my loose plan, he made his choice. His face was strangely pained as he took a few steps backward toward my front door.

"I'm so sorry," he said, his voice soft. "I lost control for a second but it won't happen again. I'll make it up to you."

He had part of that right. It wouldn't happen again. I wouldn't give him the chance, no matter how much of a sweet-talker he tried to be.

So I didn't reply. Just stared at him, still holding my stinging cheek.

With another forlorn look at me, he turned and left, shutting the door behind him.

Tears streamed down my cheeks and my whole body started to shake. I darted to the door and locked it, grabbed my purse, and ran to my bedroom.

Then I did the only thing I could think to do. I called Zachary.

CHAPTER 24

Zachary

I WOKE to a weight on my chest, making it hard to breathe, and a face just inches from mine.

My nephew, Will, leaned harder into my chest, grinning at me.

"Hi kiddo," I said, my voice strained. "I guess it's morning."

Annika and Levi lived around the corner from Marigold, so I'd crashed on their couch for the night, just to be closer to her. I'd stayed in my truck for hours after Preston left, watching over her well into the night before deciding I might as well get some sleep. It didn't seem like he'd come back. And if he did, I wouldn't be far.

Will giggled and dropped his weight on top of me. Thankfully, his foot missed my junk, but only just. And the force on my full bladder was not comfortable.

"Okay, my dude, time to get off Uncle Z." I picked him up and turned him so I could pretend to bench press him a few times. "There we go, time for a morning workout."

He laughed hysterically and his twin sisters came running into the living room.

"Mom said not to wake him up," Emma scolded.

Juliet seemed to take her little brother's side. She jumped up and down with her arms overhead. "He's awake! Now we can play!"

Annika peeked her head through the doorway. "Sorry, Z. I tried to hold them off for as long as I could."

"That's okay. As long as he doesn't jump on my nuts, I'll be fine."

Emma gasped. "Uncle Z, you can't say that."

"Say what? Nuts?"

Juliet clapped a hand over her mouth and giggled.

"Nuts! Nuts! Nuts!" Will yelled. "Uncle Z has nuts!"

Oops.

"Will has nuts!"

He rolled onto the floor then popped to his feet, still chanting about nuts, and ran into the other room.

Annika was definitely going to be pissed at me for that.

Oh well.

I got up and gave each of my nieces a quick kiss on top of their heads, then headed for the bathroom. When I came out, Emma had my phone in her outstretched hand.

"Someone called you," she said.

"Thank you, sweetheart."

"Nuts! Nuts! Nuts!" came Will's voice from the other room. "Will has nuts!"

"Sorry, Annika," I called, then checked my notifications.

I had a missed call from Marigold.

Oh shit.

My chest clenched. Something was wrong.

"Uncle Z has to go." I gave Emma and Juliet another kiss on their heads. "Tell your mom and dad thanks for the couch."

I shoved my feet in my shoes, grabbed my coat, and headed out the door. I was only a minute or two away, but I called her anyway.

"Zachary?" she answered.

She was crying. Damn it, why was she crying?

"I'm on my way. What happened?"

"Just please get here."

A sense of panic rose. What had that asshole done to her? I'd kill him. I'd absolutely fucking kill him.

"I'm turning on your street. Thirty seconds, Mari. I'm almost there."

"Is anyone in the driveway?"

"No, just your car."

"Okay. I'll come to the door."

I scanned the street, up and down, looking for the douchebag's car, but I didn't see any sign of him. Nothing looked out of place. Just a sleepy neighborhood under a cloudy sky, the lawns covered with multicolored leaves and pine needles.

I parked next to her and flew out of my truck. A second later, I was at her front door.

"Marigold?"

She opened the door. One look at her and I knew.

He'd hit her.

Her cheek was bright pink and her eyes brimmed with tears. I slipped inside, shut the door behind me, and wrapped her in my arms.

Anger simmered hot in the background. But she didn't need me mad right now. She needed me to hold her. So that was what I was going to do.

Her body shook as she started to cry. Her head rested against my shoulder and she kept her arms tucked against my chest. I just held her, caressing her back without saying a word. She could tell me the details when she was ready.

And then I'd kill him.

After long moments, she pulled away and wiped beneath her eyes. "Sorry."

"Don't be sorry." I gently touched her chin and moved her face so I could see. "Here?"

"How did you know?"

"Your skin is pink, but mostly a gut feeling. I was afraid of that when I heard your voice on the phone."

She sniffed and gingerly touched her cheek. "He hit me, Zachary. He actually hit me."

Rage warred with compassion. I needed to keep control of my temper for now, but it wasn't easy. "Can you tell me what happened?"

She nodded and we went to the couch to sit down. I wanted to haul her into my lap—keep her as close as I could —but I didn't want to overwhelm her. This wasn't about me.

"I was supposed to meet him for coffee." She dabbed the cuff of her sweater beneath her eyes. "I was going to tell him I don't want to see him anymore and after last night, I felt like I should do it in public."

"That was smart."

"But he came here first. He barged in, so I told him. Obviously he didn't take it well." She pointed to her cheek.

"Did he leave on his own? How'd you get rid of him?"

"He tried to apologize, like it had been an accident or something. I was trying to decide if I needed to run out the back door when he left."

"Oh, Marigold." I nudged her closer and when she nestled against my chest, I put my arms around her again. "I'm so sorry this happened to you."

"I feel so stupid. How could I have dated someone who would do that?"

"You didn't know."

"I should have."

"Should you, though? You weren't seeing him that long and I'm sure he didn't raise a hand to you before."

"No, he didn't."

"This isn't your fault. You hear me? You did nothing to deserve this."

She nodded against my chest.

"What do you want to do? Should I call Garrett?"

"In a minute."

I tightened my arms around her. "Take your time."

Her body relaxed against me and I closed my eyes for a moment, savoring the feel of her. I hated that this had happened, but I was so glad she'd called me. Warmth spread through my chest as I thought about that. When she'd needed someone, she'd called me.

That felt good.

After a while, she shifted and I let go so she could sit up. She dabbed beneath her eyes and her cheek didn't look quite as red.

"I can just call the police," she said. "We don't have to bother Garrett specifically."

"No, I'll call him. He'd want me to." I grabbed my phone and brought up his number. I didn't always get along with my brother, but I trusted him.

"Yeah," he answered.

"Can you come to Marigold's house? She was assaulted this morning."

"Oh, shit," he said. "Does she need medical attention?"

"No, she's okay. She's at home and I'm with her."

"Got it. Stay with her. I'm on my way."

"I'm not going anywhere. See you when you get here."

I ended the call.

She sniffed again. "Thank you."

"Yeah, of course."

I gently drew her close again and let her rest her head on my chest while we waited. Thankfully my ill-fated piercing site was healing well, but I was still glad she was on my right side.

It didn't take long for Garrett to arrive. We saw him pull up in his police cruiser and come to the door. Marigold got up and let him in.

"Hey, Mari," he said. "Z said you're not injured, but can you confirm that?"

"I'm not injured. It was just a slap." She pointed to her cheek.

"I see. Go ahead and walk me through it."

She sat down next to me and I took her hand while she told Garrett the entire story. How she'd decided to end things with Preston and planned to do it in public, but he'd come over unannounced. I clenched my teeth as she described the tone of the conversation, how he'd refused to take no for an answer.

"And then he slapped me," she said.

"What happened after that?" Garrett asked.

"He started apologizing. I told him to get out. I think I had to repeat it two or maybe three times. I don't remember exactly. But he did leave."

"You did the right thing in calling me," he said. "I'm so glad he didn't injure you seriously, but it's still assault."

"What's going to happen now?" she asked.

"Please tell me you're going to arrest that fucker," I said. "Can I come when you do?"

"No," he said, but there was amusement in his voice. Or maybe he just understood. "But yes, I'm going to arrest him. Any idea where he might be?"

Marigold shook her head. "I'm not sure. He's building a house outside of town and he has a room at the Grand Peak."

"Let me come, I'll show you his construction site."

"You working up there?" he asked.

"I was. They fired me."

"Oh, no," Marigold said. "Why?"

"Because of you."

Her eyes widened. "What? No. I'm so sorry."

I grinned. "Don't be. I was going to quit anyway."

"I'm sure I can find it," Garrett said.

He asked Marigold a few more questions about Preston's

car, the helicopter at the airport, and his hotel. Then he made sure he had her number and said he'd be in touch. We both stood and walked him to the door. She thanked him for coming and he gave her a friendly hug before he left.

She shut the door behind him and locked the deadbolt. "This is all so surreal."

"Don't worry. Garrett will take care of it."

She nodded, then met my eyes. "Can I ask you a question?"

"Sure."

"How did you get here so fast?"

"I crashed at Annika and Levi's last night."

"Why?"

I shrugged. "I wanted to be close in case you needed me."

She stared at me for a long moment, and I thought she might cry again. Without another word, she marched over, grabbed me by the back of the neck, and pulled my mouth to hers.

My entire body exploded with sensation. Groaning, I wrapped my arms around her, pulling her tight against me. Her lips were soft but hungry and I parted them with my tongue so I could delve into her mouth.

I had no idea if she'd planned on kissing me like this, but now that we'd started, I couldn't stop.

Her arms wound around my shoulders and her body pressed against me as I took the kiss deeper. I tasted her, savored her. Kissed her for every time I'd wanted to, but couldn't, wishing I could make up for all the years I'd been an idiot and pretended to ignore her.

A part of me wanted to start pulling her clothes off, but I had just enough blood in my brain to know better. I ached for her, but with what she'd been through, now wasn't the time.

And I was just really fucking happy she was kissing me.

This was only the beginning. Now she was mine.

CHAPTER 25
Marigold

I LOST myself in Zachary's kiss.

He'd been the subject of countless daydreams since my teens, but kissing him was better than I could have imagined. I'd thought he hated me, but the truth was, tension had been building between us for years. And in that moment, it exploded.

My body pressed against his while he devoured me. I was helpless. The sting in my cheek was forgotten, eclipsed by Zachary's brain-melting kiss.

Eventually, he pulled back and our lips parted. He held me close, his nose brushing mine.

"I didn't mean to do that," I said, my voice breathy.

"I'm glad you did. Does this mean you aren't mad at me?"

"Why would I be mad at you?"

"For crashing your date. And I don't really want to make a list, but all the other stuff."

I smiled. "I'm not mad at you."

"Good."

"Besides, I'm the one who kept dating that jerk even after you told me how you felt."

"I guess we'll call it even." He grinned and brushed another soft kiss across my lips. "Are you okay?"

"So much better."

"For the record, I really want to burn down that asshole's life. But I'll try to be a responsible adult and let the authorities handle it."

"I'm sure that's for the best. Did you really get fired?"

"Yeah, I think Preston figured out I was a threat. Joke's on him though; I was about to quit."

"Are you going to be okay?"

"I'll be fine. I don't think my new girlfriend expects caviar and diamonds."

I leaned back. "New girlfriend?"

"Too soon?" There was that cocky half-grin of his. "You can call me your boyfriend anytime. I'm not afraid of commitment."

"I don't know what to do with you."

"Just let me kiss you again. I've been wanting to do that for a long time."

With a smile, I tilted my chin up. His lips met mine, soft at first, then demanding. I sank into his kiss, reveling in the strength of his arms around me.

Nothing had ever felt so right.

Eventually, my thoughts drifted back to reality—specifically to the time. My entire morning had slipped away, and I had clients to think about.

"I need to get to work," I said reluctantly.

"Are you sure that's a good idea? You've had one hell of a morning."

"I'd rather not reschedule everyone. Things are tight already and I can't afford to lose clients." I paused, a spark of defiance flaring to life deep inside me. "And you know what? I'm not going to let him hurt me like that. He won't ruin my day."

Zachary smiled, then leaned in to kiss my forehead. "You're amazing."

I gazed at him. He meant that. He was proud of me. And at that moment, it was exactly what I needed to hear.

"I'm coming with you, though," he added.

"To the salon? Why?"

"Until Garrett tells me the douchebag is in custody, I'm not leaving you alone."

"You don't have to do that."

"Of course I do."

He said that with such self-assurance, I decided not to argue. I didn't think Preston would hurt me in public—he was too concerned with his outward appearance and reputation for that. I didn't need Zachary to follow me around like a body-guard, but I also knew him well enough to know he wouldn't last long. He was too restless to hang out at my salon all day.

I texted Stacey to let her know I'd be in soon, then spent a few minutes touching up my makeup. I was relieved to see the redness in my cheek was almost gone. The entire situation felt so surreal. Had it really happened? Had a man actually hit me?

It was a lot to process, but I still wanted to go to work. Like I'd told Zachary, I didn't want Preston to hurt me more than he already had. Going to work—facing the world and my responsibilities—felt like an act of defiance. It felt right.

And it helped to know Zachary would be there, even if he only stayed for a little while.

We left together and drove downtown. Zachary got a text from Garrett that made him scowl. They hadn't located Preston yet. I wondered if he'd gone back to Seattle. Did he assume I'd call the police and leave town as a precaution? It was hard to say.

When we got to my salon, Stacey looked up from the front desk with a smile.

"Hi," she said. "Is everything okay?"

"It's a long story."

Zachary came in behind me and placed his hand on the small of my back. Stacey's eyebrows drew together.

"A really long story." My eyes flicked to my first client of the day, sitting in the waiting area. I didn't want the incident with Preston to become the next topic of the Tilikum gossip line. "I'll fill you in later."

She looked between me and Zachary, clearly noting not only his presence, but his slightly possessive touch.

Girlfriend. He'd called me his new girlfriend.

In the wake of what had happened with Preston, how could I be giddy over something Zachary had said? It seemed absurd. But there I was, hesitating in the lobby of my salon, reeling with the implications of Zachary's words.

You can call me your boyfriend anytime. I'm not afraid of commitment.

Who was this man and what had he done with the carefree Zachary Haven I'd thought I knew?

I took a quick breath to clear my head and greeted my client. "Hi, I'll be right with you."

She glanced up from her magazine. "Take your time. I'm early anyway."

I went to the back office to take off my coat and put my purse on my desk. Zachary stepped in behind me, put his hands on my hips, and kissed my neck.

"Sorry," he murmured low into my ear. "I know you have to work. I just really like kissing you."

I was quickly learning that I liked being kissed by him. I tilted my head and he moved my hair aside so he could pepper my neck with a few more kisses. My body lit up at the heat of his lips on my skin. If he didn't stop soon, I was going to have a very hard time focusing on my client.

After one last kiss, he let go. I turned around and he

grinned at me, like he wouldn't have been happier anywhere else.

"I need to go get started."

"Go do your thing, gorgeous. I won't get in the way."

True to his word, he didn't. And he didn't leave, either. I'd expected him to get bored within the first hour and decide he didn't need to stay all day. He could go do something else and stop by, or even just call, to check on me.

But he didn't go anywhere.

Not only did he stay, he chatted with my clients while they waited. He listened intently while Sarah Jean Simpson told him all about her arthritis, and gushed over photos of Linda Mayfair's grandkids. He discussed the latest in the celebrity gossip magazines and even helped Mildred Winnaker decide on a new hairstyle.

A little after one, Theo popped in with chicken soup and roast turkey sandwiches—my favorite—from the Copper Kettle. Apparently Zachary had ordered lunch and recruited his brother to pick it up. I ate a little between clients, but it wasn't until an hour or so later that I got a long enough break to tell Stacey what had happened with Preston.

She was horrified, of course, but seemed particularly curious about Zachary's presence in the salon.

I glanced at him where he sat, sprawled on a velvet chaise with a magazine.

"He's just worried about me since they haven't found Preston yet."

Her eyebrows lifted. "Just your best friend's brother suddenly developing a chivalric streak?"

"It's possible he also gave me the most brain-melting kiss I've ever experienced."

"I knew it!"

Zachary lowered his magazine for a second, then seemed to decide we were fine and went back to reading.

"I knew it," she said again, this time in a whisper. "I knew there was something going on between the two of you."

"I'm still not entirely sure what's happening."

"What are you worried about? He's obviously crazy about you."

"I just feel like everything has been such a roller coaster lately."

"Isn't that the truth. Speaking of Preston, I need to tell my husband to dump that job. No way is my man working for a guy who'll hit a woman." She took out her phone and started typing with a wicked grin. "I bet a day or two from now, Preston won't be able to find a subcontractor in a fifty-mile radius. Good luck building your mansion, now, asshole."

"Don't feel like he has to quit on my account. I wouldn't want you guys to struggle because of me."

"Not at all. Jason is a smart guy and a good businessman. People like Preston might scoff at guys in the trades, but we do just fine."

A walk-in arrived and I got up to take care of her. Zachary dozed off with his magazine on his chest. It was so endearing, I wanted to dart over there and kiss him all over his face.

I was grateful for the busy day, but by my last client, I felt the weight of not only my full schedule, but my awful morning. It wasn't the typical tired feet at the end of a day feeling. I wanted to collapse into a little ball and possibly cry.

I held myself together while Zachary helped Stacey and I clean up for the day, but I could feel the knot of emotion growing in my chest. By the time we left the salon and got to my house, I thought I might crumble.

Zachary walked me in and I felt a twinge of panic. Despite how I'd felt earlier about him coming to work with me, now I didn't want him to go.

"Are you okay?" he asked, brushing my hair back from my face.

I nodded but tears welled up in my eyes. "It's just been a very long day."

He drew me against him and wrapped his arms around me. Although my emotions still threatened to overwhelm me, his steady presence kept me calm.

I felt safe and secure in a way I'd never experienced before.

"Will you stay?" I whispered.

His arms tightened around me. "I'll only leave if you make me."

My body relaxed and the knot of chaotic feelings eased.

We were both hungry, so we ordered from one of the few places in Tilikum that delivered, Home Slice Pizza. After dinner, we curled up on the couch together. Garrett texted with a final update for the day—Preston was definitely not in town and they hadn't yet located him. But I didn't let it get to me. They'd find him. And in the meantime, Zachary was here and he wasn't going anywhere.

My eyes grew heavy and I found myself almost falling asleep against his chest.

"Do you want to go to bed?" he asked.

"I probably should. I can barely stay awake."

He kissed my head and we got up off the couch. I showed him the extra toiletries I kept in the guest room, in case he wanted to shower or brush his teeth, and went to my bathroom to get ready for bed. When I came out, he was waiting in the doorway to my bedroom, leaning casually against the door frame.

"Do you want me in the guest room, or…"

The way he trailed off made it clear where he wanted to sleep. And who was I kidding? I wanted him close.

"Can you sleep here with me?"

One corner of his mouth turned up in a grin. "Sounds like a dream come true."

That made me laugh. He came in and shut the door, then

stripped down to his boxer briefs. His body was muscular and toned and I let my eyes flick down from the dusting of chest hair to the trail leading below his waistband.

Dream come true indeed.

I took off my robe, revealing my tank top and shorts. I could see the heat in his eyes, but I also knew I was safe with him, no matter what we were wearing.

We got into bed and he pulled me close, my back to his front. The cadence of his deep breathing and his arm draped over my waist felt natural, like we'd been made for this all along.

And as I drifted off to sleep, I wondered if it had all been a crazy dream.

Change of plans

BRIELLE

THE CABIN DOOR OPENED ABRUPTLY, letting in a blast of cold air. Brielle gasped and instinctively pulled the throw blanket up to her chin, as if she could hide beneath it.

But it was only John.

He shut the door and she popped up from the couch. She'd made banana bread for him that morning, hoping he'd come visit her soon enough to try it.

"Go upstairs and pack your things," he said before she even got to the kitchen to unwrap the loaf.

She stared at him for a second, confused. His brow was furrowed, his dark eyes angry.

"Is someone coming?"

"No. There's just been a change of plans."

"Well, if no one's coming here, can you try my banana bread first? I made it for you."

"Just go pack."

"Oh." Her shoulders drooped. "Where are we going?"

"Seattle."

Her eyes lit up. "Really? How long are we staying?"

"I don't know yet."

There was something wrong. She could see it in the set of

his shoulders, the tension in his forehead. She stepped closer. "What's wrong?"

He hesitated, raw anger flashing across his features. "My girlfriend thinks she can break up with me. She's wrong. But I need to get out of town for a little while, so I'm taking you with me."

His words hit her like a slap. Girlfriend? John had a girlfriend? What was he talking about? She staggered backward, her stomach hurting and tears blurring her vision.

"Girlfriend?"

He groaned with frustration. "It's not important, just go upstairs and pack."

"But... I thought... How could you have a girlfriend? I thought you didn't. I thought I was."

He regarded her with a look she knew all too well. Just like the expression her mother used to give her when she'd asked too many questions. Annoyance. Frustration. As if he were thinking, *why do I have to deal with you*?

But he took a deep breath and his face changed. His eyes softened and he unclenched his fists.

"She doesn't have anything to do with you," he said, his voice soft. "You're special, Brielle. You're my kitten."

She sniffed back the tears. "But if she was your girlfriend..."

He stepped closer and brushed her hair back from her face. "She was never my kitten. Never my pet, like you."

Her lower lip quivered. She wanted to believe him. But how could she be his kitten if he had a girlfriend somewhere else?

"I have to go out of town for a while." His voice was quiet and he touched her hair again. "I didn't have to come here first. And I could still go. I could leave you out here, all alone. Is that what you want?"

She shook her head.

"How long before you run out of food, do you think? I bet

a few days, unless you stretch it out. Then you'll have to try to walk. Do you know how far it is to the next town?"

She shook her head again.

"Too far. And it's getting colder by the day. You wouldn't last a night." He gripped her chin so she couldn't look away. "Is that what you want, Brielle? Do you want to die all alone in the cold?"

"No."

"Are you sure?"

"Yes. Please."

"Do you want to stay with me?"

"Yes."

"After everything I've done for you." He tightened his grip on her chin. "I have too much invested in you to leave you here."

"No, don't leave me."

He held her eyes. "That's why I came. You should appreciate that. I didn't have to."

"I do appreciate it. Promise."

"Do you?"

"Yes. Please don't leave me alone."

"Okay. Since you asked nicely. Go pack."

She nodded. He let her go and she hurried up the stairs.

Her backpack was stuffed under the bed. She dug it out and started filling it. She wondered how long they'd be gone and how much stuff she'd need, but she kept her questions to herself. She didn't want John to change his mind and leave her behind.

She didn't want to be left alone.

With her full backpack slung over one shoulder, she went downstairs. John stood near the door. He looked impatient, his eyes darting around, his shoulders tense. She didn't understand what was really going on. Why did they have to leave so suddenly? But she didn't dare ask that question either.

"Let's go," he said.

She followed him outside to a car she didn't recognize. It was black, but different than the one he usually drove. He opened the trunk and put her backpack inside. Then he stepped close and put an arm around her waist, drawing her against him.

What was he doing?

"Hold still," he whispered in her ear.

She felt a prick in the side of her neck and tried to pull away from the sting, but John held her in place.

"What are you doing?"

"Shh," he said. "It's for the best."

Her vision blurred and her head swam. Before she lost consciousness, she had the strangest thought. John had stuck a needle in her and he was putting her in the trunk of his car.

CHAPTER 26

Zachary

WAKING up in bed with Marigold put me in an instant good mood.

She'd rolled away from me in the night, so I moved closer and drew her against me. Her body was warm, her skin soft. And how did this woman smell so good? Closing my eyes, I breathed her in.

I was such a goner.

She made a little noise in her throat as she nestled into me. I groaned as her ass pressed into my groin.

"Morning," I murmured into her ear and kissed her shoulder.

"You really are here. I was afraid I'd dreamed it."

I kissed her shoulder again. "I'm here."

She let out a long exhale. I held her for a while, enjoying the feel of her body molding to mine. I'd wanted this for so long, even before I'd finally admitted it to myself.

I couldn't screw this up.

After a while, we both decided we needed to take care of biological necessities. It was early, so instead of getting up for the day, we crawled back into bed. I hauled her against me, more aggressively this time, and she giggled.

"Why didn't I know you could be so sweet?" she asked.

"I don't know about sweet." I pressed my groin against her. "I'm just trying to feel your ass."

She laughed again. "Maybe you're unintentionally sweet."

"Maybe I just really like you."

"Did all this really start when you got shocked in my salon?"

"No." I kissed her shoulder. "I've had a thing for you for a long time, I just tried to ignore it."

"Why?"

I hesitated. This was tough to admit. "I didn't think I deserved you."

She rolled over so we were facing each other and placed her hand alongside my face. "I'm sorry you felt that way."

"I'm just glad I got my head out of my ass before it was too late. All things considered, I cut this one pretty close."

She smiled. "Can I tell you a secret?"

"Yeah."

"I've had a crush on you since I was a teenager."

I both loved and hated hearing that. I loved it because I wanted her to want me as much as I wanted her. But I hated it because I'd wasted so much time.

The perfect woman had been right in front of me for so long. And I'd been too much of an idiot to do the right thing.

"That kills me. I love it, but the thought that I could have been with you years ago makes me crazy."

"Maybe it wouldn't have worked out, though. Maybe we both needed to be ready."

I rolled her onto her back and leaned over so I could kiss her. "Does this mean I can call you my girlfriend?"

She started to answer, but I covered her mouth with mine. I couldn't get enough.

Finally, I stopped so she could say something.

"If you keep kissing me like that, I'll be anything you want me to be."

"Mine." I growled and kissed her again. "You're mine."

"Yours," she said between kisses, her voice breathy. "Oh my god, Zachary, I can't believe this is happening."

I slid on top of her, nestling between her legs. I could feel her heat, even through our clothes. "Do you want this?"

"Yes."

"Are you sure? I'll wait until you're ready."

She rolled her hips against me. "I'm ready."

I had just enough blood in my brain to be practical. "Do I need protection?"

"I stay on the pill to keep me regular. Are you safe?"

"Oh yeah. I'm safe."

"Me too. We're good then."

I dove for her mouth as I pressed myself against her. Our lips crashed together as we ground into each other, suddenly too obsessed to even get our clothes off. Her body moved with mine as I kissed her deeply. I wanted to take it slow— make this last—but I couldn't get enough.

We disentangled slightly, groping at our clothes, unable to stop our lips and tongues from connecting. It was wet and messy and frantic, a mad rush to undress. To remove the last barriers between us.

She pulled me on top of her and wrapped her legs around me as I sank inside. She nearly undid me right there. I groaned into her mouth, kissing her as we began to move.

We fit together perfectly, as if we'd been made for each other. Despite our frenzied start, we easily found our rhythm, our bodies connecting in the heat of pleasure. She was every- thing. Soft, silky, delicious. I wanted all of her, every last inch.

I wanted her forever.

All the years of tension between us broke wide open. I rolled us over so I could caress her skin, feeling her soft curves beneath my calloused hands. Her eyes drifted closed and her lips parted, her breath coming fast.

She was so fucking beautiful.

The heat and pressure built to a breaking point. I felt her release and couldn't hold back. The surge was overwhelming, the waves of pleasure crashing through me.

She collapsed on top of me. I caressed her back and kissed her neck, drowning in euphoria.

"You feel so good," I murmured in her ear.

"That was amazing."

I grinned. "Yeah it was. Best you've ever had, right? It's okay, you don't have to say it."

"It really was."

"Me too."

She lifted up to look at me, a playful smile on her lips. "Really?"

"Absolutely." I put my hand around the back of her neck and brought her mouth to mine for a kiss. "Marigold, I've never felt this way about anyone. I've never wanted someone like I want you. And I don't mean just your body. I mean all of you."

"I wanted you to want me for so long. I thought I was so stupid for wanting it. But I did. And now that we're... I don't even know what to think."

"Now that we're what?" The corner of my mouth lifted.

"Together?"

"Mm, good girl. I like when you admit you're mine."

"I'm yours, Zachary. I think I always have been."

I brought her in for another kiss then rolled her over so I could kiss her more. I had a lot of lost time to make up for.

She ran her fingers through my hair, kissing me eagerly.

"You better be careful," I said. "Or I'm not going to be able to stop. And you probably have to get to work."

Her lips turned up in a wicked smile. "The salon doesn't open until noon today."

Groaning, I climbed between her legs again. That was exactly what I wanted to hear.

———

Eventually, we peeled ourselves out of bed. Reluctantly. I was sated and mellow, but I could have spent all day just kissing her, feeling her soft skin against mine. Unfortunately, the real world didn't stop moving just because the woman of my dreams was finally mine.

We had a problem to deal with. A big one.

I called Garrett.

"Hey, man," he answered. "Sorry, no news yet."

"What the hell happened? He just skipped town?"

"Apparently. He didn't check out of his hotel and his car is in the lot, but he's not there. No record of him leaving via the airport, and no sign of him at his construction site, either."

"Damn it." I gazed out the front window as a car drove by. "I don't like that he's still out there."

"I don't either. We've alerted the Seattle PD and the state patrol, but I doubt they'll be much help. It's not their fault, they're just maxed out. They have bigger problems than a guy who slapped his girlfriend."

"She's not his girlfriend."

"Fine, a guy who slapped a girl he was dating. Look, don't stress about it. He's building a multi-million-dollar mansion. He's not going to stay away for long. Besides, once his pride stops hurting, he'll probably let it go."

"I don't know about that. It was a heat of the moment thing, I get it. She rejected him and he got pissed. Lost his temper. But I have a bad feeling about that guy. I think he's dangerous."

"Just keep an eye on her when you can."

"She won't be out of my sight until that piece of shit is locked up."

"How does she feel about that?"

I grinned. "I'll make it up to her."

"All right, I gotta go."

"Call me if you find anything."

"I will as long as it doesn't impede the investigation."

I rolled my eyes. There he was, captain rule follower. "Whatever, just find him and deal with him so I don't have to."

"Z, don't do anything stupid."

Marigold came out of her room, wearing just my red flannel over her bra and underwear. No woman in the history of the world had ever looked hotter.

"I won't. For now." I ended the call before he could argue with me, my eyes glued to Marigold. "Look at you. Could you be any more beautiful?"

She smiled. "Stop. I haven't even put makeup on yet."

I stepped in and wrapped my arms around her. "I won't stop, because I'm right. You're stunning."

"Thank you."

I kissed the tip of her nose. "I hate to break the post sex buzz, because I don't know about you, but I feel fantastic."

She giggled a little. "Me too. But what's wrong?"

"No sign of Preston. Do I have to call him by his name? I don't want to give him that kind of respect. How about cockmuppet?"

"What does cockmuppet even mean?"

"I don't know, but it sounds insulting. Anyway, no sign of cockmuppet. Garrett said he hasn't checked out of his hotel and his car is still there, but he's not. No record of him flying out and he's not at the construction site. Did he have another vehicle or anything?"

"Not that I know of, at least not here in Tilikum."

"Don't worry. They'll find him. In the meantime, I won't let him get anywhere near you."

"Is it stupid of me to hope he'll let this go? It's not like we were in a relationship. We'd only been on a handful of dates."

"My gut tells me he won't. I don't know why, he just

seems like the kind of guy who doesn't like it when his toys get taken away."

She glanced away. "You're probably right."

The solution came to me in a flash. It was so simple. "How about I move in?"

"Move in where? Here?"

"Yeah."

"Don't you think that's a little sudden?"

"Well yeah, under normal circumstances. I'm not saying I have to move in permanently." Actually, that was exactly what I was saying, but I didn't want to push her too hard. Not yet, anyway. "Just while cockmuppet is on the loose. That way you'll always have someone here to protect you."

"Zachary, it's not like I need a bodyguard twenty-four-seven."

"You do, actually. And not just any bodyguard. You need me."

She smiled. "You seem very confident of that."

I pulled her in tighter. "You know you want me here. You're just worried things are moving too fast. But they're not. We're not strangers, Marigold. We've both wanted this for a long time. Why hold back now?"

"I'm just nervous."

"About what?"

She slid her hands up my chest and locked them behind my neck. "I don't know how to explain it."

I leaned in and kissed her forehead. "I get it. You don't know if you can trust me. That's okay. I'll prove it to you. Just give me a chance."

"No, it's not that I don't trust you. I do. I'm just afraid this is too good to be true."

"It's not. Marigold, I'm in love with you. You're the oxygen I need to live. I can't get enough of you."

She lifted up on her tiptoes and kissed me. "I'm in love with you too."

It was the best thing I'd ever heard in my life. I cupped her cheeks and kissed her hard. "See? It's all good, gorgeous."

"Does this mean you're coming to work with me again?"

"Obviously."

She laughed. "Okay, then. I guess I should finish getting ready."

I watched her go back to her bedroom. The undercurrent of rage against the cockmuppet was still there, but for the first time in a long time—maybe ever—the biggest thing I felt was simply happy. Marigold was mine. She didn't know it yet, but I was going to marry her. Hopefully sooner rather than later.

I didn't want to waste another minute.

CHAPTER 27

Marigold

THE SCENT of coffee filled the air as the hum of the espresso machine whirred against the backdrop of acoustic guitar music. The Steaming Mug was only about half full, a few people milling around the front counter waiting for their orders and others seated at tables.

I took a sip of my London fog—an Earl Grey tea latte with a hint of vanilla. Audrey was already here, enjoying her coffee while we waited for Annika to join us. I'd recently freshened up Audrey's dark hair with some face-framing layers and she looked fabulous.

We chatted about her wedding, catching up on details and gushing over the bridesmaid dresses as we savored our drinks. I was so honored to join Annika and Audrey's coworker Sandra as one of her bridesmaids. She'd decided on a deep wine color to match her overall color palette.

As we scrolled through dress photos, it occurred to me that for the first time in a very long time, talking about someone else's wedding didn't elicit a little ache of longing in my chest.

Zachary and I certainly weren't engaged, so I didn't quite understand the change. But even after just a few days, there was a sense of stability and permanence to our relationship. Like he'd said, we weren't strangers. We weren't two people navigating the beginnings of a relationship, getting to know each other to see if we might be compatible.

Maybe we really had been meant to be all along.

Annika arrived dressed in a sweater and jeans with her blond hair up in a ponytail. She waved to us and went to the counter to order a drink before coming to our table.

"We need to talk," she said, looking straight at me as she took her seat. "The town is abuzz and I'm freaking out. In a good way."

"I'm so glad you're here." Audrey practically bounced in her seat. "I was trying not to ask her about Zachary until you got here and it's been killing me."

"So?" Annika asked, her eyes widening. "Did you and Zachary actually get together?"

I bit my bottom lip as I smiled. "Yes."

Annika grabbed Audrey's arm and they both squealed. A few people glanced in our direction.

"Sorry." Annika put a hand on her chest. "This is just so amazing. I'm overwhelmed."

"I'm so sorry I didn't tell you immediately," I said. "So much has happened, I wanted to wait until I could talk to you in person."

"That's okay," Annika said. "And leave it to the Tilikum gossip line to make sure no one can keep a secret in this town. So, what happened?"

"First of all, I decided to end things with Preston, and he didn't take it well. In fact," I said, leaning closer and lowering my voice, "he slapped me."

Both Audrey and Annika gasped.

"What?" Audrey asked, her voice filled with shock.

I put a finger to my lips. "Shh. I'd rather have everyone in town talking about me and Zachary, not this. I filed a police report and they were going to arrest him, but he left town. They haven't been able to find him."

"Oh, honey," Annika reached over and clasped my hands in hers, "I'm so sorry that happened to you."

Audrey touched my arm. "Me too. That must have been awful."

"It was scary, but I'm glad it wasn't worse. Even before that happened, I knew Preston had been a mistake. That certainly solidified it."

"That jerk," Audrey said.

"Jerk is too nice for him," Annika said.

"If they still haven't found him, we should alert the Squirrel Protection Squad," Audrey suggested. "I know this isn't squirrel related, but they'd be great at keeping a lookout for him."

"That's a good point," Annika said. "I bet they'd love a new mission."

"It's not a bad idea," I said. "Especially because I've been having a hard time convincing Zachary I can be out of his sight. The only reason he isn't on bodyguard duty right now is that I convinced him I'll be fine with you two, especially in a public place."

"Good, get back to my brother, because I need to know how this happened," Annika said.

I took a deep breath. "After the incident with Preston, I called Zachary. He'd slept on your couch that night to be closer to me because he had a feeling something bad might happen."

"That was why? He didn't tell us what he was doing."

"Oh my gosh, that's so sweet," Audrey said.

"It was so romantic. I was standing there, staring at him, and it hit me. All those times he said he had feelings for me, he was absolutely and completely serious. None of it was a joke to him. It was real. Then I sort of lost my mind for a minute and threw myself at him and kissed him."

"You know, if you'd told me a few months ago you were with Zachary, I would have been worried," Annika said. "I love my brother, but he's always been kind of a mess. But now? This is the best news ever."

"He's definitely crazy about you," Audrey said.

Annika nodded. "For sure."

"I've never really admitted this to you out loud, because it made me feel so foolish, but I've had a crush on him for almost as long as I can remember."

"I wondered if you did." Annika gave me a knowing smile. "I'll never forget, there was this moment at the masquerade ball, the one where Levi and I kissed for the first time. I saw you looking at someone and you had this beautiful, wistful gaze, full of longing. It seemed like you might have been looking at Zachary, and I thought uh-oh."

"I remember that. He looked so mysterious and handsome."

"And now it's finally happening," she said. "I'm so, so happy for you."

"There's a little more." I wrapped my hands around my mug. "He's kind of moving in with me."

"Oh my gosh, wow," Audrey said, her eyes widening.

"It might only be temporary. And it's less about jumping ahead on the relationship timeline and more about the bodyguard thing he's doing. He doesn't want me to be alone in case Preston decides to retaliate or something."

"Good," Annika said. "I'm so glad you won't be alone."

"Absolutely," Audrey said. "We need to keep you safe until they find that jerk."

"I agree. And you guys, I have to be honest, I hope he stays. Is that crazy?"

"Not at all," Annika said. "When you know, you know. Besides, you grew up with him. This is obviously a new dimension to your relationship, but in a way, it's been a long time coming."

"If you're crazy, so am I," Audrey said. "I haven't even known Josiah for half a year and we're already engaged. But there's no doubt in my mind that it's right."

Annika clutched her hands to her chest. "I don't want to get ahead of myself, but we could all be sisters someday."

Audrey pressed her lips together, like she was trying to stop herself from shrieking.

"I know!" Happy tears stung my eyes and I dabbed them away. "I don't want to get ahead of myself, either. I'm just really happy right now."

"Let's just breathe in the moment," Annika said.

We took a deep breath together and the blissful feelings that bubbled up almost made me laugh.

"So what is Zachary doing while you're here?" Annika asked.

"Moving his stuff. He brought over a few things the other day, but he's getting the rest. Or at least the rest of what he's bringing for now."

"So good," Annika said. "I love happy news."

"Thanks," I said. "But enough about me. Audrey and I need to show you these bridesmaid dresses and I want to hear about the kids."

We spent some time chatting about Annika's kids. She always had cute stories to share. Her oldest son, Thomas, had recently been able to go on a ride-along with the fire department and hadn't stopped talking about it since. Her twin daughters were currently obsessed with mermaids, and her youngest, Will, was keeping her on her toes as usual.

Then we looked at the dresses and gushed about how beautiful the wedding was going to be. I could practically feel Audrey's excitement. It made my heart so happy.

Eventually Annika had to get home to her kids. Audrey and I both hugged her goodbye.

"Is Zachary picking you up or did you bring your car?"

Audrey asked. "I feel like I shouldn't leave until someone else is here to watch over you."

"I appreciate it, but I'll be fine." My phone buzzed with a call, so I gestured for Audrey to give me a second while I checked to see who it was. "I should take this. It's my mom."

"No problem."

"Hi, Mom. What's up?"

"Hi, flower. Do you have time to stop by?"

"Actually, yes. I'm just saying goodbye to Audrey, so I can swing by on my way home."

"Perfect. See you then."

I ended the call. "I guess I'm stopping by my parents' place."

"Have fun," Audrey said. "It was good to hang out and I'm so thrilled for you."

"Thank you."

We hugged goodbye and I went to my car. I didn't think I needed to worry about Preston—the cops were looking for him and they'd take him in as soon as he showed up in town—but I still glanced around, wary of my surroundings, just in case.

I got in the car and called Zachary to let him know where I was going.

"Hi, gorgeous," he answered. "How was your girl time?"

"It was wonderful. I love them so much. I'm just calling to let you know I'm stopping by my parents' house."

"Sure, yeah. Are you coming home after that?"

"I was planning on it, yes."

"Good. I miss you. I can't wait to kiss you all over."

That sent a rush of tingles down my spine. "I can't wait either. How is everything going?"

"Not bad. Luke was around, so he's been helping. We're just bringing over the stuff I need, so it's not much."

"Sounds good. I don't think I'll be there too long, so I'll see you in a little bit."

"Okay, baby. Love you."

Oh how I loved hearing him say that. "I love you too."

I ended the call and drove over to my parents' house. As usual, it looked cozy from the outside and I found myself smiling and humming softly as I parked and went in.

"Mom? Dad?" I called.

"We're in the kitchen, flower," Mom said.

Dad was dressed in a faded flannel and jeans with a battered baseball cap on his head. The flecks of sawdust on his shirt made me wonder what he was building. Mom's shirt had a yellow paint splatter on the front and her hair was up.

"Hi." I gave them each a hug then took a seat at the table with them. "You two look like you've been busy. What are you up to?"

"Just chopping wood," Dad said. "Had to take down a tree in the back, but it'll make great firewood."

I reached over and brushed his shoulder. "That explains the sawdust."

"Thanks," he said. "Honey, we need to talk to you about something."

His tone made me nervous. He sounded so serious. "Is everything all right?"

"We're fine. But your mom and I are concerned about you."

I wondered what they'd heard. Generally, my parents were more insulated from town gossip than most people. Dad didn't bother listening and Mom tended to be in her own world too much to get caught up in other people's business. But had they heard about me and Zachary? I wasn't sure why that would make them concerned. It must have had to do with Preston.

I'd been hoping to avoid telling them the whole story. I knew Dad would overreact. But it was probably best to fill them in.

"There have been some things going on, and I haven't had

a chance to share everything yet."

"All right then, go ahead," Dad said.

"You know I started seeing a man named Preston Bradford. That's over. He wasn't right for me. But he got angry when I told him, and there was… an altercation."

Dad's eyes widened and he almost got up from the table.

I put up my hands. "It's okay. I'm fine. And I told the police. They're handling it now."

His nostrils flared and Mom put a consoling arm around him.

"I promise I'm okay. I'm not minimizing what he did, but he didn't injure me and it's all over now."

"When did this happen?" Mom asked.

"A few days ago."

"You should have called me," Dad said.

I didn't blame my dad for being upset at hearing someone had hurt his daughter. Of course he would be. But I didn't know how to tell him I hadn't called him first because having him rampage around town wouldn't have done anything to actually help me. It would have made the whole situation worse.

"I'm sorry, I felt it was better to call the police. And I wasn't alone. I called Zachary Haven as soon as it happened and he came over."

My parents didn't seem to react to that, which was odd. They just watched me, as if waiting for me to continue.

"Which leads me to a little bit of news. Zachary and I are together. As a couple. That might seem like it's coming out of nowhere, but we've had feelings for each other for a long time. And I know it will make you feel better to hear he's moving in for a while so I won't be alone. At least until we know what's going to happen with Preston."

"How is that supposed to make me feel better?" Dad asked.

"I thought you wouldn't want me to be alone."

"Is this Preston guy dangerous?"

"I honestly don't know. The police were going to arrest him but he seems to have left town."

He stood up, his expression stony. "Zachary Haven is not taking responsibility for my daughter."

"What?"

"If you're in danger, you need to come home."

"No, Dad, that's not necessary."

"There are a few things in your room, but I'll clear them out." He walked off, as if my reply didn't matter.

I looked at my mom. "Is he serious?"

"You're his baby. Can you blame him?"

"Of course he's upset. But that doesn't mean I need to move home."

"What would it hurt? At least he could be sure you're safe."

"I'll be safe at my house."

She reached over and clasped my hands. "It'll be fine, flower. We love having you here."

I squeezed her hands, but didn't reply. There wasn't any point in arguing with her, so I got up. "I should get going."

"Just pack a few things for now. Your dad can take care of the rest later."

The rest? What did she think I was going to do, sell my house and move in with them? "I love you and I appreciate that you want to help, but like I said, this isn't necessary. Can you please talk some sense into Dad?"

She laughed. "Oh, honey."

I knew this conversation wasn't over, but I decided to go. My dad couldn't make me move out of my own house. Hopefully I'd be able to help him see reason once he'd calmed down. I said goodbye to my mom and told her I'd call soon.

When I got back in my car, the weight of my parents' overprotectiveness lifted. I was going home to Zachary, and nothing was better than that.

CHAPTER 28
Marigold

AT HOME, I found Zachary on the couch and a pile of garbage bags near the door.

"What's all this?" I asked.

"Clothes and stuff."

I laughed. "You packed your things in garbage bags?"

"Yeah." He furrowed his brow as if that were an odd question. "But you're going to have to tell me where to unpack because you're already hogging every closet in this house."

"No I'm not."

He gave me a crooked smile. "Baby, I looked everywhere. There's no room for me."

That couldn't be right. I admit, I had a lot of clothes, but this was a three-bedroom house. There had to be empty closet space somewhere.

I set down my things and took off my coat, then headed for the guest room. "Did you check in here? We can move some of my stuff from the master bedroom into this closet for now. I'm sure there's room."

"Yeah, I looked."

The guest room had a queen bed with a lavender duvet and one of my mom's paintings of a meadow filled with wildflowers on the wall. I went to the closet, expecting it to have a few things that were spread out, making it look fuller than it was.

I was wrong.

Oops.

I remembered storing my bridesmaid dresses from Isabelle and Annika's weddings there. And it wouldn't have surprised me to find a few coats. I kind of had a thing for coats. But I didn't expect to find it stuffed full of clothes.

The third bedroom was my little library, with bookshelves and a big, comfy chair. Surely that closet was almost empty.

Nope. Full.

I went out to the living room feeling a bit sheepish. Zachary just grinned at me from his spot on the couch.

"You were right," I said. "I have way too much stuff."

"I didn't say you had too much stuff. Just that your closets are full."

I laughed. "Thank you for not judging, but I do have too much stuff. I should go through it all and donate what I don't need. I guess I've lived alone for so long, I didn't even think about it."

He stood and walked over to me, then brushed my hair back from my face.

I loved it when he did that.

"I can just live out of bags for a while. Wouldn't be the first time."

"No, I don't want you to leave your stuff in garbage bags. I can make room. It's just going to take a little more work than I thought."

"Need help?"

"Please."

He leaned in and kissed my forehead.

I loved it when he did that, too.

Since the guest room wasn't being used, I decided the

easiest thing would be to empty out that closet as best as I could. Then we could move some of my things from the master bedroom into that closet to make room for Zachary's stuff. We'd pile the excess on the guest bed and I could go through it later.

Or maybe just take it all to be donated so I didn't over-think it.

"How was coffee with my sister and soon-to-be-sister?" Zachary asked as we got started emptying the guest closet.

"It was lovely. There's been so much going on, it was great to catch up. They were excited to hear that things between us have, well, changed."

He grinned. "Of course they were."

I almost blurted out that we'd squealed over the possi-bility of being sisters someday. Thankfully, I stopped myself. The last thing I needed was to freak Zachary out by implying we might get married.

It was too soon to even think about that. Wasn't it?

I filled him in on some of the details of Audrey and Josi-ah's wedding. I didn't know how interesting that was to a guy, but he didn't seem to mind.

"And you stopped by your parents' place?" he asked.

"I did." I let out a long sigh.

"Uh-oh. Your voice did that thing you do when you're sad."

I set an armful of coats on the guest bed. "I hadn't told them about the assault yet. Of course they were upset and worried when they heard. I expected that. What I didn't expect was my dad deciding I should move home."

He snort-laughed, then paused for a second. "Wait, you're serious?"

"Yes. He immediately started clearing out my old room. I told them we're together now and they didn't seem all that surprised. I figured when I told them you were moving in so I wouldn't be alone, that would be the end of it. But Dad said you weren't going to be responsible for protecting his daughter."

Zachary's body stiffened and I could see the tension in his clenched jaw. "What did you tell him?"

"He got up and left the room and I didn't want to argue. I told my mom to talk some sense into him."

"Is this going to be a problem?"

"I'm a grown woman. He can't make me move home."

"No, but he could try."

"I don't think it's going to come to that. Someone hurt his daughter, of course he's going to be angry. And it's possible my parents are a little bit overprotective."

"A little?"

"Okay, a lot."

"I don't want to make trouble for you and your family. But I need you to know, I'm going to stand my ground. He's not going to push me out of your life."

"He wouldn't do that."

Zachary raised his eyebrows.

"I won't let him do that," I said, my voice resolute.

"You're hot when you're being defiant." He grinned and pulled me close. "I like it."

His mouth dipped to mine and, for a moment, I forgot what we were doing. I wound my arms around his neck, losing myself in his intoxicating kiss.

Until someone pounded on the front door.

I gasped, my heart jumping. What if it was Preston?

Zachary clearly had the same thought. His expression was hard, intense. "Wait here."

I peeked out into the hallway while he went to the front door. I couldn't see him from where I was standing, so I strained to hear what was going on.

The front door opened, then closed a moment later. That had to mean it wasn't Preston. There was no way Zachary would let him in.

Then I heard a voice. Familiar and male.

Dad.

Oh no.

I went out to the front room, half expecting to see a moving truck through the window. Fortunately, it was just his car in the driveway. But the tension in the room was so thick, it stopped me in my tracks.

My dad stood in front of the door, back stick-straight, arms crossed. He didn't so much as glance in my direction, just leveled Zachary with a hard stare.

I recognized the upward twitch in Zachary's lip. I'd seen it before, usually right before he got himself into some kind of trouble.

"Dad," I said, hoping to head this off before it turned into something unpleasant. "What are you doing here?"

He didn't take his eyes off Zachary. "I came to help you move your stuff."

"I told you that's not necessary."

Dad didn't answer. Zachary just watched him.

I marched over and moved in between them. "I know you're concerned, but I'm not going to let that man drive me out of my own house."

Something about that finally tore Dad's attention from Zachary. "Flower, I can't leave you here in danger."

"I'm not in danger."

"You could be and that's enough. Just come home until this blows over."

Zachary touched the small of my back, silently lending his support. It was such a small gesture, but it filled me with warmth and gratitude. He didn't take over. He didn't step in front of me and start a fight with my dad.

But he was there, on my side.

I looked my dad in the eyes and for once in my life, I stood my ground. "Dad, I really appreciate the offer. I understand that you're worried, but this is my home. And I'm not leaving."

His brow furrowed and his eyes flicked to Zachary again. "If anything happens to her."

"It won't," Zachary said.

Dad hesitated for a long moment, as if deciding what to do. "All right. But if anything changes, you're coming home."

I sighed. My dad wasn't one to let things go, but he was going to have to concede eventually. I stepped in and hugged him.

"Love you, Dad."

He hugged me back. "Love you too, flower."

With a hard glare at Zachary, he turned and left.

"He really doesn't like me," Zachary said.

"It's not about you. He doesn't like Preston. And he doesn't like having to let go of his daughter."

"I still don't think he likes me. But that's okay, I'll win him over eventually."

He gathered me into his arms and I rested my head against his chest. I was ready for everything to calm down.

I didn't know why, but I had the strangest feeling things were going to get worse before they could get better.

Where am I?

BRIELLE

IT TOOK a while for the drowsiness to lift enough that Brielle could comfortably open her eyes. She didn't know where she was or exactly how long she'd been there. It was hard to remember.

He'd drugged her. Put her in the trunk.

She didn't remember much after that. When she'd come to, she was in a room, lying in bed. John had come and told her she'd done a good job. He was so proud of her. He'd done it to keep her safe and he wasn't going to let anyone take her away from him.

Since then, he'd kept her high.

He said the pills were just to help her sleep and keep her from feeling scared. He wouldn't want his kitten to be afraid while he was gone.

She sat up and rubbed her eyes. At first, she'd believed him. Someone must have figured out where she was and they were coming for her. John was just protecting her. She was his pet.

But even her drug-addled mind couldn't ignore the fact that he'd put her in a trunk. If they'd been questioned, she would have lied. She wasn't going to tell anyone who she really was.

She got up to use the bathroom. Wherever she was, it was clean but sparse. The room had a wood floor, an old bed, and a dresser with drawers that stuck. The window was painted shut and all she could see was the side of another building. The adjoining bathroom was tiny, with a pedestal sink and a small shower. Her backpack had been brought in for her, but she was going to run out of clean clothes soon. She'd have to remember to tell John when he came again.

Her grogginess lingered, but for the first time since she'd been brought there, her head was beginning to clear. A craving in the back of her mind made her wonder if she was getting addicted to whatever John had been giving her. She glanced around the bathroom, wondering if he'd left her more pills. Should she search for some, or would that confirm she was hooked? Could she hold out until he came back?

She decided to wait. She'd always liked partying—it was one of the things she'd fought about with her parents. But she didn't want to turn into a drug addict.

Instead, she took a shower, hoping it would help her clear her head. Part of her wanted to sink back into hazy oblivion so she didn't have to think too deeply about her situation. Yet her old self was in there somewhere, telling her things weren't right.

Her old self? When had she started thinking of herself that way? When had she become different?

It was all so confusing.

After finishing her shower, she put on her last clean outfit —a gray sweatshirt and jeans. It was raining outside, and the room was a little chilly.

She wished she knew what time it was. And where she was. And when John was coming back. Her stomach rumbled and she wondered how long it had been since he'd brought her something to eat.

Which made her think about the other thing she couldn't keep ignoring. The door was locked.

She was being held there.

John had said it was for her safety. But why? Couldn't she at least have access to the rest of the apartment? She was capable, she could get her own meals. And eventually she'd need to do some laundry.

That made her wonder, was the door still locked? Maybe this was like the cabin. She'd thought he was locking her in, but when she'd finally decided to try the door, she'd found it was just stuck.

She was almost afraid to try.

But her mind kept clearing, things coming into sharper focus. She needed to know.

Her heart beat hard and her body trembled as she walked to the door and put her hand on the doorknob. She twisted.

Locked.

She tried again, twisting it the other direction. It didn't move.

Panic rose like a lump in her throat and tears stung her eyes. She pounded on the door a few times. "Hello? Is anyone out there?"

Nothing. No sound.

Had he abandoned her?

She knocked louder, using the side of her fist. "Hello? Please, is anyone there?"

Footsteps came from outside the door. She stepped back, her heart racing.

The doorknob turned and she braced herself to see John. He'd be calm and soothing and tell her everything was all right.

But it wasn't John.

A young woman she didn't know came in, smiling warmly. She was dressed in a tight-fitting blouse and high waisted black pants with tall stilettos, and her dark hair was curled in a vintage pinup style.

"Hey," she said, her voice friendly. "Sorry, I didn't know you were awake."

"Who are you?"

"I'm Desi."

"Where am I?"

"Don't worry." She walked over to the bed and sat. "You're safe here."

"But where is here?"

"We're in Seattle."

Brielle glanced at the rain streaming down the window. Seattle. Why had he brought her to the city?

"Where's John?"

"He had to work or whatever. He told me to take care of you when you woke up."

"How do you know him? Are you his sister? I thought she ran away."

Did John even have a sister? She was starting to doubt it.

Desi smiled again. She didn't look much older than Brielle —maybe mid-twenties—but her eyes seemed older somehow. She patted the bed next to her. "Come here, sweetie."

Brielle wasn't sure she wanted to sit, but Desi patted the bed again, so she took a seat next to her.

"You are so pretty," Desi said, her eyes flicking up and down. "I can see why he likes you so much."

That didn't make Brielle feel better. "I don't understand what's going on. Who are you really?"

"I'm one of his girls."

"What does that mean? One of whose girls?"

"John's. I've been with him since I was eighteen."

"With him?"

"Not like that. John doesn't, um, partake. At least not that I've seen. It seems weird to me. He could have any one of us whenever he wanted. I know I'd be more than willing. But to each his own, I guess." She reached over and moved a lock of Brielle's hair. "Maybe you'll be the exception. He might be keeping you for himself. I don't know, he didn't really tell me anything. How did you meet him?"

Trying to process what Desi was saying, she answered almost robotically. "He gave me a ride."

"Hitchhiking?"

She nodded.

"Okay, things are making more sense."

This wasn't making any sense to Brielle. "How?"

"I overheard him arguing with someone on the phone. He said something about not knowing the town would turn out to be such a pain in the ass and he didn't expect anyone to still be looking for you. And then he said something about unexpected legal problems but he was handling it."

"Is that why he brought me here?"

Desi shrugged. "Seems like it."

"He said he was going to keep me safe." She didn't know why she said that. It was getting harder to believe.

"Of course." Desi rubbed her arm. "I've probably said too much. I thought you knew more about our setup, but maybe he hasn't brought you in on it yet. And that's totally okay. It took a while for me to understand it too."

"What setup?"

"The thing is, it's going to be so amazing once the lodge is done. He's going to bring us all there and we'll get to live in luxury. I can't wait."

"What lodge? Who gets to live there? And why did you say you're one of John's girls?"

"John is a very powerful man with a lot of important connections. He knows some of the richest men in the country. We're talking actual billionaires."

Brielle had no idea what to say to that, so she kept listening.

"He provides companionship to his friends and colleagues. That's where his girls come in."

"Companionship?"

"Trust me, it's a great gig. When I first left home, I tried turning tricks on my own and it was a total nightmare. The guys were so gross. Our clients are rich, so it's a totally different world."

The truth of what Desi was saying hit Brielle like a slap to the face. "You're prostitutes."

"No, no, no." She wagged her finger. "We don't use that word. We're not whores, hookers, prostitutes, or escorts. We're luxury companions."

"So you don't sleep with them?"

"Oh no, we do."

"Then how is that not prostitution?"

"It's a subtle distinction. Don't worry, sweetie, John will explain everything. Although I kind of wonder if you're going to be able to live in the lodge with us. I think it's near where you're from, and if you're still considered a missing person, that might be a problem."

"What's the lodge?"

"Oh my god, it's going to be the best. John is building a huge lodge in the mountains. Right now, most of us live in a couple of apartments, but we're right on top of each other. There's no space. And we mostly spend time with clients in hotel rooms. The lodge is going to change everything. John's going to have us live there and he'll bring clients to us. We get to attend parties and service our clients right there." She let out a wistful sigh. "It's going to be the best."

Brielle felt oddly numb. She sat there, gaping at her.

"That was why he picked me up that night," Brielle said, her voice sounding far away. "To make me one of his girls."

Desi rubbed her arm again. "Sweetie, it's okay. He'll take good care of you. He takes good care of all of us. Trust me, I've seen what it's like out there for a girl on her own. You don't want that. Besides, we get to keep any gifts our clients give us. I'll probably be able to retire on the jewelry alone."

"I wasn't going to be on the street. I was going to Vegas to get a job. A real job."

She scoffed. "Oh honey, he did you such a big favor. You don't know how lucky you are. You just have to do what you're told and he won't send you away."

"Send me away where?"

A flash of fear crossed her face. "No one really knows. Girls who get sent away don't come back. They get sold. I figure they end up in Mexico or South America or something."

"Sold?"

"Don't worry about it. He obviously really likes you. I'm sure you'll be fine."

"He put me in the trunk," she said weakly.

"Sounds like he had to make a quick getaway. Sometimes things get a little crazy in our line of work. It's not a big deal." She patted Brielle's leg. "Are you hungry? You probably haven't eaten in a while."

She nodded.

Desi glanced around. "I'm not supposed to do this, but why don't you come out there with me? Do you cook?"

She nodded again.

Desi smiled. "Fabulous. I'll let you out and we can have some dinner. Just don't tell, okay? A little secret between friends?"

A secret? It seemed like there were more secrets than Brielle had realized. What was one more?

She felt so stupid. She'd thought she was special. His kitten.

Turned out, he had an entire litter of them.

But she didn't know what to do. She was in a city she didn't know with no money, no phone. If she left, where would she go? What would she do?

For a second, as she followed Desi out to the kitchen, she thought about making a run for it. If she could get outside, she could find a way to alert the police. She could yell for help. Someone would probably call the cops just because of the disturbance.

But then what? Where would she go? She didn't have anywhere to live. And her parents would never forgive her for this. Never forgive her for being so stupid and naïve.

They'd never take her back, even if she'd wanted them to.

Her stomach rumbled again, feeling raw and empty. It was almost as if someone else took over her body. She went through the motions, getting things out of cupboards to cook dinner.

It was the new Brielle. The one who believed John. Who just wanted another pill so she could go numb—feel good and stop worrying about all these big things she couldn't control.

She let that Brielle take the lead.

But her old self was still in there, shouting at her in the darkness, begging to be let out.

CHAPTER 29

Zachary

CHECKING my surroundings had already become second nature. As I drove Marigold to the salon, I didn't notice anything suspicious. Wet leaves covered the ground. A storm had blown through the night before, stripping the trees bare and leaving the mountains suspended between late fall and the onset of winter.

Marigold huddled in her wool coat and clasped her hands together. I reached forward and turned up the heat so she wouldn't be cold. Her smile warmed me from the inside.

I freaking loved her so much.

We pulled up to the salon and although there was no sign of the cockmuppet, I did notice someone waiting in the parking lot for her.

Her dad.

He stood next to his car, leaning against the driver's side door, arms crossed. I hoped he wasn't there to try to convince Marigold to move home again. I really didn't want to get into it with her dad, but if he kept pushing, I was going to have to say something.

I'd never been a guy to shy away from confrontation—I was usually the one starting shit—but this was different. I had to tread carefully where my girl's parents were concerned. Not so much for my sake as for Marigold's. It wasn't so much that I didn't care what they thought of me—after all, I was planning on marrying their daughter—it was more that I didn't want to make things worse for Mari.

But damn, the urge to tell Craig he needed to back off and let me handle this was hard to resist.

"Oh, Dad." Marigold sighed. "I really hope he hasn't decided he needs to stand guard out here all day."

"That's my job."

She glanced at me. "You don't need to stand guard all day, either."

No one had seen Preston. Chances were, he'd lay low for a while. And when he did reappear, it would probably be to get his construction project moving again, not to harass Marigold. Rumor had it, his project had ground to a halt. Word had gotten around about what he'd done to Mari and all the local subcontractors had quit.

Still, I didn't trust him. And I couldn't shake the feeling he could show up and cause trouble.

But I also had my own job to do. I couldn't afford to put off work forever and I was supposed to swing by Tilikum Hardware to give the owner a quote for a rewiring project.

Maybe it wasn't so bad Craig was here.

I tucked her hair behind her ear. "I actually can't stay. Work stuff. I know your dad is driving you crazy, but it'll make me feel better to know he's looking out for you."

"I wish he'd just stop by a couple of times instead of standing out there. It's going to start getting weird for my clients. And the rumors in this town are going from silly to absolutely ridiculous. Someone came in yesterday and asked if I was involved with the mafia."

"So you're saying I should call off the private security detail who look like the Secret Service."

She laughed. "Yes."

"I don't know what to tell you about your dad. Do you want me to talk to him?" I braced myself, kind of hoping she'd say no. I wasn't sure I trusted myself to have that conversation with Craig.

"No," she said, and I breathed out a sigh of relief. "If he tries to stay, I'll talk to him."

"Okay." I leaned in and pressed my lips to hers. "Have a good day, gorgeous."

"You too."

"I'll swing by when I'm done. Maybe we can get lunch if you have time for a break."

"I'd love that."

"I love you." I kissed her again.

She smiled against my mouth. "I love you too."

I was never going to get tired of hearing her say that.

The heat of Craig's glare beat at me through the wind-shield. My gaze flicked to him, then back to Marigold. He didn't like me kissing his daughter?

Too bad.

For Marigold's sake, I wouldn't confront him. But I could only contain my troublemaker tendencies to a point. I slid my fingers into her hair and brought her mouth to mine, kissing her deeply. She didn't hesitate or hold back, opening for me, her tongue sliding against mine.

Was it juvenile to kiss her like that just to provoke Craig? Probably. But no one had ever accused me of maturity.

She pulled away and laughed softly. "I think my dad is watching."

"He is."

"Serves him right. I'm not a kid anymore."

"No, baby, you are not." I licked the taste of her off my lips. "You're all woman."

"I really have to go. I have a client first thing." She gathered up her purse. "I'll see you later."

"Bye, baby. Love you."

"Love you too."

She got out of my truck and I waited until she got inside the salon. Craig didn't follow her in and I wondered how long he was going to hang around. Truthfully, I kind of hoped he wouldn't leave; at least not for a while. Whether either of us liked it or not, we were in this together.

Reluctantly, I left and headed to Tilikum Hardware. The wiring issue was bigger than I'd expected. His building needed a lot of work, which was good for me. As much as I would have rather spent every waking moment with Marigold, life didn't actually work that way.

I went to my truck and got out my laptop so I could put together a quote. I ran the numbers then sent it to him, letting him know my schedule was pretty open for now. I could get started as soon as he was ready.

A few seconds after I hit send, my phone rang. It was my dad.

"Hey, Dad."

"Do you have some time today? We closed on that house on Maple Street. The wiring is a mess. I'm hoping you can take a look."

"Yeah, sure." It was too early for lunch anyway. "Are you there now? I can swing by."

"I'm heading over. I'll meet you there."

"Sounds good."

I ended the call and headed over to their latest acquisition.

Josiah and my dad were turning into small-town real estate moguls. They owned several rentals already, and typically as soon as they finished one remodel, they were on to the next. Their newest house wasn't far from Marigold's, on a quiet street lined with trees. From the outside, it didn't look too bad, but they always bought houses that needed a lot of work. Sweat equity was a big part of their business model.

Dad's truck was already outside. I parked next to him and went in.

As expected, the interior was a mess. Old, stained carpet, holes in the walls. Everything was drab and dated, but a few months from now, the place would look like new.

"Hey, Dad?"

He came around the corner from the kitchen, dressed in his usual flannel, jeans, and work boots. "The wiring is a mess. We knew that going in, but I have a feeling it's worse than we thought."

"Luckily you have me." I grinned at him but he just glowered at me like he wasn't amused.

Typical.

And that wasn't just me being cocky. I was good at my job. I'd always been fascinated with electricity, from the time I was a kid. And owning my own business meant I didn't have to take orders very often. That was probably why I'd never asked to partner with Dad and Josiah—just worked with them as a contractor. It was better for everyone that way.

I showed myself around, flipping switches and testing outlets. Some of them were getting juice, some weren't. One of the upstairs bathrooms was completely dead. That wasn't a great sign, but I could fix it. I went down to the garage and checked the panel. Whoever had lived there before had clearly been a DIYer. It was a mess.

"How bad is it?" Dad asked.

I shrugged. "Not great, but I've seen worse."

He grunted.

"I might be doing some work over at Tilikum Hardware next week, but I can get started after that."

"Sure. And check with Josiah about the fixtures. We need to replace them all, but I don't know if he wants to add anything. Especially in the kitchen."

"Will do."

"How's Marigold?" he asked.

His question was out of the blue, but that was my dad for you. Abrupt. "She's fine."

"You sure?"

"Yeah, why? What did you hear?"

He scowled. "Probably nothing that's true. I doubt she won the lottery and now she has long lost family members trying to blackmail her for her money."

"Uh, no."

"That arrogant son of a bitch show his face again yet?"

"Not yet. How'd you hear about him?"

"Annika."

Made sense. I kept thinking of Marigold as mine, but she'd been friends with my sister for most of our lives. My parents knew her as well as anyone.

"How much did she tell you?"

Dad's voice was hard. "Enough to know he laid a hand on her."

I nodded, anger simmering beneath the surface.

"Just make sure you stay out of it," he said. "Let the authorities do their job."

"What do you think I've been doing? The first thing I did was call Garrett."

He narrowed his eyes, skepticism written all over his expression. "Still."

"Still, what? What do you think I'm going to do? Go all vigilante?"

His eyebrows lifted.

"Thanks, Dad."

"We all want to rearrange the guy's face. I just don't want you getting in the way. Let Garrett handle this."

I knew what my dad meant, and he wasn't wrong. As satisfying as it would be to beat the shit out of the cockmuppet, that wouldn't help Marigold. And she was my main concern.

But it still irked me that my dad assumed I was going to cause problems.

"I get it," I said. "Sit down, shut up, and let Garrett the wonder boy save the day."

"It's his job."

"I know it's his job. Not that he's getting anywhere. Preston skips town and I don't know what the fuck Garrett and his buddies are doing, other than playing grab ass down at the station. Certainly not arresting the guy who assaulted my girl."

"That's not your brother's fault."

"Yeah, well, it sucks that Marigold still has to worry about that piece of shit."

"That's why I'm glad she's with you."

I stared at my dad, stunned. Had he meant that? He usually assumed the worst when it came to me.

He cleared his throat. "She's like one of ours. You know that. I'm glad she has you, especially now." He glared at me again. "Just don't screw it up."

A grin stole over my face and I patted his shoulder. "Don't worry, Dad. Now that I've got her, there's no way I'm messing this up."

He grunted. I wasn't sure if that meant he believed me or not.

Didn't matter. Marigold was mine and I wasn't ever letting her go.

CHAPTER 30
Marigold

IT WOULD HAVE BEEN easy to forget I'd ever met Preston, except for the fact that my dad and Zachary were maintaining bodyguard duty. As far as I knew, they weren't coordinating with each other. But they were clearly going out of their way to check on me regularly while I was at work.

Maybe it wasn't fair to my dad, but his vigilance was wearing on me, while Zachary's wasn't. Zachary could have spent all day hanging around the salon and it wouldn't have bothered me. It helped that when he was there, he was unobtrusive and spent most of his time charming my clients. Dad looked more like a bouncer at a club.

At least he seemed to have let go of the notion I was going to move back to their house. That was something.

Aside from that, I worried less and less about Preston as the days went by. Our brief relationship, such as it was, faded from my mind. I didn't regret it, necessarily. I certainly wouldn't have wanted to go through it again, but it had been a learning experience. A reminder to trust my instincts when something felt wrong.

And when it came to Zachary Haven, everything felt right.

I'd loved him in secret for so long. And now that I could finally set my feelings free, they'd burst to life like wildflowers in spring. I marveled at how easily our lives fit together, how our hearts seemed to click in place like pieces of a puzzle.

He was everything I'd ever wished for and so much more.

The bell on the door of the salon tinkled as I was tidying up to go home. I glanced up and the sight of Zachary warmed me from the inside. The corners of his mouth turned up and the heat in his gaze sent a pleasant tingle down my spine.

"Hi, gorgeous." He came close, slipped a hand around my waist, and brought me in for a kiss. "How was your day?"

I leaned into his neck and inhaled. He smelled so good—woodsy and clean and manly. It was soothing and arousing all at once.

"So busy. There's been a sudden influx of men wanting haircuts, and half of them hardly need one."

"Weird."

"Do you know something about that?"

He shrugged. "Maybe."

I playfully pushed against his chest. "What did you do?"

"Maybe I happened to mention to Rob Landon that the cockmuppet was still a problem. And maybe he's the current captain of the Squirrel Protection Squad."

"The SPS has a captain now?"

"Yeah, they're surprisingly organized."

"They do realize there aren't any squirrels involved, right?"

"What does that have to do with it?"

I laughed. That was true. Only in Tilikum.

"I know this is last minute, but I talked to my mom a little bit ago and she invited us to come over for dinner tonight. Are you up for it?"

"I'd love to."

"You're sure? I can reschedule if you're tired."

"I'm sure." I glanced down at my feet. "Although I'd like to change my shoes. Do we have time to run home?"

"Yeah. You can change into pajamas and slippers if you want. It's just my parents."

That made me smile. I'd been in pajamas and slippers at the Havens' house hundreds of times growing up.

I finished cleaning up and we left. On the way home, I asked about Zachary's day. He'd stopped by the salon to have lunch with me, but spent the rest of his day working on a rewiring project for the hardware store. So far it was going well and he assured me that after the incident at my salon, he was careful to triple check everything before he got to work.

At home, I took a few minutes to change into a sweater, jeans, and comfortable shoes. Not quite pajamas and slippers, but comfortable enough for a casual dinner with my boyfriend's family. I touched up my makeup, grabbed a bottle of wine from the kitchen to give to Marlene, and we headed out again.

Anticipation, and maybe even nervousness, swirled in my stomach as we drove to Zachary's parents' house. Growing up with Annika, I'd been there more times than I could count. But this was different. It was the first time I'd be walking in the door at Zachary's side—as his girlfriend.

It was my teenage fantasy come true. Only better.

The log home the Havens had grown up in was rustic and cozy. I loved it there. Family photos adorned the walls and mantle, the furniture was comfortable, and Marlene's hand-made throw blankets were everywhere. We walked in and the scent of beef stew and fresh baked bread filled the air.

I'd never lived there, but somehow it still smelled like home.

Zachary shut the door behind us, then took my hand and led me inside. Paul and Marlene were both in the kitchen prepping dinner, Marlene dressed in a sweater with her hair up and Paul in his usual flannel.

The flannels were such a Haven thing. Even Zachary was wearing one.

"About time," Paul grumbled as he looked up from slicing bread. "I've been smelling this all day."

Marlene rolled her eyes and nudged him with her elbow. "Stop. You're fine."

"Not my fault you know how to drive a man crazy," he said with a slight smile.

My parents were adorable, but Paul and Marlene were the epitome of couple goals. They hadn't sailed into marriage after a lifetime of friendship. They'd both been hurt and managed to pick up the broken pieces of their lives and put them back together in a new family. That had to have come with challenges, but they'd fought for it. I'd always admired them, even when I'd been too young to understand why.

"Dad, don't be gross," Zachary said.

"I'm so glad you were able to make it," Marlene said, ignoring her son. "I can't seem to figure out how to cook stew for just two people."

"It smells great, Mom."

I lifted the bottle of wine. "I brought this. We can open it now or you can keep it for later."

"Thank you." She came around the counter and pulled me in for a warm hug before taking the bottle. "Would you like a glass?"

"Yes, please."

"Honey, would you mind opening this for me? Zachary, do you want some?"

"Sure," he said.

While Paul busied himself with the wine, I took off my coat and set down my things so I could help get dinner on the table. I got the bowls and plates out of the cupboard and

Zachary set out silverware. Then I poured us all ice waters to have alongside our wine.

All things I'd done before. And yet, this time it was different.

The Havens had always made me feel like part of the family. It was one of their gifts. And I realized as I sat down to dinner with them that this was a little piece of what my heart had longed for. Maybe this was a part of why I hadn't been able to give up my crush on Zachary, even when it had felt like folly. I loved his family too.

Zachary set his hand on my thigh underneath the table while we ate. It felt the tiniest bit naughty.

I loved it.

"Did they ever find that missing girl?" Marlene asked. "It seems like no one's talking about it anymore."

"Don't think so," Paul said.

"So sad," Marlene said.

My heart hurt for the poor girl. "I hope she's somewhere safe."

"I do too," she said. "I can't imagine not knowing what happened to my child."

Zachary paused with his fork halfway to his mouth. "I hate to bring up a sore subject, but don't you know exactly what that's like?"

Paul's expression hardened and he kept his eyes on his plate.

Marlene's gaze darted to her husband. "I've heard from him."

Zachary's fork clattered to the table. "You've heard from Reese? When?"

"He's called a few times over the years. Not often, and he never tells me anything. Just enough that I know he's alive and well."

"Did you know about this?" Zachary asked his dad.

Paul just grunted.

Zachary started to speak but I recognized I could read this situation better than he could. The subject of Reese Haven was a painful one for both Paul and Marlene, and it was clear to me they'd each handled the reality of their wayward son in their own way. This was not something Paul wanted to talk about.

I put a hand on Zachary's arm. "I'm glad you've heard from him, at least to know he's okay."

"I'm sorry, Zachary. I thought I'd mentioned it," she said.

"No, it's okay, Mom."

"I hope the missing girl reaches out to her family," I said. "Or to someone, if her family isn't safe."

"I don't know her parents well, but it sounds like it wasn't a good situation," Marlene said.

"Don't think it was," Paul said. "Poor kid."

"So, Zachary." Marlene's tone said we were changing the subject. "Are you all settled at Marigold's?"

He put his arm around the back of my chair. "Yeah. She managed to clear out some space for me."

I laughed softly. "I had no idea I had so much stuff. Especially coats. It's kind of embarrassing."

"If you still have things that need a home, Stitch and Sip is hosting a clothing drive," Marlene said.

Stitch and Sip, Tilikum's knitting group, was the ideal solution to my clothing overindulgence. "I do, that's perfect. Where can I bring them?"

"The Knotty Knitter. We have a collection table set up in the front of the store."

"The salon doesn't open until noon tomorrow, so I'll take care of it in the morning." I turned to Zachary. "Can you help before you go to work?"

"Of course." He smiled, and for a second, I got lost in his blue eyes.

My cheeks flushed but Marlene just smiled at me.

After dinner, I finished my last swallow of wine, then helped clear the table. Paul shooed me out of the kitchen, saying he'd handle the dishes. Zachary and I chatted with his mom for a few more minutes, then decided it was time to go.

I was filled with warm fuzzies as we drove home. There was something so special about sharing dinner with Zachary and his parents. The combination of the familiarity of their home and the thrill of Zachary's touch was intoxicating.

Zachary seemed to feel it too. I could see it in his eyes, feel it in the way he laid his hand on my thigh on the way home.

When we got to my house—which I was already starting to think of as our house—he went around and opened the door for me, then offered his hand to help me out of his truck.

"What a gentleman you are."

"I have my moments." He grinned as he led me to the front door. "Or maybe I'm just trying to get in your pants."

I tilted my face up to his. "You don't have to try."

His lips met mine, his tongue brushing against them. A knot of sensation burst between my legs and I was suddenly very, very glad we were no longer at his parents' house.

As he opened the door, he hooked an arm around my waist and hauled me inside. Coats fell to the floor and he kicked off his shoes. Sliding his hands through my hair, he kissed me deeply. I loved the feel of his mouth tangled with mine, the way he devoured me.

He picked me up and pressed me against the wall. I wrapped my legs around his waist and moaned into his mouth.

"I wanted to do this to you so many times," he said, his voice deep, and pressed himself against me.

"I wanted you to do this to me."

"It's probably good that I didn't." He brushed his nose against mine. "I wanted you so bad but I would have screwed it up."

"Maybe."

"I won't this time, Marigold. You make me want to be the kind of man who deserves you."

I smiled, both giddy and on fire for him. "I love you so much."

"I love you too." He kissed me, his lips hungry for more. "I know you love a gentleman, but how about I fuck you like a rogue?"

My voice was breathy, almost desperate. "Oh, yes."

I held on while he carried me to the bedroom. He laid me on the bed, then took his time, kissing my skin while he undressed me. His fingers moved between my legs, driving me into a frenzy. By the time he'd finished taking his clothes off and climbed on top of me, I was ready to burst.

He took me hard while I clutched the sheets, reveling in every movement. He was rough but tender, demanding but sweet. Teeth nipped and hands caressed. I gasped and moaned, the waves of pleasure washing over me with every thrust. The heat of his body and the feel of him inside me overwhelmed my senses.

Manhandling me, he turned me over. I felt uninhibited, watching over my shoulder as he took me from behind. Our gazes met and the raw intensity in his eyes almost undid me. I'd never felt so wanted, so desired. So loved.

With his hands gripping my hips and his body moving with mine, my climax overtook me. I spiraled in ecstasy, crying out as he found his release.

We collapsed to catch our breath, laying tangled together for a few moments before I went to the bathroom to clean up. He drew me back in bed with him, holding me close, his arms tight around me.

"I love that you're mine," he murmured.

"Me too."

"I'm going to marry you, Marigold Martin." He kissed my head.

I leaned back a little. "Are you trying to propose?"

"No." He grinned. "Not yet. But I will. Just so you know."

I smiled. "Thanks for the heads up."

He kissed my forehead, then down my cheek. "Anytime."

I nestled in his arms, happier than I'd ever been. Because Zachary Haven really was going to marry me.

Can't Do It

Brielle

BRIELLE RELAXED, sinking into the couch cushions, enjoying her buzz. Desi lounged on the armchair, her legs stretched out, eyes half-closed and glassy. Whatever she'd given her, Brielle liked it. It made the voice in the back of her head—the one that was afraid—go quiet.

Despite Brielle's promise to stay in the apartment, Desi still locked Brielle in the bedroom any time she had to leave. Brielle told herself she didn't mind and the last thing she wanted to do was get her in trouble. Desi assured her that, eventually, she'd have all the freedom she needed. This was all for her own good; to keep her safe.

When Brielle was high, it was easy to believe that. Easy to push away the thoughts that made her scared.

Like being one of John's girls.

She still couldn't remember how long it had been since she'd seen John. A few days? A week? Desi seemed concerned that he hadn't been back. She said something must have happened—something business related.

Brielle tried not to think about it too much. She tried not to think at all.

The sound of a key in the door made Brielle jump. Desi sat up, her eyes wide.

"Get in the bedroom," she whispered.

She jumped up but couldn't seem to move fast enough. The door opened and John walked in.

Anger clouded his usually handsome features. It was the same look he'd had the day he'd taken her from the cabin.

When he'd put her in the trunk.

Brielle froze like a terrified rabbit, her heart pounding in her chest. John's angry glare moved from her to Desi.

"What is she doing out here?" he snapped.

"You left us here for days." Desi got to her feet, and although she squared her shoulders, her eyes seemed uncertain. "What was I supposed to do? Leave her in there?"

He took slow steps until he was standing in front of Desi. "You're supposed to do what you're told."

"She was scared. You didn't even tell her anything."

"What did you say to her?"

"Nothing."

He moved a fraction of an inch closer and raised his eyebrows. Somehow that was more terrifying than if he'd yelled at her.

She crossed her arms. "I had to say something. We couldn't just sit here in silence all the time. I told her about the lodge and how great it's going to be."

Without warning, John's hand flew, cracking across Desi's face. She spun with the impact and clutched her cheek.

Brielle gasped and jumped back. She thought she might be sick.

"You're supposed to do what you're told," he said through clenched teeth.

Desi straightened, still holding a hand to her face. She didn't reply.

He moved her hand and stroked his finger down the side of her face where he'd slapped her. "I thought I could trust you to be a good girl, Desi."

"You can," she said, her voice weak.

"Then why did you disobey me?"

"I was just trying to help."

He stroked her face again. "After everything I've done for you, this is how you repay me? Do you want me to send you away, Desi?"

"No. No, please." Her voice held an edge of panic. "Don't send me away."

"I can, you know. You won't have it nearly as good as you do with me."

"I know. Look, she's fine. I took care of her."

His eyes flicked to Brielle, then back to Desi. "Did you let anyone else in?"

"No." She shook her head vehemently. "No one. I swear."

"Did you leave with her?"

"No."

He looked at Brielle again. "Is she lying?"

"No," Brielle said, her voice trembling. "She was just being nice to me. I haven't gone anywhere, I promise."

His expression softened as he moved around Desi to approach Brielle. "Look at you. Such a good girl. You've been through so much, kitten."

She swallowed hard, her stomach knotting with fear and indecision. She wanted to trust him.

The old Brielle called to her from deep inside. *It's all a lie.*

He gently touched her face, tipping her chin so she had to look up at him. "It's time to go."

"Where?"

"Home."

"What home? The cabin again?"

"Of course, kitten."

He stroked her cheek, just like he'd stroked Desi's. "You're a risk, there's no doubt about that. But I have a plan. We're going to make sure they stop looking for you. Then you'll be mine forever."

"How?"

"Don't worry about it right now. First, we need to get you out of here."

Brielle stepped back. She had to know. "Are you going to make me one of your girls? Is that why you picked me up?"

A flash of anger crossed his features. "We were going to talk about that later. Desi wasn't supposed to scare you like that."

"I'm not scared, I just want to know. Are you building a lodge to have parties and invite all your rich friends and I'm going to live there and be a..." She hesitated, then decided to use the word anyway. "A prostitute?"

"Oh, kitten." He stepped closer. "You're going to be so much more than that. I told you, you're my special one."

"What does that mean? I need to know."

"It means you're mine." His voice had the edge of a knife. "I'll take care of you and only give you to a select few. You get the best of everything. And in return, you're going to help me find more pets, like you. You'll take care of them and teach them everything they need to know." He looked her up and down, brushing her hair away from her face. "You look so sweet. So fucking innocent. They'll trust you. And if you're a good girl, like I know you are, I'll reward you."

She took another step back. "What if I say no? What if I don't want to?"

"You don't have a choice anymore. Where are you going to go? Your family doesn't want you. You don't have anyone else." He paused and stroked her face again. "And if you don't obey me, I'll send you away."

"Where?"

"Does it matter? You're fresh and pretty, I'd get plenty for you. But I have bigger plans." He checked his watch. "We've been here long enough. It's time to go."

"Am I coming with you?" Desi asked.

John didn't bother looking at her. "No. You stay here. Keep your appointments."

"Why? John, please. Take me with you."

He turned slowly. "I do not have the patience for your whining. If I get any complaints, I'm sending you to the docks."

"No, don't do that."

The old Brielle almost broke free. She almost told Desi to run—to leave, get out, and never look back.

But John grabbed her wrist and led her toward the door.

"I don't have my stuff."

"You don't need it." He hauled her out and paused in the hallway to lock the door.

Brielle's heart raced and her stomach turned. "Please don't put me in the trunk again."

"I told you, that was for your protection." He grabbed her wrist again and led her to a flight of stairs.

"I know it was, I know. Just please don't do it again."

He whirled on her, hand raised. She flinched away, holding an arm over her face so he wouldn't backhand her. But the blow didn't come.

"I'm sorry, kitten." He lowered his hand. "I've been under a tremendous amount of stress. I didn't want to leave you here with Desi this long but I had to wait until I was sure we could get back to the cabin safely."

"It's okay, she was nice to me."

"Girls like her are only good for certain things. You understand that, right? She knows her place and she does her job. But I have a lot more planned for you."

"Why?"

"I had a feeling about you from the first time I saw you.

You're going to make me a lot of money, kitten. And don't worry, I'm going to take very good care of you."

She had no doubt that he would. At least, according to his standards.

He'd manipulated her, convinced her. And she'd gone along with it, even when she'd been afraid and unsure. She felt so stupid. She really was stupid, just like her mother had said.

But she knew one thing. She couldn't do what John was asking. She couldn't be one of his girls.

She just didn't know how she was going to get away, or where she would go once she did.

CHAPTER 31

Zachary

MY NECK and shoulders were knotted with tension after a long day at work. The Tilikum Hardware project was pretty straightforward, but it involved a lot of holding my arms overhead while I worked on ceiling fixtures and wiring. And I had to admit, being on a ladder and rewiring things was still slightly disconcerting. I was extra careful—double and triple checking everything—but I remembered the feeling of being shocked all too well. I did not want to go through that again.

I rolled my shoulders as I walked out to my truck. A hot shower sounded good. Maybe I'd do that after I picked up Marigold from the salon.

A hot shower with Marigold sounded even better.

The thought of her put a smile on my face. I loaded up my tools as a few drops of rain started to fall. It was miserably cold, but Mari would call it cozy weather. I wondered if I had time to stop by the Steaming Mug to get her a London fog, her favorite drink. She'd like that, especially on a rainy day.

A beige Buick pulled up behind me, blocking me in, and the driver tapped the horn. I was about to get annoyed when I saw it was just my aunt Louise.

"Hi, honey," she called out as she rolled down the passenger side window.

"Hi, Aunt Louise." I grinned at her. "What's up?"

"Come here." She waved me over. "I don't want to get out. The rain will ruin my hair and I just got it done."

I walked over to her passenger side and leaned in the window. "Looks good. Did you see Marigold?"

"Of course I did. She's the best. What's this I hear about you and the lovely Miss Martin? She said you're an item now."

"She's my girl."

"Who would have thought? I figured I'd have my work cut out for me, getting you to settle down. Turns out the right woman was there all along."

"She absolutely was. I was just too much of an idiot to see it for a while."

"Glad you got yourself straightened out, honey." She narrowed her eyes. "Marigold is a sweet girl, you know. Don't you dare go breaking her heart."

"Not gonna happen, Aunt Louise. So what does this do to my standing on the bachelor hierarchy?"

"Well, I'm not saying you should marry her just so your Aunt Louise wins a wager, but I do have my money on you being next."

"I've got you." I winked.

She laughed and grabbed a round tin off the passenger seat. "I have some cookies for you. Baked them this morning."

I reached in and took the tin from her. "How'd you know you were going to see me today?"

She tapped her temple. "Your Aunt Louise knows things, honey. That's why I'm going to win that wager."

I laughed. She was so weird. I loved it. And she baked great cookies. They'd be perfect with Mari's London fog. "Thanks, Aunt Louise."

"See you later, honey."

I straightened and waved as she drove off. The rain was picking up, so I hurried back to my truck and got in, then checked the clock. I had just enough time to make a quick stop before Mari would be done with work.

The Steaming Mug wasn't busy and I was in and out in no time. I headed to the salon and parked out front. A trio of squirrels darted past, probably seeking shelter from the rain.

I went inside and there was my girl, looking as beautiful as ever. She smiled when she saw me, and I held up her drink.

"I got you something."

She took it and inhaled. "A London fog? Perfect for a rainy day."

"Exactly." I gave her a quick kiss. "Let me help you clean up and we can get home."

"Thank you."

She and Stacey had already done most of the work, but I did what I could. The rain was really coming down when we left, so I shielded her from it with my coat while she locked up, then took her home. Neither of us were particularly hungry for a meal—we'd both had a late lunch—so after changing out of our work clothes, we settled on the couch with the cookies from Aunt Louise.

We chatted for a while about our days. The electricity blinked once and we paused, wondering if the power would go out. The wind was picking up outside, so it wouldn't be surprising if it did. But the lights stayed on.

"Do you want dinner?" I asked.

"Actually, I kind of want to finish reorganizing the closets. I still need to take a load of clothes to donate to the clothing drive."

"Need help?"

She smiled. "Sure."

The bedroom was pretty well organized, with plenty of

space for my stuff, but that had come at the expense of the other rooms in the house. The guest bed was piled with clothes she hadn't sorted yet and the closet in the library was still full.

We started with the guest room closet. She pulled things out one at a time, gave them a quick once over, and handed them off to me, declaring keep or donate. Most were donate, but she had a few things she said were special or she thought she'd wear again, even if only on special occasions. I didn't have any strong opinions about it. She looked gorgeous in anything—or nothing—so it was all the same to me. Whatever made her happy.

Besides, I just liked being with her. Even if all we were doing was sorting clothes and cleaning out closets.

We got to the end of the closet and I helped her hang up the keep pile alongside her old bridesmaid dresses. Which is to say, I handed her clothes and then grabbed her ass every chance I got.

Because, damn, that ass.

"I think we should bring the rest in here to sort it," she said, and eyed the closet with her hands on her hips. "I want to give away enough stuff that everything fits in here."

"What do you want to do with the other closet once it's empty?"

She smiled. "I'll probably end up filling it with books."

I moved in and brushed a kiss across her lips. "Whatever makes you happy, baby."

The closet in her library had a lot of dresses in garment bags in addition to more coats and winter clothes. My girl definitely had a thing for coats. We moved it all to the guest room so she could sort what she wanted to keep.

"These are tough," she said, opening one of the garment bags. She held up a dress that reminded me of the *Pride and Prejudice* musical. "I was really into period costumes for a while. They're so pretty but I almost never have a reason to wear them."

I shrugged. "Up to you."

"They're also not the sort of thing you take to a clothing drive. I'll make a costume pile and then go from there."

"Maybe the library can be books and costumes," I said.

"That was my idea before things got a little out of control. I swear, I don't have a shopping addiction. I just never get rid of anything."

I took the dress and tucked it back in the garment bag for her. "I want to see this on you. I bet it's hot."

"Careful, I might get scandalous and show a little ankle."

I slid my hand down her backside and squeezed. "My bad girl."

She giggled. "I do love how they used to dress, especially during the Regency era. Empire waists and long gowns. They were so pretty and flattering."

"Were the costumes in that musical the kind of thing they wore?"

"They were fairly accurate, yes."

"I was into it. Even the men. They looked badass."

"They did. So gentlemanly."

She opened another garment bag and paused.

"What's that?" I asked, glancing at the pink fabric showing through. "Another costume?"

"No." She zipped it back up. "This was going to be my prom dress."

Oh, shit.

She set it aside. "I didn't remember I still had it."

I needed to say something. She shifted some of the clothes so she could keep sorting through them, but I could tell by her body language she was upset. The mood in the room had changed—even I wasn't clueless enough to miss it.

But what the hell was I supposed to say? I wanted to go

back to ignoring it; pretending it hadn't happened. But it had, and it clearly still bothered her.

"Hey. Are you okay?" I ran a hand down her arm, hoping I could draw her in and kiss it all away, but she moved out of my reach.

"I'm fine. It was such a long time ago, there's no reason for it to still bother me. It's silly."

I opened and closed my fists a couple of times, almost groaning with dread. I could take her *I'm fine* at face value and change the subject, but my gut was throwing danger signals I couldn't ignore. It didn't matter that it had been a long time. It had changed the course of our relationship for years.

And it was my fault.

I didn't want something I'd done when I was young and stupid to get in the way of what we had now. I couldn't ignore this like I'd ignored her for so long.

"Mari, can we just talk about it?"

"Talk about what?"

"Baby, you know." I took her hand and turned her toward me. "It was a long time ago, but that doesn't mean it didn't happen. I hurt you and I'm so sorry."

Tears gathered in the corners of her eyes. It felt like having an ice pick rammed straight into my chest.

She dabbed the tears away. "This is so stupid. I shouldn't cry about it now."

I wasn't sure what else to say. Just let her cry? Hold her? Apologize again?

"Why did you do it?" she asked, her voice suddenly a whisper. "Why would you play a joke like that on me?"

"It wasn't a joke."

Her teary eyes lifted to meet mine. "I know it was just a high school prom, but at the time, that dance meant everything to me. My friends all had dates, but I was Marigold, the quiet bookworm who was too scared to even talk to boys. So of course no one asked me. And then, out of the blue, there you were. I had such a crush on you, I could hardly speak when you were around. And you, the boy of my dreams, my best friend's big brother who seemed as out of reach as the stars—you were asking me to prom. I thought I'd died and gone to heaven."

She paused and wiped her tears again. I knew how this ended and I didn't want to hear it.

"I was so excited. Mom took me shopping to buy that dress and she even let me get shoes to match. I got my hopes up that maybe you actually liked me. Maybe all those years we'd been around each other at your family's house, you'd secretly harbored a crush on me. Just like I had a crush on you. And then Annika told me the truth. It was just a joke. Somebody paid you to ask me to the prom. It wasn't real at all."

"That's not…" I trailed off, not sure what to say. How could I explain myself? It had been an awful thing to do to her, even if I'd never meant it that way. "It wasn't a joke."

"Then why?"

Closing my eyes, I let out a long breath. I'd made a promise back then and now I was faced with a choice. Break that promise, but tell her the truth. Or lie to her again.

I couldn't lie to her.

"Someone did pay me to ask you to that dance. But it wasn't a joke. And I did have a crush on you. It drove me absolutely crazy to have you at my parents' house all the time. I wanted to be near you, but you were younger and I didn't know what the hell I was doing. You seemed so forbidden, I didn't know how to handle it."

"If it wasn't a joke, why would someone give you money to ask me to prom? Who would do something like that?"

I met her eyes. I had to just tell her. "Your dad."

Her mouth opened and she took a step backward. "What?"

"He knew you were sad because you didn't have a date. So he came to me and offered to pay for it if I'd take you—the tickets, tux rental, limo, dinner, plus a little extra. I don't know why he thought I was a good choice. I guess because he knows our family and I wasn't too much older than you."

"Why didn't you tell me?"

"I wasn't supposed to tell anyone. Your dad made me swear. But of course I screwed up. Garrett started interrogating me about where I got the money to rent a limo and take you to a fancy dinner, and I let slip that someone paid me to take you. I figured that was the end of it, but the jerk told Annika. And then you found out and the whole thing blew up.

"After that, your dad cornered me in the parking lot outside the Quick Stop and put the fear of God in me. He threatened to take me out and make my body disappear if I ever told anyone he was involved. So I kept my mouth shut. I wanted to apologize, but I was afraid to say anything to you. I didn't know if I could keep it a secret, and then it was like the more I avoided you, the more I felt like I had to avoid you."

She shook her head slowly and took another step back.

Panic rose in my chest. "Baby, I'm so sorry. I was stupid and wrong. It's totally my fault."

"It's not only your fault," she said. "It's his fault too."

I moved closer, desperate to gather her in my arms. To hold her tight against me until this awful feeling went away.

But she shied away. "I just need to process this. And I need to talk to my dad."

She turned and walked out of the room. I fucking hated this. I hated that something I'd done had hurt her. That one glance at an old dress had ripped the wound open again.

I followed her out to the front room. "Marigold."

She put on one of her coats, grabbed her purse, and stepped into a pair of shoes. "I'll be back in a little while. I need to talk to him in person."

"At least let me drive you."

"No." She finally met my eyes. "I need to do this on my own."

As I watched her go, it felt like my heart went out the door with her. It was ripped free from my chest and firmly in her possession.

I just hoped she'd bring it back.

CHAPTER 32

Marigold

I SHOULD HAVE KNOWN.

Then again, what teenage girl expected her father to go behind her back and pay someone to be her prom date? That was a lot, even for my dad.

Rain pelted the windshield as I drove to my parents' house and tried to make sense of my feelings. The prom incident had been a formative experience in my young life. I'd gone from the highest of highs to the lowest of lows. The worst part had been the sheer embarrassment of it. I had already been a self-conscious teenager. Being the butt of a joke —or so I thought—had been mortifying.

Enough time had gone by that my relationship with Zachary felt disconnected from that long-ago embarrassment. I wasn't mad at him anymore. Or, at the very least, I didn't want to be. I wanted to let it go—maybe even pretend it hadn't happened. But hearing that my dad had been the one behind it all along sent me into a tailspin. All those chaotic, insecure feelings came roaring to the surface.

I needed to know why. Why would he go so far as to pay someone to date me? I already knew he and my mom had a hard time seeing me as a capable adult who could handle her own life. But had he believed he'd need to intervene at every turn, even when it came to my relationships?

Had he ever done it again? Had any of the men I'd dated over the years asked me out at the behest of my father?

I parked outside my parents' house and noticed I'd stepped into a pair of high heels. Not exactly the smartest choice, but they'd been nearby. At least they had ankle straps. I fastened them before getting out of the car and darted through the driving rain to their front door. My coat didn't have a hood, but I didn't care what the stormy weather did to my hair. I knocked and let myself in.

"Mom? Dad? Are you home?"

Thunder boomed outside as I shut the door behind me.

"Back here," Mom called.

I found them in my mom's studio. Dad had long ago set up a recliner in the corner where he'd read or watch sports with headphones on so he didn't bother my mom while she painted. He sat with his phone propped up while my mom regarded her latest painting. She had a small brush in her hand and a palette sitting nearby.

Dad set his phone on a side table and took off his head-phones. "Hi, flower. Is something wrong?"

I probably looked oddly disheveled with stringy damp hair and an unbuttoned coat.

"I need to talk to you."

"Sure, what's going on?"

"Did you pay Zachary Haven to take me to prom?"

He hesitated, and I could practically see him trying to figure out how he was going to spin this. "That was a long time ago."

"Yes, it was, but I'm sure you remember. Did you?"

"Flower—"

"Dad, please just answer my question."

"That dance meant the world to you. It was all you could talk about. You had a bulletin board filled with prom dress pictures you cut out from magazines. You started it when you were a freshman."

That was true, I had done that. "I remember."

"First Isabelle had a date. Then Annika. And you were left wondering if your prom dreams were going to come true. I kept hoping you were going to come home and tell us someone had finally asked. And believe me, a father wanting some teenage idiot to ask his daughter to a dance is rare. I didn't want you to go, so you could be safe at home with us, and wanted you to go because you wanted it so badly. So I decided to step in and make sure you had your night."

Mom's eyes widened in shock. He'd probably kept it from her too.

"But why Zachary? If you were worried about me going out with a boy, why choose him?"

"Paul and Marlene love you almost as much as we do. I knew they'd never let one of their sons treat you badly. And let's be honest, you only had eyes for Zachary, even back then."

"So you bribed him."

"It wasn't a bribe. I gave him what he needed to cover the cost of the dance."

"How is that not a bribe?"

"I was just trying to help."

"Paying someone to date me did not help. Do you have any idea how mortified I was when I found out?"

"That's his fault." He crossed his arms. "He was sworn to secrecy."

"But that's the thing. How could you have expected him to keep that a secret? What if we'd gone to that dance and had such a good time that he asked me out again and we started dating? He'd have had to come clean eventually. What was I supposed to think?"

"It was just a prom," Dad said.

"What you don't understand is what that says about how

you see me as a person. It's like you don't think I'm capable of doing things on my own."

"That's not true."

"Maybe you don't mean it that way, but how else am I supposed to see it? How often have you intervened in my life because something wasn't going my way or I was in danger of being disappointed? It makes me feel like you don't think I can face hard things or make my own decisions or even find love on my own."

"I only want you to be happy."

"I know you do. But finding out someone paid Zachary to ask me out hurt. I was embarrassed and ashamed. I thought it was all a big joke and everyone was laughing at me behind my back. I missed the prom anyway. And while that didn't hurt me, thinking Zachary had played a mean prank on me for so many years did."

His expression fell. "Flower, I didn't want to hurt you."

"I just wish you would have told me. No, first, I wish you hadn't done it. But since you did, I wish you would have told me the truth. I spent so many years thinking Zachary hated me because of this."

He nodded slowly.

"I don't want you to think I don't appreciate that you want to help. You and Mom do a lot for me. But when you step in without asking, whether it's to get me a prom date or to replace appliances in my house or anything in between, it makes me feel like you don't think I'm a capable person. At least ask me if I need help instead of assuming. I'm a grown woman with a house and a business. I'm doing okay for myself and I wish you could see that."

"We do," Mom said. "We're nothing but proud of you."

"No, she's right." Dad shook his head. "I'm always trying to smooth out the road for you. You're my little girl, it's hard to see you struggle."

"I know, Dad. But struggle is a part of life."

"Don't I know it." He took a deep breath. "I'm sorry if I've been a little overbearing. And I'm sorry about the prom. That was a mistake and I knew it back then. I just hoped everyone would forget and we could move on."

I stepped in and gave him a hug. "Thanks, Dad."

"Don't be too hard on Zachary about it," Mom said. "He was practically a kid himself."

"I know he was. He's sorry for his part in it and I can accept his apology. This whole thing just stirred up a lot of big feelings." I dabbed the tears at the corners of my eyes.

"Oh, flower, you get those big feelings from me, I'm afraid," Mom said. "It's why I paint. I don't have anywhere else to keep them."

I gave my mom a hug, careful to stay out of the way of her wet paintbrush.

"Speaking of Zachary, I left pretty abruptly. I should get back."

"Are we okay?" Dad asked, his brow furrowed with concern. "I don't know if I can change overnight, but I'll try not to butt in so much."

"Yes, we're okay," I said. "And that's a good start."

"Bring Zachary by for dinner soon," Mom said. "We need to let your dad interrogate him as to his intent with his daughter."

I laughed. That conversation didn't scare me in the least. I knew Zachary's intent, and I had no doubt he'd be forthright with my dad.

In fact, I was looking forward to hearing Zachary tell my parents he was planning on making me a Haven. That was better than any dance could have been.

After another round of hugs, I said goodbye to my parents, feeling freer than I had in a long time. A weight had been lifted from my shoulders and an invisible but very real boundary between me and Zachary was gone. Now that the truth was in the open, we were free of the hurts of the past—free to move on with our future.

The wind howled outside. It blew my hair around my face as soon as I stepped out the front door. I hurried to my car as the rain pelted me. It was shaping up to be quite a storm.

I got in and left, anxious to get home to Zachary. I wanted to change out of my wet clothes and crawl into his arms. He'd keep me safe and warm.

The windshield wipers could hardly keep up. It was difficult to see, so I slowed down. Another car passed me, going in the opposite direction, their headlights reflecting off all the water.

A car was stopped in the road up ahead, yellow hazard lights flashing. I wondered if something had blown into the road or if a tree had fallen. Sometimes the wind blew hard enough to knock trees down.

I pulled closer to see if I could tell who it was. There wasn't much I could do—especially since I'd thoughtlessly put on heels as I walked out the door—but I could at least call for help if they needed it.

I slowed to a stop behind them. Sure enough, there was a tree lying across the road.

A man got out and put up his hood as he ran back to my car. I rolled down the window.

"Are you okay?" I asked.

"Yeah, fine," he said. "It was already down. I called it in."

"Good, I just wanted to make sure."

"Appreciate it." He gestured the way I'd come. "Afraid you'll have to find a way around."

"That's fine. Be careful."

"You too."

I rolled up my window, shutting out the wind and rain. Checking my surroundings, I made sure it was clear, then maneuvered so I could turn around. I took a left onto a side street. The route would take me a little bit out of my way, but it wouldn't take too long.

No lights were on in the houses I passed. The tree must have knocked out the power. Hopefully it wouldn't be out too long. Although the thought of snuggling up with Zachary by candlelight and listening to the storm didn't sound bad at all —so cozy and romantic.

Out of nowhere, a dark shape crashed to the ground in front of me. I slammed on my brakes to keep from hitting it, my tires skidding on the wet road. Tree branches scraped across my windshield, pine needles flying everywhere.

Adrenaline rushed through my veins and my heart raced. A tree had fallen across the road.

If I'd been there a second later, it might have crushed me.

I put the car in park, then closed my eyes for a moment and took deep breaths to steady myself. I was fine. I hadn't hit it. Just came close.

When I opened my eyes, lightning flashed overhead, and for an instant, I could see all around me.

Someone was standing next to my car.

I fumbled for the lock, but he was already opening the door. Cold wind whipped around us as he grabbed me, reached across to unfasten my seat belt, and dragged me out of the car. I started to scream but he had his arms tight around me and a hand clamped over my mouth. Something pricked my neck. My head swam and it felt like my arms and legs were completely detached from my body. I couldn't make them move. Couldn't resist.

Couldn't even scream.

As he dragged me to the car I hadn't seen pull up behind me, all I could do was wonder why Preston was putting me in the trunk.

CHAPTER 33

Zachary

PACING AROUND THE HOUSE, I checked my phone about every twenty seconds. As if I'd somehow miss her call with my ringer on and my phone in my hand. She hadn't been gone that long. Only a little over an hour. Her parents were across town, maybe fifteen minutes from here. That meant half an hour just to get there and back, plus however long she spent talking to them. There was no real reason to be alarmed that she wasn't home yet.

But I couldn't sit still.

Deep down, I'd known the truth had to come out eventually. We couldn't go the rest of our lives without ever talking about the stupid prom incident. And of course she'd be upset. I didn't blame her for that. I just wanted this whole thing to be over.

I wanted her to come home so she could do what she needed to do, say what she needed to say. Yell at me, cry, punch me if it would help. I'd take it all. And then I'd spend the rest of the night apologizing, making it right.

Loving her hard so I could show her I meant it. That I loved her and I'd never hurt her like that again.

The storm wasn't making me feel any better. She was a

capable woman, it wasn't like she couldn't drive in torrential rain. But every flash of lightning and crack of thunder made my back ripple with tension.

I just wanted her here in my arms.

My eyes kept darting to the clock on the wall outside the kitchen. It didn't make noise, but I swore I could hear it ticking. Mocking me with the slowness of each second. It was like the last half hour of the last day of school before summer break. Every minute might as well have taken an hour.

I checked my phone again, although I knew she hadn't called, then slipped it in my pocket. I had to keep telling myself I'd done the right thing by letting her go. She'd asked for space, and I was giving it to her—trusting her to handle the situation with her dad on her own. That was what she needed.

But I didn't like it.

I sat down and tried to distract myself with a mindless game on my phone. It didn't really work but at least I wasn't wearing a groove in the floor with my pacing.

Time went on and my restlessness grew. Was she still at her parents'? How long would it take to talk this out with her dad? Was she staying for dinner? That could explain it, but she probably would have at least texted to let me know.

Where was she?

A nagging feeling ate at me. It was like being poked in the back over and over. Something was wrong.

I was just being paranoid. I was worried because she'd left upset and I didn't like the way that felt. That's all it was.

But no matter how many times I told myself she had to be fine, I didn't believe it.

Something was definitely wrong.

"Fuck it."

I got up and put on my shoes and coat. I'd drive by her parents' place. I wouldn't intrude, just confirm her car was there and come back to wait for her.

The weather sucked balls. Icy cold rain soaked everything and the wind howled down from the mountain peaks.

All the more reason to make sure she was okay.

My windshield fogged up almost before I'd backed out of the driveway. I leaned forward and wiped it with my arm so I could see.

There weren't many people out and about. I passed one other car but it looked like most of the town had hunkered down for the storm.

I wasn't far from her parents' house when I came upon flashing lights in the road. A cop car was blocking the way and it looked like another car with hazards on farther up. I stopped and peered into the rainy darkness.

A tree lay across the road. A few guys were already working on clearing it.

I opened my window and leaned out. "Hey, need help?"

A guy looked up and waved. "We got it. But thanks."

"Stay safe," I called.

I rolled up the window and wiped the rain off my forehead. It was pouring out there.

Since I couldn't get to their house that way, I took a side street and wound my way through a neighborhood. The porch light was on at her parents' place, but her car wasn't in the driveway.

Well, shit.

I got out my phone and called her. She'd probably gone a different way to get around the tree and we'd just missed each other.

I expected her to answer and tell me she was pulling into her driveway, but it rang until it went to voicemail.

That was weird.

It wasn't just weird. Given the circumstances, it was alarming.

I decided to check with her parents first. See how long ago she'd left. I parked outside and went up to their door.

Her dad answered and his eyebrows lifted in surprise. "Zachary. What are you doing here? Is everything okay?"

"Is Marigold here?"

"No, she left quite a while ago. She isn't home?"

"Maybe she is now, but she wasn't when I left. I just called her and it went to voicemail."

He fished his phone out of his pocket. "I'll try her."

I waited while Craig tried to call his daughter. For the first couple of rings, he seemed relaxed, like he was convinced she'd answer. Maybe he assumed we were fighting and she'd ignored my call.

His face fell and he tapped his phone to end the call. "Voicemail."

I glanced over my shoulder into the stormy darkness. "There was at least one tree down. I had to go around."

He was already shoving his arms into his coat. "Let's split up. You go east and I'll go west. Follow the likely routes back to her house and call me if you see any sign of her."

"Done."

I didn't have his number, so I got it and texted him so he'd have mine. I left while he called to Alyssa that he had to run out for a bit.

Dread knotted in the pit of my stomach as I headed out. The downed tree I'd seen had been sprawled across the road but it didn't look like it had hit anyone. The only cars I'd seen were the cop car and the guys clearing it. And there weren't any places for her to run off the road—not there, at least.

That tree might have been down already when she came through, so she'd have detoured around it. There were a couple of options, including the way I'd come. I hadn't seen her car on the way over, although if she'd gone into a ditch or something, I could have missed it. It was hard to see anything with the heavy rain.

I decided to take a different turn, winding around another

road that led roughly in the direction of her house. She might have gone that way.

Adrenaline pumped through my veins. I drove slowly, peering out through the storm, hoping I didn't miss anything. Had she rolled down a hillside? Or stopped to help someone?

Where was she?

I came around a corner and my heart felt like it jumped right into my throat.

Marigold's car was stopped in the road with another downed tree in front of it. I slammed on the brakes, flew out of my truck, and ran to the driver's side.

"Marigold?"

It was empty. And her car was still running.

I opened the door, as if she'd somehow appear. Her purse was on the passenger's seat, her phone on the center console.

"Marigold!" I called.

No reply.

"Fuck." I fumbled for my phone and started looking around. Why was her car sitting there? Where the hell was she? I did a circle around her car and used my phone as a flashlight, desperate to find some sign of her. But I couldn't see a damn thing. The tree was partially blocking the road, but she hadn't hit it.

Finally, I stopped and called her dad.

"Find her?" he answered.

"Just her car. There's a downed tree but it doesn't look like it hit her. But she's not here."

"Where are you?"

I told him the street.

"Call the police. I'll be right there."

"Done."

I ended the call and went straight for Garrett's number.

"Yeah?" he answered.

"Marigold is missing."

"What?"

"Just listen. She left her parents' house but didn't make it home. I found her car on Stonybrook Lane. There's a tree in the road, but it didn't hit her. She's not here, Garrett. Her car is just sitting here, empty. She left her purse and everything."

"What's the cross street?"

"I don't know. Pine, I think."

"Okay, I'm only about five minutes from there. Keep looking. I'll call it in."

"Thanks, man."

Rain pelted me, soaking my hair and my coat, but I didn't feel the cold. Only the panic rising in my chest. Where was she? Why was her car here? What had happened to her?

I checked both sides of the road, shining my flashlight into the dark, calling her name. Even with a tree in the road, she wouldn't have left her car like that.

And then it hit me. Preston.

That bastard piece of shit motherfucker. He'd taken her.

"Fuck!"

Headlights lit up the road behind my truck. Her dad parked next to me and flew out of his car as fast as I had.

"Where is she? What happened? Did she hit the tree?"

"No." I looked around, wondering which way they'd gone. Where he'd taken her. "She was abducted."

"Now you're talking crazy. Who would kidnap my sweet Marigold?"

"Preston Bradford."

"Where is he? I'll kill him."

The seriousness in her dad's voice spoke to the rage ready to explode inside me. Only, I wanted to be the one to do it.

If he so much as touched her—

"I don't know." My voice was oddly calm. "Garrett is on his way."

Garrett arrived a moment later, approaching from the other side of the downed tree in his cruiser, blue and red lights flashing. He got out and shined his flashlight on her car, then stepped over the tree.

"Preston took her." I didn't want him to waste a second. "I've looked, there's no sign of her. Her car's still running and her purse is in there."

"Shit," Garrett muttered. Using his flashlight, he took in the scene, walking around the car and checking inside. He lit up the trees on the side of the road as rain pelted us. "She wouldn't just walk away in a storm."

"Yeah, no shit."

"You need to find my daughter," Craig said, his voice almost breaking.

Garrett nodded and walked back toward his car, talking into his radio.

I felt like I was going to rip out of my own skin. I looked at Craig. "If you tell me we need to wait while the cops do their job, I might punch you in the face."

"Fuck that, son. I'm calling in reinforcements."

"Who?"

"The SPS. Let's go."

The Squirrel Protection Squad? I looked at him like he'd lost his mind, but he was already on the phone and heading to his car.

I could either stand out there in the rain and wait for Garrett to tell me to stay out of the way while he handled this, or follow Craig.

I got in my truck and followed.

CHAPTER 34

Marigold

MY HEAD SWAM, nausea roiled in my stomach, and my mouth was so dry. I pried open my eyes, trying to make sense of things. Why did I feel so awful? And where was I?

Memories started to come back to me. Driving home in the storm. A downed tree. Someone dragging me out of my car. Then everything going dark.

Panic made my chest tighten. I'd been abducted. Pulled out of my car on a side street and knocked out with something.

Had it been Preston? Did I remember that right?

I realized my eyes had closed again. Whatever he'd used to render me unconscious was obviously still in my system—and probably what was making me feel like vomiting.

Deep breaths, Marigold. Deep breaths.

I tried to breathe slowly, but fear compressed my lungs, making it hard to fill them with air. I finally got my eyes open but my vision was blurry. Blinking, I lifted my head and tried to make sense of my surroundings.

A bed. I was lying on my back on a bed, but nothing about the room was familiar. It was too dark to see much, just the light of a small lamp illuminating the space. But it looked like a loft with a pitched ceiling. My clothes were still on, as were my coat and shoes.

Had he really put me in a trunk? It seemed like he had, but it was hard to be sure. My mind was so fuzzy.

I let my head drop onto the pillow and rubbed my eyes. I hated the way this felt, like my limbs weren't quite connected to my body and my head was full of cotton. At least the nausea was gradually subsiding.

The sudden sense that I was being watched made me freeze. I slowly opened my eyes, keeping my hands up, as if I wasn't as weak as a kitten and stood a chance of actually defending myself if I needed to.

But it wasn't Preston. It wasn't even a man.

A young woman stood near the bed, dressed in a sweat-shirt and jeans. Her long blond hair was down and slightly disheveled, like she'd just woken up. Even in the dim light, I could see dark circles beneath her eyes, and she gazed at me with a haunted expression.

Wait. I knew that face. How did I know her?

"You're awake." Her voice sounded so young.

She couldn't have been the one to take me. It had been a man. "Where am I?"

"John's cabin."

"John?" Was I supposed to know who that was?

"I thought you were his girlfriend."

"I don't know John. Did you help bring me here?"

"No. He left me here for a while, then came back with you."

"Is he here?"

She shook her head. "He said he wouldn't be gone for very long. Did he use a needle?"

"I think so."

She nodded, like she understood. "I'll get you some water. It helps when you're first waking up."

The girl turned and disappeared down a set of stairs.

I sat up and my stomach protested. A few deep breaths and the nausea abated, for the moment at least. My head hurt but at least my vision was coming back.

A needle. He'd injected something into me that had knocked me out.

What was happening?

The girl returned with a glass of water. She handed it to me and I took a careful sip.

"Thank you."

"You're welcome."

I put the glass on a side table. The girl eyed me with an odd expression, her brow slightly furrowed and her lips pressed together.

"What's your name?" I asked.

"Brielle."

I gaped at her. "Brielle Thayer? From Tilikum?"

She nodded.

"Is this where you've been?" I glanced around, as if that would tell me something about why I was sitting in a loft with a missing teenager.

"Mostly. John brought me."

"Did John take you like he took me?"

She shook her head. "No. He gave me a ride. Told me I could stay here for a while until I figured things out."

I wished I understood what she was talking about, but I couldn't quite string my thoughts together.

"I thought he was a good guy, but I don't think he is anymore," she said, her voice lowering to a whisper. "I don't know why he wants you, but I know why he wants me. It isn't good. But I don't know how to get away."

Fear tightened my chest again and made my throat dry. Who was John? Who had taken me? Had I imagined it was Preston?

What was going on?

"We're going to get out of here." I didn't know how, but I had to hear myself say it. "We're going to get away. Okay?"

She nodded. It was hard to tell in the dark, but it seemed like she had tears in her eyes.

Poor thing.

I scooted to the edge of the bed and swung my legs over. "How long have I been here?"

"A few hours."

My stomach protested again and I had to pause to breathe through it. A few hours. That meant Zachary was already looking for me.

If I knew Zachary, it meant half the town was already looking for me.

"Okay," I said. "Do you know where we are? In relation to Tilikum?"

"I'm not sure, but I know it's far."

"Well, we'll figure it out."

"No."

I looked up. "Why not?"

"He locked us in."

Locked in. What did she mean we were locked in? I'd have to try the doors and windows for myself to be sure. I didn't know if I could actually trust this girl. Whoever John was, he'd apparently had her in this cabin for quite a while. She seemed afraid, but it could be an act.

"John didn't say when he was coming back?"

"He just said soon."

I took a breath to steady myself, then tried standing. My legs were weak, but I could stay upright. And I didn't vomit. That was good.

A noise came from downstairs and Brielle's eyes widened. Without a word, she dashed down the stairs.

The door opened, letting in the sound of the storm outside. I'd never been so terrified. I could hardly breathe. My body was so weak and I was stuck; there was nowhere to go.

A man's voice drifted up into the loft. He spoke low, too quiet for me to hear what he was saying.

A moment later, footsteps. I swayed on my feet. With nowhere to go, I decided to sit on the edge of the bed. That might give me a better chance of remaining conscious.

Oh my god. It was Preston.

"Good, you're awake."

I stared at him, my lips parted. I didn't know what to say, where to begin.

He came closer and reached out, trying to brush the hair back from my face, but I flinched away.

"It's okay, beautiful," he said, his tone soothing. "You'll feel better soon."

"Where am I?"

"It's a little cabin I happen to own. Not my most impressive property, I admit, but it's useful."

"You abducted me."

"That's how it appears now. But in time, you'll come to see things my way."

"It doesn't *appear* that you abducted me. You did. You drugged me."

"I'm sorry about that. I know it's disconcerting. But it was better for you."

This man was delusional.

He sat on the bed next to me and tried to take my hand, but I pulled away. "Marigold, you're going to have to understand, when I want something, I get it. No matter what it is, no matter the cost. I've gotten to where I am in life because I don't take no for an answer. Ever. And what I want now is you."

I shook my head slowly. "We hardly know each other. We only went out a handful of times."

"Doesn't matter." He took my hand, this time holding it so tight I couldn't draw away. "I decided you were mine the first time I met you. And nothing and no one is going to take you from me."

"I told you I didn't want to see you anymore."

His dark eyes were hard as steel. "You will want me. I'm going to make sure of it."

"You can't do this. You can't keep me here."

He kept my hand in a tight grip. "Of course I can."

"This is crazy. What do you think is going to happen? You're going to keep me locked up in some cabin and eventually I'm going to fall in love with you?"

The corner of his mouth turned up. "Believe me, it won't be a problem."

"You're delusional."

"No, you just underestimate my determination. I tried to tell you, Marigold, I'm going to elevate you. You're going to associate with people you only read about now; some of the most powerful people in the world. And you'll be the envy of all because you're with me."

"I'll never be with you."

"You will." He grabbed my chin so I couldn't look away. "You're spirited. It's one of the things I like about you. So I'll have to take my time. I don't want to have to break you too quickly. But trust me, it won't be a problem. I'm a very patient man."

Brielle appeared at the top of the stairs. I hoped she'd raise a big frying pan and knock him out with it. No such luck. She just inched her way onto the loft, like a little girl who wanted attention but was afraid of making the grown-ups mad.

"Did you kidnap her too?" I asked.

Preston glanced at her. "No. I saved her. Didn't I, kitten?"

She nodded but kept her lips pressed closed.

"You've been a very good girl," he said to her. "I know it's been scary, but isn't it good to be back home?"

She nodded again.

"I told you everything would be okay. You've been very brave."

Her face almost lit up and I could tell that not too long ago, that kind of praise from him would have had her beaming with pleasure. Now she seemed uncertain and afraid.

His brow furrowed and he pulled out his phone. Without another word to me, or to Brielle, he got up and started down the stairs.

"Yeah," he answered.

Brielle stood at the top of the stairs, watching him. I waited, not sure what I should do. It was dark outside, probably late at night. Or maybe early in the morning. I had no idea where we were or how long we'd driven to get here. Even if I could make it out the door, I couldn't just leave.

"Don't worry about it," Preston said, his voice hard. "Because I have it under control."

He paused and Brielle looked at me as if to say she didn't know what was going on.

"The fuck you are. Drew, when have I ever been wrong?" His tone grew angrier. "I made you a fucking millionaire and now you're questioning me?" Another pause. "I realize that, but the risks are worth it." He paused again. "Don't. Drew, don't fucking talk about her. She's not part of this discussion."

Were they talking about me? Brielle? Someone else? I didn't know.

"They won't... No, they won't. I told you, I have everything under control so stay the fuck out of it."

He got quiet again and I wondered if he'd ended the call. But a moment later, he spoke.

"Are you fucking kidding me? Damn it, Drew. Fine. No, do not come here. Stay where you are. I'm on my way."

He came back upstairs and pocketed his phone. His face

was hard and angry. Brielle shrank away, as if afraid he'd hurt her.

Her fear was certainly justified.

"Nothing good comes without struggle," he said. "Kitten, I need you to keep being a good girl for me. This is Marigold. She's special, just like you. I want you to take good care of her tonight. I'll be back in the morning."

"Can't I come with you?" she asked.

"No. This is a big responsibility I'm giving you. If you do a good job with Marigold, you'll show me I can trust you."

"Okay," she said.

"Just stay here and you'll be safe. There's a storm outside. I wouldn't want my girls getting hurt." He turned to me. "Don't worry, beautiful. I know this is a lot to take in. This isn't how I wanted things to unfold, but I've had to make a lot of adjustments recently. We'll get through this together."

He was absolutely insane. But saying so wasn't going to do me any good. So I didn't say anything. He went back down the stairs and out the door. I didn't have to hear the lock to know we were trapped.

CHAPTER 35

Zachary

STILL NO SIGN OF HER.

I'd heard those words so many times over the last however many hours. They knocked around in my brain, giving me a headache.

I stared at the mug of lukewarm black coffee on the table in front of me. Activity swirled in the Copper Kettle. Sometime in the night, it had become unofficial Marigold search headquarters. Sheriff Jack and his guys were doing their thing at the station, but the rest of the town had mobilized under the direction of the Squirrel Protection Squad.

Fortunately, law enforcement wasn't wasting time treating this like some kind of accident or misunderstanding. We'd checked with everyone—Isabelle, Audrey, Annika, Stacey. None of Marigold's friends had seen or heard from her. Her car was fine. There was no reason for her to have left it. And no one had given her a ride.

She was officially missing.

The SPS were still out there, taking shifts looking for her. The sheriff had alerted police in neighboring towns, as well as the state patrol. But every hour that went by increased the dread in my gut.

Where was she?

He'd taken her in the dark in the middle of the worst storm we'd had so far this season. No one had seen a thing, nobody's camera had caught it. We had no idea where to even begin looking, let alone anything like an actual lead.

Garrett put a hand on my shoulder. He'd changed into street clothes and the circles beneath his eyes betrayed his lack of sleep. His shift must have ended the night before, but he hadn't gone to bed. We'd both been up all night.

"You should crash for a couple of hours," he said.

"Not gonna happen."

He shrugged, as if he'd known I'd say that. "Sun is coming up. That'll make looking for her easier."

I shook my head. "She's not wandering around town. She could be anywhere by now."

"I know."

"How does a guy roll into town, grab a woman out of her car, and disappear again? There has to be something."

"Seattle PD checked his known residence there," he said. "Nothing unusual, but they'll keep an eye out."

"He's not going to take her to his place in the city. He's not stupid. He'll know we're looking for her."

"Yeah, but we have to start somewhere."

"Can't you guys track his phone or something?"

"His known number isn't moving. If he has a phone on him, it's either a burner or a number we don't have."

I raked my hands through my hair. "We've got nothing. Not a fucking thing."

His jaw hitched. "I know."

At least he wasn't bullshitting me. And I knew the cops were doing what they could. I just hated feeling so helpless. I didn't want to be here, in some stupid diner. I wanted to be out there, finding her.

The door swung open and a group of SPS members trudged in, wet and bedraggled.

"Nothing new to report," one of them said, his voice somber.

Of course there wasn't. She wasn't here.

"Can't we track his credit cards?" I asked. "There's no way they're on foot. Won't he stop for gas eventually?"

"We're working on it, but bank records require a lot more paperwork," Garrett said.

"We don't have time for fucking court orders and warrants and all that bullshit."

"All that bullshit is the law, Z. We'll get it as soon as we can."

"Not soon enough."

Rob Landon walked over with a fresh cup of coffee. He wore a reflective jacket over his SPS t-shirt. "We'll find her, Zachary. Too many people out there looking not to."

"She's not in town," I said. "If that piece of shit took her, and we all know he did, they've been gone for hours. Who knows how far they've gotten."

"We've got people out on the highways in every direction. They'll ask around everywhere. Diners, gas stations, hotels."

"State patrol is on it too," Garrett said.

"Shame we don't know what he's driving," Rob said, then took a sip of his coffee. "It would help if we knew what we were looking for. Did his car turn up?"

"It's in Seattle, parked at his building," Garrett said. "Whatever he's driving, it isn't his."

"How is this guy so fucking elusive?" I asked. "There's been a warrant out for his arrest since he assaulted Marigold. How is he just out there doing shit and no one can track him down?"

Rob's brow furrowed. "Do you think…"

"What?" I asked.

"Sorry, my memory isn't what it used to be. But do you think he could be using an alias?"

"He could be," Garrett said. "But what does that have to do with your memory?"

"He came in here quite a few times. The whole town was buzzing about him, he was hard not to notice. I could have sworn he used a credit card with a different name one of those times. It struck me because Preston Bradford isn't a name you hear around these parts. Has a city ring to it. But that time, he used a card that said John something-or-other. I didn't think much of it at the time."

It was all I could do to let Rob finish talking. "John what? What last name did he use?"

"I wish I could remember."

"Damn it," I muttered. "Do you have receipts? Could we find it?"

"That would be like searching for a needle in a haystack, especially without a date or last name."

"I'll do it. It's the closest thing we have to a lead." I glanced at my brother. He looked uneasy. "Just walk away. If there's anything illegal in going through restaurant receipts, I don't want to know and you don't need to know what I'm doing."

He shook his head and wandered over to where some of the other SPS members had congregated.

"Show me the way," I said to Rob.

I followed him to a back office that made my childhood bedroom—that I'd shared with two of my brothers—look organized by comparison. Stacks of paperwork covered the two desks, and shoe boxes of various sizes were stuffed in the shelves along with random utensils that were undoubtedly meant to be in the kitchen.

"Let's see here." He ran his finger along a row of boxes. They were labeled with the month and year in black marker. "This would be easier if we were sure of the dates, but this will get us started."

He handed me several boxes and took down more. We

brought them out to the breakfast bar and I took a seat. I opened the first box and found a mess of receipts and paperwork.

Rob slid a coffee across the bar. "Sorry about all that. I'm not the best at staying organized. But the receipts are in there and they should be in the right box according to date. Hopefully."

"That's okay," I said. "I'd probably mess up your organization anyway."

I took a sip of coffee and got to work. Rob helped from his side of the breakfast bar. The early morning sun streamed in through the windows and people came and went around me. I was running on caffeine and adrenaline, pure determination keeping me alert.

"Here's a John," Rob said. "No, this is John Miller. He lives over on Evergreen."

I sorted through receipts, trying not to thumb through them too fast. The names started going by in a blur until I got to another John Miller. I put his receipt aside anyway, just in case.

The next few stacks produced nothing. I pulled out another one and toward the middle, I finally found something.

"This is him." I held up a receipt for Preston Bradford. "It's his real name, but at least it has a signature on it."

"That's something," Rob said.

Finding at least one receipt with Preston's name on it gave me a renewed burst of energy. I found another John Miller—definitely a regular—but even though I finished out the box with no potential leads on an alias for Preston, I was determined to keep looking. Even if I had to go through every old receipt in this place.

The next box had a few Johns, although I doubted any of them were actually Preston. The handwriting on one was completely different. Another had been spilled on and the last name was obscured, so it wouldn't have been any help. And the third was just John Miller again.

Heidi, a local girl who worked at the Copper Kettle, came up behind the counter. "Morning, Rob."

"Oh hi there, Heidi," he said. "Have you been filled in on what's going on?"

"Yeah. I just got here for my shift. It's terrible." She pulled her hair back and tied it in a low ponytail. "What are you doing with those? Can I help?"

"Sure. The man we think took Marigold is Preston Bradford. He started coming in here pretty regularly and I could have sworn at least once he used a credit card with a different name. Seems like it was John something."

"Do you mean the crappy tipper?"

I glanced up. "What?"

"He was the rich guy, right? Always dressed nice. He looked like he had plenty of money but his tips were terrible."

"Figures," I said. "Do you remember him using a different name?"

"No."

"Damn. Actually, that gives us one more clue. A guy named John who tips like shit."

"Are you going through all the receipts?" Heidi asked, pulling a box toward her.

"Yep. If the cops come up with a better lead, great," I said. "Until then, I'm going to track that fucker down any way I can."

I had to. I had to find Marigold. Maybe digging through receipts was useless, but so was driving up and down the highways with no idea which way he'd taken her. What else were we supposed to do?

Keep doing stupid shit until something worked.

Rob brought out more boxes. Heidi found a Preston receipt and we came up with a few more Johns, but nothing that seemed like it could be Preston's alias. I started to wonder if Rob had remembered it correctly. What if the name on his credit card had been something else? James or Josh or Jake. Was it definitely John? Had we missed it already in one of the boxes we'd searched?

I was in such a rhythm—grabbing a receipt, checking the name, setting it aside—I almost missed it. A receipt with the name John Saladin.

It wasn't just the crappy tip that caught my attention. It was the signature. The name on the receipt was John Saladin, but the signature read Preston Bradford.

He'd made a mistake. Used the wrong card. Signed the wrong name.

"I got him." I jumped off the stool and took the receipt, along with one that had his real name and signature, over to Garrett. "Check this out. This one says John Saladin, but that's his signature."

"Holy shit," Garrett muttered. "You're right."

"What can we find out about him? There's gotta be something."

He pulled out his phone and made a call. "Hey. Can you run the name John Saladin? Anything you can find." He moved the phone and spoke to me. "Brenna at the station. She's a research genius."

I nodded. Standing with my arms crossed, I tried to hold still while my body buzzed with anticipation.

"You're kidding," Garrett said. "Yeah, I'd say that's significant."

"What?" I asked.

"Property records show a piece of land about two hours north of here owned by a John Saladin. It's pretty deep in the woods, but it looks like there's a cabin on it."

"Let's go."

"Z, it might be a total dead end."

"He said something about a cabin. Or his friend did. I overheard them."

He spoke into his phone again. "Can you send me the address?"

"Text it to me." I was already heading out the door.

"Z, wait up," Garrett called, jogging to catch up with me.

"You coming?"

"You're sure as hell not going alone."

I opened the driver's side door of my truck. "Then get in."

CHAPTER 36

Marigold

AS SOON AS PRESTON LEFT, I'd checked the doors and windows. Unsurprisingly, the doors were locked from the outside and none of the windows opened. I'd already considered smashing through the glass, but the windows on the ground floor were paned and I wasn't sure if I'd be able to break the structure between the panes of glass. The one window in the loft was so high off the ground, I didn't know how we'd make it down even if we broke it open.

Bedsheets, maybe? Was that a trick that actually worked?

I also had to consider whether Brielle would try to stop me.

Could I convince her I'd help her escape too? Or was she too afraid of Preston to try? So far, she'd just watched me. But her eyes seemed to be clearing, making me wonder if he'd drugged her too. That might have accounted for her glassy expression and her compliance.

Other than doors that locked from the outside, the cabin was disturbingly ordinary. It had a couch and TV, a few books and games on a shelf nearby, as well as a collection of old DVDs. The kitchen had clearly been in use. The garbage was half full and there were a few dishes in the sink. A decorative sign on the wall read Cabin Life is the Best Life, and soft throw pillows and blankets gave it a cozy vibe.

"So, Brielle," I said, hoping to get her talking. I needed to figure out if she was going to help or hinder. "You said John brought you here? And you've been living here since then?"

"Mostly," she said. "We had to leave for a while but for the most part, I've been here."

"Was he living here with you?" I asked. I was still confused as to why she was calling him John, but maybe it was the name he'd given her. For all I knew, it was his real name. Preston could have been made up.

"No, he never stayed here. He came and went a lot."

"Did he lock you in like this? Or did you want to stay?"

She glanced away. "Both, I guess. I think I was locked in at first, even though he said the door just stuck. I got out once, but I don't know if he forgot to lock it or if he was testing me." She paused. "I thought he was going to take care of me."

"Is that what he told you?"

"I'm so stupid." Her voice went quiet. "He told me he had a sister who ran away and that was why he wanted to help me. I don't know if he even has a sister. Do you know?"

"No, I don't."

"It doesn't matter. I should have figured it out, but I kept telling myself he was just a really cool guy. Even when he brought a friend here. He gave me something, so I was pretty high, but I know what he made me do. John just watched."

She didn't have to give me the details. I understood what she was getting at and it broke my heart. "Oh, Brielle. That's so wrong."

"He didn't want to help me, he just wanted me to become one of his girls."

A chill ran down my spine. "What does that mean, exactly? One of his girls?"

"I met one of them when we had to leave for a while. They're prostitutes. She said they don't like that word. They say luxury companions. But it's the same thing. Doesn't matter how rich the clients are, you're still selling your body."

I put my hand over my mouth, feeling nauseated again. "Oh, Brielle."

"That's what the lodge is for," she continued, and I got the feeling she just needed to get this all out. "The other girl, Desi, was really excited about the lodge. She said the best girls will get to live there. They'll go to big parties with rich people and service their clients there instead of in hotels."

"Oh my god, that's why he's building that mansion?"

She nodded. "But Desi said to do what I'm told or he'll send me away. She said girls who are sent away don't come back. They're sold."

"Sold?" I couldn't keep the shock out of my voice. "To whom?"

"I don't know. But I know it can't be good."

"No, that's definitely not good." I took a deep breath, hoping to ease the returning nausea.

Preston Bradford was a sex trafficker.

And he had me locked in his cabin.

This was so surreal, it was hard to acknowledge the depth of my fear. Was this actually happening?

"What are we going to do?" Brielle asked, her voice breaking. "I don't know what he's going to do to me when he comes back."

I moved in close and took her by the upper arms. "He's not going to do anything. Do you hear me? We're going to get away and he's not going to have the chance."

She nodded.

"But we have to be in this together. I can't help you if you're trying to sabotage me because you're afraid of him."

"I won't. I want to get away. I don't know where I'll go when I do, but I can't stay with him."

"We're not going to. We're going to find a way out of here."

How, was another story. As was what we would do once we got free. I had no way of knowing where we were. The drive here was a black hole in my memory. I had no direction, no time frame, nothing. At least the sun was coming up. It would be easier to find our way in the light.

I closed my eyes and said a silent prayer that Zachary was looking for me. In my heart of hearts, I knew he was. That he'd stop at nothing until he found me. If we could get out, someone would find us eventually. Even if we were in the middle of nowhere, hours from Tilikum, there had to be people searching. I had to believe we'd be rescued, if we could just get out.

"First things first," I said. "We need to break a window or something."

"I don't think we can get out any of those."

"What about upstairs? We could make a rope out of bed sheets and lower ourselves down."

"Will that work?"

"We'll only know if we try."

I went to the kitchen and found a frying pan. It was sturdy and hard. I hoped it would be strong enough to break the glass.

Brielle followed me upstairs and started stripping the bed. I told her to stand back while I took a whack at the window.

I swung the pan as hard as I could, smashing it against the glass. It left a deep indent and cracks snaked out from the center, but it didn't break. I hit it a few more times, hoping the sharp glass didn't come flying back at me. Finally, I broke through, the glass shattering outward.

Cold air blew in as I used the pan to push the remaining shards outside. The window wasn't large, so I needed to make sure as much of the glass was gone as possible, otherwise we'd shred ourselves to ribbons on the way out. We didn't need to add bleeding cuts to our list of problems. Especially when we were about to head into the wilderness in late fall without any way of knowing where we were or how to get to safety.

One problem at a time, Marigold.

"I don't think this is going to be long enough," Brielle said.

She'd tied the sheets together, but we needed to tie it off on something sturdy to anchor it. And she was right, it wasn't going to reach very far.

But maybe it would be far enough. We just had to get down without breaking any bones.

The urgency to get out made my heart race. Preston could return any minute. I took a few seconds to look for more sheets so we could make our rope longer, but there was only an old quilt in a drawer. Nothing else that would help us get down.

I took the old quilt and unfolded it, then had Brielle help me drop it out the window. It wouldn't cushion our fall, but at least it might cover up some of the glass shards. Then we tied the bed sheet rope to the bed frame and pushed the bed closer to the window.

"Are you ready?" I asked Brielle.

"Where do we go once we're out? Down the road? It should meet up with the highway somewhere."

"No, too much risk of Preston coming back and catching us. We should—" I was about to say we should use the road as a guide but stay hidden in the woods, when the distinct sound of a car came from outside.

Brielle's eyes widened in terror.

I tossed the rope out the window. "You go first."

She climbed onto the bed and scrambled out the window. My heart pounded as I watched, leaning out so I could grab her if necessary. She braced herself with her feet on the side of the cabin and lowered herself down as far as she could. Then she looked up.

"Jump down," I said, trying to keep my voice low. "Roll when you hit the ground."

She squeezed her eyes shut for a second, then let go. The drop wasn't too far. She hit the ground and rolled, then got to her feet.

"I'm okay," she said. "Come down."

I didn't even look over my shoulder to see if Preston was already inside. With blood roaring in my ears, I climbed out the window, over the ledge, and held on for dear life.

It was hard to brace myself against the cabin in my stupid heels, but there was nothing I could do about that. I didn't want to be barefoot once I got outside. My arms burned with the effort as I climbed down. A voice came from inside, making my heart jump, and I let go, hoping I didn't break a leg when I hit the ground.

I didn't even try to keep my feet. I let the fall take me, rolling into the impact. A funny memory of Theo Haven teaching me how to roll when I fell off a swing came back to me. An odd thought to have while my life was in danger, but I was grateful my body seemed to remember the maneuver.

Brielle grabbed my hands to help me up and we raced away from the cabin together.

Behind us, I heard a man's voice, harsh with anger. Was it Preston? Had he come up to the loft just as we'd fled out the window?

It didn't sound like him. Although that might have been my fear-soaked imagination.

My heels sank into the wet ground, making it hard to pick up any speed. I tried to keep my head, orienting myself to the cabin and the road leading away, but everything was happening so fast.

My stomach sank as I noticed we were leaving a clear trail into the woods. There was no way to avoid leaving footprints in the muddy ground. It would be a matter of minutes before Preston—or whoever it was—found us.

"Keep going," I said, half breathless.

My back tensed as a noise came from behind us. Someone was crashing through the brush.

We were screwed.

I risked a look over my shoulder. Sure enough, a man was following us into the woods. He was dressed in a black wool coat, but it wasn't his clothes that struck me.

That wasn't Preston. It was his friend, Drew.

A shot rang out behind us and Brielle reached out to grab me. We stopped and I drew her close to me, putting an arm around her.

Slowly, I turned around. Drew stood a short distance behind us, his arm raised. A gunshot. He'd just fired a gun into the air.

His arm moved so the gun was pointing at us. "I'd rather not shoot you, but I will if you run."

I believed him. His casual tone was too honest—too matter of fact—to be a bluff.

"Come on back, girls," he said, gesturing with the gun.

Brielle clung to me, her body trembling. I took a breath to steady myself—to find some semblance of courage—and led her back toward the cabin.

Drew watched us with a dispassionate expression. "Let's go. I don't have all day. We need to get out of here before Preston comes back."

Wait, what? Preston wasn't there?

Drew couldn't be there to rescue us, could he? If he were there to help, why would he threaten to shoot us if we ran?

None of this made sense. But considering Drew was armed, I was reluctant to start asking questions.

He motioned for us to walk in front of him. The gun was still in his hand and my back tightened as I passed him. It felt like walking to my death. Any second, a bullet would rip through my body from behind.

Would Zachary ever find me? Would he know what had happened to me?

It was hard not to let fear take over. But I couldn't give up now. I held onto Brielle as Drew took us around to the front of the cabin and put us in the backseat of a car. He didn't say a word as he got in. Just set the gun in his lap and turned the car around.

I didn't know where he was taking us, but I took courage in the fact that he hadn't shot us at the cabin. If he'd been there to kill us, he could have done it easily. Moving us wasn't necessarily a good sign either, but at least it meant I still had a chance to find a way out.

I could still get away. Somehow.

CHAPTER 37

Zachary

THE DRIVE to the cabin felt like an eternity. I had zero respect for the speed limit and, to his credit, Garrett didn't say a word. We headed north on the wet highway, winding through the mountains. Thankfully the storm had let up, but the steel gray sky threatened more rain.

We didn't talk. Didn't speculate about what we were going to find or try to make a plan B in case this was a dead end. Just drove in silence, united in grim determination to find her.

The property didn't have an address so much as coordinates, and Google maps certainly didn't recognize it. I had to trust Garrett to navigate as best he could. He took us off the highway in the middle of nowhere, down a long road with enough potholes to break my suspension. I had to swerve more than once, my tires skidding on the wet pavement.

"Turn left," he said out of the blue.

I didn't see anything that looked remotely like a road. Just trees. "Where?"

"There!"

I slammed on the brakes to slow down enough to make

the turn and we flew around the corner, tires digging into the mud of a poorly maintained gravel road.

The ruts were deep and tree branches scraped the sides of the truck. I had to stop clenching my teeth or I was going to crack a molar with all the bumps. My entire body was saturated with adrenaline, no sign of the fatigue of a sleepless night.

She was out there. We were going to find her.

Hang on, Marigold. I'm almost there.

Finally, a structure emerged in the distance. A small cabin —probably one story with a loft—sat in the middle of a clearing, looking oddly cozy and innocent from the outside. I half expected to see a curl of smoke from the chimney.

Garrett and I got out and he motioned for me to wait before approaching the door. As much as I wanted to barrel inside, I knew he was right. There weren't any vehicles that I could see, but that didn't mean she wasn't here.

Maybe it just meant we got lucky and Preston had dumped her off and left.

Without saying a word, we crept up to the front door. There was a locking gate latch—a way to lock the door from the outside.

But it hung from the doorframe. Someone had dismantled it.

Garrett shrugged. I didn't know what that meant, either. He nodded, indicating he was ready to go inside, and drew his weapon, so I let him take the lead, and followed him in.

No one jumped out or pointed a gun at us, so that was a good first step.

The first thing I noticed was the cold. It wasn't any warmer inside than out. We took slow steps around the ground floor, checking in the kitchen and bathroom.

Once again, no sign of her.

It seemed like a breeze was blowing in from the loft. I nodded toward the stairs and started up.

If it was hard to tell anything from the ground floor, the loft was another story. Something had clearly gone down. The bed was at an odd angle, pushed up against the one wall with a window in it. The glass was broken out almost completely and cold air streamed in. My eyes widened as I saw there was a sheet tied to the bed, hanging out the window.

She'd escaped. My badass woman had escaped out the window.

"Outside," I said, rushing past Garrett and flying down the stairs.

He followed and we raced around the building. A quilt was on the ground below the window and shards of broken glass sparkled, even with the sun hidden behind dark clouds.

"That way," Garrett said, pointing to the ground.

Her path was clear, footsteps in the wet ground leading to the trees. I took a deep breath so I could start calling for her, but Garrett stopped me.

"Wait," he hissed. "We don't know who's out here."

We followed the tracks into the trees. I was no expert, but I'd grown up running around the woods, and it looked to me like there was more than one set of footprints. In some places, there were multiple tracks on top of each other.

Someone following her? Had she been caught?

Then the footprints stopped.

Garrett went ahead a little farther, but came back shaking his head. "They stop here. She must have turned around."

"Was she followed?" I asked, pointing to what looked like a sneaker print. "That doesn't look like her shoes."

Garrett tilted his head, looking at the ground. "That's not very big. It's either a woman's shoe or a guy with really small feet."

I looked around, my heart sinking into the pit of my stomach. Where was she?

What might have been another set of footprints led toward the front of the cabin. "I see them too," Garrett said. "I have a feeling she got out the window and someone caught up with her here, then left in a vehicle. But I don't know why Preston would bring her all the way out here only to move her again so soon."

"Other than the fact that she broke a window and escaped?"

"True."

"What the fuck do we do now?"

He put his gun away and pulled out his phone. "I need to get back to where I have a signal so I can call in this location. Get search and rescue out here in case she's still on foot. And make sure state patrol knows to be on the lookout this far north."

A coal of rage simmered in my gut. I was not giving in to despair. She wasn't here, but she'd been here. I was sure of it. That meant we were on the right track. We were going to find her.

Garrett kept trying to get a call to go through as we hurried to my truck. I went back inside the cabin to make sure we hadn't missed anything. Maybe she'd left a clue behind. But there wasn't anything I could see, and we needed to get closer to civilization so Garrett could get in touch with the cops back in Tilikum.

I went outside and paused at a noise. Was that a vehicle? Garrett looked up in alarm. He'd heard it too.

There was only one road in or out, at least that I could see. If someone was coming down that road, we were trapped.

We didn't have time to think about a plan before a black full-size sedan appeared. The driver stopped abruptly and the door flew open.

Preston Bradford stepped out of the car.

"Where the fuck is she?" I started toward him, ready to tear him to pieces, but Garrett grabbed me before I could get far. "What did you do with her?"

"What are you doing here?"

"I'm asking the questions. Where is she?"

And then the weirdest thing happened. He blinked and a flash of alarm crossed his features. He looked past us, at the open cabin door, his eyes widening. "Oh, fuck."

Garrett let me go, and while I still wanted to kill the fucker, I was too confused to go at him. Yet. "What?"

Preston jogged by, giving us a wide berth, and went to the front door. He touched the dismantled gate latch, then barreled his way in.

Garrett followed with me close on his heels. We watched Preston tear through the cabin, swearing under his breath.

I lowered my voice. "What the fuck is happening?"

"I don't know," Garrett said. "But I don't think he knows I'm a cop."

"Let's keep it that way."

"That piece of shit." Preston's voice rose as he stormed outside. "I never should have trusted him."

"Who? Where's Marigold?"

Garrett and I followed him outside. He stopped, and when he turned, I almost flinched away. His face was red and I'd be lying if I said his expression didn't scare me a little. It would have scared any man with half a brain. He wasn't simply angry, he was unhinged.

"Fucking Drew." Preston practically spat out the words. "He has her."

"Who the hell is Drew?"

"My partner. He's the only one who knows this place exists."

"Are you saying you abducted Marigold and then your fucking partner abducted her from you?"

"I didn't abduct her," Preston snapped. "I brought her home."

"Oh great, he's batshit," I muttered. "This will be fun."

"Careful," Garrett said, his voice low. "We don't know if he's armed."

At this point, I didn't give a shit whether or not he was armed, although I probably should have. "Where would Drew take her?"

He let out a breath and shook his head slowly. "He's trying to get rid of her."

The hit of fear almost knocked me over. "Is he going to kill her?"

"No. Too messy. And there's no money in it. He'll offload her to one of our runners. In forty-eight hours, she'll be in Moscow. Maybe Bogata, I don't know. Depends on which container she ends up in."

"He's going to fucking sell her?" I shouted, not quite believing what I'd just said.

"He'll try. It makes sense. He thinks she's too big of a risk to keep. I never should have left her here. Fuck."

"Fuck is right, you psycho piece of shit." Garrett tried to stop me, but I wasn't done. "You're going to take us to them. Now."

He hesitated, his eyes on me. This wasn't the Preston I remembered from the job site. That man had been tightly controlled—and totally in charge. This guy had a wildness in his eyes, like one wrong step and he'd lose it.

I knew that look. I'd worn it many times. Usually right before I did something stupid, like punch a guy in the face in front of my cop brother.

A guy like that—about to lose control—was dangerous. But he could also be manipulated. I just had to turn the tables and be the one to stay calm.

Not my best skill, I admit, but I could do anything if it would save Marigold.

I had a hunch about him and I just hoped I was right. I took the intensity out of my voice. "You have a choice. Show us where he's taking her. Or let him keep her. Which means you lose."

The flash of fury that rippled across his features told me

I'd nailed it. This guy couldn't stand losing. He was going to help us rescue Marigold, even if only to make sure he won.

I had no idea what we were going to do about him after that. Obviously he wasn't going to just let us take Marigold home. But one thing at a time. Especially since he'd just said his partner was taking her to be fucking *sold*.

I could see Preston weighing his options. There were two of us, one of him. I was betting he wasn't armed, otherwise he would have gone for his weapon already. He was trying to decide if he wanted to try to take us out now, or after we got Marigold.

"Fine." He adjusted his jacket, but the gesture did nothing to calm the ferocity in his eyes. If anything, his buttoned-up exterior made him look crazier. Those eyes didn't look right in that face. "Follow me."

"Where are we going?" Garrett asked.

"Pasco," he said, and got in his car.

"What the fuck is in Pasco?" Garrett asked as we got in my truck.

A sick feeling spread through my stomach. "A port. It's right on the Columbia."

"That's got to be like five hours from here."

I turned around and started down the road, following Preston. "Probably."

"Do you actually think he's going to take us to her?"

"He's not thinking straight. I can see it in his eyes. So yeah, I do think he's going to take us to her."

I glanced at my brother. He wasn't acting like Garrett the cop. That guy wouldn't have let Preston get in his car, let alone agree to follow the psycho five hours south hoping he'd lead us to my abducted girlfriend.

"Are you going to get fired for this?"

"Maybe."

"Then why didn't you arrest him back there or something?"

"Because, God help me, I think you're right. He's the only chance we have of finding Marigold before it's too late." He turned to look at me. "I'll break every fucking rule in the book if that's what it takes to get her back."

Damn. Maybe my brother wasn't a robot after all.

I nodded. He nodded back. And for once in our lives, we understood each other.

Preston's partner was going to put her in a shipping container. If he managed that, finding her would be basically impossible. And if Preston was right, in a few days, she'd be long gone.

Once again, Garrett and I drove in silence. We didn't try to figure out what we were going to do with Preston once we found Marigold.

One thing at a time. Find her. Then figure out the rest.

Only Marigold mattered.

CHAPTER 38

Marigold

WE'D BEEN in the car for hours, and I still had no idea where we were going. Drew drove exactly the speed limit, slowed through every town the highway passed through, and even stopped once for gas. Naturally, he threatened to kill us if we tried anything, and the empty gas station in the middle of nowhere wasn't going to do us much good anyway.

I held Brielle close, doing my best to give her what little comfort I could. Her body was stiff with terror but she hardly made a sound. If there were tears to be cried, they'd come later. I had a feeling the poor girl was going to need an awful lot of therapy if we ever got out of this.

My eyes grew heavy as the miles passed. I'd been rendered unconscious, but that didn't really count as sleep. My mouth was dry with thirst and I had no idea when I'd last eaten. It was hard to tell if the knots in my stomach were fear, hunger, or maybe a bit of both.

But mostly fear.

I shifted to ease the pressure on my hip and readjusted my arm around Brielle. Drew's eyes flicked to me in the rearview mirror.

For the first time since the cabin, I spoke up. "Where are you taking us?"

He watched me for a moment, his gaze moving from the mirror to the road, then back again. "I'm taking you to one of our associates."

"What is he going to do with us?"

"Do you really want to know?"

I nodded.

"Depends on what he thinks of you. And where his people are headed in the near future. That one," he said, his eyes moving to Brielle, "is going to make me a good amount of money. You? You're older than we usually deal in and a hell of a lot feistier than I'd like. But some money is better than none. And it's certainly better than you ruining our entire operation."

The reality of what he was saying threatened to suck the air from my lungs, but I forced myself to speak. I wanted to keep him talking. "I don't know anything about your operation. How could I ruin it?"

"Preston has his eccentricities. Most of the time, I'm willing to overlook them. But you're a risk he never should have taken. He actually thought he could keep you at the lodge. Her, I can see. He knows how to get in their heads. A couple more months, he'd have had her drinking milk from a saucer and thanking him for it. But you? No way. I don't care if he kept you at his cabin for years, the first chance you got, you'd have bolted. And then we'd all be screwed."

He was right about that. I'd never have stopped trying to escape.

I wasn't going to stop now, either. Unfortunately, Drew obviously knew it.

"Does your wife know about all this?" I asked.

He chuckled. "She doesn't want to know. She's happy to look the other way as long as the money doesn't run out."

I couldn't decide if I felt sorry for Tess or not. Being

married to this nightmare of a man? Horrible. But was she willfully ignorant, or did she actually not know? It was hard to say.

"Are we going to be kept together?" I asked.

He shrugged. "Once I have my money, you're not my problem anymore. He can do whatever he wants with you."

Brielle's arms tightened around me. I squeezed her back.

Eventually, we came to a small city. The signs said Pasco. I'd heard of it, but I'd never been there. He got off the highway and made his way through town, clearly familiar with the route. A few raindrops splattered on the windshield and I vaguely wondered if a storm would work in our favor.

Or make things worse.

He turned into a large parking lot with warehouses. The complex was surrounded by a chain link fence, but the gate was open and the entire place seemed deserted. Concrete buildings were littered with graffiti and there were stacks of crates and boxes stacked haphazardly against the walls. He pulled around one of the buildings, out of sight of the road, and parked. Then he twisted in his seat to look at us.

"Anyone within earshot of us works for me. There's no one to hear you scream. No one to help you. And if you try to get away, I'll just kill you and be done with it. Understand?"

Brielle and I nodded.

"Good girls."

He took his gun and got out of the car, then used his key fob to lock the doors. He glanced at us and held up his weapon, making his point clear. Then he walked toward one of the warehouse buildings and disappeared around the corner.

"He's going to sell us," Brielle said. "Just like Desi said. They sell the girls they don't want to keep."

"No one is getting sold." I had to dig deep to sound as determined as I did, but there was no way this was happening. "We almost got away once. We're going to get away for good."

I tried the door, but of course it didn't open. Child locks. But there wouldn't be child locks on the driver's side. I hesitated. He wouldn't have left sight of the car if we could just open the door and get out, would he?

I started picturing snipers positioned around the rooftops of the warehouse. But that was silly, right? No one was going to pick us off if we escaped the car. Although, could opening the door from the inside set off the alarm?

It was a risk I'd have to take. Maybe Drew would come back around the corner and shoot me. But I couldn't sit here and wait for him to sell me to some human trafficker.

I crawled between the front seats and tried the driver's side door.

Locked.

"How is this locked?" I jerked on the handle a few times, then pressed the unlock button over and over, but it was like it had no power.

I reached across to the passenger side door. It was locked too. I tried the unlock button on the door again, but nothing happened.

"This isn't normal," I said.

"Could he have done something to the car so it stays locked without the remote?"

"He must have." A shiver ran down my spine. We clearly weren't the first women he'd transported in this car, for this purpose.

I checked the glove box, but it was empty. There weren't even service records inside. Same with the center console.

I knew from a safety video my dad had made me watch that windshields would break from the inside if you were ever stuck in your car after an accident. But there was nothing we could use to break it.

Then I looked down at my shoes. The stupid heels I'd put

on in my hurry to confront my dad.

That thought almost brought tears to my eyes. It seemed so long ago. Had it really only been a day? And had I really been so concerned about something that had happened back in high school? It all seemed so ridiculous now.

I had to get out.

My heart beat fast, but otherwise, I was strangely calm. "Get ready to run."

I scrambled to the passenger seat so I had more room, put my feet up, bent my knees, and kicked.

My heels stuck into the windshield, leaving cracks around them. Grateful for that little ankle strap, I pulled back, dislodging them, and kicked again.

The windshield shattered.

"Let's go."

Fortunately, the safety glass didn't slice us open as we got enough of the debris out of the way to climb out. I got out first, then helped Brielle. I could feel panic trying to take hold —Drew could come back around that corner any second—but I forced myself to stay calm.

We needed to get out of sight. There was another building in the opposite direction of where Drew had gone. I grabbed Brielle's hand and we took off toward it. With every breath, I feared I'd feel the impact of a bullet. Would Drew try to stop us, or just mow us down without a word?

Somehow, we reached the building and took cover on one side. I pressed my back against the wall, hoping we hadn't made things worse.

Before I could figure out what to do next—we were still within the fence and all too easy to find—all hell broke loose.

Drew started yelling obscenities but was cut off by the sound of vehicle engines. Someone else had arrived.

I froze, hope surging through me like heat from a flame. I didn't know how I knew—how I could be sure. But I was.

It was Zachary.

CHAPTER 39

Zachary

PRESTON PULLED into what looked like an abandoned warehouse complex on the river. A chain-link gate was open and we drove right in.

Two things immediately caught my attention. One, the lone car parked up ahead. It was angled just enough that I could see the broken windshield. And two, the boat tied up to the dock.

That had to be the boat that was going to take Marigold west where they'd smuggle her out of the country. Was she on it already?

I didn't have time to consider our options or make a plan. Preston got out of his car and started talking to another man —and that dude was pissed.

"All we have to do is stall for time until local law enforcement gets here," Garrett said. "Don't do anything stupid."

"If she's on that boat, we can't let it leave."

"I know."

We got out and I could see Garrett ready to draw his weapon. I held up a hand, hoping he wouldn't. Not yet.

"Drew," Preston said, taking a few steps closer to the other guy. "Where are they?"

"Who the fuck are they?" Drew asked, gesturing toward me and Garrett.

"Don't worry about them," Preston said.

I caught sight of a third man, hanging back, closer to the dock. Shit. I'd been in bar fights with worse odds—and won —but I had to assume these guys were armed. That was a totally different situation.

"I am going to worry about them," Drew said. "You're losing it, Preston."

"Just give me the girls."

Girls? Garrett mouthed.

I shrugged.

Drew shook his head. "You've gotten too arrogant, my friend. You think you can get away with anything."

"My track record speaks for itself."

"You never took risks like this before. We both know she's a liability now."

Even from a slight distance, I could see Preston's jaw hitch and fury flashing across his features. "She's mine. Do you hear me? She's mine and you're going to give her to me."

The third guy backed up slowly toward the dock. I cast around, wondering where Marigold was. She had to be on that boat. And by the looks of it, that other dude wanted out of there.

"I can't do that," Drew said. "You're putting our entire operation at risk. Look at yourself. You're losing your mind."

"Where is she?" Preston asked through clenched teeth.

"You're making a mess of this." Drew's eyes flicked to us. "And now I have to clean it up."

Drew reached under his jacket and the third guy bolted for the boat.

"Get down." Garrett was already drawing his weapon.

Heedless of the danger, I took off running for the dock. I was not letting that asshole leave if my woman was on board.

"Drop your weapon!" Garrett said.

I didn't stop.

"Drop it!"

A shot fired. I kept running until the third guy turned, pointing a gun at me. I skidded to a halt and dropped to the ground.

More shots fired in rapid succession. I looked back in time to see Drew fall to the ground. Garrett took aim at the third guy and fired until he crumpled onto the dock.

"Holy shit," I said, practically breathless.

"You okay, Z?" Garrett called.

"Yeah."

Preston was still standing. He had his hands slightly up, as if considering surrender. Then his features transformed, his cool confidence melting into abject malevolence. He dove for Drew's gun and I watched in horror as he raised it, not pointing it at Garrett—the only armed man left standing—but at me.

I started to shout for my brother when an engine revved and tires squealed. Preston's car came roaring toward him. It hit him head on, throwing him backward onto the concrete with a sickening crunch.

The driver's door opened and Marigold got out.

For a split second, I couldn't move. The clouds broke behind her and a beam of light lit her up from behind. It was like that day at her salon when I'd been shocked. She was an angel, glowing with beauty.

"Zachary!"

I scrambled to my feet as she ran toward me. She landed in my arms and I held her tight. My heart felt like it would beat right out of my chest as waves of relief washed over me.

She was here. We'd found her. She was here.

"Are you okay?" I kissed her hair. "Baby, are you all right?"

"I'm okay." Her voice was slightly breathless. "Are you?"

"I am now."

Several cop cars sped onto the scene, blue and red lights flashing. I caught Garrett's eyes and nodded to him. I'd never be able to repay him for what he'd done for Marigold today. I resolved never to do something so stupid that he might have to arrest me ever again. Probably not enough, but it was a start.

He set down his weapon and held up his hands, shouting that he was law enforcement. I let him handle that side of things while I held Marigold. I didn't want to let her go.

Finally she pulled away and started to turn toward Preston. I touched her face and turned her to me. "You don't have to look."

"Oh my god, Brielle."

"Brielle?"

She twisted around. "Brielle? Are you okay? It's safe to come out."

"Wait, wasn't the missing girl from Tilikum named Brielle?"

Marigold nodded. "Preston had her."

A blond woman came out from behind a stack of wooden crates. She ran to Marigold, eyes streaming with tears.

Marigold wrapped her arms around her. "It's okay. We're safe. It's over now."

I stared at my girl in absolute awe. I didn't know the details of what had happened, but I had a feeling I could figure it out. Drew had brought them here to sell them off to human traffickers. And Marigold had been well on her way to escaping on her own. She must have broken out the windshield of Drew's car. And when it counted, she'd done what she had to do.

She'd saved my life. And Preston couldn't hurt anyone, ever again.

She let go of Brielle and I grabbed her, hauling her against me. I needed to feel her breathe. Feel the warmth of her body next to mine.

"I love you." I kissed her forehead. "I love you so much."

"I love you too. How did you find us?"

"It's a long story."

She smiled. "I knew you would. I knew you were looking for me."

"Baby, I would have gone to the ends of the earth to find you."

I leaned down and kissed her, savoring the softness of her lips. She was alive. And I was never, ever letting her go.

CHAPTER 40

Marigold

THE SUN HAD GONE DOWN by the time we got to Tilikum. I'd spent the drive cuddled up next to Zachary with Garrett on my other side. I'd dozed off and on, my body feeling the strain of everything I'd been through. Each time my eyes fluttered open, I'd been greeted by the warmth of Zachary next to me.

I was safe.

Once law enforcement had arrived on the scene in Pasco, paramedics had looked us over. Thankfully, we'd all escaped without major injuries. I was a little banged up, probably from the jump out the cabin window.

They'd taken us to the local police station to get our statements and it was clear they believed we were the victims, not the perpetrators. Fortunately, they were sympathetic and compassionate. Someone brought us food, and once they had the full story, they let us go home.

Although Brielle didn't have serious injuries, it had been determined the best thing for her would be to go to the hospital in Tilikum, where she'd spend the night. Law enforcement would drive her there.

I didn't know what would happen to her then. She'd

made it clear she didn't want to go home. And from what I'd seen of her family, I didn't blame her. She was an adult, so she didn't have to. But I wasn't sure what her other options would be.

A problem for another day. For now, I just wanted to get home.

Zachary pulled up to the house after we'd dropped Garrett off at his place. I'd already called my parents to let them know I was safe and unhurt, but it didn't surprise me to see their car in my driveway. They jumped out of the car and ran to me as soon as I got out of Zachary's truck, catching me in a tight hug between them. Surprisingly, I didn't cry. I was probably too exhausted. But I did rest in the relief of seeing them again.

When my dad pulled away, he had tears in his eyes. "I'm so glad you're safe."

"Me too," I said.

Mom kissed me on the cheek. "We were so scared. It's so good to have you back."

Dad met Zachary's eyes and, without a word, stepped in to hug him too.

"Thank you," he said, his voice breaking. "Thank you for bringing her home."

Zachary hugged him back. "I wasn't coming back without her."

"You must be exhausted," Mom said, brushing my hair back from my face. "We'll let you go. We just had to see you."

"I'm glad you were here," I said.

"Get some rest," Dad said. "If you want to tell us more about what happened, we can do that later."

"Where's Brielle tonight?" Mom asked.

"They're taking her to the hospital here in town."

"Good." Mom glanced at Dad and I wasn't sure what her look meant. "Poor thing."

"She's been through a lot," I said. "And she's definitely going to need help."

"At least she's safe now," Dad said. He cleared his throat. "All right, flower. Get some rest. I'm sure you need it."

We finished our goodbyes and I was a little bit surprised they hadn't either insisted I go home with them or that they stay at my place. But they didn't even ask to come in. They'd actually understood I was exhausted and just needed to go to bed.

And maybe they finally trusted Zachary to be the one to take care of me when I needed it.

He led me inside and relief washed over me. It felt so good to be home. And not just home, but home with him. I was right where I was supposed to be, safe and loved.

We went straight for the shower to wash off the horrors of the previous twenty-four hours. Then we tucked into bed. Despite my exhaustion, I drifted on the brink of sleep for a while. I was warm and relaxed, content in Zachary's arms.

————

Zachary held my hand as we walked down the hospital hallway. We'd hardly broken physical contact since he'd found me, only separating to deal with biological necessities. Touching made us both feel better, even if it was just our hands clasped together.

Garrett had called first thing and let us know the FBI had been called in to investigate Preston's sex trafficking operation. It turned out, they were already onto some of his associates, including Drew. But discovering Preston was at the center of it had the potential to blow their investigation wide open. They hadn't given Garrett any more details, but they were working on following all the trails of evidence so they could take down as many of the people involved as possible.

We paused outside Brielle's room. Now that we were free, I wasn't sure what more I could do to help her. But I needed to at least see her—let her know I was here for her as she processed everything she'd been through.

The girl in the bed almost looked like someone else. Her blond hair was clean and glossy and her cheeks a healthy pink. The bright smile she gave me as I walked in warmed my heart.

Preston hadn't broken her. She had a lot of healing to do—and she'd need professional help to do it—but I could see the life in her eyes. She was going to make it.

"Look at you, lovely," I said, coming to sit on the edge of the bed. "You look so much better today."

"I feel better," she said. "A shower helped a lot and one of the nurses brought me a hair dryer."

"Did you do this blowout?" I gently touched her hair. "It looks great."

She nodded. "The bathroom is really small but I managed."

"How do you feel today?"

She took a deep breath. "Better. A lot of it still feels like a blur, you know? It's almost like a dream. I can't believe it happened."

"And you told the police everything?"

"Everything I could remember." Her eyes moved to Zachary. "Thank you for rescuing us."

He grinned. "You two were doing a pretty good job rescuing yourselves. But I'm glad I was there to help out."

"Marigold, you saved my life. I know it's not a good thing John... I mean, Preston, kidnapped you like that. But if you hadn't been there, I don't know what would have happened to me. Actually, I do know, and it isn't good."

"I'm so glad we got you out. The whole town was looking for you. Did you know that?"

"My parents weren't."

I glanced at Zachary. She wasn't wrong about that and it broke my heart. "Sounds like there's a lot of brokenness in your family."

"Life sucked at home. I'd moved out and was living with my boyfriend, but I found out he was cheating. That was why I left town. I wanted to disappear and start a new life. I don't know what I'm going to do now, but I can't live with my parents."

Zachary nudged me. "Can I see you in the hall for a second?"

"Sure." I took Brielle's hand and squeezed. "I'll be right back."

I followed him out. He leaned in and lowered his voice.

"I wonder if we can find a place for her to stay."

My eyes widened. "I wonder if my parents would take her in."

"That's not a bad idea. Seems like they could use another kid to overprotect for a while."

"Exactly. I don't want to offer before talking to them, but it could be good for everyone. I'll call Dad. Mom would definitely say yes, but she'd probably forget within ten minutes."

"I'll go sit with her. Keep her company."

I popped up on my tiptoes to kiss him. "You're so good."

He went back into the room while I took out my phone and called my dad.

"Hi, flower. Everything okay this morning?"

"Yes, I'm doing well. A lot better after a good night's sleep."

"So glad to hear that."

"We're actually down at the hospital visiting Brielle. She looks good. A lot healthier already."

"Hang on, I'll tell your mom." His voice grew muffled as he relayed the news.

"I have something big I want to talk to you about. Can you put me on speaker?"

"Sure, what's going on?"

"Hi, flower," Mom said.

"Hi, Mom. Listen, I know this might sound like a lot to ask, so feel free to take your time and think about it. But Brielle doesn't really have a lot of good options. Her family seems…"

"Awful," Mom said.

"Basically. I was thinking, what if she stayed with you guys for a little while? I know that's so much to ask. She's a young woman who's been through some very serious trauma. But—"

"Yes," Dad said.

"Of course we'll take her in," Mom said, almost at the same time.

"This is a lot. You don't have to decide so fast."

"I knew this was coming," Mom said. "I already had a feeling about it."

"She's right," Dad said. "She told me last night."

"You guys already talked about this? You're kidding."

"I can't say I'm psychic," Mom said, "but I do have strong intuition."

"Is she up for visitors?" Dad asked.

"I'll talk to her and then let you know. Oh my gosh, you two are so wonderful. Thank you. This is going to help her so much."

"We'll help fix her up," Mom said. "Us and a good therapy team."

I said goodbye to my parents, my heart filled with love for them. We'd had our struggles and challenges, but they were genuinely good people. They'd always wanted the best for me, even when they went overboard. I knew they'd always wished I hadn't been an only child. Maybe Brielle would give them a way to channel of that parental love they had in such abundance.

Zachary was sitting in a chair near Brielle's bed. Like the

true gentleman he was, he was giving her space—not getting too close so she'd be uncomfortable. He'd clearly just told her a joke or said something that made her laugh. She giggled a little more as I walked in the door. It was great to see her smiling.

I went back to the edge of her bed and sat down. "So, I have an idea, and of course it's totally up to you, but my parents would love to have you stay with them. Even if it's just for a little while. They really want to help. If you're up for it, they can come by sometime today so you can meet them."

"Your mom and dad?"

"Yeah. They're both very nice. They'd give you a safe place to land. No pressure, of course. It's entirely up to you."

Tears gathered in the corners of her eyes. "I don't know what to say. All morning I've been trying not to think about what comes next. But obviously I can't stay here."

"How about you just meet them," I said. "If you feel good about it, you can give it a try. I have to warn you, my mom is sweet, but she forgets things a lot. And my dad is a good man, but he can be a little overprotective."

"I'd love to meet them."

"Good. I'll let them know."

We visited with Brielle and eventually my parents arrived. Mom gushed over how brave she was and Dad formally invited her to stay with them. He sheepishly admitted he wasn't good at letting go of his daughter, but he'd try to treat her like an adult as much as he could. Mom promised to teach her how to paint if she was interested.

But I think what clinched it was when Dad addressed the issue of Brielle's parents.

"I'm not usually one to judge," he said, "but I can't fathom what they did when you were missing. If you were my daughter, I wouldn't have rested until I had you back, safe and sound."

"We're not your parents and we won't try to be," Mom

added. "But if you need a place to heal, we can give that to you."

Brielle looked at me. "Are you sure they aren't too good to be true?"

"Wait until you move into your own place and he shows up to replace appliances that aren't broken." I winked at him.

Brielle was being discharged later that day, so my parents went home to get things ready for her. I didn't know if she'd be there for a few weeks, a few months, or longer. But I knew she'd be in good hands.

Zachary and I went home together. He was the best anti-dote to the chaos of the previous days. We made love, slow and tender, then fell asleep in each other's arms again.

CHAPTER 41

Zachary

BY THE FUSS the town made over Marigold's return, you'd have thought she'd been missing for years, not a day. Of course, they were lumping her in with Brielle, who had been missing for quite a while. Tilikum was happy to have their girls home, and they pulled out all the stops.

A banner welcoming them home hung across Main Street and truckloads of marigolds had been brought in to decorate the storefronts downtown. Someone had decided Brielle needed a flower too, so they'd picked begonias. I guess because they started with the letter B. They didn't last long in the cold, but for a few days at least, the town was awash in color.

I had a feeling the Squirrel Protection Squad was behind most of it.

My mom had come into town to see me and Marigold several times since we'd returned. Mom kept knitting things for her and bringing baked goods. I certainly didn't mind. Especially when she dropped off one of Gram Bailey's famous pumpkin pies. Apparently they'd been doing the same for Brielle, who was getting settled at Craig and Alyssa's place. I wasn't sure how much throw blankets and food were going to help her, but Marigold said it was about making her feel loved. That made sense. And reminded me why men—especially men like me—needed a good woman.

Marigold made everything make sense.

By the Saturday after the rescue, the clouds had gone. It wasn't exactly warm, but the November sun shone on the mountains and the air was crisp rather than frigid. Apparently in Tilikum, that meant an impromptu party in Lumberjack Park.

Tables were set up with food and Tilikum's resident taco truck had a long line. Some college kids had formed a band and they played an assortment of folk rock tunes. They weren't bad. Most of the town seemed to be in attendance—families with little kids, teenagers, elderly folks. They milled around and ate and talked, and a handful of people had even started dancing.

I wandered with Marigold, her hand clasped in mine, and munched on a roasted turkey leg. My family was there. I'd spotted my parents across the park, but they'd been busy talking to some friends. Josiah and Audrey had brought their dogs and Garrett had Owen with him. The kid was getting tall—looked like his dad. Theo and Luke were tossing a football with some high school kids in the street, moving whenever a car came, and Annika and Levi were keeping their kids corralled.

"How you doing?" I asked, pulling Marigold a little closer. "Warm enough? Are you hungry?"

"I'm fine, just wondering if Brielle is here."

"I haven't seen her yet, but I haven't seen your parents either."

"My mom probably forgot."

I laughed. "Your dad won't. I'm sure they'll be here soon."

Sandra and Rocco walked arm in arm toward us. Clearly they'd made up after whatever fight they'd had. I winced at the memory of the nipple piercing I'd been stupid enough to get. It had healed pretty fast, but that pain wasn't something I'd soon forget.

She dropped Rocco's arm and rushed over to give Marigold a hug. "Oh sweetie. What an ordeal you've been through. We're so glad you're home."

"Thank you."

"This," Sandra said, gesturing between me and Marigold, "is the cutest thing I've ever seen."

Marigold tucked her arm in mine. "It was a long time coming."

"I guess so. And way to be the hero, Z. Well done."

Rocco nodded. "Impressive."

"I had help," I said with a shrug.

"A little humility is very charming on you." Sandra grinned, then pursed her lips a little. "By the way, how is the, uh…" Her eyes flicked to my chest. "Healing okay?"

Inadvertently, I hunched my shoulders, as if I had to protect my chest. "Fine. Gone, and fine."

"You didn't keep it? That's too bad." She stepped closer and lowered her voice. "I thought Rocco would hate them. Turns out I was wrong. All's well that ends well."

I laughed and lifted my hand for a high give. "You're a badass, Sandra."

She slapped my hand. "You're not so bad yourself, kid. Take care of her. She's a special one."

I slipped my arm around Marigold's waist and drew her close. "Don't I know it."

She took Rocco's arm and they said goodbye before wandering farther into the park.

"What was that about?" Marigold asked. "What needed healing?"

I groaned. This was not a flattering story. "I don't want to tell you."

"Well now I really need to know."

"Fine. One night when I was feeling particularly shitty

because I thought you were too good for me, I ran into Sandra. She was drinking her feelings after a fight with Rocco. I joined her and, after way too many drinks, we wound up at the tattoo shop. She wanted to get her nips pierced and I thought it sounded like a great idea, so I did one of mine too."

She pulled away, her eyes wide. "You had your nipples pierced?"

"Just one and I took it out right away." I rolled my eyes. "Actually, I had to get my mom to take it out because I couldn't make myself do it. Can we change the subject now? This story does not make me look manly."

She laughed and ran her hands gently up my chest. "Don't worry. I find you very manly. And I'm also glad you took it out."

"Yeah, not my thing."

"Could have been worse. I heard one of Grace Bailey's older brothers once got a unicorn tattoo across his ribs. Apparently he didn't remember getting it."

"That would be Cooper Miles. I met him once and he showed me the tattoo. He was pretty proud of it."

She laughed. "That's hilarious."

I pulled her in for a kiss, just because I could. She kept smiling while I kissed her and I couldn't help but think I was the luckiest guy in the whole damn town.

Marigold's friend Isabelle came over with her husband, Elias, and their two kids. Isabelle gave her a long hug.

"How are you feeling? Are you doing okay?" she asked.

"Yes, I'm fine. Promise."

Garrett approached and nodded to the side. I stepped back, letting Mari talk to Isabelle, and stood next to my brother.

He lowered his voice. "I'm not supposed to say too much, but what was left of Preston's network is already unraveling.

They've found at least half a dozen girls who'd been missing, some of them underage."

I shuddered. "That bastard."

"No shit. They've made a couple of arrests, but it sounds like he kept his operation pretty lean. A few guys who ferried the girls around, kept tabs on them, that sort of thing. But they flew under the radar by staying small."

"Is that why there was only one other guy at that dock in Pasco?"

"Probably. Their guy in Pasco was just a middle man. He'd have taken them on that boat out to a port where they'd have been smuggled onto a larger vessel, bound for who knows where. It sounds like Preston liked to keep most of the girls he coerced into working for him. But if they didn't behave, being sold off was their punishment."

"Fucking disgusting."

"How's Marigold? Don't forget, she took a guy out. That can be hard to live with, no matter the circumstances."

"She's okay. It's definitely a lot and I think she's still processing the whole thing." I gazed at her. "She saved my life, man."

"Yeah, she did."

"How are you?" I asked. "You're trained for it, but you had to drop two guys that day."

"I don't ever want to have to draw my weapon. But sometimes it's part of the job. And in this case, I have no regrets."

"Thank you. You saved my life, too."

"Anytime, brother."

We hugged it out and I mentally renewed my resolution not to do anything stupid that would make Garrett need to arrest me.

Thankfully, now I had Marigold to keep me on the up and up. I didn't think I'd have too much trouble keeping my promise.

She hugged Isabelle again, then came over to me. "Any news?"

"Garrett said the feds are doing their thing. They made some arrests and rescued half a dozen girls."

"I'm so glad. I hope those poor girls have families to go home to." Her face lit up. "Speaking of, there they are."

Her parents walked across the grass with Brielle between them. She looked good—much better than when we'd rescued her in Pasco. The color had returned to her face, but the biggest difference was in her eyes. They were still a bit haunted—and who could blame her—but they were brighter. And I understood on a certain level what had changed. She had hope.

I hadn't been through everything she'd experienced, but I kind of knew what that felt like.

There were hugs all around. It was nice to feel like the awkwardness between me and Craig was a thing of the past.

Especially since I had every intention of marrying his daughter.

"Isn't this beautiful?" Alyssa said. "It makes me want to paint begonias."

"It's wonderful," Marigold said, then turned to Brielle. "How do you feel about all this attention?"

"It's kind of hard to believe."

"Have you seen your parents at all?"

Brielle nodded. "Just once. It didn't exactly go well, but I expected that. Your mom and dad were with me so that helped a lot."

"And look at all this. You have an entire town who's thrilled to have you home."

Brielle's cheeks flushed. "It's a little bit embarrassing, but not in a bad way. I don't know if that makes sense."

"I totally understand," Marigold said.

"I have an idea I want to run by you," Brielle said. "My

therapist says not to rush things, but I think I know what I want to do next."

"What's that?"

She took a breath, like she needed a little courage. "I want to go to beauty school."

Marigold's smile was like the sun—big and radiant. "Really? That's a great idea."

"Do you think so? I don't know if I'll ever be as good as you, but I thought it would be a good next step for me."

"You'll be amazing. And as soon as you finish school, you can start apprenticing with me at my salon."

She grabbed Marigold's hands. "Oh my gosh, seriously? That would be a dream come true."

"Absolutely. I need the help anyway. And I can teach you all the tips and tricks you don't learn in beauty school."

Craig put an arm around Alyssa and held her close. They both smiled at Brielle, clearly proud of her. The whole thing was so damn wholesome, it almost brought a tear to my eye.

Almost.

"We should go get in line for tacos," Craig said. "I want to make sure we get lunch before they run out. Are you hungry, flower?"

"No, I already ate."

"How about you, Zachary?"

"Usually I wouldn't say no to street tacos, but I just had a roasted turkey leg. I'm good for now."

Craig reached out and shook my hand. There was unspoken thanks in his expression.

We said our goodbyes so they could get lunch and they walked away with Brielle between them.

More people came to hug Marigold, telling her how happy they were that she was okay. Some had questions about her ordeal. The Tilikum gossip line had been in full swing and, surprisingly, most of the stories going around town were scarily close to the truth. Her clients gushed that they couldn't live without her.

I knew exactly how that felt.

A pat on my shoulder caught my attention and I turned around. It was my dad. Mom stood next to him, holding a plate of food.

"Hey, Dad."

He didn't say anything right away. Just nodded slowly, like he was working out what to say. Finally, he cleared his throat, stepped closer, and wrapped me in a tight hug.

I was stunned. It wasn't that my dad had never hugged me before. He had. But this was different. He held me tight for a long moment, his big arms almost crushing me.

When he dropped his arms and stepped back, he met my eyes. "I'm proud of you, son."

My chest tightened with emotion and a lump rose in my throat. For a second, I couldn't speak. He'd never said those words to me. Not once. And until that moment, I'd never realized just how badly I'd needed to hear them.

"Thanks, Dad," I finally choked out.

He nodded again, a quick tip of his chin. It wasn't a lengthy conversation about why he was proud or what it all meant. That wasn't his style. Paul Haven had always been a man of few words, and somehow, that made the words he did say all the more powerful.

Mom took off her glasses and dabbed beneath her eyes. Annika and Levi had made their way to Marigold and my nieces and nephews were jumping all over her. Except Thomas. He took his big brother job very seriously and made sure Will didn't get Mari's dress dirty.

A chorus of "Auntie Mari" rang out around her from the kids.

Just you wait, my dudes. She's going to be your real auntie soon enough.

Not for the first time, my spontaneous streak kicked in. I

had an almost uncontrollable urge to drop to one knee right there and propose.

A guy could have worse timing. Word on the street had it that my brother Josiah had first proposed to Audrey right after rescuing her from the man who'd been stalking her. When I heard that, I thought he was nuts. Who would be thinking about marriage in the immediate aftermath of a life and death crisis?

Now, I got it.

I'd almost done it at the dock in Pasco. All the adrenaline and fear of losing her had come to a head, and in the midst of my relief I'd had this crazy urge to seal the deal. To lock things down so I knew she'd be mine forever.

But I'd resisted the urge to blurt out that I wanted her to marry me as soon as humanly possible. That had been the right call. Marriage meant a lot to Marigold. I knew from my sister she'd been keeping a wedding binder since they were kids, so I was going to do things right. Give her everything she deserved. Including a proposal worthy of my beautiful girl.

So once again, I resisted the urge. I had the beginnings of a plan and it was going to be worth the wait.

CHAPTER 42

Marigold

I HADN'T BEEN this excited for a birthday party in years.

My Regency costume still fit—thank goodness. I turned to the side, smoothing down the pale blue empire waist dress, checking my reflection in the full length mirror. I loved the bit of a bustle effect the drawstring at the high waistline added to the silhouette.

Annika, Audrey, and Isabelle had come to me with the idea for a costume party for my birthday. I wasn't sure why— it was just an ordinary birthday—but I'd been thrilled with the idea, even if only to have a reason to wear my costume dress again.

It was being held at the Grand Peak hotel, which seemed awfully opulent. But Annika had assured me they'd been given a great deal, since it was the off season.

It was going to be an actual ball, just like in some of my favorite books.

I checked my hair, making sure I'd pinned it securely. I'd put it up in the back and curled ringlets around my face. It wasn't perfectly authentic, but it was close. My phone rang, so I hurried out to the bedroom to answer it. It was Zachary.

"Hello?"

"Hi, baby. Slight change of plans. I'm going to be a little late for the party. I'm really sorry, it's a work thing. If I leave things the way they are, it'll be dangerous. I have to finish up. But I'll meet you there as soon as I can."

He'd been called in that morning for an emergency electrical issue at one of his client's businesses. I was the tiniest bit disappointed he'd be late, but of course he couldn't leave a problem that could be dangerous.

"That's totally fine."

"You sure? It's your day, I don't want you to be sad."

"I'm not sad. Promise. I'll just be that much more excited to see you."

"You're the best. I love you."

"Love you too. I'll see you there."

"Sounds good, baby."

He ended the call and I finished getting ready, donning a pair of ballet-style slippers that matched my gown. They were surprisingly comfortable, and one of the reasons I loved the clothing from that period. Trends had changed from binding corsets and stiff shoes to flowy, feminine gowns and wearable slippers.

Outside, the air was cold, although it hadn't snowed yet. We'd had a few flakes earlier in the week, which meant it wouldn't be long before the mountains were blanketed in white. My costume didn't have a proper coat, but it wouldn't be cold indoors. I hurried to my car and drove to the Grand Peak Hotel.

I parked and went in through the lobby, glad to be out of the chill. A pretty chalkboard sign pointed the way to the room where my party was being held.

Walking in was like stepping back in time. String ensemble music played in the background and, to my amazement, everyone was in costume. I'd expected my friends and I to be among the only ones to dress up. But the women all wore gowns with short sleeves and empire waists, and the men were in suits with tails and trousers. It wasn't a large gathering, but the effect almost made me burst into tears.

Annika and Isabelle rushed to greet me. They looked so pretty, Annika in a striped green dress and Isabelle in cream with a touch of lace at the neckline. Their husbands stood a short distance away, talking with drinks in their hands. They were similarly dressed with short tailed jackets, white shirts, and black trousers.

"Look at you," Annika said, grabbing my hands. "You're a vision."

"Where did everyone get costumes?" I asked.

"The Tilikum College theater," Annika said. "Audrey interviewed the director a few months ago for a Hometown Spotlight in the newspaper. Of course they became friends and she asked if they had anything we could borrow. Turns out, they had trunks full of stuff."

"Everyone looks so pretty," I said. "This is amazing. It's way too much for just my birthday."

"Don't be silly," Isabelle said. "Your birthday is a great reason for a costume party."

"Where's Zachary?" Annika asked.

"He's running late. Work issue."

She shared a quick look with Isabelle. "Oh, okay. I'm sure he'll be here soon."

They led me deeper into the room so I could start saying hello to the other guests. A number of my clients had come, and my parents were there, of course. Brielle looked like a dream in her lavender gown. She was starting beauty school after the first of the year but had been shadowing me at the salon. She had real talent.

The Havens were also there. Paul looked so uncomfortable in his outfit, I felt bad for him. Marlene looked radiant and gushed about how Brielle had done her hair for her. She wore hairpins with little pearls on the ends and had ringlets framing her face.

Zachary's brothers looked great. Garrett and Luke wandered around the room, looking confident, as if they always dressed that way. Theo and Josiah mirrored their dad's discomfort, although they both wore their suits well. They gave me brotherly hugs and wished me happy birthday.

A murmur ran through the small crowd, and as I turned toward the entrance, I almost couldn't believe my eyes.

As if it had been choreographed, the guests parted, moving to each side to create an aisle down the center of the room. Zachary stood just inside the door, dressed in a short black tailcoat, white shirt with a tall collar, tan trousers, and riding boots. He flipped the tail of his coat back and strode toward me.

He looked like he owned the place. He certainly owned me.

I walked out to meet my dashing gentleman. He grinned and his eyes swept up and down, as if he liked what he saw. He stopped in front of me, took my hand, and placed a gentle kiss on my knuckles.

"Miss Martin. Would you do me the honor of a dance?"

"The honor is mine, Mr. Haven."

He looked to someone else in the crowd and nodded. A new song began. He stepped back and bowed. I curtsied. He moved closer, putting one hand around the small of my back and took my hand in the other.

"I don't actually know how to do the right kind of dance. I tried researching but it was surprisingly confusing."

"That's okay," I said as we moved to the music, waltz-style. "This is lovely."

He led me in gentle, sweeping circles. A few people around us joined the fun. It wasn't the coordinated cotillion or Scotch reel of a regency ball, but it left me giddy none-theless. Zachary was so handsome, so dashing, such a gentleman.

The man of my dreams, indeed.

"Are you having a good birthday?" he asked as another song began. We kept right on dancing.

"The best ever."

He smiled. "Good. I thought you'd like this."

"You?" I narrowed my eyes. "I've been under the impression this was Annika or Audrey's idea. But it wasn't them, was it? It was you."

"Guilty."

"You rogue."

"Guilty there too. I also have a little confession."

"Besides being secretly behind my party?"

He nodded. "This isn't actually a birthday party."

"Then what is it?"

He stopped dancing right in the middle of the song. His eyes didn't leave mine as he slowly lowered himself to one knee.

The guests around me faded away as Zachary produced a ring from an inside pocket. My eyes widened and I gasped as I recognized what was happening.

"Marigold, I love you more than anything. You're the kindest, most beautiful, most compassionate, most amazing woman I've ever known. I want nothing more than to spend the rest of my life with you. Will you marry me?"

I nodded, trying to get the word out around the lump in my throat. "Yes. Yes, I'll marry you."

With that brain-melting, sexy grin, he rose and took my hand. The crowd erupted in applause as he slid the ring onto my finger. Then he drew me close, placed a knuckle beneath my chin to lift my face to his, and kissed me.

I melted in his arms. He picked me up off my feet and twirled me around. I couldn't tell if I was laughing or crying. Probably a bit of both.

Finally, he set me down and kissed me again.

"You orchestrated this whole thing so you could propose?" I asked.

"Your birthday was a good excuse. I wasn't sure how else I was going to pull off a regency costume party without making you suspicious."

I held out my hand to stare in awe at the dazzling vintage-style halo with an emerald cut center diamond set in a rose gold band. "I had no idea."

"I told you I was going to marry you."

I met his eyes. My heart felt like it could burst right out of my chest. I loved him so much. After everything we'd been through, it had been him all along. I was going to be Mrs. Zachary Haven. And I couldn't imagine a better happily ever after than that.

Epilogue
MARIGOLD

THE DAY of my wedding dawned clear and crisp after days of spring rain. A few puffy clouds lingered in the sky and the air smelled fresh. It was absolute perfection.

Zachary had wanted to get married as soon as possible, while also letting me have my dream of a beautiful wedding. We'd decided to wait until spring so we wouldn't be stealing Audrey and Josiah's thunder for their January wedding and I'd have enough time to plan our day.

Now it was finally here. I could hardly believe it.

Audrey and Josiah's wedding had been amazing. She'd been a vision in white, and Josiah cleaned up well. People were still talking about how much fun their reception had been. Especially because it had culminated in a moonlit snowball fight outside.

As I'd gone through the familiar steps to plan my own wedding—consulting all the ideas I'd saved, pictures I'd cut out, plans I'd made— I'd realized something. It wasn't the colors or the flowers or the dress that really mattered. Those things were nice, and I enjoyed every minute of planning for them. But what I actually wanted, more than the perfect day, was to become Zachary's wife.

That took a lot of the pressure off the details.

So when the centerpieces weren't quite right and Audrey's bridesmaid dress had been hemmed too long and the cake was late and I didn't know if it would arrive, I let it all go.

Because I was becoming Mrs. Zachary Haven.

We were at Salishan Cellars Winery, my favorite wedding venue, surrounded by dusty blue and blush with gold decorations—understated, soft, and romantic. Annika, my matron of honor and oldest friend, looked lovely in her blue dress, as did the rest of my bridesmaids—Isabelle, Audrey, and Brielle.

Zachary's brothers rounded out our wedding party. He'd asked Garrett to be his best man, which had kind of surprised me. They hadn't always gotten along. Apparently the rescue down in Pasco had helped them bond. They certainly seemed to understand each other better.

Before I knew it, I was standing at the back of the room in my wedding gown, holding a bouquet, ready to take my dad's arm. My dress was elegant, with a v-neckline and lace at the shoulders, a wide a-line skirt, and a train. Brielle had done my hair in a sweeping updo with romantic tendrils around my face, and my white veil fastened with a pearl clip.

Dad turned to me with tears in his eyes. He was so handsome in his black tux. "Oh, flower. Look at you."

I smiled, hoping I wouldn't cry. Yet. "Thanks, Dad."

"A father looks forward to and dreads his daughter's wedding day. But I couldn't be happier for you." He leaned in and kissed my cheek.

Zoe Miles, the head of events at Salishan, motioned me and Dad forward. As the wedding party started walking up the aisle in pairs, my stomach fluttered with excitement and anticipation.

"Ready?" Zoe whispered. She made a quick adjustment to my veil.

"Ready."

Dad and I stepped into the doorway and our guests stood.

It was happening.

There was probably music. I didn't hear it. There were probably smiles and maybe a few tears as Dad walked me up the aisle. I didn't see them. All that existed was Zachary Haven, waiting for me at the front in his tux, ready to make me his wife.

He grinned as I approached, and that smile nearly undid me. I fought back happy tears and smiled right back.

The ceremony went by in a blur. I gazed at Zachary as we said our vows, pledging our hearts and lives to each other, until death do us part. We exchanged rings, and as the officiant pronounced us man and wife, the tears came.

Zachary pulled me against him, and with his signature mischievous grin, took my mouth in a kiss.

It wasn't exactly a wedding kiss, but I didn't care. I threw my arms around his neck and kissed him back.

He was mine. My husband. My dream.

It was the best moment of my life.

We walked down the aisle, hand in hand, to cheers, whistles, and applause. Zachary stopped at the end, turned around, and pumped his fist in the air. I laughed, positively giddy. It felt like I was floating on a cloud of marital bliss.

The reception began with hugs, greetings, congratulations, and champagne. I had a feeling my face was going to hurt from smiling so much. But I didn't mind. I couldn't have stopped if I'd tried.

As we wandered and chatted with guests, Zachary fed me hors d'oeuvres. Which was good because he also made sure my champagne was always full. Eventually, we took our seats at our table and dinner was served.

Partway through the meal, I noticed Zoe come in with another woman. She was pretty with gorgeous blond hair. She caught my attention because she had a flour-covered apron on over a blue dress.

The cake.

I got up so I could take a closer look as they set it on a side table. It had light blue frosting with large blush pink flowers trailing down one side and everything was rimmed in a hint of gold.

"Cake disaster averted," Zoe said.

"I'm so sorry," the other woman said. "I'm Harper Tilburn, Doris's niece. My aunt has been having health problems lately but she didn't tell anyone. She finally came clean to my mom this morning, so I rushed out here to help her."

"It's totally fine. I'm sorry Doris isn't feeling well."

"I told you Marigold wouldn't be upset," Zoe said. "She's one of the best brides I've ever worked with."

"Congratulations," Harper said. "You're stunning, by the way."

"Thank you so much."

"I hope the cake is what you wanted. I did my best."

"It's absolutely beautiful."

"Good. I'm so glad."

Zachary put a hand on the small of my back. "Is it cake time already?"

"Not quite," I said. "But isn't it beautiful?"

"Looks great."

I thanked Harper and Zoe again and Zachary and I went back to our table.

Garrett stood and clinked a fork against his glass to get the guests' attention.

"Hi, everyone," he said when the room quieted. "I'm Garrett Haven, Zachary's brother. And, for some reason, his best man."

Applause filled the air and someone shouted his name.

"Thanks," he said. "I don't think I'm the only one who wouldn't have predicted Z would be the next of my brothers to get married. And that's not because he isn't a great guy. He is. He just stayed wild a little longer than the rest of us."

That earned a laugh from the guests. And from me.

"But sometimes what a man needs isn't his family or the people around him telling him what to do or how to live. What he really needs is a reason. A mission. He needs a purpose. Something bigger than his job or career or hobbies or interests. Something bigger than himself. And Zachary is lucky enough to have found his purpose—found his mission. Turns out, she was right there all along. All it took was almost getting electrocuted for him to figure it out."

Zachary shook his head and laughed, squeezing my hand.

"Zachary, I'm really happy for you. You couldn't have picked a better wife. And Marigold, you've been like our sister since you and Annika were little. So allow me to be the first to officially say, welcome to the Haven family. We love you guys. Cheers."

I didn't bother dabbing the tears at the corners of my eyes as we raised our glasses to toast. That was why waterproof mascara had been invented.

And thank goodness for that.

After dinner, we cut the cake. Zachary dabbed a little bit of frosting on my nose and kissed it off. While servers sliced the cake for our guests, Zachary led me onto the dance floor for our first dance. He took me in his arms and I gazed into his eyes as we moved to the music.

"You look so good, I want to eat you up," he said.

I smiled. "You just had cake."

"You're so much better than cake."

"That might be one of the best compliments a man can give his wife."

He grinned. "My wife. Man, I like hearing that."

"Thank you for marrying me, Zachary Haven."

"Thank you for becoming my wife, Marigold Haven."

Hearing my name with his made me tingle with pleasure. It was a dream come true. I'd loved him for so long and thought it was a mistake. That he could never feel the same way. Garrett might have been right about it taking an almost electrocution to open his eyes to what was right in front of him, but somehow, it made sense. It was Zachary Haven. Of course it would be explosive.

And now he was mine, and I was his. My dream man. My husband. My love. Forever.

Bonus Epilogue

ZACHARY

SEVERAL YEARS LATER...

Blowing up balloons was making me dizzy.

I tied one off and let it bounce on the floor with the others while I waited for my head to clear. The kitchen was quiet, the only sound the soft movement of the balloons as they bumped against each other.

Our cat, Mr. Darcy, sat watching me with an air of mild disdain, as if my early morning project was interrupting his routine.

Or maybe he just wanted food.

I grabbed another purple balloon and blew air into it, then tied the end. I wasn't sure how many I needed, but I figured too many would be better than too few. After all, it wasn't every day my little girl was turning four.

Four. It was hard to believe it had been four years since our Emily had been born. It seemed like just days ago she'd been a tiny newborn, so small I could practically hold her in the palms of my hands.

She'd grown into the most amazing little girl with big blue

eyes, long brown hair, and a smile that took me out every single time. She was also brilliant, which was both incredible and mildly terrifying. Without any help from us, other than reading to her about a million times a day, she'd started reading simple words on her own. It wouldn't be long before she was smarter than me.

I just needed to teach her to use her powers for good. Both her big brain and her big blue eyes.

A balloon drifted by the cat. He lifted a paw, claws extended.

"Hey," I whisper-yelled. I didn't want to wake up my sleeping family—especially the two-year-old force of nature that was our son, Henry. "Pop that balloon and you'll never get catnip again."

He lowered his paw and slow-blinked while the balloon bounced by.

I tipped my chin to the cat. He was Marigold's idea. Same with our other cat, Mr. Bingley. I wasn't exactly a cat person, but Marigold had fallen in love with them, so that was enough for me.

Glancing around the kitchen floor, I did a quick count of the balloons. I probably had enough.

Dad prank commencing.

I grabbed a roll of purple crepe paper and some tape, then shuffled the balloons down the hall toward Emily's room. Careful to be as quiet as I could, I taped crepe paper across her closed door and tucked the balloons inside.

When she woke up, she'd open the door and an avalanche of purple birthday balloons would bounce all over her.

It was going to be great.

I'd gotten the idea from Gavin Bailey. He'd started doing the balloon avalanche prank on his kids years ago. He said it didn't seem to matter how many times he did it, they always loved it.

Once I'd stuffed as many balloons as I could into my

contraption, I stepped back and admired my handywork. It wasn't a complex prank, but sometimes the simple ones were the best.

Pop!

I froze at the sound. Shit. Emily probably wouldn't wake up—she was a sound sleeper. But Henry? His something-fun-is-happening radar was sure to go off, and once he was up, there'd be no getting him back to sleep. If I woke him up too early, Marigold might very well unalive me.

The house stayed silent. No sound of two-year-old feet hitting the floor. No bedroom door flinging open.

I let out a breath. Crisis averted.

There'd been a time when I teased Annika and Levi about their youngest son, Will. He'd been a handful from the day he was born. Little did I know my son would give Will a run for his money.

My dad liked to remind me that I deserved it.

He wasn't wrong.

Emily was soft spoken and sweet—so much like her mom. Henry? Just like me, down to the little dimple in his chin. He had a big personality and an endless well of energy.

I loved them both more than I could have imagined.

Don't get me wrong, I knew I'd love my kids. I'd already known what it was like to love my nieces and nephews. But my kids were everything. I loved them so much I ached with it.

And they made me love Marigold even more.

I tip toed to the end of the hall and slipped into our bedroom. Marigold was still in bed, the shape of her body tantalizing beneath the covers. The sun was rising and light filtered in from a gap in the curtains. But maybe we'd have time for some grown-up fun before the day began.

She murmured as I caressed her and brushed her hair back from her face. I waited while she stretched and her eyes fluttered open.

"Morning," she said, her voice sleepy.

"Morning, gorgeous."

"What are you doing up?"

I leaned down and brushed a kiss across her lips. "Just making a little surprise for Emily."

"Kids aren't awake yet?"

"Nope."

She smiled and reached up to wrap her hand around the back of my neck and brought me in for another kiss. I growled into her mouth, hoping we had time to—

The bedroom door creaked.

"Daddy." Henry's whisper was about as loud as a normal person's voice. "Morning?"

I loved that kid so much, I couldn't even be annoyed. Besides, Marigold and I had gotten good at finding naked time together. Or making it. I'd lost count of the number of times we'd enjoyed a quick fuck in the bathroom while the kids watched a cartoon.

"Morning, big man." I crouched and opened my arms.

He ran to me and I wrapped him in a tight hug. His little arms wound around my neck. "Emmy birfday?"

"Yep, it's Emily's birthday."

"Cake?"

I laughed. "How did you know there's cake on birthdays?"

He shrugged.

"Smart kid." I glanced at Marigold and grinned. "Should we let him loose so she wakes up?"

"Bawoons, Mommy!"

I stood and picked him up. "Did you see the balloons?"

He pointed toward the open door. "Bawoons!"

"What balloons?" Marigold asked.

"You'll see."

I held Henry while Marigold got up and went to the bathroom. She came out in a t-shirt and black joggers, her hair loose around her shoulders. I set Henry on the bed so I could pull her in for a kiss.

"We'll finish what we started later." I kissed her again.

She smiled against my lips. "I have something I need to—"

"Daddy! Emmy!"

I scooped Henry off the bed and grabbed Marigold by the hand. I didn't want to miss it. We rushed into the hall and I let go of Marigold so I could put a finger to my lips.

Marigold's mouth dropped open and she pointed to Emily's door. I just nodded.

It was ridiculous how excited I was.

The sound of little feet came from Emily's room. Henry wiggled in my arms and I motioned for him to stay quiet. Her doorknob turned and I held my breath.

Emily opened her door and squealed as purple balloons cascaded all over her.

"Happy birthday!" Marigold and I said in a chorus.

Emily's eyes were bright and her smile could have lit up the entire sky. She looked around at the balloons bouncing all around her. "Daddy, did you do that?"

"I have no idea what you're talking about."

She put her hands on her hips. "Daddy."

"Okay, maybe it was me." I set Henry down so he could play with the balloons. "Happy birthday, pumpkin."

She ran to me and I scooped her into my arms. A sharp pop made us both jump a little, but it was inevitable with her brother on the loose.

"Mommy, I'm four." She held up four fingers.

"Yes you are, my big girl." Marigold reached for her and Emily practically dove into her arms. "Happy birthday."

"Daddy, can I have balloons again tomorrow?"

I grinned. "Your birthday is today."

"But it's fun."

She had a point.

Henry was busy kicking balloons and spitting with his sound effects. Mr. Bingley the cat had ventured out to see what was happening. He wandered around the hallway, rubbing against the doorframes, ignoring the two-year-old chaos. Mr. Darcy avoided Henry at all costs, but Mr. Bingley didn't seem to mind him.

We kicked some balloons into the living room so the kids could play with them, then went to the kitchen. The birthday girl requested pancakes, so I got to work while Marigold made tea.

The sun was rising, illuminating our view of the river. My dad had scored a great deal on this house for us and he and Josiah had helped us fix it up. It hadn't been in the best shape when we'd bought it before Emily was born, but the location couldn't be beat. We were up on a little rise, far enough from the river that flooding wouldn't be an issue, and we'd put up a small fence to keep the kids safe. But we could still see— and hear—the water rushing by.

A house on the river had been a dream of Marigold's. It was the best damn thing in the world to make her dreams come true.

I cooked our pancakes while Marigold got the kids their tea. Emily's was actual tea with a bit of ice to cool it down. Henry's was watered down juice in a mug. With her soft voice, Marigold calmed the chaos that was our son and coaxed him into a seat at the table. Emily sat next to him, a crown she'd made with her aunties on her head and her nose already in a book.

So like her mommy.

We sat down together for Emily's birthday breakfast. Because it was a special day, Marigold let them have whipped cream and sprinkles on their pancakes.

I leaned in and whispered, "Save some of that whipped cream. I want to eat it off you later."

She bit her bottom lip and giggled, then gave me a sultry smile.

Oh, man. The things I was going to do to my wife.

Emily's birthday party was scheduled for later in the afternoon. We were having it up at my parents' place, since they had more space—and these days, there were a lot more Havens than there used to be.

So. Many. Cousins.

We lingered over breakfast, even after the kids got down to play. Henry drove his dump truck around the kitchen, trying to run over the balloons. Emily tucked herself into a corner of the couch with a stack of picture books, her crown still on her head.

I took Marigold's hand and brought it to my lips. "I love you."

Her smile was the sun—my sun. "I love you, too."

"Think she's having a good birthday?"

She glanced at our daughter. "It looks like it."

I kissed her hand again. "How did I get so lucky?"

"If I remember correctly, I almost electrocuted you."

"That's true, you did. Although it wasn't your fault. And I'm sure glad it happened."

"Me too." She threaded her fingers through mine and leaned closer. "I have something to tell you."

There was a hint of excitement in her voice that made my mouth turn up in the hint of a grin. "Yeah? What is it?"

Meeting my eyes, she hesitated for a moment, then lowered her voice to a whisper. "I'm pregnant."

I stood so fast I almost knocked my chair over. My chest tightened as my heart swelled, and I grabbed my wife, hauling her against me. She wound her arms around my neck as I held her tight.

"Baby?" I whispered.

"Baby."

I laughed and kissed her head. Another baby. I felt like I might burst.

Henry's body collided with our legs and he held his arms up. "Me!"

Marigold picked him up. "You want a hug too?"

"Hug!"

We hugged him between us. Emily put her book down and ran into the kitchen. I scooped her up and settled her on my hip so I could put my other arm around my wife and son.

I'm man enough to admit to the tears that stung my eyes as I hugged my family. Tears of contentment and unadulterated joy.

They were my everything. My wife, my kids, and the new baby we'd be meeting soon. Marigold was the best thing that had ever happened to me. It had taken a brush with death to make me realize what had been right in front of me all along, but I'd suffer that shock a thousand times if it brought me to her.

And now she was mine. We were a family, and it didn't get any better than that.

Dear reader

I don't know if you saw this book coming. But if you did, that makes one of us.

I sure didn't.

While I was writing this book, but before it was public that Zachary and Marigold were indeed the couple, a reader posted an "unpopular opinion" on social media—that they hoped Marigold didn't end up with any of the Havens, because they wanted her to have a light, fluffy, sweet, and angst-free story. A happily ever after without the conflict or struggle.

T'was not to be.

But you know what? Marigold deserved this.

Not that she deserved to be manipulated and abducted by someone so vile. But she did deserve to be challenged. She deserved the chance to grow into who she is—to prove to herself that she can handle anything.

And Zachary Haven. Oh my sweet, sweet Z.

Did you guess Zachary Haven would fall first? I didn't.

He burst onto the page, as I knew he would, with all the bravado I expected of him—and so much heart. I really didn't see him coming. He had all this bottled up love and affection and he was absolutely dying to give it all to Marigold. He just didn't know how.

I love writing a story where the characters learn to let go of the past and embrace who they've become. Who can forgive and grow. And these two did all of that and more.

And can we talk about his cosplay at the end? Writing that scene gave me all kinds of warm fuzzies. Marigold didn't get her Mr. Darcy, she got someone much better. The real love of her life.

The suspense side of this book was a unique challenge for me. Weaving Brielle into the story added another dimension and gave you a peek behind the curtain. You probably guessed right away that "John" wasn't who he seemed.

He was such a predator (he totally made my skin crawl) and Brielle was so vulnerable. I loved being able to walk with her as she came through her own storm and found hope in her future.

I hope you enjoyed Storms and Secrets! I loved writing it and there's much more to come from this family.

Love,

Claire

Acknowledgments

Thank you to everyone who helped make this book a reality.

To my dad, for making our morning coffee. We all know that's a vital necessity.

To my son Grayson, for the many steaks and other delicious foods you grilled, roasted, and smoked. Your culinary explorations were not only delicious, they gave me extra writing time.

To Nikki and Alex, for brainstorming, hand-holding, beta reading, and listening to me be dramatic.

To the rest of my admin team for all your help. Stacey, Jess, Jessica, and Emily, you're awesome and I appreciate you!

To Eliza for your editing prowess and especially for helping me untangle some of the technical details.

To Michelle, for even more editing prowess, feedback, and gentle encouragement.

And to Erma, for once again taking the time to hunt for pesky typos.

Finally, to my readers. I hope Zachary and Marigold were everything you wanted them to be. I love your faces!

Also by Claire Kingsley

For a full and up-to-date listing of Claire Kingsley books visit www.clairekingsleybooks.com/books/

For comprehensive reading order, visit www.clairekingsleybooks. com/reading-order/

————

The Haven Brothers

Small-town romantic suspense with CK's signature endearing characters and heartwarming happily ever afters. Can be read as stand-alones.

Obsession Falls (Josiah and Audrey)

Storms and Secrets (Zachary and Marigold)

The rest of the Haven brothers will be getting their own happily ever afters!

————

How the Grump Saved Christmas (Elias and Isabelle)

A stand-alone, small-town Christmas romance.

————

The Bailey Brothers

Steamy, small-town family series with a dash of suspense. Five unruly brothers. Epic pranks. A quirky, feuding town. Big HEAs. Best read in order.

Protecting You (Asher and Grace part 1)

Fighting for Us (Asher and Grace part 2)

Unraveling Him (Evan and Fiona)

Rushing In (Gavin and Skylar)

Chasing Her Fire (Logan and Cara)

Rewriting the Stars (Levi and Annika)

————

The Miles Family

Sexy, sweet, funny, and heartfelt family series with a dash of suspense. Messy family. Epic bromance. Super romantic. Best read in order.

Broken Miles (Roland and Zoe)

Forbidden Miles (Brynn and Chase)

Reckless Miles (Cooper and Amelia)

Hidden Miles (Leo and Hannah)

Gaining Miles: A Miles Family Novella (Ben and Shannon)

————

Dirty Martini Running Club

Sexy, fun, feel-good romantic comedies with huge… hearts. Can be read as stand-alones.

Everly Dalton's Dating Disasters (Prequel with Everly, Hazel, and Nora)

Faking Ms. Right (Everly and Shepherd)

Falling for My Enemy (Hazel and Corban)

Marrying Mr. Wrong (Sophie and Cox)

Flirting with Forever (Nora and Dex)

————

Bluewater Billionaires

Hot romantic comedies. Lady billionaire BFFs and the badass heroes who love them. Can be read as stand-alones.

The Mogul and the Muscle (Cameron and Jude)

The Price of Scandal, Wild Open Hearts, and Crazy for Loving You

More Bluewater Billionaire shared-world romantic comedies by Lucy Score, Kathryn Nolan, and Pippa Grant

————

Bootleg Springs
by Claire Kingsley and Lucy Score

Hot and hilarious small-town romcom series with a dash of mystery and suspense. Best read in order.

Whiskey Chaser (Scarlett and Devlin)

Sidecar Crush (Jameson and Leah Mae)

Moonshine Kiss (Bowie and Cassidy)

Bourbon Bliss (June and George)

Gin Fling (Jonah and Shelby)

Highball Rush (Gibson and I can't tell you)

————

Book Boyfriends

Hot romcoms that will make you laugh and make you swoon. Can be read as stand-alones.

Book Boyfriend (Alex and Mia)

Cocky Roommate (Weston and Kendra)

Hot Single Dad (Caleb and Linnea)

————

Finding Ivy (William and Ivy)

A unique contemporary romance with a hint of mystery. Stand-alone.

His Heart (Sebastian and Brooke)

A poignant and emotionally intense story about grief, loss, and the transcendent power of love. Stand-alone.

The Always Series

Smoking hot, dirty talking bad boys with some angsty intensity. Can be read as stand-alones.

Always Have (Braxton and Kylie)

Always Will (Selene and Ronan)

Always Ever After (Braxton and Kylie)

The Jetty Beach Series

Sexy small-town romance series with swoony heroes, romantic HEAs, and lots of big feels. Can be read as stand-alones.

Behind His Eyes (Ryan and Nicole)

One Crazy Week (Melissa and Jackson)

Messy Perfect Love (Cody and Clover)

Operation Get Her Back (Hunter and Emma)

Weekend Fling (Finn and Juliet)

Good Girl Next Door (Lucas and Becca)

The Path to You (Gabriel and Sadie)

About the Author

Claire Kingsley is a #1 Amazon bestselling author of sexy, heartfelt contemporary romance and romantic comedies. She writes sassy, quirky heroines, swoony heroes who love their women hard, romantic happily ever afters, and all the big feels.

She can't imagine life without coffee, her Kindle, and the sexy heroes who inhabit her imagination. She lives in the inland Pacific Northwest with her three kids.

www.clairekingsleybooks.com

9 781959 809142